P9-DFK-536

# *"You okay?"*

"Uh-huh," Sue Ann managed, intensely aware that both his hands were now molded to her hips. "Just stood up too fast. Plus I've had some wine, so I'm probably a little wobbly. Like a little drunk."

And she was pretty sure she was right about that part, since it was the only way she could account for her next move—she lifted her free hand to the navy tee Adam wore under an open flannel shirt. She rested her fingertips on his chest, as if it were about keeping her balance, but in reality she was fairly certain she was actually testing it out, seeing how it felt to touch him.

Even with only the tips of her fingers pressed there, she sensed the firm muscle underneath. It made her heart beat faster, harder.

But wait.

God.

This is Adam.

"The perfect small-town romance."
Eloisa James, Barnes & Noble Review
on *One Reckless Summer*

## By Toni Blake

HOLLY LANE
WHISPER FALLS
SUGAR CREEK
ONE RECKLESS SUMMER
LETTERS TO A SECRET LOVER
TEMPT ME TONIGHT
SWEPT AWAY

**ATTENTION: ORGANIZATIONS AND CORPORATIONS**
Most Avon Books paperbacks are available at special quantity
discounts for bulk purchases for sales promotions, premiums,
or fund raising. For information, please call or write:

**Special Markets Department, HarperCollins Publishers,**
**10 East 53rd Street, New York, New York 10022-5299.**
**Telephone: (212) 207-7528.     Fax: (212) 207-7222.**

# TONI BLAKE

# HOLLY LANE

## A DESTINY NOVEL

**AVON**

*An Imprint of HarperCollinsPublishers*

This is a work of fiction. Names, characters, places, and incidents are products of the author's imagination or are used fictitiously and are not to be construed as real. Any resemblance to actual events, locales, organizations, or persons, living or dead, is entirely coincidental.

AVON BOOKS
*An Imprint of* HarperCollins*Publishers*
10 East 53rd Street
New York, New York 10022-5299

Copyright © 2011 by Toni Herzog
ISBN 978-0-06-202460-2
**www.avonromance.com**

All rights reserved. No part of this book may be used or reproduced in any manner whatsoever without written permission, except in the case of brief quotations embodied in critical articles and reviews. For information address Avon Books, an Imprint of HarperCollins Publishers.

First Avon Books mass market printing: November 2011

Avon Trademark Reg. U.S. Pat. Off. and in Other Countries, Marca Registrada, Hecho en U.S.A.
HarperCollins® is a registered trademark of HarperCollins Publishers.

Printed in the U.S.A.

10 9 8 7 6 5 4 3 2 1

If you purchased this book without a cover, you should be aware that this book is stolen property. It was reported as "unsold and destroyed" to the publisher, and neither the author nor the publisher has received any payment for this "stripped book."

*To my dear friend, Renee,*
*who makes every day a holiday*

# Acknowledgments

As always, I am indebted to Lindsey Faber, for so patiently brainstorming this story with me, and to Renee Norris, for tirelessly reading and critiquing version after version of it on short notice, and also for coming up with brilliant ways to solve plot problems! How blessed am I to have close friends who just happen to be gifted at this stuff? You guys are the best!

I also want to thank my New York team of professionals for all they do—May Chen, Meg Ruley, Christina Hogrebe, Pam Jaffee, Jessie Edwards, and Amanda Bergeron. You all rock the publishing world and I'm thankful to have you in my corner!

"What right have you to be merry? What reason have you to be merry?"

Charles Dickens, A *Christmas Carol*

# *Prologue*

The car barreled around a curve next to Blue Valley Lake, tires squealing, barely staying on the pavement. Sue Ann gripped the wheel tight, trying to see the headlight-illuminated road through tears and hoping she wouldn't go plummeting into the water at any second. *I shouldn't be driving right now. I'm someone's mother. I'm supposed to be more careful than this.*

But it was difficult to think about things like being careful at the moment. It was difficult to think at all when she felt like someone had just plunged a dagger into her chest.

But no—not just someone. Jeff. Her husband. This was a nightmare. And she wanted desperately to wake up. She couldn't breathe.

And—oh God, poor Sophie! She was only seven.

Home asleep in her bed, she had no idea what was going on, no notion that her perfect little life was about to change forever.

Sue Ann swung the sedan into Jenny's driveway, slamming on the brakes just in time to avoid rear-ending Mick's pickup. It was the middle of the night, but instinct had led her here. And if you couldn't show up at your best friend's house at three in the morning, whose house *could* you show up at?

Only when she felt the cool grass of Jenny's yard beneath her toes did she realize she was barefoot. And in pajamas. But she'd simply had to get away—the only thing she'd grabbed walking out were her keys.

She didn't hesitate to bang on the door. Her chest still felt like it was about to explode and everything inside her hurt. This didn't feel real—couldn't be real. But it *was* real. Painfully, sickeningly real.

When Jenny's husband, Mick, yanked the door open a minute later, he at first looked perturbed—but then his expression transformed into one of worry. "Sue Ann?"

She must look awful—or maybe crazed. She suddenly felt very fragile. And embarrassed for Mick to see her this way. "I need Jenny," she said, her voice coming out small and desperate. She knew her cheeks were tearstained, her eyes red.

"Come inside," Mick said, reaching for her elbow, guiding her toward the couch. "I'll get her." Then he took off up the cottage's narrow staircase.

*To think—I once thought he was the bad one, the one who couldn't be trusted.* The irony rose thick in her throat, nearly gagging her.

When Jenny came rushing down the stairs in a flowy white nightgown, something about the mere sight of her friend made Sue Ann burst back into fresh tears.

*Now I have to tell her this. And I'm not even sure I can bear to say the words.*

"Sue Ann?" Jenny blinked, her gaze fraught with concern. "What is it? What's happened?"

"It's Jeff," Sue Ann managed, even though her throat threatened to close up at any second.

Jenny's jaw dropped. "Is he hurt?"

Yet Sue Ann just gave her head a short shake. The area behind her eyes throbbed. "No, I am."

"What?"

"He's—He's . . . there's another woman."

The news literally knocked the breath out of Jenny, just as Sue Ann had known it would, making her sag onto the couch as well. Because Sue Ann and Jeff, they were . . . solid. They were the couple everyone wanted to be. High school sweethearts. Happy and in love. Always. Jeff was the good, handsome, dependable man every woman in Destiny wished she had. They all envied Sue Ann.

They wouldn't anymore.

*"What?"* Jenny whispered in horror. "Are you sure? Because . . . because . . . " Yes, because this didn't sound like Jeff. Sue Ann knew that. She knew it to the marrow of her bones. And it made this all the more devastating.

"He admitted it. He told me all about it. It's someone he works with." Sue Ann felt as if she could barely draw air into her lungs. Now she'd said it. And giving voice to it had made it even more heartbreakingly true.

"Is . . . is the affair over?" Jenny asked.

Oh God. The question forced Sue Ann to expel a rough, deflating breath. Because Jenny didn't even know the really bad part yet. "It's . . . much worse than just an affair, Jen. He . . . " It felt as if something clawed at her stomach from the inside. "He *loves* her. And he . . . he hasn't even actually cheated on me yet—technically, physically. But he's *in love* with her. And that's much worse than just some affair. Much, much worse." She dissolved into new tears at the raw reality in her own words. Jeff had always been in love with *her*, devoted to *her*. She'd never had any doubt that it would be that way forever, until the day they died. But now, suddenly, without warning, he loved someone else. As her heart seized anew, she found herself reaching out, clutching at Jenny's shoulder, leaning over onto her.

"Oh, Sue Ann," Jenny said. Just that. Because they both knew there were no words to console her now, or make it better. "And you're sure? That he . . . still feels that way about this woman?"

Sue Ann just nodded.

"Oh Lord," Jenny whispered.

"How can this be?" Sue Ann burst out then. "I mean, how could this happen? How is it even possible?"

"I don't know," her best friend murmured as her arm came around her in a tight hug. "I don't know."

Sue Ann simply shook her head once more, as if doing so could somehow take this all away, take her back to the safe little world she'd lived in so happily until just a few hours ago when she'd innocently asked her husband if something was wrong because he'd seemed oddly withdrawn the last few weeks. She'd never in her wildest dreams expected to hear that he'd spent the recent months falling in love with someone else.

"I've . . . never felt so empty, Jen. Never. Like one day you're loved and the world makes sense—and the next day, the love you thought you'd have forever is just . . . gone."

"Bah," said Scrooge. "Humbug!"

Charles Dickens, A *Christmas Carol*

# *One*

*S*ue Ann trudged through the department store, feet tired, shopping bags in hand, and the spirit of Christmas nowhere to be found despite— or maybe because of—the sound of "Grandma Got Run Over by a Reindeer" echoing through loudspeakers overhead.

Oh God, it was only the day after Thanksgiving— she had a whole month of this private hell to go. Or a lifetime, depending upon which particular private hell she chose to focus on. The private hell of this first Christmas without Jeff would last a month, but the private hell of losing her husband and their life together would keep right on lingering.

*One day at a time. Just take one day at a time.* That was the advice in the divorce self-help guide her bookstore-owner friend, Amy, had foisted on her. And the truth was, it was a simple but good rule to live by during tough times. So she resolved not to look ahead to all the potential problems she'd face in the future, and not to even let herself anticipate all the awkward, sad moments she would experience at holiday events in the coming weeks—*just get through today. Finish your shopping, then get the hell out of Dodge.*

Dodge, in this case, was her hometown of Destiny, Ohio, where she'd been born and raised and had lovingly refurbished a big Victorian house with Jeff on Holly Lane, just a few blocks from the town square—a house that suddenly felt much emptier since he'd left nearly six months ago. So now she was escaping the house and everything else, just for the weekend—she'd rented a cabin on nearby Bear Lake to sort of just . . . collect herself, center herself, and gear up for the coming holiday season.

To her surprise, she'd learned that even in a small town where everyone knew you, it was possible to keep a low profile if you tried. Somewhat, anyway. And that was exactly what she'd instinctively done since Jeff's departure. But Christmastime brought invitations to all sorts of parties and events, and she had a child whose happiness meant the world to her—and all things considered, she knew it was time to face her loss and start living her life again, as best she could. Whether she felt ready for it or not.

It was her friend Tessa who'd suggested the cabin for Thanksgiving weekend—and Jenny and Amy, as well as their other friend, Rachel, had all thought it sounded like a good idea. Tessa had actually *bought* a cabin out in the woods when she'd been looking for some peace, and not only had she found it—she'd also inadvertently stumbled across the love of her life there as well. And though a man was the last thing Sue Ann sought, the peace and solace sounded good. Like one final retreat inside her sorrows, and a time to gather enough courage to break out of this lonely shell she'd built around herself.

She headed for the department store's side door, thinking of the cooler full of Thanksgiving leftovers in the trunk of her car just outside. She was already in Crestview, the larger nearby town where Destinyites came for any significant retail needs, and Bear Lake wasn't far away. She'd also tossed Christmas cards and her real estate study guide in the car, just in case she got in the mood for such tasks. But mostly, her plan was to relax. Read a book. Sit by the fire. Maybe bundle up and take a walk outside to enjoy the scenery.

And perhaps it was all just some grand test she was giving herself—maybe she thought a woman who could enjoy a weekend alone in a cabin was a woman who was stronger than she'd felt these last months. But whether it was about relaxing, or gathering courage, or proving something to herself, she was ready to make her way to the lake and leave all the shoppers, music, and early holiday stress behind. *Quiet cabin, here I come.*

"Hi."

The deep male voice had come from somewhere nearby—but she was the only person currently in this part of the store. Taken aback, she stopped, looked around, and wondered if she was losing her mind.

And she was just about to continue on her way—when she heard it again. "Over here." It made her flinch. Then look around once more. And this time her eyes caught on a wooden structure to one side of the store aisle—with a life-size fake furry reindeer head protruding from it.

"What's wrong?" The reindeer's mouth moved as it spoke, and its head even tilted pointedly, as if challenging her. "Haven't you ever talked to a reindeer before?"

Oh brother, this felt weird. Because someone was in there who she couldn't see, but he could see *her*. It didn't seem quite fair and left her feeling oddly intimidated. "Um . . . no," she finally said. Quietly. Because she didn't really want to be seen conversing with a reindeer.

"I mostly talk to kids," the reindeer said.

"Then . . . um . . . how did *I* get so lucky?"

"Because you're pretty."

"Oh." Dear God, was she blushing? Because a reindeer had told her she was pretty? She felt like an idiot. And yet . . . still oddly flattered. She hadn't felt anything remotely close to pretty in a long time.

"And I'm supposed to tell you the Cub Scouts are doing free gift wrapping by the Customer Service desk," the reindeer added. "I'd help them, but when it comes to scissors and tape, I'm all hooves."

"I see," Sue Ann replied, unwittingly amused but still wary. "Well, I'm on my way out."

"My loss," said the reindeer.

Which made Sue Ann blink, then pull in her breath. This was ridiculous. A reindeer *was* making her blush.

"Wanna come back to my stable for a while?" he asked then—and this time she had to stifle a laugh. "We could have an eggnog or two. Then maybe, you know, play some reindeer games."

Her cheeks heated up all over again. Over reindeer games? Or was it that the reindeer's antlers now slanted at a jaunty angle that somehow actually felt suggestive?—even though that made no sense at all.

And she wanted to be offended that the reindeer was being so forward—but she couldn't. Because he was funny. And sounded cute. And was making her feel . . . like a woman, a desirable woman, for the first time since Jeff had announced he'd fallen out of love with her.

"That's, um, flattering," she finally said, unable to hide a small smile now, "but I really have to go."

"You'd break a poor reindeer's heart? At Christmastime?"

She tilted her head and couldn't believe she was still having a conversation with a fake deer. "I'm sure some cute doe will catch your eye when you get back to the North Pole."

The reindeer actually managed to shrug, as if to say: *Maybe, maybe not.*

And Sue Ann tried to suppress a grin as she turned to go.

"Merry Christmas," called the reindeer.

"You, too," she said with a last glance in his direction, then headed for the door. She was still eager to get out of the store, away from the music, away from the crowds, away from everything.

But as silly as it seemed, that reindeer had made her day.

Seven rustic log cabins lined the arm of Bear Lake that cut through Snow Valley, and Sue Ann sat in the third one, making out Christmas cards. It hadn't taken her long to fall back on needing an activity. After she'd carried in her cooler and overnight case, started a fire, and put on some pajamas—even though it was just now getting dark—she'd realized she felt at loose ends. As a young mom used to being on the run, she was accustomed to staying busy.

*But you came here to relax, unwind, and maybe—finally—get over the divorce. You don't have to keep busy every second.*

So she stopped writing out the card in front of her and set it aside on the small coffee table she was using as a desk. Then she pushed to her feet from the braided rug where she sat, walked to the cooler, and pulled out the bottle of chardonnay she'd packed, in hopes of bringing on that relaxation. She listened to the crackle of the fire behind her as she maneuvered the corkscrew and poured some into a wineglass from home. After which she settled into one of the two easy chairs facing the stone hearth, stared into the almost hypnotic fire, and allowed herself to . . . think.

Unfortunately, however, what she thought about was Jeff. More specifically, Jeff and Veronica—who he called Ronni and which made Sue Ann want to puke, not because she really disliked the nickname but because the two were so sickeningly into each other. And because as careful as Jeff had been about not sleeping with "Ronni" before separating from Sue Ann, once they'd officially split, he'd begun parading his new woman all over town. As if it were normal for him to be with someone else. As if it weren't disrespectful to Sue Ann and potentially harmful to Sophie to be flaunting the chick he now lived with, hanging all over her everywhere they went. He'd brought her to the summer carnival in Creekside Park, Jenny had seen them at the fall Apple Festival, and they'd been spotted together everywhere from the Whippy Dip to Dolly's Main Street Café. And they didn't even live in Destiny—Jeff had moved into her small house in Crestview.

*He's like a schoolboy with her. The way he once was with me.* But he wasn't that schoolboy anymore—he only behaved like one.

So pretty much *any* thought having to do with Jeff and Ronni made her want to puke. Instead, though, she just took a sip of her wine.

"I feel like our whole relationship has been a lie, a sham, where I thought you loved me but you don't. I feel like a fool." That's one of the many things she'd said to Jeff that horrible night he'd told her about Veronica.

"You're not a fool, Sue Ann—I *have* loved you. I just . . . don't anymore. Not in that way, I mean. You're Sophie's mom and you've been in my life forever, so I'll *always* love you—I'm just not *in* love with you anymore." That's what he'd said. Like it would make her feel better. Idiot. She made the next sip of wine a bigger one.

And possibly the worst thing about Veronica was that Sue Ann couldn't even hate her for being younger or silly or gorgeous—because she wasn't any of those things. She was thirty-one, only two years younger than Sue Ann. And she was slightly plump with plain, somewhat frizzy hair and boring fashion taste. Which meant Jeff's love for her wasn't based on anything superficial—it was genuine, bone deep. And all the more agonizing for Sue Ann when she couldn't blame it on anything physical or shallow. It was real, true love. One more thought that made her sick. Time for another swig of wine.

Okay, so working on Christmas cards had been better than this. She'd come here committed to shaking off all these hurtful thoughts that still haunted her—but so far, it wasn't working very well. Maybe it was a real blessing that she led a busy life. Maybe coming to this cabin had been a stupid idea.

Wine in hand, she stood and padded to the window, glancing out on the serene lake across the narrow blacktop road. Oh, it was starting to snow. She hadn't heard that in the forecast—but snow this early wasn't the norm in southeast Ohio, so it would stop soon. Yet it was one more reminder that winter was here, and Christmas with it. Sophie's first Christmas in a broken home.

Sophie had spent Thanksgiving yesterday with Sue Ann at her mother's house with all the relatives—then Jeff had stopped by to pick her up, dumbly telling Sue Ann all the fun stuff he and Ronni were going to do with their daughter over the weekend.

Don't you see how wrong this is, she'd wanted to say. You're supposed to be *here*, with me, with us—and now we're supposed to get in the car and go to your mother's for pumpkin pie and Pictionary, like every year. We're supposed to be a family.

And yet at the same time, she'd realized she could barely stand to look at him. Because he'd betrayed her. Broken their vow—and her trust. And now he kept walking around acting like it was all okay, like the divorce was long in the past, like they were all already adjusted to this new life they led.

Once, she'd respected Jeff's easygoing social manner, the way he was always comfortable in any crowd. But now she sort of loathed it, because at the very least, she wanted him to be as uncomfortable as her when they saw each other. She wanted him to feel bad for uprooting their lives, changing everything. And he just didn't seem to feel very bad about it at all. He was too busy flashing Veronica all over Destiny like a new—even if not very flashy—piece of jewelry.

But then, maybe the fact that she could barely stand to see him was a step in the right direction. Loathing him seemed healthier than missing him. Didn't it?

Though, even if she was starting to loathe Jeff . . . well, at moments it was pretty easy not to like *herself* very much, either. This whole ugly drama had forced her to start being more critical of herself than ever before.

Was it unappealing that she'd been perfectly happy with her part-time job at Destiny Properties and was otherwise fulfilled by just being a mom? Was she supposed to want more simply because so many other people did? Had Jeff's feelings for her changed because she tended to laugh too loud, or because she brought home takeout too often, or because she sometimes couldn't keep a secret? She was working on that last one, though, and had gotten better about it. God knew she was learning just how painful it was when your dirty laundry was hung out for the whole world to see.

Karmic payback? It was hard not to wonder.

Every time she got on jags like this, Jenny talked her down, making her see that it was all just fruitless pondering. But Jenny wasn't here to stop the useless spinning of her mind this time.

Letting out a sigh and taking another sip of wine, she decided that maybe tomorrow she'd rise early, bundle up, and take a refreshing walk by the lake. She'd try to soak in nature, look inward for peace, stuff like that. But for now, returning to her Christmas cards seemed like a much safer way to occupy her time than all this thinking.

An hour later, she'd finished the cards plus another glass of wine, and darkness had fallen silent and deep outside. Next up, studying for her real estate license. She'd done part-time administrative work at the real estate office for years, but now that she needed more money, this was the obvious direction to go in. If things went well, she might even be able to keep the house. She'd been waffling back and forth—to sell or not to sell—but she *loved* the house and she'd put a lot of herself into it.

And everyone said she had a knack for matching people with the right home and for helping people see a property's potential even if it wasn't obvious. She'd known Logan Whitaker would love her Great Aunt Celia's lake cottage when it had been vacated summer before last, after all. And she'd seen the potential in her own house on picturesque Holly Lane when she'd talked Jeff into buying it—and following her vision, they'd turned the once run-down old place into a warm, wonderful home. And she'd actually started rehabbing and redecorating houses when she was a little girl—only they'd been *doll*houses. Back then, her mother would buy old dollhouses at yard sales and she would repaint and revitalize them until they were showplaces. So going for her real estate license was about the only *positive* change caused by Jeff's departure.

Just then, her cell phone rang. She hadn't been sure she'd get reception here in the valley, but she rushed to the table where her purse rested, digging it out to answer. "Hello?"

"Sue Ann, it's Barry Clayton." Her lawyer. Hmm. She hadn't talked to Barry since the divorce was final.

"And I'm afraid I'm calling with some bad news. Are you sitting down?"

Fifteen minutes later, Sue Ann disconnected from Barry, then slumped back into one of the easy chairs across from the fireplace, numb. Life had felt pretty crappy lately, but she'd been coping, doing the one-day-at-a-time thing, getting by, getting stronger. Yet this—this changed everything.

As she stared blankly into the low-burning flames, snippets of all he'd just told her echoed in her head. "Jeff's petitioning to stop his alimony payments . . . He's arguing he'll no longer be able to afford it because he and Veronica are getting married—tomorrow. And I'm sorry to tell you this, but they plan to have a baby. Right away . . . One and potentially two more dependents—he'll have a reasonable case . . . And I don't want to scare you, but—worst case scenario if you have trouble making ends meet because of this, he *could* go after full custody of Sophie."

Trying to wrap her head around it all, Sue Ann got dizzy, even while sitting down, and finally blew out a long breath. Whoa. *Jeff, how could you? Marrying her, already? And . . . oh God, having a baby?* She felt as if someone had punched her in the gut. But not just someone—her ex-husband. He'd behaved pretty selfishly in many ways lately, but this took the cake. It was almost unimaginable. And at the same time that he was getting married and preparing to start a family with someone else, he was cutting her off financially? Before she even had a chance to get her feet under her? Yes, she was studying for her real estate exam, but now . . . well, it sounded like there was no time for that, like she had to come up with a bigger income *immediately*.

Or else she could lose Sophie. Another *whooshing* breath left her. Surely Jeff wouldn't do that? Surely. And yet—Jeff had done a lot in the past six months that she wouldn't have thought possible.

*What am I going to do? How on earth am I going to make this work?*

Before that phone call, she'd been getting ready to grab the binder containing her real estate study materials, but now . . . well, again, she was gonna need a bigger, quicker miracle than a real estate license to keep her afloat. So she reached past the binder for the bottle of wine and took a big drink. That wouldn't save her either, but in this particular moment, it made more sense to her than trying to study.

So she drank more and tried to think. About options.

She considered calling Jenny, or maybe her mom, but realized she was still absorbing the news and couldn't quite face sharing it just yet, not even with the people closest to her. *Block out the hurt. That he's marrying her. That he's ready to have a child with her. Focus on Sophie and you. What are you going to do to save yourself? And to ensure keeping Sophie with you?*

Deep down inside, tears of rage threatened to burst free—*but don't you dare cry. You've shed enough tears over this whole situation already. No more.*

And to her surprise, she held them back.

Maybe it had finally happened. Maybe Jeff had finally hurt her so much that she was no longer just sad—she was mad. Angry as hell, as a matter of fact.

She took another long swig from the bottle, then resisted the urge to throw it across the room and send it crashing into grate where the fire still burned. After which she set the wine aside, emotionally exhausted. Oh God, this was too much to think about. *But don't panic here. Just give yourself a little time to get used to it all. You don't have to solve the world's problems right this second. So let yourself rest. And maybe tomorrow you'll wake up with an answer. Of some kind. Maybe everything will be clearer in the morning.*

The fire could have used another log, but . . . she was suddenly feeling sleepy, like she could nod off any second. Must be the wine. Okay, and the mental collapse, too. So she simply let herself lean back into the comfortable easy chair. Fire, schmire.

It felt good to let her eyes fall shut, good to feel herself drifting into a peaceful place. *You're strong, you're capable, and everything will be fine,* she promised herself silently—another simple mantra from the book Amy had given her. *Everything will be fine.* God, she hoped so.

And then . . . what was that? Sue Ann had no idea how much time had passed when she flinched awake—from a sound. It had come from her right, near the door, like a click. And it was followed by a jiggle.

Lethargic from her nap, she tried to get her wits about her, tried to force herself to sit up straight and think.

Then the jiggle came again, louder this time. And holy crap, it wasn't just *near* the door—it *was* the door! Someone was outside—trying to get in!

Still disoriented, she leaped to feet. *Weapon, weapon, I need a weapon.*

She glanced around but could barely focus and her limbs moved too slow.

*Come on, do something. You're someone's mother—*

*you're supposed to be quick-thinking in the face of danger, and you can't let yourself get killed because Sophie needs you now more than ever.*

In full desperation mode as the jiggling grew louder and she sensed the door about to open at any second, she spotted an old wooden broom leaning against a doorjamb near the fireplace. She snatched it up, her heart beating wildly, painfully now, and just as the cabin door began to move, she followed the instinct to jump up onto her easy chair. She held the broom like a battering ram.

When the door opened and a man's form entered the room along with a cold burst of air, she let out a yelp of fright. But then she remembered to be brave. Tough. *What would you do if Sophie were here, if it were up to you to protect her?* "Don't come near me—I'm armed!" she yelled.

And then she realized the man, looking completely unalarmed, was squinting at her.

And that he was dark and . . . hmm, maybe handsome.

And that he was . . . "Adam?" she said. Adam Becker had been a fixture in her life since they were kids at Destiny Elementary, as well as being her ex-husband's best friend for nearly as long. With dark hair and classic good looks, Adam was Destiny's all around good guy, so it was a relief to see *him* instead of some mad killer—but what on earth had brought him to Bear Lake on Thanksgiving weekend?

Adam squinted even harder in the room left dimly lit by the dying fire, and continued looking confused as he said, "Sue Ann? What the hell are you doing here?"

"Me? I'm wondering the same thing about you. What are *you* doing here? In my cabin?"

That's when Adam drew back slightly, his usually friendly expression suddenly filling with a clear disdain. Whoa, what was that about? And who *was* this masked man? In all the years she'd known him, she'd never seen Adam look so snarly.

"*Your* cabin?" he spat. "Uh, I hate to break this to you, Sue Ann, but this cabin belongs to me."

By this time it was getting dark, and snowing pretty heavily . . .

Charles Dickens, A *Christmas Carol*

## *Two*

*O*kay, was it just her or did Adam look hotter than usual? Maybe it was the pale lighting. Or maybe the wine? But wait. What he'd just said didn't make any sense.

"How can it be yours?" she snapped back at him. "Especially since I'm in it?"

"I rent this cabin on Thanksgiving weekend every year—including this year. That's how," he said.

"Well, you must have rented some *other* cabin, because I rented one, too, and this is the one they gave me."

In response, he simply held up a key attached to a wooden key chain the size of his fist with the Bear Lake logo imprinted on it, as if that proved his ownership of the building.

"I have one of those, too," she informed him smartly.

But he still wore a look she couldn't quite read, because—again—it wasn't like any expression she'd ever seen Adam wearing in all the time she'd known him. He appeared disgusted bordering on angry. That's when his gaze dropped to the broom she held . . . more like a low-slung guitar now. "So what were you gonna do if I was some crazed cabin killer, sweep me to death?"

Embarrassment heated her cheeks. "I'm not sure. It was all I could find."

He swung his glance toward the hearth, then back at her. "Um, next time, try the fire poker—I would have been a little more worried."

Crap—how had she missed the poker! Sleep, wine, distress. But still . . .

"And what the hell are you doing on that chair? I'm a crazed cabin killer, remember—not a mouse."

Okay, he was officially starting to make her feel stupid—which was not Adam's usual style. What had come over him? "I was disoriented and . . . I guess I thought it would make me feel more powerful if I was towering *over* the crazed cabin killer."

Yet he didn't look the least bit impressed. Or as if he thought she was at all powerful. "Well, you can come down now," he said dryly. Then he looked around. "So . . . are you, like, alone here? By yourself?" He made it sound like that was insane, even though he, too, appeared to be alone.

"Yep."

"Weird," he said, seemingly more to himself than to her, but it rankled just the same.

"What's wrong with you?" she asked. Usually, Adam

was friendly, responsible, and likable—and most people in Destiny would go so far as to describe the owner of Becker Landscaping as a "people person." Even at his worst, he might be quiet and a little brooding, but he was never snide or condescending like this.

"I thought we covered that already," he said. "You're in my cabin."

*Never before now, that is.* She didn't know what his problem was, but he was starting to piss her off. "I thought we also covered that when I checked in, they gave this cabin to *me*. So there must be some sort of mix-up, but I'm sure if you go back to the office, they can give you a different cabin." She enunciated very clearly, just to make sure he got it this time. Sheesh, to think she was the one who'd been drinking.

A few feet away from her, he let his narrowed eyes run the length of her body, brow tightly knit, as if sizing up the situation yet again and realizing that she really wasn't going to just disappear. "Fine," he finally bit off, then turned to go. But as he reached the door, he stopped and looked back, and this time he spoke with a little less contempt. "What *are* you doing here anyway? I mean, since when are you the rent-a-cabin type?"

She didn't let her gaze waver from his. "Since my husband left me for another woman," she reminded him sharply. Although her sharpness faded regrettably as she added, "I just . . . wanted to get away from everything for a couple of days before the holidays, that's all."

"Oh." Apparently he'd been so caught up in his own . . . issues, problems—or whatever was going on with him—that for a moment he'd forgotten hers. And then his eyes softened, his angry look fading to something like . . . sadness. For her. Kind of like pity. Yuck. "Just so you know, I think he's an idiot."

And despite the fact that Adam still wasn't acting like himself, and that she didn't want to be the object of sympathy, the sentiment warmed something in her chest, just a little. "Thanks," she said softly.

And then the door closed behind him and she stood there staring at it.

What had just happened here? And what the hell had Adam in such a nasty mood? She hadn't talked to him much since she and Jeff had split, and it did help a little to find out he thought Jeff had made a mistake, but that aside—what had turned Mr. All American good guy Adam Becker into the snotty jerk she'd just encountered?

Oh well—whatever the case, at least now she had her cabin back to herself.

Adam wasn't acting like himself and he knew it. Problem was, he just didn't care much at the moment. Too many thoughts spun through his head as he trod back through the falling snow toward the small office that served the cabins and nearby campground.

Damn, when had it started coming down this hard? He pulled the collar of his denim jacket up around his neck to ward off the cold wind that kept the thick, heavy flakes swirling around him.

He still couldn't believe he'd walked into his cabin to find Sue Ann there. Sue Ann and all her girlfriends—that he could have believed. But Sue Ann alone, in a cabin—it just didn't make sense.

*Aw hell, cut her a break. Her world's been turned upside down—she doesn't have to do things that make sense right now.* Still, what were the chances? Of all the places she could retreat to, she'd had to choose *his* place? His actual cabin, the same one he and his twin boys, Jacob and Joey, came to every year on Thanksgiving weekend.

Not that the twins were with him this year. That's what had him in such a Grinchy mood. When his ex-wife, Sheila, had told him just over a week ago that her parents wanted to take the boys out west to Aspen for the entire month of December . . . well, it had shot his holidays to hell before they'd even started. Of course, he shared custody and could have said no, but he'd have seemed like an ass, especially the way his kids' eyes had lit up at the thought of all that snow. Hell—even their second-grade teacher, Miss Wallace, had agreed to the plan, citing that travel was educational, so long as the twins kept up with their work via a laptop he'd given them to take on the trip.

Adam and his dad had camped here in the valley a lot when he was a kid—in summer the fishing was good, there were canoes and paddleboats, and hiking trails crisscrossed the hills surrounding the lake. So nearly as soon as his boys could walk, he'd started packing them up and bringing them over here—and Thanksgiving weekend had become an easy time to do it because Sheila had always used that weekend to drive to Columbus and shop with her friends. And even still, since the divorce, she and the guy she now lived with usually went away for those few days. It wasn't the warmest time of year, but he and the boys still found plenty to do—hiking, roasting marshmallows, telling ghost stories, and just generally hanging out and doing guy stuff.

And since he had a standing reservation, he hadn't

bothered cancelling it this year despite the fact that the twins couldn't come—in fact, he'd decided it might be a good place to blow off some steam and see if he could get back in his normal state of mind.

But so far, coming here had only made him more irate. Even with only a little snow falling, the roads had gotten slippery on the way over, making for an unpleasant drive. And then he'd found his cabin inhabited by his best friend's ex-wife. And not only that—she'd been wearing some skimpy pajama top that had given him far too good a view of her breasts, which had made him a little uncomfortable even as it had tightened his groin.

But maybe it was silly to feel weird about that. After all, he'd known Sue Ann since they were kids, and he'd seen her in a two-piece bathing suit plenty of times over their years of hanging out with the same friends. Yet something about this, right now, had felt different, had felt . . . personal. Even though she hadn't caught on that he'd been unwittingly staring at her chest half the time they were talking. Damn—the whole situation was beginning to feel a little surreal.

Snow blew around the entrance to the log-hewn office as he opened the door to see Grayson Collier, the skinny old man who'd been renting him the cabin all these years. "Back so soon?" he asked, friendly as ever.

Adam pulled the door shut behind him, blocking out the blowing snow and now-whistling wind. He tried not to sound too put out as he replied, though it required effort. "Not by choice. There's a woman in my cabin."

Grayson just laughed. "And you left? I mean, I'd like a woman in *my* cabin, if ya know what I mean, son," he ended with a wink.

Adam just glared at him, unamused. Grayson had picked now to start being a funny guy?

When Grayson caught on, though, he wiped away his smile and cleared his throat. "Oh, you wasn't jokin' around? There's really a woman in your cabin?"

"Yep."

His eyebrows knit. "Don't see how that could be, but . . . well, give me just a minute to investigate this." And with that, he pulled out an old-fashioned registry book that looked like it had been in service for decades. You didn't find anything modern like a computer at the Snow Valley rental office. "Hmm," Grayson said, studying the book. Then, "Oh," "Hmm," and finally, "Uh-oh."

"Uh-oh?" Adam asked.

"Uh-oh," Grayson confirmed.

Adam's fuse grew shorter by the moment, so it was through slightly gritted teeth that he said, "Uh-oh what?"

"Well, we got us a new feller workin' here, and it looks like he took a reservation for your cabin, not re-alizin' you'd booked it already. And he musta checked her in before my shift."

"I see," Adam said dryly, trying to keep his cool. "Well then, how about you just give me a different cabin?" He liked his usual cabin, but he'd take *any* cabin at this point. He slapped the key he'd been given on the counter, ready to trade it in for another.

"Can't," Grayson said.

And Adam felt his eyebrows shoot up. "Can't?"

"They're all full."

At this, Adam simply blinked his disbelief. Usually it was empty here this time of year. "You're kidding. How the hell many people rent cabins on Thanksgiving weekend, for God's sake?"

"Well, 'bout eight from the looks of things. Given that we got seven cabins plus you. Turley family decided to have a Thanksgiving family reunion sorta shindig, and most of 'em's stayin' *here*."

"You're seriously telling me you don't have a cabin for me?" Adam barked. "When I've had this booked since last year?"

Now Grayson finally began to look as remorseful as Adam felt he should. "Sure am sorry, and I'll be givin' the new feller a lecture about it, that's for certain. But . . . guess the good news is—at least your little boys ain't with ya this year, so you don't have to fret about disappointin' 'em."

A thick sigh that bordered on a growl left Adam's lungs. The old man made a decent point, but it didn't make him any happier. He'd packed up enough food and clothes for a couple of days, enlisted his mom to feed the dog, and . . . hell, more than that, he'd just been counting on this getaway. It wasn't a big thing—but it was the one thing he'd felt stood a chance of helping him get back in a better mood and ready to face the holidays. Damn it.

Yet it looked like fate—or something—had taken away his options. "Well then, like it or not, guess as soon as you put my money back on my credit card, I'm heading home."

So it surprised him when Grayson appeared just as uncertain about this as he had everything else in their conversation. "You sure about that?" he asked, glancing toward the window. "I mean, you notice how fast that snow's fallin'?"

"I saw it," Adam said, giving the window no more than a sideways glance. "But so what? I've got four-wheel drive—a little snow doesn't slow me down."

"Hmm," Grayson replied as if he knew something Adam didn't. "You remember that hill you just come down to get here? I just got a call from up top sayin' nothin's movin' up or down it now—road's slick as snot. And besides, this is Snow Valley, ya know."

"So?" Adam asked, squinting slightly.

"Well, it ain't just a name. When it snows here, it piles up faster, falls harder. Somethin' about the lay of the land and the air flow into the valley. A clipper that leaves an inch or two everywhere else leaves more like four or five down here. And that hill's a bear—steep enough in good weather, and pert near impossible in bad."

Huh. He'd never heard any of this before—but he was used to driving in bad conditions given that he did a lot of snow removal to tide him over during the winter, and Grayson was probably prone to exaggeration. "Well, you just told me you don't have any place for me to sleep tonight," Adam said, "so looks like I don't have much choice. I'm getting out of here." Then he trudged back out into the cold, wrestling his keys from his pocket.

The first thing he noticed was the way his work boots sank deeper into the snow than they had a few minutes ago. Then he lifted his head to look around.

Shit. In a very short time, the whole valley had taken on blizzardlike conditions—everything covered in white and the snow blowing harder than before. He could barely see the first cabin less than twenty yards away.

The next thing to catch his attention was the sound of slipping, sliding tires somewhere behind him, and he turned back to spot a dark shadow through the heavy snow—a big, sturdy-looking SUV struggled to make the first turn where the narrow road began sloping upward.

Aw, damn. In truth, it was a hell of a road, and he *had* been sliding around more than he liked getting down here—and that was when the snow had been light. And now the behemoth SUV in the distance was making no headway.

That's when he glanced to his right to see Grayson standing next to him, having followed him out into the cold. "Told ya," Grayson said.

Adam only glowered—then said, "Where will *you* be sleepin' tonight?" Since it appeared he might be bunking with the old man.

"Office floor, I reckon. I keep a sleepin' bag here for just such occasions."

Huh. Adam hadn't even *brought* a sleeping bag. Since he'd rented a cabin. With bunk beds. Usually he took the bottom and the boys shared the top. His chest tightened with irritation all over again.

"You can join me if you like," Grayson offered. "Ain't exactly comfy, but it's better than freezin' to death in your truck."

"You're a ray of sunshine, old man," Adam bit off in his direction. "But . . . the fact is, the woman in the cabin happens to be an old friend of mine. And since the place has bunks, it makes more sense for me to stay with her. Whether she likes it or not."

This was starting to feel like a bad movie. If things kept going like this, a crazed cabin killer probably *would* show up soon. And if Adam had been in a sour mood when he'd first gotten here, now it had progressed to being downright rotten. To think he had a perfectly nice house that he'd willingly chosen to leave behind for this.

He stomped back in through the cabin door, not bothering to knock since it was damn cold out. And Sue Ann looked up with a start, now sitting in the same chair where she'd been standing a few minutes ago. Apparently, she hadn't meant to leave the door unlocked.

"I've got some bad news for ya," he said without ceremony. "You've got a roommate."

Her eyebrows shot up. "What?"

"All the cabins are booked for the night, and I've gotta sleep *somewhere*."

He watched as she sucked in her breath, an expression of disbelief on her pretty face, her blond hair pulled up into a messy knot behind her head, loose tendrils falling down and calling attention to her slender neck. And like before, something about seeing skin that was usually covered, here, now, in such a private setting, felt more personal than any other time she might have worn her hair that way over the years. Strange. Strange in a way he couldn't explain to himself.

*You flirted with her earlier. Behind that silly reindeer head.*

Damn, he had. And he hadn't quite known why, just like he couldn't understand the way he was feeling *now*. At the time, he'd been bored, pressed into the situation by virtue of being den leader—it had been his last official act of fatherhood before driving the twins to Sheila's parents' house for their trip. He'd assumed Sue Ann would recognize his voice. And when she hadn't, something uncharacteristically devilish had perked to life inside him, urging him to play with her a little—and before he'd known it, it had turned into flirting.

It had, if nothing else, provided a momentary distraction from his crappy mood. And it had been . . . fun, even if a little weird. But he didn't think this was the time to break the news that he was the bold reindeer, because, pretty or not, she looked completely upset, even more than before.

"Well, if you insist on staying," she said, "then I'll just leave. Because if you're here . . . " She let out a heavy sigh. "It just ruins the whole thing."

Adam heaved out a hot breath. "Thanks a lot," he said, trying to be more offended than . . . aroused. Since she'd just pushed to her feet to face him—and she apparently still hadn't noticed what she was wearing in front of him. And hell, he *wished* she could leave, but . . . "If it was that simple, Sue Ann, *I'd* have left."

"What do you mean by simple?"

"There's a freaking blizzard going on outside."

She blinked up at him, confusion now shading her brown eyes. "Really? How can that be? It's only November." The bulk of southern Ohio's snow typically showed up after the holiday, and it was downright rare to get a full-blown snowstorm this early.

But he only gave a disgusted nod. "Really. And November or not, nothing's making it up or down the hill, so we're trapped here, at least 'til morning. Afraid you're stuck with me."

This forced another thick sigh from her, the kind that came with a heavy shrug—which drew his attention back to her boobs, to the fact that her nipples were clearly visible through that pajama top. The bottoms, they were okay—flannel, with different colored snowflakes on them. The top, though—the top was getting a little hard to take. It was strappy, pale pink—paler than her nipples, he could attest, since the darker shade shone through—and ridiculously thin. Did the woman not know it was winter, for God's sake?

He'd always been kind of a boob man, and maybe somewhere in the back of his mind he'd always been vaguely aware that Sue Ann's were probably nice, but now he knew for sure and the knowledge had his groin tightening again. Maybe more than tightening. Aw, hell. He wished he'd already grabbed his duffel bag from the truck on his way back in—so he could hold it in front of him in case his jeans were getting snugger there. Damn it. This was not what he needed. And the sad truth of it was, at this moment, he felt almost physically incapable of pulling his eyes away from her chest.

So he felt he had as little choice in what he said next as in where he was sleeping tonight. "Um, do you have anything you can put on?"

"Huh?" she asked, oblivious.

But then he dropped his gaze pointedly back from her face to her breasts, so she finally looked down, too—then let out a horrified gasp.

"I just thought maybe those pants might come with, like, a big matching flannel top or something," he offered, squinting uncertainly. God, this was awkward. And since he *had* known Sue Ann for so long, it probably shouldn't be, but it was and that somehow made it worse.

She crossed her arms over herself as a bright blush blossomed on her cheeks. "Um, no—no matching flannel top, and I, um, don't really have anything since I thought I'd be alone here, but . . . "

Her gaze darted frantically around until she finally grabbed up an afghan from the back of the other easy chair and wrapped it around her like a cape. Crocheted in warm, woodsy shades of green, it covered her up well, which should have made it better for him—only . . . hell, somehow it wasn't helping. Seemed the damage was done; he was seeing her breasts in his mind now anyway.

"Better?" she asked.

"Yes," he lied. Then repeated it—"Yes"—as if that might magically make it more true.

Peering toward the window now, Sue Ann walked over to it in her afghan to stare out at the snow, looking completely distressed.

And he almost felt bad for barging in on her—but mostly, he just continued being angry about the whole situation. "Look, it's not my fault," he said. "I mean, what's the big problem? With any luck I'll be out of your hair in the morning."

"The big problem is " She stopped, sighed, still peering forlornly out the dark pane "—that I just really needed some time alone. To help me face the holidays—and some other stuff, too, it turns out. And maybe it wouldn't have helped anyway, but I'm still just . . . " She shook her head, appearing tired. "I'm just exhausted and humiliated by it all. And the truth is—between dealing with the holidays, trying to keep Sophie happy and acceptant of all this, and just trying to build a new life for myself, some days I feel like I'm barely holding it all together."

She pursed her lips then, looking more vulnerable than he'd known Sue Ann could, and despite himself, he felt the weight of her troubles in his chest and sort of wished he could give her a hug.

"You probably don't get that, though," she went on,

almost sounding resentful. "Guys are so sturdy. You went through your divorce so easy."

The words forced him to expel a heavy breath that echoed through his lungs. Adam didn't talk about his divorce three years ago to anyone, ever. But right now, he was going to make one very small, quick exception. "It, uh, might not have been as easy as I made it seem," he told her quietly. "And . . . I really am sorry you're going through this."

Finally, she shifted her gaze from the window to him, and the sadness in her warm eyes brought him down even further. "Thanks," she said softly. "And I'm sorry I just dumped all that on you. It's just . . . that's why I came here. To try to start getting on with my life. And so far . . . well, I got some really bad news after getting here, so it hasn't exactly turned out like I planned. Then again, *nothing* has turned out like I planned, so why am I surprised?"

Adam tilted his head, asking the obvious question. "What kind of bad news?"

She met his gaze for a long moment, then let out a heavy sigh before answering. "Maybe you already know all this from Jeff—"

"I haven't talked to Jeff in a while," he interrupted. So whatever was going on, he probably hadn't heard.

Still, she hesitated again, and he got the idea it had grown difficult for her to speak. "The thing is—" She stopped, bit her lip. "My lawyer called right before you got here. To tell me Jeff and Ronni are getting married. And want to have a baby. And he's trying to cut off my alimony already. And I'm not sure what I'm gonna do."

"Holy shit." That's all Adam could muster for a moment. Talk about being kicked when you're down. "That sucks. I'm sorry, Sue Ann."

"Thanks. But, um, let's not talk about it, okay? And the fact that I just spilled all that . . . " She made the same face as if she'd just eaten something unpleasant. "Please don't tell Jeff I did that, okay?"

"I wouldn't," he reassured her quickly. "And you don't need to be embarrassed in front of me."

She didn't look wholly convinced—and maybe he couldn't blame her given the way he'd been acting and the stiffness in his voice even now as he tried to comfort her—but she gave him a short nod anyway. Then said, "So now that you know why *I'm* upset, what's *your* problem? You've been a bear since you got here."

Being a guy who tended to keep his troubles to himself—and not usually let them show so damn much—he normally would have brushed off the question, changed the subject. But he supposed it was only fair. And besides, now that Sue Ann had seen the worst of him, maybe he wanted to explain, let her know there was a reason. "Sheila's parents took the boys out West for the whole month, from now 'til after Christmas."

Though this clearly didn't surprise her at all. "Sophie told me. It was all the talk at school."

Ah, made sense—her daughter and his sons were in the same class. "Well, it's just a long time for them to be gone, especially this time of year, you know?"

She nodded but said, "Well, at least you know they're coming back." Unlike her husband, she meant. And he supposed she made a good point. And maybe compared to her current troubles, this sounded small—because yeah, this fresh news about Jeff seemed pretty devastating. Even so, though, that didn't take away his problems or make him feel any better. There was so much she didn't know about him, so much no one knew. And things that weren't coming back, ever.

He didn't tell her that, though—instead he just let the stark silence of a snow-filled night settle around them. Even the fire in the hearth stayed quiet—until finally a pop and a hiss from that direction broke the moment. "I'll go get my stuff from the truck," he said. "Give you a minute to . . . do anything you want to do." *Like maybe find some more flannel to cover yourself with.* But then, if the afghan wasn't working, what did it matter?

*Well, please just keep that blanket around you and maybe eventually I'll quit seeing your breasts in my mind.*

"You want to be on top or bottom?" Adam asked.

Sue Ann turned to look at him from where she sat by the fire. "Huh?"

"The bunks," he said, standing next to them with a duffel bag in hand.

"Oh. Um, I'll go with bottom." *And I'm feeling pretty relieved that you're not talking about sex.* Not that she knew why she'd expect Adam to be talking about sex— they'd never talked about it *before.* She was probably just still a little embarrassed about him seeing her in such a revealing top, which hadn't even occurred to her given all the other general unrest of the evening—until he'd so pointedly called it to her attention. She pulled the afghan closed a bit tighter in front, though it was sort of itchy on her shoulders.

Or maybe it was because she'd been right upon first seeing him—he somehow looked more handsome to her tonight than usual, a little more . . . rugged or something. He'd always possessed classic good looks, but tonight his usually tidy dark hair was slightly mussed around the edges and maybe he needed a trim. Looked like he'd forgotten to shave today, too.

Not that she could really think of Adam in a sexual way. He'd been her friend for too long and she wasn't wired to make that sort of switch. Even back when he'd been the quarterback of the Destiny Bulldogs and every girl in school had had the hots for him, she never had—because he'd been Jeff's best friend and Jenny's boyfriend, her first love. They'd double-dated to the prom, for heaven's sake.

Or hell— maybe it was just more pleasant to think about something like sex than the very new, very real problems that had just been dropped in her lap. Maybe she was in denial, happy to think about anything else besides financial stability and keeping custody of her child.

"You want a turkey sandwich?" she asked. Another distraction from ugly subjects. "I was about to make one for myself." Besides, it was high time she ate something to soak up all the wine she'd been drinking. And—oh, maybe that was it. Maybe the wine had her feeling sort of . . . amorous or something. After all, she'd parted from Jeff six months ago and hadn't actually had sex for at least a month or two before that, so . . . well, her body was probably just letting her know it missed sex.

*Oh, good. I needed something else to add to my list of troubles.*

"Okay, sure," Adam said behind her, still sounding mildly belligerent but at least as if he was making an effort. "I brought some stuff, too. I'll head back out to the truck to get it."

A few minutes later they sat in front of the fire feasting on turkey sandwiches, cranberry relish, cold stuffing, pumpkin bread, and pumpkin pie—a mishmash from both their coolers and bags. Adam drank the beer he'd brought and Sue Ann kept working on the wine.

"Fire's dying," Adam said, then set his plate aside to grab up a couple of logs from the nearby pile—and Sue Ann watched as he bent to place them strategically onto the low burning blaze. *Hmm. I've never noticed what a nice butt he has.*

Only then she caught herself. *The wine—it's just the wine. And you're looking for any distraction from your troubles. But for God's sake, stop thinking of Adam like that.*

"You still seem kind of . . . growly," she observed. He was usually more talkative than this, and now, when he did talk, he remained brusque and kept things short.

In response, he flashed yet one more un-Adam-like expression in her direction. "That's because I'm still in a shitty mood."

She gave a superior sort of shrug and pointed out, "Me, too. But I'm trying not to take it out on you. If we're stuck here together, I'm trying to be as pleasant as possible."

"Don't feel obligated," he told her.

Sheesh. "I don't—it's just the kind of person I am. No matter how crappy I feel, I still try to be civil. I always thought you were that type of person, too, but I'm seeing a whole new side of you tonight."

He gave her an especially cutting look. "Don't ya think, Sue Ann, that maybe just once in my life I'm entitled to be in a cruddy mood? I tried to do it privately," he groused, "but turns out you're in my cabin."

"Okay, fine—be in your cruddy mood. But the issue of this cabin being yours is still debatable. If you ask me, you're lucky I'm being nice enough to share."

"I've had the place reserved for a year," he said. "So if we're gonna debate ownership, I win."

"But I got here first."

At this, he went quiet, simply casting her a solemn, steely sort of glare—and when he finally spoke, his voice came out at once quiet yet acerbic. "Sue Ann, do you really want to keep arguing over something stupid when we both have bigger things to be upset about?"

Wow. "Thanks for reminding me."

"You forced my hand," he snipped. "And now, if you don't mind, I'm gonna just sit here and look at the fire."

"Fine," she said, back to feeling a little snippy herself. But also suddenly wondering what the deal was—what was the bigger thing he had to be upset about? Yeah, he was going to be alone for Christmas, but that didn't seem like enough to make Adam this distraught.

And she almost considered asking, but another glance at him from within the afghan that still draped her shoulders warned her not to. He stared into the flames before them, now crackling hotly and adding light to the room, his expression troubled and even a little bitter. *What the heck is really wrong with you tonight, Adam Becker?*

Finally, she stood up, now wearing the afghan sort of like a shawl, her empty plate in one hand, and reached down to take his with the other, saying, "Done?"

"No," he answered, closing a fist snug around her wrist—since she'd actually grabbed for his plate before asking. "Still working on my pie."

That's when he turned his head toward her and peered . . . right into her chest, given the way she was leaning over him. And, with her hands full, the afghan had fallen open. "Oh." She pulled back, upright, maybe a little too quickly—because his touch had felt a little too . . . warm. "Sorry."

And that's when she stumbled slightly backward, bumping into the chair behind her before regaining her balance—and Adam shot to his feet, abandoning his plate swiftly on the coffee table before catching her in his arms. Even though by that time she didn't really need to be caught. And then he kind of . . . held on. "You okay?"

"Uh-huh," she managed, nodding and still holding tight to her own plate, intensely aware that both his hands now molded to her hips. And that they felt strong, and capable. And something in her panties fluttered, just a bit. Oh God.

"Okay," he said. But he was still holding on.

"Just stood up too fast," she told him. "Plus I've had some wine, so I'm probably a little wobbly."

"Wobbly," he repeated, those warm hands still supporting her.

"Like a little drunk." And she was pretty sure she was right about that part, since it was the only way she could account for her next move—she lifted her free hand to the navy tee Adam wore under an open flannel shirt. She rested her fingertips on his chest, as if it were about keeping her balance, but in reality, she was fairly certain she was actually just testing it out, seeing how it felt to touch him.

They both stayed quiet, still, and she kind of liked the chest-touching. Even with only the tips of her fingers pressed there, she sensed the firm muscle underneath. It made her heart beat faster, harder. And a surreptitious glance down revealed that her nipples were front and center on display—which could be because it was cold outside . . . but it was rather warm in here at the moment, convincing her the weather had nothing to do with it.

*But wait.*

*God.*

*This is Adam.*

"What, um, are we doing?" she whispered in the still air.

"I don't know," he whispered back, sounding earnest and yet . . . maybe a little needful.

And then she lifted her gaze to his and their eyes met and she had the feeling she was looking at him like she wanted him to kiss her.

And she must have been right about that, too, because that was when he leaned slowly, tentatively forward and brushed his lips ever-so-gently across hers. She let out a little gasp as the pleasure it delivered cascaded through her deprived body. Oh boy. Oh wow. Oh Lord.

When their eyes met again, she noticed how blue his sparkled in the firelight and that her chest now heaved a little. And she said, dumbly, "I have a plate in my hand." Because it seemed like it was going to be hard to kiss him that way.

But he never acted like it was dumb at all—instead he just rushed to take the plate and set it on the coffee table with his—and then he took her back into his arms, pulled her close enough that there was no mistaking the hard bulge in his pants, and lowered his mouth to hers in the most powerful kiss she'd ever received.

Whoa.

She wasn't usually thankful for blizzards, but suddenly, all she could think was—let it snow!

The joy, and gratitude, and ecstasy!

Charles Dickens, A *Christmas Carol*

# *Three*

*I*f that last kiss had been filled with power, the ones
that followed were stunningly . . . smooth, controlled,
and skilled. Wow. Adam definitely knew how to kiss a
woman. As his hands skimmed her curves—one roam-
ing her back, the other drifting seductively up her side
toward her breast—it all left her breathless, the plea-
sures at once simple yet profound. The lack of urgency
in his kisses combined with the confident way he delivered them gave the impression that he wasn't racing
toward some better end—but that he was completely
and wholly satisfied by the moment, that he was enjoying the passion passing between them just as much as
she was.

She found herself shocked by how easy it was to
stand there and kiss him, how her body seemed to take
over, instantly comfortable moving against his. Since

that's what was happening now, very naturally—her breasts shifted sensually against his chest, her fingers twined in his thick, mussed hair. His hands had eased onto her ass now, which, of course, meant that in front she was grinding against him where he was hard and thick—and wow, talk about being breathless.

*This should be more awkward.* But instead, it was just . . . pleasure, plain and simple.

Was it the wine? Was the wine responsible for all of this?

Maybe, but she didn't think so anymore.

"How drunk are you?" he asked then, as if reading her mind.

The pause in kissing left their faces but an inch apart as she looked into his eyes, then lifted one hand, holding her thumb and index finger close together. "Just a little." She could smell the manly, musky scent of him and wanted to get back to the kissing.

"Promise?" he asked.

She nodded profusely.

"Okay, good."

But . . . "Why?"

He sounded a little breathless now, too, when he said, "That means I can keep kissing you without feeling like a jerk."

*Oh, okay. Kissing, more kissing—good.* That was all she wanted in the world right now, to keep kissing and being kissed. And once he resumed kissing her, she pretty much ceased thinking, letting good old-fashioned feeling take over. And even if she was a little drunk, it wasn't in the not-capable-of-good-judgment way; it was more in the maybe-I'm-finally-relaxing, finally-letting-go way. It was the first time in six long months that she hadn't been letting herself worry about something, that she was just living in this moment, soaking up every sexy second of it.

So when Adam pulled back without warning, it jarred her—until she saw that he was only stopping to push the coffee table out of the way, leaving the big braided rug in front of the fireplace vacant. Then he took her hand and silently pulled her down until they were both on their knees, kissing some more as the fire roared next to them, warming their faces—and maybe making her warm in other places, too.

Soon, he lay her down on the rug until both of them had stretched out fully there—and as his hands roamed her body once more, she began to experiment with that, too, with more touching. She glided her palms over his chest, slid them around to explore the sinews of his back, shoulders. And at some point she'd stopped thinking about this being Adam, because that part was weird and it was much easier to just focus on the rest: that a strong, handsome man who knew how to use his mouth and hands was indeed using them—on her. She could scarcely remember a time since high school when kissing and touching had felt so new, when she'd found herself so swept up in a passion so pure and fresh and easy.

He never stopped kissing her even as the back of his hand grazed her breast, making her let out a little gasp against his mouth and igniting fresh heat between her thighs. And then he was cupping the curved side, sensually kneading the flesh—just before he stroked his thumb over the taut peak. She sucked in her breath once more and Adam pulled back slightly—but he didn't look alarmed, just maybe a little more passion-

ate. His gaze fell on her mouth, and even as he continued caressing her breast in one hand, he lifted the other
to run his fingertip over her bottom lip, studying it, as
if getting to know that simple part of her in a whole
new way.

Kissing her again, this time he pressed his tongue
into her mouth for the first time, and it felt like being
entered by him, gently taken, so much that the burst
of pleasure in her panties echoed through her whole
body. Such simple things—touches, kisses—she'd enjoyed them thousands of times before. But they were
suddenly more intense than she remembered, and that
made it so utterly easy to sink into them and forget
about everything else. Maybe because this was someone new? When she least expected it? Or did it have
anything to do with the sudden and amazing chemistry
she felt with a guy she'd known all her life?

When he lifted up, glanced down to her stomach, and
reached for the hem of her top, she pulled in her breath,
watching, too. He rolled the cami slowly upward,
upward, finally pushing the fabric past her breasts to
put them on display. Only one guy had ever seen them
before—until now—and that knowledge left her feeling both nervous and . . . wildly alive. And—oh God,
they ached beneath his scrutiny. Ached for more. She
bit her lip. Did he think they were pretty? He didn't
say, but his eyes went a bit glassy, lustful, and his jaw
slack.

Framing them with his hands, he leaned down, licking his way around one hardened nipple before pulling
it skillfully into his mouth. She didn't try to suppress
her moan—she couldn't have anyway. The pleasure
stretched through her as taut as a rubber band connect-

ing all her sensitive spots, and the more he kissed and
suckled her breasts, the more connected it all felt, like
her body was becoming simply one big sensual tool for
his pleasure—and for hers.

When he began to ease his flannel shirt off, she
helped him, then watched patiently as he removed his
dark T-shirt over his head. She'd seen him shirtless
plenty of times in her life—swimming, putting up hay
with Jeff at her ex-in-laws' farm—but seeing him shirtless and hovering above her was a bit more powerful,
and made it more difficult not to notice his muscular
stomach and biceps, or the dark smattering of hair on
his chest.

"Lift up," he whispered then, his hands back at her
top—he wanted it off of her. She held her arms over her
head so he could remove it.

Then he reached for the drawstring on her snowflake
pants. And that move threw her off a little, forcing her
back from feeling to thinking. Because it meant—oh
wow, this wasn't stopping. *He* wasn't stopping. And she
wasn't stopping. Were they actually going to . . . ?

For a lot of women, maybe it wouldn't be a big deal
to have casual sex at this moment, but for her . . . she'd
only ever slept with one man, her ex-husband. So it felt
sort of like . . . being a virgin all over again in a way.
She didn't know anymore what other people did in bed;
she'd never known, in fact. She'd fallen into patterns,
habits, the kind that are built over years between two
people. And God knew she'd never thought anything
would break those patterns—she'd thought she knew
exactly what her sexual future held.

So realizing what was about to happen here suddenly
made her . . . crazily nervous. She felt wildly inexperi-

enced. And suddenly sorry she'd wasted so many precious years on one person who was only going to throw her away in the end.

*Then quit thinking about it. Quit thinking about it and just do this. Feel this.*

*Okay, I can do that. I'm strong, I'm capable, and everything will be fine. I can lift up and let Adam pull my pants down like it's a completely normal thing to be happening between us.*

And that's exactly what she did, the move leaving her in only a pair of bikini panties with a smiling gingerbread man below her belly button—which she might have rethought when she'd gotten dressed if she'd known anyone else would be seeing them. She caught the glint of amusement in Adam's eye just before he said, "Cute."

" 'Tis the season," she whispered.

"Thought you were hating the holidays this year."

"I am. But I'm trying to make myself snap out of it."

"Maybe this'll snap you out of it," he said—just before he smoothly parted her legs, bent down, and delivered a passionate open-mouthed kiss just below the gingerbread man.

"Ohhhh," she moaned—the sound echoing through the room. Talk about catching her off guard—yowsa.

And without quite planning it, the second he rose up above her again, she found herself reaching for the waistband of his jeans. And then going for his belt, starting to undo it. It wasn't a decision—just an instinct. Okay, looked like she was back from thinking to feeling again. And she liked feeling much better.

Things began to move faster then—despite Adam's unrushed, seductive charm, the time had come for a little more urgency. Even so, it remained a steady progression that now simply came with firmer grips, more rhythmic movements, deeper kisses. Slowly but surely, Sue Ann's body had taken over completely, now following a blinding, driving urge to join with Adam's.

She'd told Jenny recently that she couldn't imagine being with someone new, that despite her previous sexual comfort and confidence, she feared she'd turn nervous and clumsy and unsure—but apparently she'd been wrong since her apprehension was suddenly a thing of the past. Who could have known how well her body would move with Adam's, that something about his would simply inspire her response without thought. Every nerve in her flesh tingled at his touch.

When she helped him push his jeans down, the sight of what stood prominently between his legs made her stomach contract. And she tried not to stare, but it was difficult, especially the way the firelight shone upon it, enhancing every ridge, vein, and contour. Adam's penis was one more thing she hadn't expected to be confronted with on this trip, but—oh my—she was ready to meet it without hesitation now.

As she studied it, Adam stayed busy, lowering her panties, digging in his jeans for a condom, ripping it open, rolling it on. And then he was parting her thighs with strong hands, leaning into her warm and firm, and then—oh, he was pressing his way inside her.

After which they both gasped and went still. Wow. Had anything ever felt better than suddenly being filled up by him, connected with him? She lay on her back on the rug, her arms tight around his neck, her legs curling up around his ass, her cheeks heating with the knowledge of that blunt connection, the rawness of sharing it with someone new.

It shocked her to discover she almost wanted to cry. Not out of any sadness or remorse—but simply from how good it felt, how lovely it was to be desired, how right it seemed to be appreciated this way, pleasured this way, by someone she'd always known.

Things she wanted to say flitted through her mind, but ultimately she kept them inside, afraid that speaking would somehow break the spell holding them in its grasp. So she only sighed in his ear, kissed his neck, breathed in the masculine scent of him again—then felt him begin to move in her. And then she held to him tight, absorbing the wonder of his body moving over hers, moving *in* hers. Oh God—*yes, yes.* Each deep stroke plunged straight to her core, left her feeling every ounce a woman, pleasure erupting from her as hot sighs and unrestrained moans.

It surprised her a little when Adam wrapped his arms around her and rolled them both until he lay on his back, putting her on top. But it didn't surprise her after she thought about it—it didn't surprise her to learn that Adam was a considerate lover and wanted her to come and probably figured it was more likely this way.

Just as from the moment he'd first kissed her, her body took over, moving on him of its own volition as fresh heat skittered through her from head to toe. And somehow she grew more aware of everything around her: the gentle pop and crackle of the warming blaze a few feet away, the way her knees dug into the rug of blue and green beneath them, the light sheen of perspiration on Adam's forehead, the sway of her breasts in the firelight, the vibrant blue of his eyes as he watched her. She'd have thought it would feel strange, embarrassing, to have him see her naked—but it was just the opposite. Adam's eyes on her made her feel beautiful, and natural, and free.

She rode him with pure recklessness as the waves of pleasure rose higher and higher inside her. She arched her back and pressed her palms to his chest, feeling his gaze on her breasts as her arms pushed them together. She leaned her head back in abandon and let those waves finally wash over her in a stunning orgasm that rocked her body more deeply than she could ever recall. Then she closed her eyes and cried out as it swept through her, again, again, again.

And just as she began to slump onto him in exhaustion, his hands tightened on her hips and he said, "Aw God—me, too," and thrust up into her powerful and deep, lifting her body to leave her totally impaled on him as he yelled out his climax as well.

"Oh God," she whispered against his chest when it was all over. "Oh God." It had been the most unexpected sex of her life. And the *best* sex of her life. And all with her ex-husband's best friend. Oh boy.

Adam woke up on the rug by the fire and glanced over to see—holy crap—Sue Ann. He tried to swallow back his shock, though, since he'd known good and well what he was doing the whole time he'd been kissing her and then moving inside her.

He could blame it on his weird bad mood. Or he could blame it on her slinky pajama top. Or he could blame it on the snowstorm. All of them definitely had a hand in this, after all. But as he watched her now, asleep, pretty, her bared skin aglow in the waning firelight, he began to get hard all over again, that fast. Which meant it hadn't just been a heat-of-the-moment indiscretion. He'd really wanted her. Sue Ann Kinman—who'd later become Sue Ann Simpkins. He'd been the best man at her wedding, for God's sake. And he'd just never thought of her like this before. Even when he'd flirted with her today behind that reindeer head . . . well, that was a hell of a far cry from *this*. And it had been a hell of a lot simpler than this, too.

Still, now that he was thinking of her that way, he wasn't inclined to stop. At least not yet. The afghan that had fallen from her shoulders earlier was now pulled across both their bodies, covering them from the waist down, but he was glad her breasts—just as gorgeous as he'd suspected—remained on display. Hell, it was hard to believe that he'd *had* them now—he'd held them, kissed them. And he'd been between her slender, welcoming legs.

God, the truth was, it made him feel lucky—damn lucky. Since he was fairly certain that up until now only Jeff had gotten to experience that. Which seemed like a crying shame in a way. Since he clearly hadn't appreciated what he had.

Most people—including Adam—thought of Sue Ann as the outgoing, funny, happy, dependable wife and mom, as someone who showed up at every town event in support of every person she knew. But he was pretty sure people didn't think of Sue Ann as . . . this gorgeous, sensual woman lying naked next to him, this woman who'd panted and moaned and writhed against him so passionately on this rug. He knew a secret side of her now, a hot and amazing side, and he felt . . . privileged.

As she stirred next to him, her breasts shifting slightly, his cock tightened. It was hard to believe this was happening, but they were in this now, and at the moment he didn't feel like holding back. Narrowing his gaze on those breasts that had so captured his attention from the first time he'd seen her tonight, he bent and gently raked his tongue across one deliciously distended peak. The sensation raised the hair on the back of his neck and made him still harder.

And when he did it again, delivering just a light little lick across that stiffened bit of pink flesh, it brought a sexy smile to her face, even though her eyes remained closed.

"What are you thinking about that's making you grin?" he teased, now that he knew she was awake.

"Um . . . would you believe me if I said visions of sugar plums were dancing in my head?"

He let out a laugh and said, "Not even a little."

"What do you *think* I'm thinking about?"

He considered the question. "Maybe something like, 'Oh my God, I just had sex with Adam.' But I hope it's more like, 'Wow, that feels good and I don't ever want him to stop.'"

She bit her lip, eyes still shut. "It's probably . . . a little of both."

"I can live with that," he told her, then heard his voice go deeper without quite planning it. "But . . . for now, how about we just focus on the second one?"

"And I can live with *that*," she said, finally opening her eyes to meet his.

And damn, how had he never noticed that before? How pretty her eyes were. How warm and sensual. They were the comforting, cozy sort of brown you found all around you in nature, but . . . somehow deeper, like they held secrets. Yet . . . maybe they only got that way when she was *feeling* sensual. And as he began to slowly kiss his way down her body, he continued being grateful for seeing this side of her. Maybe that was the secret in her eyes, that underneath the responsible but fun-loving mom hid this very sexy, very *sexual* woman.

He liked the hot, gentle way she hissed in her breath with each kiss he lowered to her skin—he'd started just beneath her pert breast and now moved slowly down her smooth stomach, dotted with a few freckles, and over the rounded flesh just below her belly button.

Her eyes went sort of dreamy then, her mouth dropping open halfway—maybe it had just struck her where he was headed. He wanted to make her feel good again. And he also wanted to taste her.

He heard her pretty gasp when he gently parted her legs, and she let out a hot little "Oh . . ." as he stroked his middle finger down through her moist center. Good God, she was wet for him, fueling his lust even more. He slipped two fingers inside her at the precise moment he lowered his tongue to her tender, waiting flesh—and he loved it when her moan echoed toward the ceiling.

Sue Ann bit her lip as she watched Adam's ministrations—because otherwise her mouth would be trembling. She couldn't deny how excited she was by the openness of what he was doing, by how wild it felt—how very uninhibited—to be that intimate with someone new. Oh Lord—*yes, yes.* "Good," she heard herself whisper toward the ceiling. "So good."

She'd always been happy being a small town wife, living a small town life. Yet there was a part of her that had at least understood the desire for more, the yearning for something bigger, freer, the idea of taking life by the horns—and this, right now, felt like that, like living. So even now that she was coming back down to earth after their first sultry round of sex, even though she was feeling the wine less than before, she didn't try to rein in her instinctive response—instead, she let herself go completely. And within moments she'd reached the pinnacle of ecstasy with him again and was crying out as—*oh God*—another powerful orgasm rushed through her like . . . well, like a blizzard. Except much hotter.

Wow.

And then she lay there basking in the afterglow, biting her lip, and once again thinking: Adam just did that to me? Really? Adam?

When he rose up and their eyes met, she said, a bit timidly, "That was . . . nice."

He raised his eyebrows, his dark, sexy gaze pinning her in place. "Nice?"

"Okay, would spectacular make you happier?" she asked with a grin.

"Damn straight," he said, the arrogance in his expression turning him even a little more handsome.

She went a little sheepish then—not sure what came next. "Thank you."

"I . . . didn't mind," he said. Then he shut his eyes, looking like he might suddenly feel a bit weird, too. "What I mean is . . . I wanted to." Then he shook his head, appearing slightly embarrassed. "I don't know how to talk to you about sex," he told her.

"I know," she whispered.

"So how about if we just kiss instead of talk?"

She nodded, liking that idea, and he moved up along-

side her on the rug, lifted his hand to her cheek, and
resumed giving her more of those delicious kisses that
seemed at once pure yet . . . not, since now she tasted
herself on his mouth.

Soon, though, Adam disentangled himself from her
and the afghan to silently rise up into the same chair
he'd occupied earlier, and she wasn't sure what that
meant—were they done, taking a break, what? But from
the looks of his erection—nope, there was definitely
more to come, so she just knelt on the rug, waiting.

Next, he reached for the bottle of wine she hadn't
quite finished with dinner and took a big drink from
it, then handed it down to her. She followed suit with
one sip, then another, before holding it back out to say,
"Last drink?"

"You finish it off," he said, "and then come up here
with me."

*Oh. Okay. We're just going to try a new position. I
can get into that.* So she drained the wine bottle, got to
her feet, and eased her way into Adam's lap, straddling
him.

And God—it felt . . . so personal to be that way with
him, face-to-face without a shred of clothing. And sure,
she knew sex was personal, but it was something about
the nearness of his eyes right now, the unavoidability
of looking at each other, of somehow acknowledging
that they were really doing this, *still* doing this, quite a
while after it had started.

"Will you kiss me some more?" she requested without quite planning it.

"Absolutely," he said, his tenor deep, full of promise.
And like everything else so far, once their mouths were
moving against each other, Sue Ann stopped think-

ing so much and resumed just feeling it all, letting her soft breasts rub against his muscled chest, and letting the juncture of her thighs connect with the hard length arcing up between his legs.

She heard her own breath then, turning labored, hot—his, too—and found herself reaching between them, curling her hand around his arousal, beginning to stroke it with a firm, rhythmic caress that forced a muffled groan from his throat between kisses.

She didn't know why she was suddenly getting aggressive, but—*mmm*—she liked being the giver of the pleasure suddenly; she liked the way he felt in her grip. And maybe those last few gulps of wine had something to do with it, but she suffered the desire to simply . . . follow her every impulse right now. Even when she was struck with a somewhat surprising one.

Because this was the one moment in life when she could do that, follow every urge. When she didn't have to worry about Sophie. Or Destiny. Or the future. Or anything. And the honest truth was, who knew how long it might be before she was with a man again?

So she didn't stop herself . . . from lifting, backing off his body. From easing herself down onto the floor—on her knees, between his. She still held his erection in her hand and now she studied it again, thinking it was strong and sturdy, just like Adam himself. And then she leaned inward, closer, closer, ready to follow that impulse—but unable to resist looking up at him first. "Am I shocking you?"

"Yes," he said, appearing a little breathless.

"Is it okay?"

"God, yes."

As best she could tell, they were the only words he

could eke out, and they seemed to have come through slightly clenched teeth. He clearly hadn't expected this, and God knew neither had she. But letting out the breath she'd been holding the last few seconds, she then lowered her lips over him, feeling the full size of him there, listening to his hot sigh and relishing it. Then she began to move her mouth up and down, pleasuring him, which in turn meant pleasuring herself, and though she still wasn't sure what had driven her to do this particular thing at this particularly unexpected time . . . maybe she just wanted to live again, fully, without reserve. Or maybe she wanted to show Adam that she could be a generous lover, too. All she knew was that it made sense to her, and that her body wanted it.

She moved on him that way for a long while, loving the feel of his hands in her hair, his moans and murmurs—he was whispering, "God, yeah, yeah"—until finally she backed away, took the liberty of finding another condom in the wallet that lay open near his rumpled blue jeans, and knelt back between his legs to roll it on.

By which point he'd grown a little more frantic, hurried, pulling her back to where he'd wanted her in the first place, on top of him in the chair. And then he was situating her hips, pushing her down onto him, and making her cry out at the intense delight of being so forcefully filled.

She met his gaze, saw her passion reflected in his eyes, then twined her arms around his neck and kissed him for all she was worth as her body took over once more, grinding atop his, rocking and undulating in a primal dance that rose quickly to its pinnacle. They both came within a few hot, scintillating minutes, and once all the moaning and sobbing was done they rested there, bodies entangled, her head on his shoulder.

"That was amazing," he whispered.

"Uh-huh," she agreed. Now she was the one who'd lost the power of speech.

"Wanna get in bed, sugar plum?" he asked, making her giggle at the silly nickname, and a minute later they lay naked beneath the covers of the bottom bunk, that "top or bottom" question from earlier having taken on a whole new meaning now. They slept snuggled together, warm beneath the blankets, having long since forgotten the snowstorm that raged outside.

Sue Ann had no idea how late it was when she awoke to a stirring beside her, then opened her eyes to see a very firm male butt crossing the dark, shadowy room to the fireplace. She bit her lip, enjoying the view as he stoked the fire and stacked a few more logs on the grate, then waited patiently for him to rejoin her in the narrow bed that made cuddling almost a necessity.

As they settled in each other's arms, it hit her that she felt closer to Adam than she ever had before. Which was only logical, of course. But it made her wonder about earlier—and it also made her feel . . . more entitled to ask now. "Tell me something," she began. "What really had you so upset before? I mean, I understand about the boys being gone, how that could ruin your holidays, but . . . is that truly all there was to it?"

He drew back slightly in her embrace, clearly surprised by the question. "Uh, it's the middle of the night, Sue Ann."

She simply sighed. Why were men always so evasive? "Is there a law against talking in the middle of the night?" She shifted onto her side then, to peer down at his darkly stubbled face. "It's just that . . . it's not like you to be so angry—about anything."

The glance he cast made her think he might confide in her. "Maybe . . . I just don't usually let it show when I'm upset about something, and this time I did. I came here thinking I'd be alone, after all. And I guess . . . " His gaze drifted up, toward the bottom of the bunk bed above them, and she could sense him already getting distant again, possibly deciding that opening up wasn't a good idea after all. "I guess maybe it was . . . a lot of things, just building up. That's all."

"What things?"

She could read his look easily enough. It said, *You're being pushy and nosy.* But she wanted to know because she cared about him. And in that moment it occurred to her that as well as she knew Adam . . . maybe she didn't really know that much about him at all.

Thinking back to what he'd said about making his divorce look easier than it was, she said, "All right—if you won't answer that, then answer this. Why did you get divorced?"

"Christ, Sue Ann—that's . . . a little out of the blue."

"Blue shmue," she said. Because sometimes she *was* pushy, and that shouldn't come as a surprise to someone who'd known her as long as Adam had. "I've always wondered why you and Sheila broke up. And we've been friends a really long time, right? So I don't see why it would be such a big deal to tell me." He never talked about Sheila unless it involved the logistics of dropping off or picking up the boys. And he never gave anything away about what might have caused their breakup—even Jeff knew very little about it, Adam having claimed vague things like "going in different directions" and being "very different people."

Now, after what he'd said earlier, she suspected there was more to the story.

"Fine," he finally said, though he was back to sounding more belligerent than she liked. She propped herself on one elbow next to him, and he still faced the bunk above but now spared her a matter-of-fact glance. "Our marriage was crappy long before it broke up. Most people don't know that, but now you do."

Sue Ann just blinked, truly surprised. "Really? You both seemed happy."

"We were for a while," he told her on a sigh. "But we married young—passion and all that stuff—and once that part faded, we just didn't have much in common. She wanted . . . bigger things than I did."

"Bigger?"

"A bigger life. In a bigger place. She regretted moving to Destiny with me after college." Adam and Sheila had met at Ohio State, where he'd played football and she'd been a cheerleader—Sue Ann and Jeff had even gone up to see a few games and get together with the other couple afterward.

"Well, I'm not sure I agree that living in a bigger place gives you a bigger life," Sue Ann argued. "Or even a richer one."

"I guess I must agree with you or I wouldn't have come back home to start my business," he replied. "But I should have known it wasn't right for her. She'd always wanted to move to a big city—but I talked her into being a landscaper's wife in Destiny. It seemed easy then, while we were in school, living it up, living the dream—and I was young and foolish enough to think it would go on that way, no matter what choices we made. But as time passed, she made me feel like our life together was . . . small. And after the boys were born it got even worse—and we just grew further and further apart."

"And then?" she asked.

"And then what?"

"What happened that finally brought about the divorce?"

He just looked at her, as if sizing her up in some way, as if choosing his next words with care. "That's it," he finally said.

She blinked. "It?" It wasn't an outlandish claim; that wasn't what made her question it. It was the look in his eyes. They'd grown darker somehow, even in the room's pale light, and she knew he was holding back. There for a minute, he'd actually seemed open with her, like he was speaking from the heart—and then he'd suddenly clammed up, his answers growing short and clipped. "What aren't you telling me?"

"Okay, maybe I didn't tell you everything," he began—yet he sounded wholly uncertain, like maybe he still wasn't sure he wanted to. Then his look transformed into one of scolding. "But one reason for that, Little Miss Sugar Plum, is that you kinda have a big mouth sometimes. You know?"

Oh, that. Sue Ann just sighed. There it was, the fault she'd reined in lately, but no one seemed to notice the change—they only remembered past transgressions. Funny how once upon a time such flaws had seemed small—they'd been insignificant traits she'd simply accepted as part of who she was—but now they added to her insecurities. "I've stopped that," she explained. "And something like this, Adam—I would never tell anyone. Seriously."

When he still looked doubtful, though, she added, "I promise. I can keep a secret. Just ask Jenny. Back when she was secretly seeing Mick, I knew all about it and never breathed a word to anyone, not even Jeff."

He tilted his head in the other direction, his eyes narrowing on her as he said, "That's impressive, but . . . I still can't tell you."

"You can't do that," she snipped, adding a *hmmpf* sound. "You can't act like you're going to and then not."

He just flashed a challenging look. "Is that so? Sue Ann's rules of fair play?"

She nodded. "Yes, as a matter of fact."

And she couldn't completely read his expression then, but if nothing else, she sensed a certain . . . sadness in it.

"Just tell me, Adam," she whispered.

"I can't," he replied, his voice just as low, something in it almost ominous now. "Even if I trust you not to tell anyone."

Despite the warmth of the bed, his response made her skin prickle and her stomach churn. God, what was it already? What could be so horrible? "Why?"

He let out a sigh, his eyes shifting away from hers. "Because if I tell you, it'll change how you see me. Not in a good way, either."

Hmm. Adam? Really? That was hard to fathom. Despite his recent bad mood, he was the most upstanding guy in all of Destiny. "I can't imagine that," she finally said.

"Well, you will. If I tell you."

"No," she argued.

"Yes," he countered.

But she still thought it sounded improbable. "How? What could you possibly say to make me think badly of you? I mean, you're Adam Becker, for God's sake—

Mr. Becker Landscaping, Mr. Cub Scout dad, Mr. All American good guy. You bend over backward to help people. You cut Willie Hargis's grass for free all summer the year his wife died. You shovel snow for the elderly. You—"

"Sue Ann," he said sharply, cutting her off. "I cheated on her."

"Huh?" she said on a gasp, flinching.

"You heard me. I said I cheated on her."

"These are but shadows of the things that have been."

Charles Dickens, A *Christmas Carol*

## *Four*

*A*dam's chest tightened as he tried to read the expression on Sue Ann's face. But he didn't really need to read it—he could feel it. He'd committed the worst sin a man—a husband—could commit. The same her ex-husband had committed, more or less. And they'd been very different situations, but that probably didn't matter.

"You're . . . kidding," she said, her voice barely audible as she stiffened slightly in his arms.

"I wish I was," he told her and—damn, the shame washed over him then like something fresh, brand new.

God, there were reasons he never talked to anyone about this. For one, he just didn't think it was right to go around airing his or Sheila's private problems. And for another . . . he wasn't proud of what he'd done.

And as for why he'd suddenly let himself tell Sue

Ann now . . . he wasn't sure. But it had been hard lying here with her naked, having her ask him, and putting her off. Somehow, the deeper they'd gotten into the discussion, the more inevitable it had begun to feel that he would tell her the truth. And then he'd heard himself just blurting it out.

Now she lay back in the bed beside him, staring up at the bunk above, the way he'd been doing for a while—and, hell, he hated upsetting her. He should have just kept his mouth shut, especially given all the new news about Jeff she'd gotten just tonight. After all, he'd managed to keep this to himself for three years—and he'd picked now, here, *her*, to suddenly start telling? A heavy sigh echoed through his body and out as he lifted his hands to run them back through his hair. "I'm sorry I told you."

"No, don't be. I pried it out of you," she insisted—but she continued speaking more quietly than before, her voice dropping further still when she asked, "Um, do you mind if I ask who you did this with?" Her body still felt more rigid than it had a few minutes ago, like she suddenly wished she were anywhere else besides in a bed with him.

"No one you know," he told her.

"And did you . . . care about her, this person?"

Arghhhh, him and his big mouth. Suddenly, he felt like it was happening all over again, the whole rotten thing and all the ugliness and regret it had brought with it. "I . . . I . . . " *Barely knew her.* God, no, that wasn't the right thing to say. "It's a long story," he settled on instead.

"Well," Sue Ann replied, voice still whisper-soft in the confines of the cabin, "I have some time."

Yep, she did. And so did he. And now that he'd so stupidly, hastily spilled his big secret, he supposed there was nothing left to do but tell her the whole unpleasant tale. *Should have thought about that before you spit out the truth.* But even as much as it would pain him to rehash this, he had to now—because now he had to try to make Sue Ann understand.

"Okay, here goes," he started, already feeling a little short of breath. Damn, he wasn't comfortable discussing this. But again, he had no choice now. And hell, he probably shouldn't say this, but . . . "The fact is, Sheila and I had reached a point in our relationship where I was almost afraid to be out in public with her."

Sue Ann blinked, clearly taken aback, then asked, "What does that mean? Because, to be honest, Sheila was never my favorite person and I always thought you'd end up with someone nicer—but she wasn't *that* bad."

He just drew a deep breath and slanted Sue Ann a look in the shadowy light. "Listen, I really don't like saying anything negative about the mother of my kids—that's one reason I never talk about this—but . . . she really *was* kinda that bad by then. She got bored being a stay-at-home mom and resented the fact that I was out working, seeing people every day. Eventually, she got . . . a little irrational. She started accusing me of going after other women when I wasn't."

"Really?" she asked, her eyes widening on him.

He nodded, vindicated to hear she thought that sounded extreme. "I mean, I run a community-based business, so I have to be nice to people—including women. But I sure as hell wasn't *after* them—I wasn't even flirting."

"I believe you," she said very solemnly. "I know you well enough to know that."

"Thanks," he answered, appreciating her faith in him, especially at a moment when it would be easy not to have any. "And things just escalated from there—it was like we were enemies and she was out to hurt me."

"What did she do?" Sue Ann asked.

And Adam let out a long sigh, remembering the worst of times, times he'd never told anyone about . . . until now. "Okay, this is kind of embarrassing, but . . . she said I was terrible in bed."

At this, Sue Ann simply gaped at him a moment, jaw slack, then replied, "Um, she was lying."

"How do you know?"

In response, she just blinked pointedly, then reminded him, "Personal experience."

Which brought a small smile to his face and made his chest go warm. "Oh. Well . . . thanks for that, too," he said. "Because, you know, I was pretty sure I knew how to please a woman, but . . . "

That's when Sue Ann's eyebrows rose higher. "Arrogant much?"

He gave his head a sharp tilt. "What do you mean, arrogant? I'm admitting she had me doubting myself a little."

"Okay, good point. And . . . actually, I guess you can *be* arrogant if you want. You've . . . earned arrogant. Trust me on that." She looked a little sheepish as she said it, though, and he kind of wanted to kiss her some more, but he was pretty sure this wasn't the right time.

So instead he just tipped his head back slightly, *feeling* a little arrogant now, and said, "Good to know."

"So back to what happened," she prodded.

Oh yeah, that. He blew out another long, tired breath.
"I guess you could say things reached a boiling point.
We went to the wedding of an old friend of hers in
Cleveland, where she was a bridesmaid, and besides
ignoring me at the rehearsal dinner, she started openly
flirting with other men, especially the one she was
walking with in the wedding. And by the time the reception rolled around, she was hanging all over the guy.

"And it wasn't that I felt jealous exactly," he said,
thinking back to decipher the unsavory memories.
"What stung was that she was working so hard to hu-
miliate me and hurt me. It was that I couldn't figure out
how my marriage had turned into something like that."

Beside him, Sue Ann murmured, "Wow, that's awful.
I'm sorry."

He just looked at her then—and felt his throat growing so thick it was tough to swallow. Because she
wouldn't feel so sorry for him after he told her the next
part, the hard part. Strange, at the time, it had seemed
. . . too easy. Because it had made him feel human
again—masculine. But trying to tell Sue Ann about it
now . . . made him feel small.

"I didn't know anybody there," he went on, "and I was
seated next to a pretty woman who was nice enough to
make conversation with me. Watching Sheila embar-
rass us both all night got hard to take, and I guess I had
too much to drink. And I was just fed up. And it felt . . .
hell, it felt good to have a woman show some interest
in me and make me laugh. And . . ." He stopped then,
because, damn it, no matter how he explained it or how
he'd felt in that moment, it still didn't justify what came
next.

"And one thing led to another?" Sue Ann supplied.

He sighed. That was pretty much the size of it. "I ended up kissing her in the little room where the wedding party had stashed all their belongings."

"Kissing," Sue Ann repeated.

"Making out," he clarified—but he still didn't go into further detail. "And that's when Sheila walked in on us."

"So you didn't actually . . . have sex."

He shook his head, sighed, and wished that simple fact actually made it better. "No. But it's still cheating," he concluded. "And despite what Sheila had been doing all night, she saw it as the proof that her accusations were true all along, that I was a womanizer out to seduce every female who crossed my path."

"Wow," Sue Ann said again, but he couldn't quite tell what she was wowing this time—Sheila's reaction, the whole distasteful story, or some other aspect of it all. "So, did you love Sheila?"

"Once upon a time, definitely," he said—yet then he paused, sighed. "I can't say I really loved her by the time we got divorced, but . . . I'm still not proud of the way it ended. Because . . ." He shook his head and felt it all rumbling through him the same way it had been for the past three years. "I thought I was that guy you and everyone else sees—that all around good guy. I thought I was a man who would do what it took to hold my marriage together and give my sons a good, normal family life. But turns out I wasn't that guy after all." Hell. He hadn't exactly meant to blurt all that out, but there it was.

And it surprised him now to see Sue Ann looking . . . completely critical. Critical a minute ago he would have understood—but not after what he'd just said. "What?" he asked.

"Listen, I'm not condoning what you did," she said pointedly, "but it doesn't sound like you *should* have held your marriage together."

Okay, he got her point, but, "Who can say? Things might've gotten better. Maybe we'd have worked through the problems, pulled it back together somehow."

Yet her gloomy expression said she wasn't even remotely convinced. "You just told me you didn't love her anymore. And once that's gone, what's the point?"

He narrowed his gaze on her, somehow seeing yet another new side of her—a smart side, a practical side, but also . . . a woman who still believed in love, even now. "You sound pretty damn wise for somebody who's still going through this."

"They're two different situations," she said, shaking her head. "Sounds like you both fell out of love. Whereas, for me, only one of us did."

Aw God. He felt her pain deep then, even deeper than usual. "You still love him?" he whispered.

But to his surprise, she looked like she had to think it over, like maybe the answer wasn't as cut and dried as he expected. "At first," she said, "I just couldn't understand how he couldn't love me anymore, how he could do this to us, and to Sophie. But over time, as I see how he's behaving, I'm realizing he's no longer the same man I fell in love with all those years ago. Every time I hear about him showing up someplace with Ronni, laughing and glad-handing people, without giving a crap how it makes me or his daughter feel, it's made me love him a little less. And after tonight's news, well . . . even more so."

"Well, between you and me, you're too good for him now."

She bit her lip, met his gaze. "You really think that?"

"I think he's a bonehead."

Sue Ann looked tired to him, and a little sad, but still pretty as hell. And the sorrow in her eyes now—he knew that was about Jeff and the things she'd just told him, but he also wondered if it was bigger than that, if she was deciding that *all* men were dogs if even Mr. All American good guy could cheat on his wife. A minute ago, he'd thought it was a victory if she still believed in love—but maybe there were times in life when it would be easier not to.

Then he glanced down to the space between their bodies; it was strange—after this talk, he couldn't decide if he felt closer to Sue Ann or further apart. She seemed understanding in a way; but on the other hand, he knew good and well how she had to feel about men who strayed, and he'd noticed she wasn't exactly snuggling up against him anymore.

It left an inevitable question in the air. "So do you think I'm an ass now?"

Like the last question he'd asked her, she seemed to consider her answer carefully before replying. "Overall, you're still probably one of the best people I know. And making out is less of a crime than sex. But . . . "

He sucked in his breath, his chest going hollow. "But?"

Instead of answering, she simply sighed, letting her eyes drop from his face to his chest. "Well, I guess I'm just sensitive about that sort of thing right now. But for what it's worth, this kind of answers my original question. I get it now."

"Get what?"

She felt his pointed glance. "What you're really upset about. Sort of, anyway."

"Is that so?" he asked.

"Like I thought, it's not just the boys' trip—it's all of this."

"All of this?" he asked cynically.

She turned her head, bringing them face-to-face on the pillow they still shared. "You feel just like I do. You had a family and a home and you thought you knew exactly what your life was going to be—and then it suddenly *wasn't* that way. You walk around acting like everything's fine, but deep down inside, you don't like being divorced any more than I do."

Huh. Was she right? Was that what he was really upset about? Well, who cared? And if she was waiting for him to agree with her, she had another thing coming. He kept his reply simple. "Are you done, Dr. Sue Ann Freud?"

Next to him, she shrugged. "I suppose."

"Well then, if you've grilled me enough, I suggest we go back to sleep."

The first rays of daylight brought Sue Ann's eyes open.

Sun shone through the window across the room, telling her the snow must have ended.

Good.

And the cabin was nice and toasty—a glance to the stone hearth revealed a roaring fire, something Adam must have tended to in the night.

Also good.

And a glimpse downward reminded her that . . . uh-oh. She was naked. She was a naked, casual-sex-having wanton who'd gone wild with Adam Becker last night like it was nothing! Oh boy.

First things first—where was he? A glance to her

right revealed that, okay, he was approximately one inch from her naked body—and equally naked. And awake, too. Sheesh. "Morning," he said.

Oh Lord, the warmth of a blush climbed her cheeks, just from that. "Morning," she returned. But she couldn't quite look at him.

He stayed quiet for a second, then said, "This is gonna be weird, isn't it?"

"Yep," she said, nodding. It was something about the morning bringing back the concept of real life. It was something about the sun shining a bright light on things that had been easier to accept in the dark. A nervousness far more severe than anything she'd experienced with him last night suddenly raced through her veins.

She heard his sigh next to her and grew unwittingly aware of the warmth of his body against hers beneath the covers. "Look, Sue Ann, there's no reason we have to act any differently to each other. This doesn't have to be a big deal."

Uh-huh, yeah, sure. "Easy for you to say," she spat out before thinking.

"It is?" he asked, sounding so surprised that she *had* to look at him now. And oh. My. He was especially sexy in the morning, all rumpled and mussed.

"Well, you probably do this all the time," she declared a bit too hysterically for her liking.

"Do what?"

"Have sex."

He looked unsure how to reply.

And she *felt* unsure about this entire conversation. Why had she started acting like having sex was the most heinous act on the planet?

"Um, yeah, sometimes," he admitted. "But . . . not with friends."

"Well, I haven't exactly been having sex with *any-body* lately, friend or foe, so you're one up on me. Or more than one, actually. However many women you've done it with since your divorce." *Dear God, be quiet. What's wrong with you?*

But she *knew* what was wrong. This "morning after" business would have been awkward enough on its own, but knowing what she knew now made it a little worse. Not only because it stung to think of Adam cheating on his wife, but because . . . she'd thought she knew him. And after what they'd just done, the comfort she'd taken with him, the intimacy they'd shared . . . well, she'd *wanted* to know him. She'd wanted to believe he was the same perfect guy she'd always thought him. She was tired of getting surprises about men, tired of thinking they were something they weren't. So it had broken her heart just a little—and changed her world still a bit more—to find out Adam wasn't completely who she'd thought he was.

And her reaction to what he'd shared wasn't his fault—she knew that. But . . . well, there for a little while, she'd felt so crazily, sexily, intimately close to him—and now, unfortunately, she'd woken up feeling closer to the opposite.

"Okay, here's the thing," she said, trying to sound smarter and more rational than she had so far this morning. "Last night was . . . um, pretty great, but—"

"You said spectacular."

"Huh?"

He looked matter-of-fact. "I'm just pointing out that you said it was spectacular."

Oh dear. The reminder warmed her face with a blush and brought back memories. Spectacular ones, of course. "Still," she tried to move on, "my point is that . . . we were both drinking, and in a weird situation, and . . . I think it's best if we just forget about it after we leave here. Forget about it and act normal."

"Of course," Adam said. As if it had never crossed his mind that it could possibly turn into more than a one-time thing. As if this were clearly the only way to handle it.

So why did she feel a little disappointed? After all, she was the one declaring they should forget it.

But that didn't matter. What mattered was that his quick agreement shored up her original conclusions. Adam might be a great guy most of the time, but when it came to romance—or sex, or whatever—she didn't need to be getting involved with him. She supposed things like trust just felt even more important to her than usual right now. And it was far too soon for something like this after her breakup anyway. And besides, he was Jeff's best friend! And ugh, he apparently wasn't even interested in her, for God's sake!

"Cold?" he asked then, pulling the covers up snugger around her shoulders. So he was suddenly back to being sweet and sexy again? Oh boy.

"Um, a little," she lied. And there was a part of her that wanted Adam to take the opportunity to cuddle against her to warm her up—even though she wasn't really cold—but a bigger, wiser part of her immediately remembered concepts like *cheating* and *too soon* and *ex's BFF*, so she said, "I wonder how the roads are."

"I heard a plow come through about an hour ago, so

that's a good sign. I can probably get out of your hair this morning."

Hmm. Funny. One minute he'd been an intruder, the next he'd been giving her multiple orgasms. "You can have the cabin for the rest of the weekend," she told him on impulse.

He blinked, looking almost skeptical, like she might be trying to pull the wool over his eyes. "Why? Last night I got the idea you really needed some peace and quiet."

*Um, yeah, this is no longer a place of peace and quiet for me. This will now and forever be the place where I had hot sex with you.* She resisted telling him that, though, and instead fell back on another version of the truth. "Well, I'm not sure it was really working— I'm more of a keep-busy kinda gal. And God knows I have plenty to do at home—gifts to wrap, trees to trim, jobs to find, all that."

"Are you sure?" he asked. "I mean, despite how it might have seemed, I don't want to run you out."

But she shook her head, wondering if she was acting as nervous as she continued to feel. "Yeah, I'm sure. Christmas is coming, whether I like it or not. Along with wondering how I'm going to support myself. Merry Christmas to *me*, right?" she asked cynically, more to the bunk bed above her than to Adam, but she still regretted it instantly. She was waking up to the troubles of real life, but there was no reason to shove them down anyone else's throat.

And from there, she simply tugged the top blanket from the bed to wrap it around her—still shy now about being naked—eased out of the lower bunk, then plucked up her overnight bag from the floor and headed to the bathroom.

She tried not to think as she stepped beneath the spray of a hot shower—she tried not to remember the way Adam had touched her or kissed her, or that her body felt . . . almost brand new in some odd sense. Because yeah, thoughts like that were still a damn nice distraction from the problems facing her now, but in another way, they were just as troubling. *I was so aggressive at moments—yikes. I don't even know if men like that. Although . . . wow—I know I liked the stuff he* did to *me. But stop thinking about it.* So she tried to focus instead on just rushing to get in and out, out of the shower, and out of the cabin.

By the time she exited the bathroom wearing a thick sweater and blue jeans, Adam had dressed and gone out to assess the road situation, informing her that a path had been cleared and that the old man in the office had assured him the hill had been salted hours ago and traffic could come and go freely in the valley again.

Well, that was a relief.

And so, as she prepared to depart, Sue Ann tried her best to start acting at least a little bit normal—especially since that's what she'd told him they should do. She made a point of asking how his parents were, and of telling him Sophie and she would be by to pick out a tree soon, since he ran a Christmas tree lot at his landscaping business every December.

Meanwhile, he used the broom she'd defended herself with the night before to clear the snow from her car, then helped her load her things in the trunk. And there were moments when, if she tried really hard, she was almost able to pretend everything really *was* normal between them. Even though it wasn't. *But that's okay—it's bound to take a little time.*

Heading back inside the cabin with Adam to grab the

last couple of things, she took a look around—at the rug where they'd lain together, the chair where they'd taken Act Two—and her stomach contracted a little. She wasn't sure why, though—if it was because of the weirdness of it all or . . . if it was the memory of the thick, burning passion they'd shared.

Bundled up in her parka with the fur-trimmed hood, keys in hand, she headed to the door where she scooped up her purse, her unopened real estate manual, and the box of finished Christmas cards. Adam had just returned the broom to its spot near the hearth, and he turned to say, "All set?"

She simply nodded.

"Um, sorry I was a crazed cabin killer last night."

She squinted slightly, not understanding. "You weren't really a crazed . . ."

"I just mean—sorry about busting in on your privacy and acting like a jerk."

She shook her head, mainly just eager to leave now and put this all behind her. No matter how hot he looked all unshaven and bundled up in flannel. And why the hell was that suddenly sexy? "Everybody's entitled now and then," she replied. "And . . . it was a weird situation."

Now he was the one who nodded, and—oh God— she was just about to get caught up in recalling how blue his eyes had been when he'd been moving inside her . . . when a funny, almost amused look came over his face.

"What?" she asked.

"I just remembered something, that's all."

"What is it?"

But he shook his head. "Nothing."

Okay, whatever—it was time to go.

And she had just opened the door when Adam said, "All right, it's that I never got a chance to tell you something. About yesterday."

"What's that?"

"It's that I was the, uh . . ." He stopped, chuckled silently, then said, "Let's put it this way. It was nice playing reindeer games with you."

Reindeer games?

Then she gasped, suddenly understanding—oh God, Adam had been the reindeer in the department store!

In reply, she simply bit her lip, met his gaze, and—despite herself—let a small smile sneak out before pulling the cabin door closed behind her.

Wow. One more surprise this weekend.

But it was time to head back to real life now. No matter how fun those reindeer games had been.

"Every idiot who goes about with 'Merry Christmas' on his lips should be boiled with his own pudding, and buried with a stake of holly through his heart."

Charles Dickens, A *Christmas Carol*

## Five

Adam swung his truck into the parking area of Becker Landscaping—newly transformed into a Christmas tree lot—just after noon on Sunday, on his way back from the cabin. He hadn't planned to return to Destiny so early, but in the end, it had seemed easier than staying at the lake. He'd thought he'd be happy when Sue Ann left, yet it had seemed . . . hell, boring after that. So boring that he'd actually ended up having dinner with Grayson last night.

So maybe going there alone hadn't been such a hot idea, after all. Sue Ann had been right—he didn't like being divorced; the radical life changes involved in that just hadn't suited him. He enjoyed being around people, had liked having someone to come home to, and he especially loved being around his kids.

Though he'd been a little taken aback by her revelation on the topic. Because he hadn't ever really bothered to draw the lines connecting them in his head, but . . . damn, the more he'd thought about it, the more he'd realized it was all true. Having his boys gone had somehow brought the divorce back, front and center, on his personal radar screen. Maybe it just reminded him that . . . well, his life hadn't turned out the way he'd planned. And that if he'd just been a little stronger and toughed things out, he might still have a family—and the normal family life he'd wanted for his kids.

As he got out of the truck, he immediately spotted a few things that irked him, making his jaw clench.

"Hey boss, didn't expect to see ya so soon," said Chuck Whaley, an amiable young guy who'd worked for him year-round since his high school graduation five years ago.

"Well, I came back early," Adam snapped. He didn't *mean* to snap, but he could tell from the expression on Chuck's face that he had. Shit, apparently he hadn't returned from his trip in any better mood than when he'd gone.

"Um, okay," Chuck said—then looked like he was tiptoeing on a thin sheet of ice when he timidly asked, "Did ya have a nice time?"

Adam took a deep breath, tried to be civil. "Not really," he replied. "And how come the snow hasn't been cleared from the parking lot? Church just let out—we'll have tree shoppers this afternoon." The accumulation wasn't deep—nothing like what he and Sue Ann had seen at Bear Lake—but it would become a slushy mess soon.

"Sorry," Chuck said, his face coloring slightly. "I'll get right on it."

And that's when Adam realized he was still acting like a jerk, civil tone or not. Until now, he'd never had a cross word with Chuck in five years.

"Chuck," he called as the young man headed for a company truck sporting a snowplow.

Chuck stopped, looked over his shoulder.

"Sorry I'm acting pissy. It's me, not you."

Chuck just nodded and said, "No problem," but Adam thought he still appeared wary as he went on his way.

*Damn, I gotta stop taking my troubles out on everybody.* First it had been Sue Ann in the cabin, and now Chuck. But hell . . . if he was honest with himself, he felt even Scroogier today than when he'd first arrived at the lake.

And at least part of that was Sue Ann's fault. For prying into the details of his divorce.

Because he didn't talk about that. To anyone. Ever. He just didn't like airing his troubles far and wide. He and Sheila didn't get along great, even now, but he'd once loved her, and to him, that was reason enough to keep their problems to himself.

As he walked over to inspect some fir trees with broken branches, he let out a sigh. Shit. Nobody wanted a damaged tree.

So he called to another employee who'd just entered his line of sight. "Tyler!"

Tyler Fleet, a senior at Destiny High who did seasonal work for Adam on weekends, looked up with a start.

"What the hell happened to these trees?"

Tyler swallowed visibly. "Uh . . . what trees?"

For God's sake. Adam's jaw clenched tighter. Then he pointed. "The ones with the broken branches!"

"Um . . . I don't know." He swallowed again—by which point Adam realized Tyler was the wrong guy to be yelling at; he probably hadn't even been here when they were delivered.

"All right—never mind," Adam muttered. And when Tyler just stood there, like a deer in headlights, Adam finally shooed him away. "Go back to whatever you were doing."

As Tyler wandered off, Adam blew out his breath, then tried to calm down. *So much for being nicer.* But the conversation with Sue Ann about his divorce still weighed on him. Maybe he didn't like being reminded of his broken marriage, or having it pointed out that it still bothered him so much.

So he couldn't help feeling a little mad at her.

Of course, at the same time, he kind of wanted to be kissing her again—those deep, rhythmic kisses that ran all through him, slow and potent. He'd never been a guy who liked to rush things when it came to sex, and kissing—simple as it was—had always been one of his favorite things.

Naturally, though, that led to thoughts of the *other* things they'd done together, the activities that went far beyond kissing. The way she'd parted her legs for him to taste her. And—mmm, God—the way she'd knelt before him and returned the favor. He hadn't seen that coming, and the mere memory had him getting hard again.

But you might as well forget all about it because you aren't gonna be kissing her anymore, or doing any of those other things with her, either.

For lots of reasons.

*She's your best friend's ex-wife.* Even if he hadn't

seen Jeff much lately, ever since he'd told him leaving Sue Ann was a bonehead move.

*The ink on her divorce papers is barely dry.* And he'd felt that, how fresh it all still was for her. Who needed that kind of drama?

*She thought it was best to keep it confined to the cabin, too.* Apparently what happened in Snow Valley stayed in Snow Valley. The truth was, he hadn't even reached the point of thinking about the future when it had come up, but when she'd declared their hot little liaison a one-time thing, there hadn't been much to do but agree.

Which led, of course, to the biggest reason of all he and Sue Ann could never be together in any real sort of way: *By telling her about the end of your marriage, you showed her you can't be trusted.*

Sue Ann stood on Jenny's porch on Sunday afternoon knocking on the door. As Mick answered, she suffered a flashback to that night six months ago when she'd first found out Jeff was leaving her, but she quickly reminded herself this was different. For one thing, Sophie stood next to her carrying a pretty box of Christmas cookies Sue Ann had whipped up this morning. For another, she was wearing shoes. They'd come to help trim the tree.

"Hey, come on in," Mick said, stepping back, and as they moved inside, the scent of fresh pine met Sue Ann's nose. She spotted a robust evergreen standing in one corner of the lake cottage's living room just awaiting tinsel and decorations.

"These are for you," Sophie said, holding up the box—decorated with dancing reindeer—to Mick. *Lord, Sophie had had to pick the box with reindeer on it, hadn't she?*

"Cookies?" he asked, taking it.

Sophie nodded. "They're to thank you for inviting us over."

He shrugged. "Well, you and your mom are like family to Jenny, and we figured this year—" He stopped then, suddenly, and Sue Ann forgave him instantly for almost referring to Jeff's departure—Mick wasn't used to being around kids or needing to think before he spoke. "Figured this year . . . we could use the help," he finally finished.

But Sophie looked baffled. "How come?"

And now Mick appeared stumped, too—but as Sue Ann prepared to jump in, he replied, "Well, I'm . . . really bad at decorating the tree. So Jenny thought you could give me some pointers."

*Nice save*, Sue Ann mouthed in Mick's direction, as Sophie cheerfully said, "Okay. I'm really good at it!"

Sue Ann had been aware of the Christmas music echoing through the room since their arrival, but only now did she hear Gene Autry singing "Rudolph the Red-Nosed Reindeer." *Oh God—reindeer, reindeer, everywhere.*

She'd been trying to get her night with Adam off her mind, but it seemed reminders lurked at every turn. Even if those reminders were only of the antlered variety. She still couldn't believe it had been Adam behind that furry deer head—and yet something about it also made her feel a little giddy. Maybe because this meant he'd flirted with her even before they'd been trapped together. Maybe it made her feel less like the nearest available woman, and more like a woman he'd already noticed . . . in that way.

Not that any of that mattered. Because she did need to get the whole event off her mind. Still, that didn't prevent a small and possibly hysterical-sounding giggle from erupting from her throat when Gene reached the part about reindeer games.

Mick and Sophie just looked at her, and Mick said, "What's funny?"

Crap. Luckily, though, her eyes fell on a framed picture perched on the room's small mantel—of Jenny, Mick, and their orange tiger cat, Trouble, all wearing Santa hats. "Cute picture," she said.

Mick, however, didn't look amused. "Yeah, that was Jenny's idea. Me and the cat are still trying to get over it."

Just then, Sue Ann's best friend came whisking into the room, looking as bright and cheerful as ever in a Christmasy red sweater, her hair pulled back into a ponytail. "Hey, you're here. How was your weekend away?"

It was a perfectly normal question, of course—yet it caught Sue Ann off guard. "It was . . . short, actually. I came home early. Yesterday."

Jenny's eyes widened. "How come? And in all that snow? I hear they get it heavier in that area."

"Yes, they do," Sue Ann reassured her. An inch or so still blanketed Destiny and the surrounding hillsides, but that was nothing compared to the brief but potent blizzard that had trapped her and Adam in the cabin.

"How much did they get?" Mick asked.

"I'm . . . not sure." *I didn't notice because I was too busy saying goodbye to my lover.* "But . . . a lot." She looked Jenny in the eye then and said, "Can we talk? Like, in the kitchen?"

"Um, yeah, sure," Jenny said, meeting Sue Ann's gaze. "Mick, maybe you and Sophie can start with the lights."

"Sounds good," Mick replied as the two women made a beeline for the next room.

"The lights are the hardest part," Sue Ann heard her daughter saying to Mick, very knowledgably, as she and Jenny ducked into privacy.

Once in the kitchen, where a string of fabric gingerbread men hung draped from the curtain rod—reminding Sue Ann of her gingerbread man panties, of course—they took a seat at the small table. "What's up?" Jenny asked with quiet concern, her eyes connecting with Sue Ann's. "Did something happen?"

"Lots of things have happened."

Jenny's eyes widened. "Like?"

Sue Ann blinked, then let out a breath. "You won't believe it. Any of it. Because *I* don't believe it." Really, if the whole encounter with Adam had seemed surreal while it was taking place, that was nothing compared to how bizarre it seemed now. And the news about Jeff and Ronni and all that came with it—oh Lord, they were married now!—remained just as devastating.

"Well, spit it out."

Though now that the moment had come to actually tell her about Adam, Sue Ann bit her lip. She'd always talked about her sex life to Jenny and their other friends with ease, but . . . this was different. So maybe she'd just start with the other stuff—and get it all over with quick, like ripping off a Band-Aid. She leaned forward, swallowed past the nervous lump in her throat, and kept her voice low. "Jeff married Ronni and they plan to have a baby. And he's petitioning to cut off my alimony, so I'm broke. And I had sex with Adam."

Jenny just looked at her as if she were speaking Chinese. Then, finally, she said, "What?"

Sue Ann simply sighed—then began again. "Jeff married Ronni and—"

Jenny held up her hands. "No, stop. I heard it all. I'm just . . . having trouble processing it."

"Understandable. It's a lot to take in at once."

Now Jenny narrowed her eyes on Sue Ann. "All right, let's start at the beginning." But her gaze began to widen as she slowly comprehended bits and pieces of what Sue Ann had said. "Jeff seriously *married* her? Already? And—and he's . . . *what*?"

So Sue Ann proceeded to share all the information Barry Clayton had given her over the phone. And as always, Jenny was her ever-supportive self, aghast on Sue Ann's behalf, reminding her she didn't need a man who would do something so cold, and assuring her the courts would never take Sophie away from her.

"But I still have to find a better job, fast," Sue Ann explained. "And make sure I look like a great mom and all that, just in case Jeff ever did take that step. I mean, I don't think he would, but . . . I never thought he'd leave me, either. And I never thought he'd marry Ronni and withdraw all financial support this fast as well. So he's turning out to be . . . "

"A giant asshole?" Jenny asked.

"Well, I was going to say unpredictable. But I think giant asshole is completely accurate, too."

"Agreed," Jenny replied, then let out a big breath as she said, "All right, now on to the next part, which I'm completely unclear on, by the way. In fact, I'm wondering if maybe I misheard you."

"You mean the part about me having sex with Adam," Sue Ann said to confirm.

And Jenny was back to looking like Sue Ann was

speaking a foreign language. "Okay, see, there are a couple of parts to that sentence that keep confusing me," she said. "Like the part about sex. And the part about Adam."

"It's confusing to me, too," Sue Ann assured her. "But that's what happened."

Again, Jenny went silent for a moment, as if trying to puzzle it all through. "So . . . " She gave her head a short shake as though trying to clear out some cobwebs. "You're saying you had sex. And that it was with Adam. Adam Becker. My high school boyfriend who you were still trying to fix me up with just a couple of years ago."

Sue Ann cringed at the irony.

And then Jenny's brow knit as the news really, finally sank in. "Whoa. You had *sex* with *Adam*! I really don't want to act like this is more important than the other stuff, but . . . start talking."

So after another deep breath, Sue Ann dove in, starting with the department store reindeer, and proceeded to tell Jen the whole tale, which now felt completely exciting and a little lurid. "You realize," Sue Ann continued, keeping her voice low, "that this is the first time I've even kissed someone other than Jeff since I was sixteen."

"Wow," Jenny said. "And . . . how was it?"

Sue Ann could only sigh. "Nice." Then, remembering Adam's reaction to that lackluster word, she added, "No, wait, that's a lie. It was incredible."

Which made Jenny's eyes light up. "He was a good kisser when we were teenagers, too."

Sue Ann cast a knowing nod. "Very smooth, confident, unhurried. Like . . . kissing is an art."

"Yeah." Jenny sounded nostalgic. "That brings back memories. But . . . how was the sex?" She hadn't gone that far with Adam back in the day.

And the question only made Sue Ann let out yet one more well-pleasured sigh. "Well, maybe this is just because I don't have a lot to compare it to, but it was almost . . . magical."

"Magical? Wow." Jenny's gaze widened. "That's saying something."

Sue Ann simply nodded.

And Jenny smiled, clearly warming to the idea now. "So . . . you and Adam."

But Sue Ann shushed her. "Keep it down—my kid's in the next room. And I don't plan on telling anyone about this—other than you. Because he and I agreed to just forget about it and move on."

In response, however, Jenny gave her head a suspicious tilt. "Um, why would you do *that*? I mean, if it was all incredible and magical. And Adam's a great guy."

Sue Ann just expelled a heavy breath. She hadn't been looking for someone to play devil's advocate; she'd just wanted Jenny to agree with whatever she said. And though she usually told Jenny everything, she couldn't tell her the story of Adam's divorce—she'd promised, after all. So she fudged a reply. "Sure, Adam's nice and all. But do I really need to be trusting another man with my heart so soon, Jen?"

Yet Jenny merely shrugged. "Look, you're gun-shy right now, which I totally get." Jenny had been through an unpleasant divorce herself before her bad boy Prince Charming had come along, so Sue Ann had thought her friend would understand her caution.

"For good reason," Sue Ann pointed out. "It's just too soon. After the divorce."

"But it was magical," Jenny reminded her. As if she could have forgotten.

"Yeah," Sue Ann confirmed, a bit sadly. "But I have plenty going on in my life without that kind of complication, you know? Especially now. I had enough to deal with already—getting settled, working toward my real estate license, making sure Sophie comes through this okay—and now on top of all that, I need to drastically increase my income, fast. Plus I'm trying to give Sophie a nice Christmas. So this is no time to bring a man into my life."

*No matter how good he made me feel.*

*No matter how much he might still be on my mind.*

It was a cold, clear winter day, with snow upon the ground.

Charles Dickens, A *Christmas Carol*

# *Six*

*J*enny headed toward the living room, and she carried a tray of red mugs filled with hot chocolate, thick peppermint sticks jutting from each. She was still trying to get over all of Sue Ann's news—wow, Jeff had married Ronni, and Sue Ann had slept with Adam Becker!—but she didn't want to leave Mick and Sophie alone too long since her big, bad, sexy husband wasn't always comfortable around kids and she didn't want to make things awkward for either of them. Mick had had a terrible home life growing up, his childhood full of dark memories, so maybe he'd just sort of somehow blocked out the part of himself that could relate to being a child. Whatever the case, she figured he'd be in need of rescue by now.

So it caught her off guard to find the two down on the floor amid a string of glowing tree lights, Mick showing Sophie how to dangle them in front of Trouble as he batted his paw at them. "Now wiggle 'em a little," Mick was saying. "He likes to chase things that move."

Such a simple sight, yet it warmed Jenny's heart. Partly because she knew how tough this particular Christmas was going to be on Sue Ann's daughter, and she figured any little bit of fun would be a distraction from the less happy parts of the holiday season, even just playing with Trouble for a few minutes. But also because she'd never seen Mick look even remotely relaxed around Sophie or any other child. Maybe his comfort now came from the accumulated time he'd spent in her presence over the past couple of years, or maybe the cat and the lights simply provided the right tools to bring the two together in this moment.

But either way . . . well, the unexpected truth was, the scene before her was doing way more than just warming Jenny's heart right now.

In fact . . . whoa. It literally stopped her in her tracks.

Because—good Lord—she wanted a baby with him.

She hadn't seen this coming, not at all. Yet she couldn't deny it. The simple moment had just awakened her maternal instinct when she'd least expected it. She felt it in her heart. And she felt it in her womb.

Wow.

Years ago, she'd begun to face the fact that she would probably never be a mom. Before Mick, she'd been in an ill-fated marriage that had never produced a child, and *since* Mick . . . well, she'd known going in that he didn't want kids. And she'd understood that, and truly respected it, too. It wasn't for everybody. And she'd even been okay with it. She loved him like crazy and she knew they could lead a happy and fulfilling life without children as part of the mix.

And yet . . . this one look at Mick with Sue Ann's little girl was tugging on her heart strings, almost instantly, making her yearn to be a mommy, and to make him a daddy. As the two laughed together now, watching as Trouble pawed madly at the twinkling lights in Sophie's little hand, it nearly stole Jenny's breath.

"Um, hello—you're blocking the doorway," Sue Ann informed her from behind.

"Oh—sorry." She moved on, making a wide path around the lights sprinkling the floor, then announced, "Hot chocolate," as she lowered the tray to the coffee table.

"And cookies," Sue Ann reminded them all, reaching to open the decorative box she'd brought. As Mick and Sophie both joined them there, Sophie went straight for a reindeer-shaped cookie, complete with a red Rudolph nose.

"So what do you want for Christmas this year, Sophie?" Jenny asked—then almost regretted the question, fearing the answer might have something to do with her parents.

So she was relieved when Sophie said, "A reindeer."

Her relief was only temporary, however, squelched by the look on Sue Ann's face. "But I keep explaining to her," Sue Ann said, "that Santa doesn't really have any reindeer to spare."

Oh. Jenny got it. Sophie wanted a completely impossible gift, and it was going to heap one more big pressure on Sue Ann during this first holiday season without Jeff. She knew Sophie's happiness was Sue Ann's top priority right now and that she didn't want to disappoint her on Christmas morning. "True," Jenny chimed in. "I'm sure Santa would bring you one if he could, but he needs them all to pull his sleigh."

At this, however, Sophie's smile faded dramatically. She clearly had her heart set on having her very own reindeer.

Hearing a knock on the door just then, Jenny said, "That must be Amy. I was in the bookstore yesterday, so I invited her to join us." Amy was the only one in their close circle of girlfriends who remained single— well, besides Sue Ann now. And while Amy never seemed to mind her single status, Jenny had sensed her feeling a little lonely lately, especially now that Rachel and Tessa were both busy making wedding plans.

"Hope I'm not late," Amy said when Jenny answered the door, then held out a small red box tied with a white ribbon. "I made buckeyes."

"Mick will love you for that," Jenny said, since he loved the regionally popular chocolate-and-peanut-butter Christmas candies, then motioned her inside.

As everyone exchanged greetings with Amy and she stooped to scratch Trouble behind the ears, Jenny stood back and watched them all. She'd built a happy life here—far happier than she'd have dreamed possible when she'd returned home to Destiny following her divorce a few years back. *I have everything a girl could want. A hot and loving husband. Dear friends. And a satisfying career.* An astronomer at heart, Jenny loved teaching science at Destiny High.

"Sophie, you should get your mom to bring you by the bookstore soon," Amy said. "We have a new stray kitten." Amy, a major cat person, was getting famous around town for taking in strays at Under the Covers, and Jenny almost suspected that people with unwanted cats were actually dropping them off now. "I'm calling him Dickens," she added.

"Because he's a little dickens," Sue Ann guessed.

But Amy just gave her a you've-got-to-be-kidding look—she always named the strays after authors she loved, after all, and this one seemed obvious.

"Ohhhh," Sue Ann said then. "After Charles."

"'Tis the season and all," Amy reminded her. "But he *is* kind of a little dickens, too, now that you mention it. And Sophie will fall in love with him."

The cat chatter continued, and soon enough Mick finally began draping lights on the tree branches with Sophie's help. And Jenny was struck once more by how the vision embedded itself deep down inside her, like . . . a vision of the way things were meant to be, or maybe a vision of . . . Christmases yet to come?

*Oh God, I want a baby. A child. With Mick. I really, really do.*

She'd never felt that tug in the same gut-wrenching way she did in this moment. And it was—oh God— downright agonizing. So much so that it forced her to amend her thought from just a few minutes ago. *I have everything a girl could want . . . except a baby.*

A baby Mick didn't desire and would never go for.

She let out a sigh. How had this happened? A little while ago, she'd been perfectly happy, perfectly thankful for all that was so good in her life. But now, in the mere blink of an eye, she hungered for something she could probably never have, and she feared her world would never again feel quite right without it.

Sue Ann's first mistake of the day: She'd taken Amy's advice and stopped into the bookstore while she and

Sophie were out running holiday-related errands. She'd thought, just like when Sophie had played with Trouble, that maybe a few minutes with the new kitten, Dickens, would be a nice little distraction for her. Something to take her mind off that impossible reindeer she wanted so badly. But instead she'd seemed . . . too attached to the tiny gray kitten when Sue Ann had announced it was time to go. Sophie hadn't wanted to leave, and Sue Ann had seen tears welling in her daughter's eyes. She knew it wasn't just the cat—it was everything Sophie was going through right now—but she'd felt like a shrew just the same.

Her second mistake of the day: going to buy a Christmas tree without realizing she no longer had an easy way to get it home. Because Jeff had taken the SUV and left her with the Corolla. She'd thought she'd been so smart going to Becker Landscaping at a time when she knew Adam wouldn't be there—he always met up with Logan Whitaker for lunch at Dolly's Main Street Café on Wednesdays—but she'd dumbly neglected to remember all the little ways her divorce affected her life, right down to no longer having a vehicle good for hauling large items. And though the guys at Adam's tree lot had suggested tying it onto the roof of her car, she hadn't felt confident about that solution. Thankfully, though, that one hadn't been a *big* problem— Chuck Whaley had taken her address and said they'd be happy to deliver it later this afternoon.

And Sue Ann's third mistake? Thinking she was capable of putting up the outside Christmas lights by herself. That's what she was doing now. Although it felt a lot more like hanging onto a ladder for dear life, wondering how you were supposed to maneuver the lights without falling to your death on the ground, and cursing Jeff all over again. At this moment, though, she wasn't cursing him because she missed him—she was cursing him for not being here to give Sophie the same, familiar Christmas traditions she'd grown accustomed to, leaving it all to her. It wasn't about love or attachment—it was only about anger, and maybe also a little about abandonment.

*But I can do this. My mother did it, after all, for all those years, without ever a complaint.* Sue Ann's father had died from a heart attack when she was just a little girl, even younger than Sophie. Her mom had never remarried—had never even appeared to have the faintest interest in any man but her dad, actually—and yet somehow she'd handled every aspect of their lives just fine. So Sue Ann tried to summon her mother's quiet strength, respecting it all the more now.

She would have gladly forgone the lights this year, but just like that dumb reindeer, it was one more thing Sophie kept asking for, and one thing Sue Ann had—crazily, it seemed—thought she could provide. So up the ladder she'd gone, and now here she was, wondering how the hell she was ever going to get the string of lights, which trailed down to the snowy yard beneath her, where they needed to go. Yes, she loved her home, situated just a few blocks from the heart of town, but it suddenly seemed so . . . tall. And wide. *Why did I ever think we needed a house this big?* She might be at this for weeks.

Unfortunately, though, her thoughts were swept rapidly back to Mistake Number Two when she glanced up to see—oh dear God!—Adam's pickup meandering down Holly Lane with her Christmas tree in back. Sheesh. She'd been trying to *avoid* seeing him, not create an awkward one-on-one, face-to-face, in-home encounter.

Despite herself, her heart pattered rapidly in her chest as he turned into her snow-covered driveway. And as he got out, wearing a flannel shirt under a dark, puffy winter vest—oh Lord, he looked good. Even in flannel, just like at the cabin. He clearly hadn't shaven in a couple of days, leaving a dark stubble on his jaw, and his hair was again mussed, this time likely from a cold, breezy afternoon at the tree lot. When on earth had she developed a thing for the outdoorsy, rugged type?

Admittedly, Adam *usually* looked good, but the effect it had on her had definitely changed. Now she felt it aching in her breasts and—oh boy—tingling between her legs. And she still couldn't quite wrap her mind around the fact that she'd had sex with him. In fact, in the days since it had happened, it had started to seem a little . . . like a dream, or a fantasy or something. But seeing him now brought the reality back with startling clarity.

That's when she glanced down at herself. She'd changed into ragged blue jeans and donned an old parka over a sweater. An ancient knit hat was tugged down over her ears, and her hair likely sprouted every which way beneath it.

Not that it really mattered what she looked like, of course. As she'd reaffirmed to Jenny the other day, it had only been a one-time thing. That was the only sane way to handle the situation . . . for oh so many reasons. And that put them back to being friends, just like always. Which was why she shouldn't feel nervous at all.

Except that she did. And why had she put on that stupid hat anyway?

The only good news here was that his arrival gave her an excellent reason to come down off the ladder of death that currently held her. Which, she suddenly realized, was easier thought than done. The lights currently looped around her arm, but coming down meant releasing the firm hug she had on the nearest rung and moving backward.

And—uh-oh—the first step gave her the sensation of falling, especially when the ladder wobbled. She let out a gasp and grabbed back on as her heart rose to her throat.

"Whoa there," she heard Adam say below her, and a glance down nearly stole what little sense of balance she had at the moment. She tightened her grip and tried not to hyperventilate.

"For God's sake, Sue Ann, you have to make sure you plant the legs on level ground," he scolded from below now, his tone calming some as he added, "All right, I'm holding it steady—you can come on down."

Hmm—that was easy for him to say. She was still breathing too fast and wondering how she'd gotten herself into this. But coming down sounded good enough that she made herself begin to take those hard, careful, backward steps, all while holding tensely to the sides of the metal ladder. Another, and another—careful, careful—and slowly the snowy ground grew nearer. And then she found herself backing . . . right into Adam's warmth.

She sucked in her breath once more, short and fast, then turned to face him as he let go of the metal. His face was right there, close enough to kiss, and he smelled like some combination of brisk winter and musky, sexy man. "Um, thanks," she said, her heartbeat kicking up again, for entirely different reasons this time.

"My pleasure," he said deeply, "but you need to be more careful."

They still stood way too close for her comfort, and if she didn't extricate herself from the position soon, she *was* going to kiss him—just from sheer instinct and feminine need—so she forced herself to slip out of the narrow space between him and the ladder.

Okay, there, that was better. Sort of. It was colder, and not nearly so inviting—but she'd had to stop the madness before it began again.

"I didn't really know what I was getting into," she admitted when she finally found her voice. "Sophie wanted the lights up, and I just want to try to make this Christmas as normal for her as possible, and it sounded like something a grown woman should be able to do—but the house is so big, and it's a lot harder than I thought."

"Sue Ann," he said as if reasoning with her, "I'll put the lights up."

Something inside her went rigid. Because he was such a good guy—but she wanted to be self-sufficient. In fact, she needed it. "I can't have you coming to my rescue."

"Why not? It's no big deal. Just some lights. It's the kind of thing I'm good at. And the kind of thing you're clearly *not* good at. I'm happy to do it. It's not rescue. It's one friend doing a favor for another."

She let out a sigh, conceding. "Okay." She had to be practical, after all. "And thanks."

He just gave his head a short shake, like it was nothing. "After I get the tree inside, I'll head back out and get started."

"Thanks for that, too. Bringing the tree." Now *she*

was the one shaking her head. "I'm just . . . out of sorts on all this holiday stuff this year."

"No sweat. Seriously," he said. Then he took off toward the truck to haul the tree, hoisting it effortlessly up onto his shoulder like some lumberjack in a way that sort of turned her on. *But yikes. You have to stop that. Adam is your friend. Your hot, sexy, skillful-in-bed friend.* Sheesh.

Adam tried not to look at Sue Ann as he carried her Christmas tree toward the old Victorian house's wrap-around porch. Because ever since she'd backed down that ladder, he'd been fighting off a monster hard-on. Hell—he'd been fighting off arousal every time she'd come to mind since Saturday.

And it wasn't like sex was a big, unusual occurrence in his life. He didn't go out looking to get laid every weekend or anything, but he'd had his fair share of female encounters in the three years since parting with Sheila. Hanging out with his buddies, Mike and Logan, who were chick magnets, had made it pretty easy to get back into the swing of things after the divorce. Of course, Mike was engaged now and didn't hit the bars as much, but by the time that had happened, he'd pretty much found his footing with women again. So what had taken place with Sue Ann wasn't some rare event.

*Then why does it keep feeling that way?* Why had she stayed on his mind so damn much?

Because she's Jeff's ex. And because you've known her your whole life. So that makes it a little weird, that's all. Those were the reasons he kept giving himself anyway. Yet at moments, he began to wonder . . .

Maybe he'd agreed to that "forget about it and act normal" thing too quickly. Maybe he'd agreed to it because he just hadn't seen any other options. Agreeing had seemed simple, sensible in so many ways, and so the words had just flowed out of his mouth.

And it really remained the smartest way to handle the situation. Especially after the phone call he'd received from Jeff last night—yep, after that, forgetting about it seemed even wiser. He didn't like the idea of being in the middle of their problems.

And yet, either way—sensible or not—he'd been cringing inside just now when he'd said the part about one friend doing a favor for another.

But then, he'd been cringing inside a lot lately. He'd continued barking at the guys who worked for him all week. He'd even caught himself yelling at his black collie, Pepper, last night for jumping up and down and being glad to see him when he got home. Which had been . . . well, ironic, given that he should have been damn grateful there was anybody at home to see him, period.

Now Sue Ann held the front door open for him and he was squeezing the evergreen through, trying not to break any branches. "To the right, to the right," she directed him, and despite himself, he liked when his body passed so closely by hers, the same way he'd liked it when she'd backed down that ladder and straight into him.

Part of him felt guilty—because she was pure, sweet Sue Ann, and he was thinking naughty thoughts about her at the moment. But on the other hand, she'd *been* a little naughty with him. And he'd loved it. So how could that not permeate his brain?

Once the tree was inside, he didn't have to ask where she wanted it—he'd been to Sue Ann's house plenty of times at Christmas and knew she erected her tree in the center of the big bay window where it could be seen from the street. She already had a container set up there, so he positioned the tree inside as Sophie ran in from the kitchen.

"You brought our tree!" she said, as wide-eyed as any kid on Christmas morning.

He paused in his work to give his god-daughter a grin. "When I heard it was yours, I made sure I was the one to deliver it."

"Really?"

"Of course. Couldn't miss a chance to see my favorite girl." And of course he meant Sophie—but just then, he unwittingly found himself glancing over at Sue Ann, who stood by the door looking both disheveled and pretty at the same time, her cheeks red from the cold, and he wondered if she could see the truth in his gaze. *Right now,* you *might be my favorite girl.*

*Whether I like it or not.*

"Can you stay and help us decorate the tree?" Sophie asked, her soft brown eyes opening even wider. And, damn, a look like that was hard to refuse, Grinch or not.

So Adam checked his watch. It was just past three, pretty early to be knocking off from work—but as the boss, he could pretty much do as he pleased.

Yet . . . a quick glance at Sue Ann said the answer was—crap—probably no. Hell. She was clearly uncomfortable with him after last weekend, and he hated that. "Well, right now I'm gonna go put up the lights outside," he told Sophie, dodging the question.

"Can I help?" asked the little blond miniature version of Sue Ann.

At this, he risked another glance at her mother. "If it's all right with your mom."

He couldn't read Sue Ann's eyes even as she expelled

a long breath. But then she managed a smile and said, "Of course you can help Adam with the lights. But let's get you bundled up first. It's cold out there."

"Look!" Sophie said then, pointing, and both Adam and Sue Ann glanced past the tall tree to peer out the window into the yard. "It's snowing again!"

Huh. How about that. Just like the clipper that had blown through last weekend, this snow hadn't been predicted, either, yet it suddenly fell from the sky in thick, pretty flakes that somehow, that quickly, made Adam feel a little bit cocooned there with Sue Ann and Sophie in the big old house on Holly Lane.

"Guess we'd better get busy," he said, looking to Sophie—but secretly feeling warm inside all over again just remembering what had happened to him the *last* time it snowed.

The night is waning fast, and it is precious time to me . . .

Charles Dickens, A *Christmas Carol*

## *Seven*

An hour later, snow still fell outside and daylight grew flat as the afternoon waned. When Sue Ann glanced out the bay window to spy Adam and Sophie beginning to build a snowman, she couldn't hold in her smile. Sophie looked happy—and distracted from her troubles—and that was all Sue Ann could ask for right now.

Well, wait, that wasn't strictly true. She could also ask for a full-time job. And though she'd been investigating possibilities the last couple of days, so far she hadn't found anything. But she wasn't going to panic. *You're strong, you're capable, and everything will be fine.*

*You won't lose the house. You won't lose Sophie.*

*Now stop thinking about the bad and focus on the good.*

And the good now even drew her toward the front door—an inexplicable urge to get closer to the scene. Maybe she just needed to latch onto a little of her daughter's joy in this moment and make it her own. Grabbing an old crocheted shawl she often wrapped up in on chilly nights from the peg board in the foyer, she tossed it around her shoulders and stepped silently out onto the front porch.

The whole neighborhood glistened with the fresh snowfall, and though dinnertime approached, most of the houses on Holly Lane sat quiet and still. The only sound was the soft trill of Sophie's laughter, warming Sue Ann's heart.

"Instead of a snowman," she heard Sophie say to Adam, "can we make a snow reindeer?"

Adam gave her daughter a come-on-get-serious sort of look. "I'm a talented snow sculptor, Soph," he said, "but I'm not a magician."

And again her daughter's giggles filled the cold air. "Then, how about a snow . . . cat?" Yes, of course—cats were on her mind now, too.

Sue Ann watched as Adam narrowed his gaze on the mound of snow they'd already amassed, as if weighing the request, then turned the same speculative look on Sophie. "Okay, a snow cat I might be able to do. But we're gonna need some twigs for whiskers, so you'd better start hunting."

"Yay," Sophie sang out merrily, then went skipping through the snow toward the tall pines in one corner of the yard—and Sue Ann leaned out beyond the covered porch to see the glowing lights that now outlined the home's eaves and windows.

And in that moment, something wrapped around her

heart like a blanket, and she realized that—wow, there it was! That cozy Christmas feeling had just begun to flutter through her when she'd least expected it. She hadn't anticipated it arriving at all this year, yet suddenly it was all around her. And just when she needed it most.

Neither Sophie nor Adam—intent on snow-sculpting now—noticed her on the porch in the fading daylight, so she quietly moved back into the house, feeling strangely at peace, at least for the moment. Which was surprising because . . . she hadn't experienced that in a long while. And extra weird that it should come now, when so many new problems had just beset her.

And as she toted boxes of ornaments and other holiday decorations down from the attic, it didn't feel like the toil she'd foreseen it being this year. After heading into the kitchen to set out mugs for hot chocolate, she even put on some Christmas music. A moment later, Chris Isaak was singing "Let it Snow," and as she continued bustling about the house, she found herself silently pushing her problems to the back of her mind, at least for now, and even feeling . . . cautiously hopeful. She wasn't sure how that had happened, or how long it might last—but she was simply thankful it had. Sometimes taking one day at a time really meant taking even just one hour or one minute at a time, and this hour was one of her better ones.

When the heavy front door burst open, she looked up to see her daughter, as red-nosed as Rudolph himself, peeking inside. "Mom! Mom! Come look!" Sophie appeared so excited that it was infectious—and God, it was good to see her acting so bubbly.

"All right, I'm coming," Sue Ann said as Sophie

waved one mitten-covered hand, hurrying her along. Instead of the shawl this time, she grabbed the old parka she'd worn earlier, completely forgetting she'd thought it seemed too ragged for Adam to see her in.

"Put on your scarf," Sophie scolded her despite the rush. "You never let *me* go out without a scarf when it's cold."

"Okay, *Mom*," she teased her daughter with a laugh, snatching her brightly striped one from the peg board and tossing it around her neck.

When they stepped outside, it was almost dark—the days were short this time of year—but snow still fell in large, lacy flakes that glittered in the rays from the porch light Sue Ann had just flicked on. Sophie grabbed her wrist and dragged her down the front steps into the snow that now lay a few inches deep, covering the front yard and the quiet street beyond, which harbored the tracks of only a few vehicles.

Adam stood behind the fat mound of snow she was being pulled toward, gloved hands in his front jeans pockets, looking chilled but cheerful and oh-so-handsome. Their eyes met briefly, and Sue Ann cast a smile in his direction without quite planning it—until Sophie finally had her where she wanted her, halting her in place, then turning her around to look. "See?" Sophie said.

And—oh! Only now could she see what a great job Adam had done with the lights—they framed the whole house in colors that glowed through the falling snow. But what Sophie was really showing her was the rather magnificent snow cat she and Adam had created. It sat proudly in the yard, back curving, front legs straight and paws neatly carved, with claws made from chips of

tree bark, probably from the woodpile in the backyard.
A long, curving tail stretched beside it on the ground,
but what made it most distinguishable as a cat were the
pointing ears and the face: A triangular piece of bark
served as the nose, with wood bits for eyes, and twigs
forming a mouth and whiskers. "It's . . . almost perfect," Sue Ann said, complimenting and teasing them
at the same time.

"Almost?" Adam argued. "Look, we tried to make
the tail stand up, but it just wasn't happening."

"No, that's not it," Sue Ann said, still studying the
snow cat. "It just needs . . . a bit of flair." And with that,
she broke her own scarf-wearing rule by whipping the
striped one from around her neck and carefully tying it
around the snow cat's, leaving the long ends to cascade
down in front. "There," she added. "*Now* it's perfect."

Sophie clapped her hands and jumped up and down in
response, then sang out, "Can we take a picture of it?"

Adam immediately whipped out his cell phone. "I
got it," he said, pointing it toward the snow cat. "Hop
in there with him, Sophie."

A few minutes later, everyone had taken turns having
pictures made with the cat—who Sophie by then had
dubbed Snowy—and Sue Ann said, "I've got stuff
ready to make hot chocolate inside. You guys must be
freezing after being out here so long."

"Some hot chocolate sounds good," Adam said, and
the three left the snow cat behind and made a trail back
through the fresh snowfall to the front door.

Once inside, everyone shed their winter gear and
Sue Ann led the way to the kitchen, where she mixed
up three mugs of cocoa and milk to heat in the micro-
wave. When it was hot, Sophie did the honors with the

whipped cream and they all carried their cups back to the living room, where the bare Christmas tree now stood.

"So are you staying to help trim the tree?" Sophie asked, clearly still just as excited about this as she'd been about everything, it seemed, since Adam's arrival.

*Maybe she just likes having a familiar man around the house again. Or . . . maybe she just likes having company, period.* The big house had felt hollow and quiet these past months. But whatever the case, Sophie's smile continued to warm Sue Ann's soul.

That's when she heard Adam waffling, though, saying, "Well, I don't know—it's getting late and the snow's really piling up out there," even as he politely looked to Sue Ann for guidance.

He was right about it getting late; it was time for dinner, in fact. And she had envisioned the tree-trimming as something she and Sophie would do alone, because Sophie needed to adjust to it being just the two of them at home now for such activities.

Yet . . . Adam had always been a part of Sophie's life. And Sue Ann couldn't help remembering that his house was lonely and quiet right now, too.

So she smiled into his sexy blue eyes and said, "Why don't you stay?"


"I think this might just be our best tree ever, Soph, don't you?" Sue Ann said as she stood back to admire the finished product. Silver snowflake garland stretched from one branch to the next in fancy scallops, and homemade ornaments blended in with the old-fashioned antique ones passed down from Sue Ann's grandma. Twinkling lights of every color glowed from top to bottom, and crowning the tree was a glittery silver star Sophie had picked out herself as a gift for Sue Ann just last year.

Sophie's beaming smile said she agreed. But the evening had gotten away from Sue Ann. After hot chocolate, she'd whipped up an easy winter meal of soup and grilled cheese for them all, and a glance at the mantel clock now told her that decorating the tree had taken longer than she'd planned. "Sophie, why don't you go call your dad and tell him we'll be on our way soon." She was late dropping Sophie at Jeff and Ronni's.

"Okay," her daughter said, scurrying up the steps just off the living room, heading for the upstairs phone.

It was the first time Sue Ann had been alone with Adam all day, the first chance she'd gotten to say, "Thank you. For all your help today. Sophie had a ball, and that doesn't happen much lately." And wow—just looking at him now . . . she couldn't deny that it brought back familiar feelings. Because the last time she'd been alone with him . . . well, they'd been having good, hot, slow-burning sex.

But Adam just gave his head a short shake, shrugging off her words. "I haven't had this much fun lately, either, so trust me, it was no sacrifice." Then he lowered his chin skeptically. "Only . . . are you planning to drive to Jeff's *now*?"

She nodded easily—but then they both glanced past the lit tree to the wintry white night outside the window. The snow had finally stopped after the completion of the snow cat, but at least three or four fresh inches had accumulated. "Don't worry," Sue Ann said, reading his thoughts. "The Corolla is pretty tough in snow. Maybe not Snow Valley snow, but luckily, Destiny roads aren't quite so steep."

The warm grin he cast in reply nearly turned her heart upside down. She'd had to mention Snow Valley, hadn't she? And now she was pretty sure he was remembering the same thing she was. "Tough or not," he finally said, "why don't you let me drop her at Jeff's? No need to take any chances when I've got four-wheel-drive."

Hmm. Adam made a considerate offer, and the truth was, she didn't look forward to the trip to Crestview. Still . . . "This will sound dumb, but I'd feel weird not to take her myself. I just feel . . . like I should spend every second with her I can. I would never want her to think it was too much trouble for me, you know?"

He shrugged. "So ride along with us."

"But then you'd have to bring me back home."

"Yeah, it'll be a whole three blocks out of my way when I pass back by." Adam lived outside of town on a pretty tract of five acres where, with his father's help, he'd built a sizable wood ranch house with stone accents and a large stone chimney. "I think I can handle it, Sue Ann."

And it was true—bringing her home afterward really wouldn't put him out. Taking Sophie to Crestview in the first place would actually be way more inconvenient. So finally, Sue Ann gave a conceding sigh and said with a cautious smile, "Okay. You talked me into it." After all, declining his offer would have been silly. She yelled up the stairs, "Soph, when you're off the phone, go get your backpack. Adam's gonna drive us over since it's snowy out."

When she turned back to Adam, she found him peering critically at the tree. "Where's that one ornament?"

"That one ornament?" she asked teasingly. "I'm gonna need a little more to go on, Mr. Becker."

"That old-fashioned glass Santa," he clarified. "It always used to be on the front of your tree, and I think once you told me it had been passed down through the family. I got the idea it was special to you."

Ah, one more reminder that Adam had known her for a long time and that his presence in her home wasn't unusual—it just felt different now; new in a way, but also familiar. Yet the mention of that particular ornament was a little depressing. "Actually, all the old ones are from my grandmother, but that one was my favorite. It got broken last year." Jeff had dropped it; it had been an honest accident and she'd been sad but not mad. "It always reminded me of Christmases at her house when I was little. She knew I liked it, so she always put it down low, on the front, so I could see it. That's why I always put it there, too. I'd hoped to give it to Sophie one day."

"Bummer," he said, and she nodded. And their eyes met—for maybe a little too long, so she looked away, out the window into the snowy night.

When she finally glanced back at him, this time she found him adjusting one of the tree's homemade pieces—a reindeer constructed of old-fashioned wooden clothespins. Sophie had made it in kindergarten. And sheesh, again it seemed this was the "year of the reindeer." Of course, reindeer were pretty common at Christmastime, but lately it almost seemed like they were . . . ganging up on her or something.

And she probably shouldn't dare bring this up, but before she could stop herself, she heard herself say, "That reminds me . . ."

He turned to face her, letting go of the ornament, his gorgeous blue eyes seeming to paralyze her a little.

Which was when she realized she *definitely* shouldn't bring this up—because it would surely lead their thoughts back to that snowbound cabin, as if they weren't both already remembering it anyway. But it was too late to stop the question, and she really was curious, so she barreled ahead. "I never got to ask you— what on earth were you doing in that reindeer head in Crestview last week?"

The question made him let out a hardy laugh. "Price you pay for being Cub Scout den leader."

"Ah," she said, tipping her head back.

"Sorry, though," he said, his smile fading into a hint of sheepishness.

She leaned forward slightly. "For?"

"Flirting with you that way. That was . . . probably weird of me." And wow, he was even sexy when he was sheepish. And though he'd just turned the conversation in the exact direction she'd not wanted it to go, something in her stomach tingled.

*Just act mature about it. Acknowledge the truth of the matter, then move on.* "Well, it caught me off guard since I couldn't see who it was. But . . ." Okay, she was being mature, but she still couldn't help lowering her eyes for this part. "Given how things turned out later, a little flirting doesn't seem all that weird."

Only then she lifted her gaze back to his just as fast, because the need to see his response overrode her discomfort. And she promptly discovered—oh dear—his gaze locking her all the more warmly in place. Paralysis complete. "Guess that's true," he said, his voice going a bit deeper than before.

Oh boy. The spot between her legs spasmed lightly. And her next words came out rushed. "But we probably shouldn't talk about that, since—you know—we agreed it would be best."

"Right," he said then, but his voice remained just as deep and sexy anyway, causing Sue Ann to start sweating a little.

And it was at that precise moment that Sophie came bounding down the steps with her backpack in tow. "Told Daddy we'd be there soon!"

*Good timing, kid.* Sue Ann thanked her daughter silently, then said, "All set and ready to go?"

Sophie nodded.

And Sue Ann broke free of her temporary paralysis.

And once again they got bundled back up for another excursion out into the wintry Destiny night.

Usually when Sue Ann sat in the driveway of Veronica's small Cape Cod style house watching Sophie go inside, it was with a sense of defeat and loneliness. On this particular night, though, it was more a feeling of: *Oh my God, I'm alone with Adam again.*

But that was okay, she told herself. *You're strong, you're capable, and everything's going to be fine.* After all, it was a twenty minute ride back to Destiny, not wild monkey sex. Well, maybe thirty on the snowy roads. But still not wild monkey sex.

No, the wild sex had been *last* week.

At moments, it all came back to her like a dream, something that couldn't really have happened, but recalling it now, with Adam only a few feet away from her in the truck's warm interior, she was reminded just how shockingly, deliciously real it had been.

As Adam maneuvered the truck back onto the main road leading home, she couldn't help wondering how her big plan to avoid him had somehow turned into them spending the entire afternoon and evening together. And so far she was doing a pretty bad job of "forgetting about it and acting normal," although she hoped she'd at least started *faking* normal better as the hours had passed.

But wait, no, not just faking. Some moments had honestly *felt* normal. Normal and real. As real as their night in that cabin—just in a different way. Standing in the snow taking pictures with him and Sophie—that had felt real. Drinking hot chocolate, trimming the tree—all that had felt real, too. Real and . . . sort of right. Sort of like . . . everything was as it *should* be.

*But that's only because it made Sophie so happy, and because Adam is a good friend—it has nothing to do with the night you spent together.*

They rode in silence, other than the Christmas music coming from the radio—the only local station played Christmas songs from the day after Thanksgiving onward through the holiday, and sometimes, during December, they even strayed from their retro theme. Now was one of those times, and Jason Mraz's peppy version of "Winter Wonderland" made her decide that, rather than being uncomfortable for the whole ride home, she should just be grateful instead, not only for Adam's help with the lights but because he'd given Sophie such a nice day.

"Thank you again," she told him as the truck rounded a curve, the headlights carving out a path on the snow-covered highway before them. "I haven't seen Sophie smile so much in a very long time."

Across the seat from her, he shrugged, keeping his eyes on the road as he answered. "Like I said earlier, it was fun for me, too." But then he cast a quick side-ways glance in her direction, one that made her feel . . . hmm, as if maybe he was talking about more kinds of fun than just building a snow cat and trimming a tree, like his fun had somehow included her as well. The look made something in her breasts tingle a little—until, that is, she gave herself a firm, *Stop it!*

"Putting up lights was fun?" she asked doubtfully—mostly just to keep the conversation going.

Adam offered up a comfortable smile as they passed the Destiny city limits sign. "All right—fun might be a stretch, but I didn't mind it."

Slowly starting to feel a little more at ease—just like during the hot chocolate drinking and tree decorating—Sue Ann elaborated on what she'd said earlier. "I just don't like finding tasks I can't handle myself, you know? I like to think I can do everything on my own now that I really am . . . on my own."

"Thing is, Sue Ann, nobody's good at everything, so we all need a little help sometimes." He slowed a bit as they drove past the town square, as silent and snow-covered as a scene on a Christmas card. "Me, I'm good at putting up lights and carrying in trees. But when it comes to things you're probably good at—like baking cookies and wrapping presents—I'm . . . "

"All hooves?" she suggested.

He let out a laugh. "Exactly." Then he said, "So, not to bring up a sore subject, but I was wondering . . . how are things going since you got the news about Jeff trying to withdraw alimony?"

She glanced over at him in the dark truck, glad he hadn't brought this up in front of Sophie but also appre-ciating that he cared. She hadn't felt like discussing it last week when it was brand new and too shocking, but she didn't mind so much now. Even if she didn't have anything positive to report. "Well, I'm trying to find a full-time job, but no luck yet. I guess if worse comes to worst, I'll keep my part-time hours at the real estate office and get a second job waiting tables someplace in Crestview. At least my mother is willing to help with childcare whenever I need her."

His expression told her he realized, though, that such a situation would be way less than ideal. "That sounds like it could create a pretty rough schedule."

But she tried to shrug it off. "Gotta do what ya gotta do, right?"

"Well, I'll keep my ears open and let you know if I hear of anything."

"Thanks," she said, then asked, "Have you talked to the boys much?" She didn't want to bring up a sore subject with him, either, but she was sure Jacob and Joey were on his mind whether or not she mentioned them.

He let out a long breath before answering, though his voice came steady and strong when he replied, "Every morning. And sometimes I get a later call, too." The truck now traveled the small grid of streets that led back to Holly Lane. "They're spending most days on the ski slopes, taking lessons—and according to their grandpa, they're getting pretty good. Then they do homework in the evenings."

"You seem like your mood about the situation has improved a lot since . . . " Oh, crap—once again, she was taking them unwittingly back to that cabin. "Since the last time I saw you."

At this, though, Adam unexpectedly cast another of those slightly sheepish—albeit very sexy—looks. "Not really. If you'd been around me an hour before I delivered your tree today, you'd have run for cover."

Hmm. She was tempted to ask him what had changed between then and his arrival at her house—but maybe she didn't really want to know. It seemed best to just keep the conversation light, not dig into anything too deeply.

As Adam pulled into her driveway and eased to a stop, she asked, "So how'd you get stuck delivering my tree anyway? Don't you have, you know, underlings for that?"

And it was then that everything shifted. After putting the four-wheel drive in park behind her Toyota, he peered over at her in the truck cab, lit only by the dash lights and the reflection of the snow all around them, the look in his eyes downright . . . smoldering. And she could have sworn his voice went an octave deeper when he said, "I volunteered for the job."

Oh. "Why?" she asked. But then she caught herself—because suddenly her heart beat too fast and her palms were starting to sweat. "Wait, don't answer that. I mean—" She stopped, swallowed. Oh Lord. So much for acting normal. Maybe the best thing to do was just make a quick escape. "Thanks again, Adam, for everything," she rushed, then reached for the door handle.

But she didn't even come close to getting it open, since that's when Adam's firm grip closed around her wrist, seeming extra warm given the weather—and the touch skittered all through her. "Sue Ann—stop."

"Huh? Why?" She found her gaze shifting from his face to where his hand circled her flesh with heat.

"I hate that I'm making you nervous."

Oh, great—her discomfort was just as obvious as she'd feared all along. "It's not you. It's me," she said, suddenly a bit short of breath. "It's . . . being alone with you. In the dark, sort of. I feel like I'm sixteen or something. Except that we've had sex. Which I hadn't quite done at sixteen. Especially not with you. So this is actually much worse than that." He let go of her now, but she just leaned her head back and rolled her eyes. Had she really just said all that? It was like verbal vomit. "Oh God, you probably think I'm a lunatic."

"No," he replied, his voice as smooth as melted chocolate. "The fact is, I think you're sweet, gorgeous, and sexy as hell."

She heard the gasp leave her before she could stop it. Then she got frank with him—and a little panicky. "Well—that's a problem."

"What's wrong with me thinking you're sweet, gor—"

"It's the sexy as hell part," she explained, still talking too fast. "You can't think that about me." Even if she thought that about *him*. Because she wasn't planning on acting on those emotions. But she suddenly had the funny feeling that maybe he was.

Across the truck from her, he let out a sigh she felt in her panties, and his next words came out slow and potent, reaching deep down inside her. "The truth is, Sue Ann, try as I might, I can't *stop* thinking that about you."

Oh. Wow. What now? "But . . . what about our agreement? To forget about what happened."

"I've been trying," he told her. "I swear. But . . . I haven't been doing very good with it."

The words hung in the air between them as her heart

continued to thump madly against her chest. It was startling—and yet also . . . deeply, wildly gratifying to hear they were having the exact same problem. "You haven't?" she finally whispered.

"Nope. What about you?" It felt as if his eyes were touching her, physically. And like earlier when he'd been looking at her, more parts of her body began to sweat besides just her palms now.

It seemed like a good time for a lie. "I've been fine with it. And I'd . . . hoped after today that we'd feel completely, um, back to normal. Like the old friends we are." Then, for good measure, she leaned over and gave him a soft punch in the arm. Buddy to buddy.

Unfortunately, though, before she could pull back her fist, Adam grabbed her wrist again. And this time he drew her arm softly closer—and lowered a terribly scintillating little kiss to the top of her hand.

Oh. My. She felt it . . . everywhere. She didn't even know a hand kiss could do that. So much for being just buddies. And so she simply sat there, frozen in place, absorbing the sensations still fluttering through her.

"Shit. Sorry. I just . . . God, I shouldn't have done that," he said, finally releasing his hold on her hand.

But . . . she couldn't seem to make herself draw it back now. So it just kind of hung there in the air for a moment, then slowly drifted downward, her still-bent fingers grazing the flannel of his sleeve before coming to rest beside him on the leather seat.

Undeniable desire moved within her. Warring. And then . . . winning.

And when she next spoke, her voice came out breathy. "Adam, I . . . "

"What?"

Oh God, she couldn't quite catch her breath.

But then she finally managed to blow outward, starting to get hold of herself. Desire had won for a very brief moment, but now she managed to say, "I should go."

"I don't want you to," he said quickly.

She grew aware of her own heartbeat yet again. "You don't?"

"Nope." Plain and simple.

So just as plain, and just as simply, she asked him, "What *do* you want?"

"To be buried back deep inside you."

Holy crap. She heard herself gasp once more as his words ran all through her—this time mostly between her legs.

*Get out of the truck. You have to. You can't afford to risk your heart again this soon—you just can't. Sure, you can tell yourself it's just sex, but there's really no such thing as that. Sex comes with emotions—deep ones you can't push away.*

But then another voice spoke up—and she feared if she glanced down she'd see an angel on one shoulder and a devil on the other, and this new voice was definitely the devil.

*It's not like he's asking you to wear his class ring and letterman jacket, for God's sake. This is sex. Good sex. Pure and simple. Why shouldn't you let yourself have that?*

"I want that," she heard herself murmur. Then she covered her mouth with her hand. "Oh God, did I say that out loud?"

"Yep," he answered, eyes warm yet steely on her, wholly determined.

"Can I take it back?"

"No way in hell, sugar plum," he said. And when his hand closed around her arm this time, it was to pull her to him across the space that separated them.

And she went, willingly, because she couldn't not anymore. She'd tried to resist. She'd spent all day trying not to feel what she felt. And when he curled his other hand seductively around her neck and drew her in for a kiss—oh God . . . oh yes.

She closed her eyes and absorbed every nuance of every pleasure assaulting her. She felt like a woman who'd been thirsty for a week and now she was finally getting to drink—of him.

And then, just like last week in the cabin, thinking gave way to only feeling, and then . . . to complete surrender.

No falling snow was more intent upon its purpose.

Charles Dickens, A *Christmas Carol*

# *Eight*

*I*n a way, Adam felt like a jerk. Because he knew she wasn't ready for this, was fighting it hard, and yet he was kissing her anyway. And because she didn't yet know about his conversation with Jeff. He'd been about to tell her a little while ago—that's why he'd brought Jeff up on the drive home. But then she'd changed the subject and they'd reached her house, and before he knew it, he'd ended up here—pressing his tongue into her mouth, letting himself get consumed by the sensation, and digging his fingertips slightly into her ass as he pulled her closer, settling her onto his lap until she straddled him.

Yeah, he might usually be a good guy, but this went beyond that. The chemistry between them was so strong he simply couldn't push it down. Maybe he'd forgotten that, the chemistry—the way it had slowly taken them both by storm in the cabin. And now that they'd shared that, the connection had grown all the more powerful and intense. He couldn't remember a time in his life when he'd felt more physically drawn to someone, when his body was operating almost independently of his brain, when he was following instincts and urges, simply giving in, giving up, following where his lust led him.

And damn, he liked kissing her. He could still taste the remnants of hot chocolate on her lips from earlier as her arms settled warm around his neck, and as—aw God, yeah—the crux of her thighs pressed against his hard-on. Before long he could hear them both emitting rough, jagged breaths between kisses.

"I have to have you," he murmured unplanned as he reached for the button on her blue jeans.

She said nothing, but didn't protest when he lifted her off of him, over into the other seat, and proceeded to tug down her jeans, the panties with them. In fact, she shrugged free of her parka at the same time, leaving her clad in only a loose sweater. He paused just long enough to crank the heat higher so she wouldn't be cold, and then he let his gaze roam her, naked from the waist down—she'd kicked off her shoes, too.

"My God, you're beautiful," he whispered deeply, and it struck him that maybe she was even more beautiful to him for the same reasons he'd originally agreed with her that this was a bad idea. Because she was Sue Ann. Because he'd known her forever. To be this way with someone he'd known so long ratcheted up the intimacy level, big time. And somehow pushed him to bend over her, lowering a kiss near her hip.

She sucked in her breath—a light, pretty, sexy

sound—but he didn't look up at her; he just let that little noise wrap around him, fuel him, as he parted her legs and delivered another soft kiss, this one to her inner thigh. It made her moan. And turned his cock still harder. A small growl echoed from his throat as he sank his mouth to where she was wet and hot for him. And then he dragged his tongue through her moist folds, listening to her heated sighs, coming thready and passionate from above.

He got lost in kissing her and licking her that way—and though part of him felt just as impatient as he had a few minutes ago, a *better* part of him wanted nothing more than to pleasure her, to show her how good he could make her feel.

He was pretty sure he achieved that when her moans grew deeper, more insistent, when she lifted herself against his mouth—when finally she cried out her orgasm in a symphony of "Oh God! Oh God!" and the small heated sobs that followed.

When she went quiet a few seconds later, her body going still, he rose up to face her. She sat biting her lip, one hand clutching tight to the back of the seat, the other curled around the handle of the glove compartment as if holding on for dear life. At some point, Harry Connick, Jr. and Lee Ann Womack had started singing a very sexy version of "Baby, It's Cold Outside," on the radio. Sue Ann's eyes looked wild.

Meeting her gaze darkly, Adam wasted no time hauling her back into his lap—then reaching to ease the seat back into the extended cab behind them. She was already working to open his jeans when he whispered in her ear, "Ride me, Sue Ann."

Sue Ann could barely breathe. She hardly knew what

had come over her. But wait—yes she did. Adam had come over her. Stark need had come over her. She'd thought she had this situation at least somewhat under control, but clearly control had fled the scene—right about the time he kissed her hand.

And so now she was reaching into his underwear, wrapping her hand around his firm erection, and relishing his sexy command.

And Lord, she wanted to feel him, flesh to hot flesh—but apparently she still possessed at least a little of her brain, since she asked, "Do you have . . . "

"Shit, almost forgot," he said, then lifted slightly to maneuver the same well-worn wallet from his back pocket that she herself had retrieved a condom from last week. This time he did the retrieving, tossing the wallet between the seats as he ripped into the foil square, but she did the rolling on, the very act of which heightened her anticipation almost immeasurably. God, she needed him. Now. Inside her.

The sound of their labored breathing filled the truck by the time she lowered herself onto him, her body taking him inch by tantalizing inch—and they both let out low groans at her slow descent. And when he was within her completely, their eyes met in the shadowy darkness, and Sue Ann knew a brand new closeness with him, an intimacy that somehow even surpassed last week. His hands curved warm and solid over her bare hips as she kissed him and then began to move, her desire guiding her instinctively.

Oh God, he felt good inside her, and just like the previous times they'd joined together like this, she let go of all the uncertainties involved and basked in the pleasure he pumped up into her. It echoed through her veins, out to her very fingers and toes—she felt each thrust everywhere.

And she knew she wouldn't climax again, because she just had—but she didn't care because this was about a different sort of pleasure, about something raw and hard and animalistic that made her feel . . . free. In this moment, there were no worries, no troubles—there was only Adam and passion and the warmth of this truck all enveloping her, making it so that nothing else in the world mattered.

She met his thrusts, ground her body against his, and delighted in his strong hands rising to her breasts to caress and massage. And she lost herself in the sensations, in the motions, in his intoxicating kisses—to her mouth, then her throat . . . until—oh God, she was wrong. She *was* going to come again. "Ohhh . . . " she moaned at the realization. And it was going to be intense.

Then her body hit that peak, that perfect point of no return where the pleasure came raining down over her, rushing all through her, hot and jagged and overwhelming, making her cry out over and over—until finally the rough pulsations faded, leaving her weak and spent as she collapsed against him, arms looped tight around his neck.

His arms closed around her waist and he continued kissing her shoulder, and then the delicate flesh just below her ear, whispering again that she was beautiful, a sentiment that kind of turned her inside out, making her flash back to that day in the department store when he'd helped her feel attractive for the first time in a long while.

But—oh God—that's when he resumed driving up

into her again, hard and deep, stealing her thoughts, making her moan.

She pulled back, met his hot gaze, liked being in his strong arms.

And even when he murmured, "I want to be on top of you," she liked that, too, for reasons she couldn't understand but didn't stop to examine.

The next thing she knew, Adam was lifting, rolling them both, him still snugly inside her, until she lay back in the newly reclined passenger seat, his body hovering above hers. And then he was thrusting again—even harder now, *hard, hard, hard*—and leaving her flushed from head to toe from the power behind every stroke, the way her body absorbed it, the pulsating sensations assaulting her again and again.

She didn't know how long they moved together that way, only that she felt profoundly well-pleasured by the time he said, "God—God, now," plunging into her with still more force as he reached that hot pinnacle himself, releasing a low groan as it overcame him.

Ten minutes later, Sue Ann was dressed, Adam's pants were zipped, and she sat on his lap, one arm around his neck, thinking: What now?

Then he kissed her.

Okay, kissing was now. And as usual, his kiss moved all through her like some warm, slow-flowing liquid, saturating her from head to toe. But once the kiss was over she had to get serious here, had to come back to herself. She had to tell him the truth that still permeated her, no matter how close she felt to him or how good the sex had been.

"Adam," she said, "what we just did . . . it can't happen again."

She waited for him to agree, as he had last week—so even despite what he'd said earlier about being unable to stop thinking about her, it took her aback when he hesitated, meeting her gaze with his, still all warm and blue in the glow of the dashboard lights. "Why not?"

Hmm. This was unexpected. "Because we agreed."

"But . . . why did we agree?" he asked. "I mean, I thought it made sense at the time, but now I'm not so sure."

Sue Ann took a deep breath and decided this would be easier if she were sitting by herself in the passenger seat instead of on top of him in the driver's seat. But even as warm and sturdy as he felt, she had to stick to her guns. It was the only thing that made sense to her. "It's . . . really soon after my divorce."

"I know," he said as if that were no reason at all.

"And I have to think of Sophie, too. I can't be bringing a new man into her life when it may not last."

"I'm not a new man in her life. I'm her godfather. I'll always be there."

But she ignored that, going on. "And . . . I have to protect myself, protect my heart. I'm . . . emotionally vulnerable right now, you know?"

He simply gave his head a pointed tilt. "I would never hurt you, Sue Ann."

She bit her lip, wanting to believe him. Yet it was impossible not to be wary. He'd probably thought he would never hurt Sheila, either. And yet, the sad truth was, as she'd learned the hard way recently, even the best of men could change, could make mistakes, could do things you'd never imagine.

"How can you know?" she ventured. "Never is a long time. And . . . it's awfully soon for a relationship. For me. And besides, I have so much to deal with right now.

I was busy enough before, but Jeff's alimony petition has opened up more than one big can of worms for me, you know?"

She was surprised, though, when that actually quieted Adam—and maybe, despite all her good reasons, there was a part of her that wanted him to keep arguing, wanted him to somehow begin convincing her that . . . well, maybe she should rethink this. Maybe she shouldn't let her worries stand in the way. Yeah, she had trust issues now, so it seemed smart to stay on guard. But what if Jenny was right about this? And what if she was wrong? What if that niggling feeling inside her, that hint of disappointment that he wasn't continuing to try to talk her into this was God or fate telling her she was supposed to stop fighting her desires and give him a chance? What if . . . what if she was somehow passing up the best thing that could possibly happen to her?

She bit her lip, peering into Adam's eyes, thinking through all this, and beginning to let it sway her, just a little. What had seemed clear and absolute just a minute ago now suddenly started turning more cloudy and uncertain.

*Maybe I shouldn't tell him no. Maybe I should tell him maybe.*

*Or hell, maybe I should just follow what my heart really wants right in this moment and tell him yes, that I want something with him, that I want more of this.*

And that's when Adam finally said, "Um, speaking of Jeff . . . Sue Ann, I couldn't tell you this earlier when Sophie was with us, but there's something you should know."

She blinked. Hmm. She hadn't seen that coming. "Oh? What should I know?"

"That Jeff asked me to testify at the alimony hearing."

The cold became intense.

Charles Dickens, A *Christmas Carol*

# *Nine*

"Testify?" she asked, stunned.

"As a character witness. On his behalf."

"Oh."

Lord. The news instantly turned her spine rigid even as she sat within his loose embrace. Despite that it wasn't his fault, it put her on the defensive, made her feel for a split second like Adam was the enemy. Or at least in the enemy camp.

And—dear God, she'd just had sex with him in a truck. After sex with him in a cabin. And that had been dramatic enough for her already, but . . . what if this came out? At the hearing? What if Jeff did decide he wanted full custody of Sophie? What kind of mother would she look like? She couldn't imagine what she'd ever done to Jeff that would make him want to hurt her that badly, but as she had to keep reminding herself, she'd never imagined he was capable of any of this.

Although, in a way, she supposed Adam's news shouldn't surprise her. It had gotten far too easy at moments to forget he was Jeff's best friend. She'd been, at the very least, careless—and at worst . . . reckless.

"I didn't say I would," Adam went on. "I told him I needed to think about it. And I don't really like him putting me in the middle of this. But . . . "

She took a deep breath, let it back out. "But?"

"But he's been my best friend for most of my life."

"Of course," she said, nodding, biting her lip, trying very hard to act unaffected but pretty sure she wasn't pulling it off. "So you're going to do it. I understand. It only makes sense."

"I didn't say that," he replied quickly. "I really do need to think it over before I give him an answer."

Still, she could barely breathe. Because it suddenly felt as if Adam held her fate in his hands. "Does he know? About . . . this?" She motioned uncertainly back and forth between them.

"No," he said. "Of course not. No reason to bring that up—that's between you and me."

"Okay, good." A sigh of relief echoed toward the truck's ceiling even as she continued trying to act as cool as possible about the whole thing. "Because, um . . . "

He held up his hands. "No need to go on. I get it, completely."

But did he really? He probably thought she was only embarrassed, or just generally wanted to keep her sex life private from her ex. She doubted he had any idea of the far-reaching ramifications flitting through her head right now, visions of ugly court scenes and custody battles and devastating loss. So much for her warm, peaceful Christmas feeling from earlier. "The thing is,

Adam, if Jeff found out about this, his lawyer could use it to paint me in a bad light. And I'm sort of jumping to the worst case scenario here, but . . . "

"No worries, Sue Ann. Seriously. I get that part, too."

"Okay," she whispered. Trying to trust in that. *Adam's a good guy. He is.*

But at the same time . . . *it would still be foolish to forget that he isn't quite as good a guy as you always thought. He once cheated on Sheila—even if not in the traditional sense, even if he'd felt backed into a corner. And despite the fact that he and Jeff aren't tight right now, they go back a long way.* And that was bound to hit Adam at some point, too—that his loyalties lay with Jeff more than with her, hot sex notwithstanding. And either way, if he was put up on a stand and asked questions at a hearing, he would have to tell the truth, whether or not that truth hurt her.

So she was right. Never was a long time to promise you wouldn't hurt someone—and right now, she just wasn't sure it was a promise Adam could really make. And as for her waffling about this a minute ago, her temptation to give in to girlish emotions—well, that was gone now. Because it had to be.

"So do I dare ask where this leaves us?" he ventured. "Though I probably picked the worst possible moment to tell you what I just told you, didn't I?"

The truth was, Sue Ann just barely heard him. She was too mired in her own thoughts now. At some point, her focus had even shifted away from Adam's face— now she stared blankly out the window into the snow and the glowing lights he'd hung across her front porch today, vaguely recalling how pleasant life had started to seem there for a few hours.

But now reality forced her to meet his gaze again.

And—oh Lord, he was handsome. And his body still felt so warm, even if she didn't exactly remain cuddled up against him the way she'd been before.

Still, she had to stay strong here—she had to do the safe thing for her and Sophie. This was no time to take risks. "I'm sorry, Adam," she said. Her voice caught slightly, yet she kept going, trying her damnedest to sound sure and resolute about this. "But it's like I told you. There's too much else that requires my complete attention right now. And I'm just in a really delicate place, emotionally. I'm sure you understand."

"I do," he said somberly, looking sincerely disappointed. "I wish you felt differently, but I do. And for the record, whatever I decide about the hearing, it has nothing to do with how I feel about you. It'll only be to say that Jeff's a decent guy. It'll only be because I know he'd do the same for me—you know?"

She nodded and said, "I get it." And she did. Even if Jenny suddenly went off the deep end or something, she wouldn't turn her back on her. So how could she expect Adam to turn his back on Jeff? She and Adam had shared a couple of nice nights together. A couple of *hot* nights. No matter how nice or how hot, though, it didn't equal twenty-plus years of friendship.

"Thanks for not holding that against me," he said.

And she just nodded softly. She wasn't enjoying turning him down, but she still knew it was best, knew it was smart. And it was simply the only answer that made any sense, especially now. "So," she said, "just like last week, can we decide to get back to normal now? As much as possible anyway?"

"Sure," he replied, even as a small, sexy smile snuck out. "But I'd be lying, Sue Ann, if I said these nights with you weren't the best thing to happen to me in a while."

In response, she bit her lip, felt her chest rise and fall in quick succession. Then she gave in to one last bit of weakness—she lifted her hand to cup his jaw and leaned in for . . . mmm, a long, slow kiss that almost made her think she had to be nuts for turning off this thing between them.

But she wasn't nuts; it had to be. No matter how that kiss echoed all through her as she whispered, "Goodnight," climbing out of his lap and back across the truck to grab up her coat and purse from the floor.

"Goodnight, Sue Ann," he said as she opened the door.

A *whooshing* burst of cold air blew in, and out into the winter evening she went.

On Sunday afternoon, after Jeff dropped Sophie off at home, Sue Ann and her daughter headed into town—the annual Destiny Christmas tree lighting on the town square would take place at dusk. Sue Ann would have been happy to skip it this year, but this was one of those holiday events Sophie looked forward to, exactly the type of outing Sue Ann had been mentally gearing up for when she'd headed for that cabin the night after Thanksgiving. So it had been nice when Jenny offered to meet the two of them at Under the Covers for a little Christmas shopping first.

Sue Ann and Sophie pushed through the cheerful little bookshop's door, the bell overhead announcing their arrival, to find Jenny and Amy sitting in the big easy chairs by the front window, sipping eggnog from festive cups.

"Wow, everything looks so nice in here," Sue Ann said to Amy. A sparkling tree stood decorated near the chairs, and a collection of cat figurines wearing Santa hats or holly wreaths sat grouped in the wide window-sill.

"Here, have a candy cane," Amy said, holding out a bowl full of them to Sophie.

Smiling, Sophie snatched one up and said, "Is Dickens here?"

And Sue Ann drew in her breath. She'd forgotten about Dickens. Oh well, too late now.

At just that moment, a book crashed to the floor somewhere back among the shelves they couldn't see, and Amy rolled her eyes. "That would be him now." And as Sophie took off to track the kitten down, Amy told Jenny and Sue Ann, "He really *is* a little trouble-maker," then set her mug aside to follow after Sophie.

"So," Jenny said, "how are things?"

Sue Ann nodded and offered up a perfunctory, "Good." Then she leaned forward slightly and lowered her voice. "I had sex with Adam again the other night."

Jenny's eyebrows shot up, and for a second Sue Ann feared her friend's cup would be the next thing to hit the hardwood. "That *is* good."

"Well, no, actually that's bad," Sue Ann corrected her.

Jenny made a face. "Why?"

"To begin with, for the reasons I already told you."

"Then why did you do it?" Jenny asked.

Hmm. "Good question," she admitted. "I guess I couldn't resist. I guess it was . . . bigger than the both of us."

"Wow," Jenny said, looking as awed as Sue Ann was

by the mere memory, which now made her face blossom with warmth.

The truth was, despite telling Adam they couldn't be together again and all the reasons why, she'd thought of him nearly nonstop since getting out of his truck. Especially with Sophie not at home to distract her. Of course, she'd been busily job searching, too—on the phone and online—but that hadn't kept him off her mind, either. And even if she wasn't excited about attending the tree lighting, in a whole different way it was almost a relief to be out and about in a social setting so that now she at least had a shot at thinking about something else. "Yeah. Wow," she finally said, her voice laced with sarcasm since she was wowing the very thing she couldn't have.

"So this is still about it being too soon and all that?" Jenny asked. "Because, I mean, if it's bigger than the both of you, shouldn't it be bigger than that reason?"

Sue Ann sighed. In a way, her best friend made a pretty good point.

But she had to consider all the stuff Jenny didn't know, as well. *He cheated on his ex-wife, and I know he's a great guy and all, but . . . does a truly great guy cheat? Ever? No matter what the circumstances?*

It still kind of killed her that she couldn't tell Jenny that part, since it might be helpful to get her feedback— but she could at least tell Jen the newer, more immediate reason. "There's more now. Jeff asked Adam to be a character witness for him." She then went on to explain that Adam had promised not to share anything having to do with her but that she couldn't be totally sure it wouldn't come out anyway. "And I don't blame Adam if he decides to do it, but face it, regardless of what does or doesn't come out, it would be pretty weird to start a relationship with a guy who's testifying for my ex-husband. Wouldn't it?"

Only instead of giving Jenny a chance to reply, she went on, adding, "Besides, when would I have time for him? I need to focus on Sophie right now, and find a full-time job, and study for my real estate license. And I have to figure out if I'm gonna sell the house or if I can afford to keep it. There's a lot going on."

So given all of her really good reasons for not diving into anything with Adam right now, it surprised her when Jenny *still* remained skeptical, saying, "A lot going on that would probably be easier if you had something good happening in your life, like Adam."

Fearing Jenny might be heard, Sue Ann waved a hand frantically downward to quiet her. "Shush!"

"And he might not even testify," Jenny went on, her voice only slightly lower. "And if he really started to care about you, like if it got serious—that would be a pretty good reason for him to turn Jeff down."

Sue Ann just shot her a look. "Are you suggesting I should bribe him with my affections?"

"Of course not," Jenny said, rolling her eyes. "I was just mentioning a possible perk, that's all. Calm down."

"Easy for you to say," Sue Ann groused. She'd had a hard enough time walking away from Adam without having her best friend tell her all the many reasons she shouldn't have. "In fact, let's talk about you. What's new in your life?"

"I want to have a baby," Jenny said without missing a beat.

And Sue Ann nearly fell out of her chair. Because she knew Jenny had casually tried to conceive during her previous marriage, around the same time she'd had

Sophie, but when it didn't happen, she hadn't seemed upset. And she hadn't brought the subject of babies up since then—except to say that Mick didn't want kids and that was okay with her.

"Um, does Mick know about this?"

Jenny gritted her teeth, hissing in her breath. "Not exactly. Not yet."

"Uh-oh."

Jenny nodded knowingly. "Yeah, the thing about him never wanting kids is gonna be a problem. I guess I'm just hoping . . . I might somehow be able to change his mind."

Yet now it was Sue Ann making a face. "Oh Jen, are you serious? Mick has never struck me as much of a mind changer—especially on something as big as that."

"I won him over on Destiny, didn't I? Once he hated Destiny, but now he likes it just fine."

Oh dear—sometimes Jenny could delude herself and needed Sue Ann to spell things out. "Um, those are two very different things, my friend. If he suddenly wakes up one day hating Destiny again, the two of you can move. But if he wakes up not wanting to have a kid—well, you can't move away from your kid, or send it back. You kinda have to be sure about it."

Across from her, Jenny let out a sigh, looking appropriately chastised. "I know. But . . . I'm just having maternal urges. Strong ones."

"It's because it's Christmas," Sue Ann assured her. "It seems fun to have a kid at Christmas. It *is* fun to have a kid at Christmas. Well, except for when she wants things you can't possibly produce on Christmas morning, like reindeer. But my point is, maybe this will pass."

Just then, Sophie and Amy appeared, exiting from

between two tall aisles of wooden bookcases, Sophie carrying Dickens in her arms. The gray kitten purred contentedly, and Sophie grinned up at Sue Ann to say, "He likes me."

And despite herself, Sue Ann couldn't hold in a smile at the sweet sight. "Well, of course he likes you. How could he *not* like you?"

"Here's the garland I told you about, Soph," Amy said, pointing to a rope of twisted gold tinsel attached to the checkout counter. It hung down, loose, all the way to the floor.

In response, Sophie lowered the cat beside it and sat down on the hardwood floor as well. Then she reached out to shake the metallic garland, drawing the kitten's attention until he began to bat at it, leaping from side to side and making them all laugh. "Silly kitty," Sophie said, and Sue Ann could sense how drawn her daughter felt to the kitten, in a way that broke her heart. *Why do we all want so many things we can't have?*

"Oh no," Amy said then from behind the counter, glaring at the floor as strawberry blond curls fell cutely around her face.

"What's wrong?" Jenny asked.

Amy turned an accusing eye on Dickens, then spoke through clenched teeth. "Somebody broke into his box of Meow Mix when I wasn't watching and made a big mess back here." But then she sighed, reaching down to pick up the kitty, looking him in the eye. "It's lucky you're cute, mister, or you would be in *so* much trouble."

"Mommy," Sophie said then, "can we adopt Dickens? Like Rachel adopted Shakespeare and Tessa adopted Brontë?"

Oh boy. She should have seen this coming—yet her mind had been too occupied with other things. Her friends had just *had* to adopt Amy's earlier strays, hadn't they? She hesitated a beat too long, then formed an answer. "Oh, honey—I'm sorry, but no, we really can't."

Sophie's face transformed into a large pout, her forehead wrinkling in distress. "Why not? All my friends have pets. Chloe at school has a cat named Whiskers. And Tiffany got a turtle for her birthday. And Jacob and Joey have Pepper."

Sue Ann released a heavy breath. "Sophie, a pet is a big responsibility." *One I just don't think I can deal with right now.* "And a big expense." *Another thing I don't need at the moment.* "And soon, I'll be working full-time, and I think a cat might get lonely being at home by himself all day." *And this particular cat would probably vandalize the place.* "Maybe        in another year or two, honey, we can think about getting a cat. But not now."

"But Dickens will be gone by then. Some other kid will get to adopt him."

Sue Ann just sighed. She was tired. From everything. And there was a part of her that was almost tempted to say okay, that Sophie could have the cat, just because it would end the tension—and God knew the two of them were cute together—but then Jenny jumped in. "Your mom's right, Sophie. Trouble gets really lonely when Mick and I aren't there. That's why he was so excited to see you last weekend—he spends a lot of long days by himself with no one to play with. You don't want Dickens to be lonely, do you?"

"No," Sophie said in a small, quiet voice.

Amy reached down to touch her shoulder. "And you can come visit him here as often as you want." Then she glanced outside and—much to Sue Ann's appreciation—changed the subject. "Look—it's getting dark. I bet they're getting ready to light the tree—we should probably all bundle up and head outside."

"Good idea," Sue Ann replied, reaching for the scarf and hat Sophie had tossed aside when they walked in. "Come here, you," she said playfully to her daughter. "You can't escape the scarf monster." Then she circled the long scarf her mom had crocheted for Sophie around her daughter's neck several times, almost covering her face with it, and making her laugh. Ah, that was music to Sue Ann's ears.

And then Sophie launched in to telling everyone where Sue Ann's scarf still happened to be—around the snow cat's neck—and how she and Adam had built it the other day, just before he helped them trim the tree. Sue Ann and Jenny exchanged looks, but fortunately Amy didn't notice, clearly thinking of Adam only as Sue Ann's good friend and Sophie's godfather.

By the time the four of them stepped outside and crossed the street to the town square, a crowd had gathered. Just like every year, a fifteen-foot cypress had been erected in the middle of the park-like area, specially ordered by Adam. Snow still carpeted the ground and people wore winter boots and coats along with hats and mittens. A few carried shopping bags from the stores situated around the square.

When Sue Ann spotted none other than Jeff and Veronica on the far side of the crowd, holding hands and looking ridiculously happy, she cringed on the inside, a little, the same way she always did. But it wasn't as bad as usual—even if knowing they were married now seemed like that should have made it worse—and it helped that Sophie hadn't seen them.

And Sue Ann had hoped to keep a low profile at the event, but that plan went awry when Amy said, "Follow me, I see a good spot!" and they all ended up at the front of the gathering, near the gazebo. After which a few people said hello or lifted their hands to wave in their direction, and . . . that was it.

After a few minutes Sue Ann realized that she didn't feel nearly as weird as she'd expected. The newness of her divorce had finally worn off in people's minds. Even with Jeff standing there in the very same crowd. And maybe the divorce was actually starting to wear off—a little—in her own mind as well; she'd been by herself now for nearly six months, after all.

*And I've had sex now. Twice. I have a life again. Sort of, anyway.* And maybe that was part of what took the edge off seeing Jeff tonight.

Still, that sex was fraught with so many mixed emotions that she could barely keep up with the constant push/pull of it in her own mind. In some ways, she still wished she could let herself trust in Adam and consider letting this thing with him go somewhere. If only she could get rid of the knot that formed in her stomach every time she remembered what he'd told her the other night. Make a mistake here and it could be critical, in so many ways. To trust her heart over her head would be no less than crazy.

And—think of the devil—that's when she heard his voice. He was snapping at Chuck Whaley, who stood on a tall easel ladder next to the tree. "No, Chuck, not that string of lights—the other one, by your hand!"

She found him in the dusk and smiled inwardly, amused on some level to hear him still acting so Scroogy and un-Adam-like. Maybe since she'd been *feeling* Scroogy since June, yet thought she'd done a far better job hiding it than he did.

"Dude," Logan Whitaker said then from the other side of the cypress, "relax. This is Destiny, not Rockefeller Center. People will wait if we're a few minutes late." Logan was a town fireman and Amy's close friend, and he always seemed to have a hand in any Destiny event.

And that's when Adam saw her, and their eyes locked across the fading, shadowy light.

And she remembered him moving in her, and touching her, and whispering all the right things. Not to mention giving her two orgasms. Again. And how it hadn't been until much later that it had even hit her that she'd had sex in her driveway where any neighbor could have seen—even if it *had* been a quiet, snowy night out. She'd been that caught up in him.

Her gut clenched. Because she knew he was remembering it, too—the rawness of it, the passion that had somehow been both hot and pure, and that he was feeling it all again and with the exact same fierceness as her in that moment. His eyes told her so. Even through the darkening air. She'd seen Adam in a lot of dimly lit spaces lately, after all—and it didn't seem to keep her from reading his thoughts.

She let out a breath. And wished like hell, just for a minute, that she didn't know the secret about his divorce, and that she didn't know he might testify for Jeff. Why did things have to be so complicated?

"Everybody ready to see this tree light up?" Logan called out then.

People in the crowd—mostly kids—answered or let out small cheers in the cold.

"Then let there be light!" he said, and the tall, majestic tree burst vividly to life with bulbs of crimson and green, blue and hot pink, amber and violet, lighting the night so brightly that she could no longer see Adam at all.

"Was it a dream or not?"

Charles Dickens, A Christmas Carol

# Ten

Adam was sweating. Probably from the itchy blanket tied onto his head with a thin piece of rope from his dad's garage. Or the big, navy blue bath robe cinched onto him backward. This was stupid. How had he ended up stuck as Joseph in the Christmas pageant?

"It's always an eighth grade boy," Mrs. Wheeler had told him when he'd tried to shove the part off on a kid in the seventh grade who had longish hair and looked a lot more like Joseph to him—if you went by paintings he'd seen anyway. "And you'll be perfect in the role."

His mom had liked the idea, too, and pressed him to do it, and next thing you know, he was sitting here on a stage behind a closed curtain, burning up in his father's robe, listening to the Destiny Middle School chorus sing "Away in a Manger" and waiting for his big moment.

*Well,* their *big moment. Sue Ann Kinman sat next to him. Her blanket and backward robe were both lighter shades of blue, typical Mary-wear, and a bald baby doll lay in a little wooden cradle in front of them. He'd known Sue Ann since his family had moved here when he was in the third grade. Mostly, he'd always thought she was a pushy, show-offy girl who never kept her opinion to herself. But lately, she'd gotten kind of . . . pretty. Especially in her cheerleading uniform. She did the splits better than any girl on the squad. He wasn't supposed to be noticing junk like that; he was supposed to have his head in the game, being the quarterback, after all. But sometimes he noticed.*

*"Are you nervous?" she whispered now.*

*"No." Then he revised his answer. "A little, I guess. Why?"*

*She shrugged her shoulders, all confidence. "You just look sorta nervous, that's all. Joseph shouldn't be nervous."*

*Nervous, huh? Her attitude irritated him. But at the same time, when she'd looked at him, that blond hair curving around her face under the blue blanket, her cheeks smooth and silky, her lips forming the slightest of pouts, he kind of felt it in his pants. That had been happening a lot lately—not just with Sue Ann, but all the time.*

*That's when impulse struck. He'd show her nervous.*

*And without an ounce of hesitation, he leaned over and kissed her. He didn't know how to kiss—he'd never kissed anyone before—but he'd had the sudden urge to do it.*

*She stiffened at first, clearly shocked. But then she seemed to relax, and he just held his mouth there, puck-*

*ered, on hers, for long enough to make sure they both felt it. And wow—he felt it all right, racing through his veins like electric.*

*What he felt afterward, though, was a little light-headed. And she looked a little light-headed.*

*"Why'd you do that?" she asked. She was trying to act mad, but he knew she'd liked it. Her voice was all breathy, her face flushed.*

*"I'm supposed to be your husband, right? Just getting into my role. Getting those nerves out," he told her.*

*She simply looked at him, eyes big and round and brown on his, lips now in the shape of a delicate O. That's when he grew aware of Jenny Tolliver's voice coming through a microphone just beyond the closed curtain: "For unto you this day, in the city of David, is born a savior . . ."*

*And the curtain opened.*

*And he really wasn't nervous anymore.*

*He was too busy still feeling his first kiss.*

Adam jerked awake in bed. A glance at the digital clock on the nightstand told him it was morning and he'd overslept. He was sweating like crazy. And his head itched. He reached up to make sure there wasn't a scratchy blanket tied there.

Okay, just hair. *Get hold of yourself. It was a dream.*

A good dream.

But more like a memory.

He'd never had that kind of dream, though, a dream that perfectly mirrored something that had happened in the past—let alone taken him back to the exact feelings he'd experienced when it had really taken place. Events were easy to remember. But maybe the feelings that

came with them . . . faded over time; maybe they felt
. . . less significant than when they happened.

Truly, until this moment, he'd not remembered—or
at least he hadn't thought about it in many years—that
his first kiss had actually been with Sue Ann on that
hot stage in those ridiculous blankets and robes.

Damn—how had he forgotten something like that?

Maybe because they'd never thought of each other
romantically since then. Hell, they'd never even talked
about it. They'd sat quietly through their manger scene,
all eyes upon them—and then it had been over, the
Christmas pageant and the kiss. Could be that he'd pondered it more right after—but soon enough, he'd gotten
bolder with other girls, too, and Sue Ann had ended up
dating Jeff after they all moved on to Destiny High.
He'd gotten to know her as his best friend's girl, and to
like her as a person, and for his entire adult life—until
Thanksgiving weekend—that's how he'd seen her: as
his friend Sue Ann.

But that dream just now had reminded him that—
wow, it had actually been a pretty great moment. He'd
felt that kiss all the way to his toes, for God's sake. And
definitely in his groin.

And now he couldn't help but wonder . . .

Had it been even more important than he realized?
After all, why would he dream about it now?

But okay, maybe in a way that made sense—now that
he'd been intimate with her, maybe his body, his brain,
was recalling that it wasn't the first time they'd kissed.

Still . . . could something bigger be happening? Was
it a sign, this reminder that his very first kiss had been
with Sue Ann?

Then he shook his head against the pillow and let out

a low, tired groan. Since when was he the kind of guy who believed in things like signs?

He wasn't. *Must be the stress getting to you.* The stress of missing his kids. Of having told Sue Ann his biggest secret, how his marriage had ended. And now, too, having this question hanging over his head about testifying on Jeff's behalf.

He still hadn't decided if he felt obligated to do what Jeff had asked of him. While the guy was still technically his best friend, he'd changed lately, and Adam had barely spoken to him since he'd left Sue Ann. But on the other hand, they'd grown up together, and even if Jeff was behaving selfishly right now, he had to believe the good guy he'd always known was still inside him somewhere. You didn't just throw a lifetime of friendship away over six months of decisions you didn't necessarily agree with.

But that aside, he couldn't exactly blame Sue Ann for not wanting to be with him. Whether or not he condoned Jeff's behavior, the two of them were friends, the long-lasting kind. And after what she knew about his divorce now . . . well, she was probably thinking that birds of a feather sure as hell seemed to flock together. All of which probably accounted, at least in part, for why he'd been in an even worse mood since their second hot encounter.

She'd stayed on his mind these last couple of days—hell, these last couple of weeks. And when he'd seen her the other night at the tree lighting ceremony, he'd felt that intense need gathering inside him again, that fast.

The phone rang then, and he thought it might be the twins—it was about time for their usual morning call.

Even though Jacob and Joey lived with him for only half of each week, his house had felt depressingly quiet without them around. So it disappointed him to see on the caller ID that it wasn't them—and perplexed him as well to see it was Caroline Meeks, a local woman involved in a lot of Destiny community groups and activities. He knew Sue Ann and her friends sometimes socialized with Caroline, even though she was a bit older than their crowd.

He picked up the receiver. "Hello?"

"Adam, it's Caroline Meeks. Sorry to call so early, but . . ."

"No problem, Caroline. What can I do for you?"

"Well, I'm glad you asked. Because I need a favor."

Uh-oh. This sounded like trouble already. His reply came a little more hesitant this time. "Um, what kind of favor?"

"Are you free Friday night?"

What on earth was this about? "Uh, can I ask why?"

"Well, it's Santa Comes to Destiny Night—you know, in the basement at the church? We host it every year for all the kids in town—it's their chance to see Santa right here at home. And usually Grampy Hoskins is our Santa, but he forgot and planned a visit to his sister upstate and couldn't reschedule. So your mother suggested that you might be kind enough to take over for him."

Huh. *Thanks, Mom.* First Joseph, now this. "Ya know, Caroline," he said, "I'm not sure I'd make the best Santa. I'm not fat. Or old. And . . . I don't look good in fur. I mean, out of all the men in Destiny, surely there's somebody else who would do a better job."

On the other end of the line, Caroline went silent,

then sighed. And Adam's stomach churned. He could almost hear it coming. And then there it was. "The truth is, Adam, I've scoured this town from top to bottom and no one will do it. You're my last hope. You wouldn't want to let down the kids, would you?"

"Mommy, look!" Sophie said on a gasp as they stepped inside. The basement of the Destiny Church of Christ had been transformed into a winter wonderland. Of course, here, the snow was fluffy cotton quilt batting with a little silver glitter sprinkled here and there—and big snowflakes constructed from silver cardboard hung on strings from the ceiling. One of Sue Ann's favorite Harry Connick, Jr. songs, "Must Have Been Ol' Santa Claus," boomed from a CD player, adding to the upbeat holiday mood in the room.

Brightly decorated cookies and cupcakes filled two tables, and her friend Rachel stood behind another with her grandma, Edna Farris, handing out slices of Edna's famous apple pie. Kids and adults alike mulled about, and Sue Ann was surprised to see that even Jenny and Mick were here. She lifted a hand to Rachel in a wave, then made her way over to Jenny. "Come to sit on Santa's lap?" she asked Jen.

"Wow," Jenny said, wide-eyed.

"Wow what?"

Jenny tilted her head. "You sound . . . almost like your old self."

Hmm. Now that Jenny mentioned it, maybe she did sound more like the fun-loving, slightly sarcastic woman she used to see in the mirror. Maybe there for a minute she'd actually gotten caught up in the holiday cheer and forgotten her troubles. "Well, don't get too used to it—I'm sure it'll pass." Though even that, she realized, had come out with a familiar old jocularity she hadn't felt in a while.

That's when Mick landed a hand on Jenny's shoulder to say, "Uh, my wife won't be sitting on anybody's lap this Christmas but mine."

"Well, if you didn't come for Santa," Sue Ann asked, "what brings you to the festivities?"

"My dad volunteered me to hand out candy to the kids," Jenny explained. Her father, Walter Tolliver, was Destiny's chief of police and this particular town event was one he personally helped organize each year.

"And he volunteered me for some heavy lifting," Mick added.

Jenny pointed toward the group of children waiting to see Santa. "Looks like Sophie's already grabbed her place in line. And by the way," she said, lowering her voice as she leaned nearer, "*you* might want to sit on Santa's lap this year."

Sue Ann just blinked, confused, and was about to tell Jenny she wasn't *that* hard-up, when Sophie called, "Mo-ommm, come on!"

"I'll . . . catch up with ya later," she told Jen, then hurried to find Sophie in line. Reaching her, she stooped down to help her daughter get unbuttoned from her coat, but left on her hat and scarf because they'd coordinated them with her outfit and Sophie wanted them in the picture. "Santa's going to think you're the prettiest little girl ever," she said to her daughter with a smile, and the grin she got in return made her feel like everything was going to be all right.

"You look pretty today, too," Sophie said. And even just coming from her own child, it made her glad she'd put a bit of effort into her appearance when getting ready for work this morning, dressing up a simple wool skirt with her chocolate brown boots and a dark green sweater with a ruffle detail. She'd never completely let herself go during the past six months, but she also hadn't taken the kind of care with herself that she used to. And today, for the first time in a while, she had.

As they moved up in line, Rachel came over to chat, complimenting both Sue Ann's and Sophie's fashion choices, and announcing that she and Mike had finally set a wedding date for next summer. Because both had large families who mostly lived out of town, it had been a challenge to find a weekend that worked for everyone. "And more good news," Rachel went on. "We're out of pie. Which means I can go home and help Mike put up our tree. His family is coming for the holidays, so I want to make everything as nice as possible."

"Who'd have thunk it?" Sue Ann quipped. "Big city girl Rachel Farris creating a hometown Christmas for her fiancé's family." Rachel had left Destiny right after high school, but after a visit home the autumn before last, hunky cop Mike Romo had coaxed her into staying.

"Well, times they really are a'changin'," Rachel acknowledged. "I never dreamed I'd find my heart's desire here of all places."

As Rachel departed, though, a little of Sue Ann's good mood was dashed—something to do with Rachel's comment about changing times. For so many of Sue Ann's friends, things had changed for the better over the last few of years—she was the only one whose life had gotten markedly worse.

"Ho-ho-ho, who's next? Step on up here, little boy, and climb onto Santa's knee."

Sue Ann looked up, squinting, not only because the last child in front of them had just been beckoned by Santa Claus, but because Santa's voice sounded weirdly familiar—weirdly . . . like Adam's. Deeper, of course, but . . . and that's when she made eye contact with him. She'd know those blue eyes anywhere, and now they sparkled on her from above a curly white beard, somehow even turning her on a little, despite the Santa suit. She was so stunned that a laugh escaped her without warning, even as their gazes remained locked.

"What are you laughing at, Mommy?"

The words drew her glance down to Sophie, whose hand she held, before she glanced back at Adam again. "Nothing, honey," she assured her, squelching her reaction, but she had to bite her lip to hold in a smile. First a reindeer, now this. How on earth had Adam gotten roped into playing Santa?

Yet then her smile faded a little, because—oh brother—he turned her on even in a freaking Santa suit? Even wearing a ridiculous red velvet jacket with a pillow under it and big white beard? Her stomach even fluttered then.

Oh no, this was awful. *I'm attracted to Santa Claus!* And a bad Santa at that! Since even with padding, the red suit was way too big for him, and his beard was the silly, curling kind. And his eyes were . . . oh, his eyes were the same eyes she'd peered into while he'd moved in her. And now the juncture of her thighs ached for him again. Yep, even as Santa.

She swallowed. Then let out a sigh. It had been bad enough that she'd still experienced that nagging yearning for him at the Christmas tree lighting last Sunday, but now . . . this seemed much worse.

Of course, it would help if she'd quit running into him everywhere. But in a small town like Destiny, that was difficult.

"A-h-hall right, Trevor," Santa Adam was saying, keeping a bit of that deep ho-ho-ho echo in his voice, "you keep doing your chores and eating your broccoli and I'll do my best on the iPod. Now down ya go."

As little Trevor went on his way, Adam shifted his gaze to Sophie, saying, "Wh-h-hell, who's this pretty little girl? Come on up, honey, and tell Santa what you'd like for Christmas."

Adam was having about as much fun playing Santa Claus as he had pretending to be a reindeer, which wasn't much, but for the sake of the kids he kept it well hidden. And he hadn't thought about the fact that Sue Ann would probably bring Sophie, but just seeing Sue Ann—even in this stupid costume—was enough to lift his mood. Even if he felt her laughing at him. He guessed it really was pretty damn funny in a way.

After he scooped Sophie onto his lap, they posed so Sue Ann could take a few pictures. Then he spoke more quietly to Sophie—already he'd figured out that most kids were more comfortable if it felt like a private conversation rather than one their parents could hear. "Have you been a good girl for your mom this year, Sophie?" he asked.

She nodded. "Most of the time."

"Good, good—that's what Santa likes to hear. Now what would you like Santa to bring you for Christmas?"

"There are only two things I want," she said, sounding very clear and decisive on the subject.

"Well, what are they?"

"First, I want a reindeer."

Adam pondered this. "Like . . . a toy reindeer? My elves make lots of nice toy reindeers."

But Sophie appeared unmoved and Adam grew worried, especially seeing the serious look on her face when she said, "No, a real reindeer. Like the ones that pull your sleigh. I saw Prancer and Dancer at the Cincinnati Zoo last year, and I got to pet them and everything. So that's what I want—my own reindeer. It can live in our backyard and I promise I'll take good care of it."

Aw, damn. She sounded so earnest, and so needful. How was he going to tell her he couldn't bring her a reindeer? Well, maybe it would be easier if her second request was something more doable, something he was sure Sue Ann—or even he—could make sure she got. "What's the other thing you want?" he asked.

And she told him softly, "I want my daddy to come home and live with us again."

Oh shit. Adam's heart broke then, right there on the spot.

And Sophie was looking up at him with such longing, such innocent desperation, that he had no idea what to do or say. So he spent a second wanting to kill Caroline Meeks for roping him into this—and then he did the best he could. "Sophie, honey," he said, "as much as I wish I could give you the things you want . . . Santa brings presents, toys, things to play with. Isn't there anything like that you'd enjoy getting?"

But Sophie just shook her little blond head, peering up at him as if he were . . . magical or something. And that's when he remembered—Santa was supposed to *be* magical. Caroline had made this sound so easy, but it wasn't, not at all. He held all these kids' hopes and dreams in his hands tonight—and right at this moment, he held Sophie's, and that was even harder because he cared about her so much. Hell, look at the mess he was in here.

And he didn't want to crush Sophie, but he also thought it unwise to give her false hope. "Sophie, about your dad . . . Santa can do a lot of special things, but something like that . . . well, I'm afraid I can't control people, or the feelings in their hearts." *In fact, if I could control the feelings in someone's heart, your mom would be spending a whole lot more time with me.* "Do you understand?"

She lowered her eyes sadly, but nodded, acceptant. And Adam felt more like a Scrooge than he had at any other time this whole holiday season. He couldn't fix her family, and he didn't know how to make her understand—since, hell, humans were complex, love was complicated, and he couldn't even claim to understand it himself.

Finally, she raised her sweet little face back up to meet his gaze and said, "What about the reindeer? Can you bring me a reindeer? I want one sooooo bad."

Aw Christ. What now? Again, this would be bad enough if it were some random kid he didn't know, but Sophie was . . . Sophie. His goddaughter, for heaven's sake. And he knew—too intimately, from his own kids—what she was going through right now. "The reindeer . . . " he began uncertainly, "will be tough."

She just kept staring at him, though, even when he'd finished, hope still shining in her eyes and almost silently begging him to go on. And that's when he heard himself saying, "But . . . if anybody can get you a reindeer, it's me, right? So . . . I'll see what I can do."

Uh-oh. He was pretty sure he'd just promised Sophie a reindeer.

But when a big smile unfurled on her face—just before she gave him a huge hug—it made it all worthwhile. Especially when he met Sue Ann's gaze over Sophie's shoulder as he warmly hugged her back.

"All right then, honey, down you go. You have a merry Christmas, okay?"

"Thanks, Santa!" she said, still beaming.

"Next," he said, glancing to a little boy wearing gigantic glasses.

And then it hit him. *What the hell did I just do? And how am I gonna fix it?* If he wasn't already on Sue Ann's "naughty list," he sure as hell would be when Sophie told her Santa was bringing her a reindeer.

Half an hour later, everyone at the Santa party was eating, drinking, and making merry. Except for Adam, who had one last child on his lap. And Sue Ann, who was absolutely livid and planning on killing him as soon as he was done. "Um, why?" Jenny asked when Sue Ann shared this with her.

She spoke through tightly clenched teeth. "He told Sophie he could get her a reindeer."

Jenny flinched, clearly as taken aback as Sue Ann had been. "Oh. Well, yeah, you should definitely kill him."

Now Sophie was dancing around with some other little kids to the Hall and Oates version of "Jingle Bell Rock," giggling and having fun, so maybe Sue Ann should be glad in a way—but what the hell was she supposed to do on Christmas morning when there wasn't a reindeer under the tree? As if a reindeer could even *fit* under a tree, for God's sake.

Just then, a glance to her right across the fake wintry scene revealed that Adam had sent the last child on her way and was standing up from the old leather wing chair they'd given him to sit in. The fact that he still looked ridiculous did nothing to calm her temper as she marched across the floor—dodging a crushed cookie and a stray red ribbon that must have fallen from some little girl's hair.

He didn't seem to see her until she was right in front of him, holding up her hand to stop him from moving forward, then even smacking his chest with her palm for good measure. "Hold it, Santa," she snapped. "I need to have a word with you."

"Uh-oh," he said. Then took her by the arm. "If you're gonna yell at me, why don't we take it someplace more private."

"Private schmivate," she said in a loud whisper, but she did allow him to lead her away from the center of the big open area and down a short hallway. After all, she didn't need to make a spectacle of herself—she was just getting *over* being Destiny's latest spectacle. And she intended to completely ignore how good Santa's hand felt on her arm.

"Okay," he said when they were secluded in the narrow hall, "go ahead, let me have it. I told Sophie that Santa would try to get her a reindeer. I'm scum. I should be beaten with candy canes or something. I know. And I'm sorry."

Hmm. Well, all that kind of took the wind out of her angry sails. So she just pursed her lips, let out a sigh, and feared she sounded more whiny than mean when she asked, "What were you thinking, Adam?"

And then Adam told her what else Sophie had asked for—for Jeff to come home—and her heart dropped to her stomach. "Oh. Wow."

"So . . . I had to say *something*. And next thing I know,

I'm telling her I can maybe come up with a reindeer. I didn't want to—it just came out, ya know? And I knew I'd screwed up the second it left my mouth. I mean, believe me, I don't want to be wearing this goofy outfit to begin with and it didn't come with a training manual."

"You do look pretty silly," she admitted, her anger all but gone now. *Except for your eyes. Your eyes are still absolutely gorgeous.* How had she gone all these years not realizing what amazing eyes he had? "And . . . I understand. About the reindeer. I'm not sure what I'm gonna do about it, but I understand."

"Maybe I can talk to her. Not as Santa," he said. "As me. Maybe I can set her up not to be too disappointed when it doesn't happen."

Sue Ann nodded appreciatively since she was tired of letting her daughter down. "That would help. A lot." And—damn it—she kind of missed Adam's touch now that it was gone. Though she still sort of felt it anyway, halfway between her wrist and elbow.

"Well, I'm the one who created the problem," he said. "I can be the one to try to fix it."

After releasing a sigh, she pointed out, "You aren't the one who really created the problem." That fell squarely on Jeff's shoulders. And then her thoughts turned back to Dickens. "She must be feeling . . . really starved for love right now or something. She asked me for a stray kitten living at Under the Covers, too—but I said no, because it's just one more responsibility to handle and my plate is already full these days. Maybe I shouldn't have been so quick to refuse, though. I probably should have gone for the kitten before the reindeer thing got so out of hand."

"Don't be too hard on yourself, Sue Ann," he said. "You're a good mom."

And that touched her—maybe more than the simple words should have. Because she tried so very hard to be a good mother. And despite his own transgressions, Adam was a pretty great parent himself. And since she hadn't felt particularly gifted at much of anything lately, she truly meant it when she said, "Thanks." She just wished she could quit feeling so tingly in his presence. Then she tugged playfully on his beard. "Bet you're ready to get out of this thing, aren't you?"

Since she, for one, was ready for him to get out of it. She still didn't particularly like being attracted to a man in a Santa suit. Even if she refused to act on her feelings for Adam, at least he was a hot, handsome guy. Lusting for Santa Claus just felt ooky to her.

"Ho-ho-ho," he said, reassuming his deeper, echoing Santa voice. "You want Santa out of his suit, huh?" Then he flashed a sexy grin the silly beard couldn't dim.

And like earlier, she was biting her lip to hide her smile even as Adam's flirtation moved all through her like something tangible, touchable. Since she didn't want to do anything to encourage him. Now if she could only hide the blush burning in her cheeks. "It's, um, not like that, Santa," she told him. But the claim came out sounding far more bashful and playful than she'd intended.

"Wh-h-hell," he said, still in Santa mode, "before Santa goes, he's got one more question for you."

"Um, what's that?" Darn it, why did her voice sound so breathy?

And when she looked back up into his eyes, there was no mistaking that they shone warm and seductive on her as he asked, "What do *you* want for Christmas, little girl?"

And yet I should have dearly liked, I own, to have touched
her lips . . .

Charles Dickens, A *Christmas Carol*


## *Eleven*

Adam could see all the heat he was feeling reflected
in her eyes, as well. And it wasn't exactly like he'd
planned to put the moves on her—he was wearing a
Santa suit, for God's sake—but it had just happened.
One minute he'd been apologizing for what he'd said
to Sophie—and the next he'd been thinking about how
much he'd like to kiss her again, soft at first, but maybe
then harder. He supposed something about Sue Ann
just brought out the animal in him these days. Even
behind a ridiculous fake beard.

And now . . . damn, he was pretty sure she wanted
to kiss him, too. She sure as hell looked like it anyway.

"I should . . . uh . . . probably go," she said then, her
voice barely audible. And yeah, the words said go, but
her eyes still said kiss.

"You haven't answered me," he reminded her. "Or . . . maybe you want to sit on Santa's lap first?" He raised his eyebrows—even though he wore big white ones glued over his own at the moment.

And like before, a smile snuck out even as she lowered her eyes and bit her lip. He felt that lip bite of hers right in his big red velvet Santa pants, directly between his legs. "That . . . sounds like a bad idea," she said.

Moving more on instinct than thought, Adam tilted his head, leaned a little closer, and tried to keep his voice Santa deep. "Why? Have you been a naughty little girl?"

He met her gaze and watched her swallow—nervously it seemed. "Lately maybe. A couple of times."

And that . . . well, that wasn't what he'd been going for at all. He'd been flirting, playing—not trying to make her feel like she'd done anything she shouldn't have. So he just tilted his head and didn't weigh his response—though he dropped the Santa voice completely. "Listen, Sue Ann—I don't think you've been naughty at all. In fact, I think you've been damn nice." In every way, he meant. As a mom, as a woman adjusting to being alone for the first time—and as a lover. Definitely as a lover.

"Well, maybe it's more a matter of dumb than naughty," she offered.

"You haven't done anything dumb, either, Little Miss Sugar Plum," he told her. He didn't like her coming down on herself for having indulged in a little pleasure—or even a lot of it. And he wasn't going to let that hesitation of hers get in the way of what he was feeling right now—because just like other recent times with her, what he was experiencing in this moment overrode everything else.

Since she'd lowered her eyes again, he used one bent finger to lift her chin. And her brown eyes looked so clear right now that he could read everything in them: the doubt, the trepidation, and the fire. But he felt the last part the most, and he wanted to kiss her almost more than he wanted to breathe. "Sue Ann," he murmured, leaning forward instinctively.

And that's when she ducked away from him, moving from the wall he'd somehow managed to back her against without having even planned it. "I should go. I'll see you later," she said, and that quick, she was walking back up the hall, the click of her boot heels on the linoleum reminding him with each passing second that she was getting farther and farther away.

Mick was ready to go. He'd moved the big Santa chair back into the storage room, carried garbage bags outside, broken down the folding tables, and hauled Caroline Meeks' boxes and bags out to her car. It was nearly ten and he was in the mood to take his wife to bed when they got home. Then again, he was *usually* in that mood. And he was damn thankful Jenny was generally in that mood, too—it was one big thing they had in common.

He'd just come back in, ready to grab her and go— when he spotted her and Sue Ann holed up in a corner on a pair of folding chairs having a heart-to-heart. This had been happening a lot since the summer and he knew to leave them alone.

Most everyone else was gone—only Caroline and a couple of other ladies remained working in the kitchen area. And Sophie knelt next to the Christmas tree, examining ornaments but otherwise looking bored.

Damn, he felt for the kid. Not just now, but for everything she and her mom were dealing with. As best he
recalled, being a kid was pretty hard at times—and a
hell of a lot harder when things went wrong.

He wasn't good with kids, but he'd at least spent
enough time around Sophie to start feeling comfortable with her. She was a lot like her mother—direct,
determined, and a little sassy at times. And since they
were both stuck waiting—hell, rather than park his ass
in a chair by himself, he figured it made more sense to
go hang out with her.

"What's up?" he asked, approaching the tree.

"Santa's bringing me a reindeer for Christmas," she
replied, peering up at him with a bright-eyed grin as
she got to her feet.

Huh. He hadn't seen that coming. Had Adam Becker
been stupid enough to promise her that? "Really?"

"Well, he said he'd try."

"Oh." Okay, that was better. But changing the
subject seemed like a good idea anyway. "Whatcha
lookin' at?"

"The baby Jesus," she said, then reached to touch a
rustic wooden ornament that he guessed was supposed
to be Jesus in a cradle. "When I grow up, I'm gonna
have lots of babies."

Crap. Another subject that just wasn't a good one for
him. "That's . . . nice, I guess." Okay, maybe it was
easier being comfortable with her when they had a cat
to play with or a tree to trim.

"How come you and Aunt Jenny don't have babies?"

Holy hell. "Well . . . um, not everybody *has* babies."

"Why not? I want lots of little kids so they can always
have lots of fun together. Don't you like kids?"

Oh God. He felt like a jerk. What now? "I like *you*," he said.

And she gave him a small smile. "I like you, too." Then she raised her hand and held his. Just held it. Like that was the natural, normal thing to do.

Mick was struck by how tiny her hand was, and how soft. It was hard to believe there'd been a time when his own had been that small. And he was sure there'd been plenty of occasions when he'd wished he had someone to hold onto, times when he'd been lonely or afraid when his parents were fighting. Sometimes his older brother, Wayne, had been there for him, trying to make him feel safe—but other times it had been only him, cowering in a corner, feeling like some scared, wounded animal.

So now, he found himself giving Sophie's little hand a small, gentle squeeze, hoping it somehow made her feel a little safer. And something inside him went warm, the sensation literally climbing up his arm and spreading outward through his body. It made him feel . . . a little frightened himself in a way—vulnerable maybe. But mostly it filled him with a powerful urge to protect her, take care of her, make sure she was all right.

It didn't make much sense—she had plenty of people in her life closer to her than him, people whose job it was to make sure she was okay. And as far as he knew, most of those people were doing their part on that, so it wasn't as if Sophie really needed him or anything.

But even so, he found himself squeezing her hand again, and then—on impulse—stooping down to face her. He wasn't sure what was driving him—just more of that unexplained urge—as he said, "You know if you ever need anything, I'm here, right?"

She tilted her blond head, looking slightly surprised, then said, "Okay."

Then he immediately felt the need to lighten what he'd just turned so serious. "I mean . . . you want a play date with Trouble, I'm your guy—I can hook you up."

And when a tiny burst of laugher erupted from her throat, he smiled at her, and everything felt normal again. "So, any cat ornaments on this tree?" he asked.

She nodded enthusiastically. "There's a white angel cat over here," she said, pointing, "with a silver halo."

"Will you show me?"

"Sure," she said, and taking his much bigger hand in hers once more, she led him to the other side of the tree, where they talked more about cats and Christmas decorations, the things that came easier to Mick with her. But it occurred to him then that maybe, now, *everything* would be different, easier, between him and Sophie. Just from this little moment they'd shared.

And when Jenny and Sue Ann finally stood and walked over to the tree a few minutes later, Mick—weirdly—was almost sorry to see Sophie go. "See ya, kiddo," he said in parting, even mussing her hair before Sue Ann slid a brightly colored winter hat onto it as they headed for the door.

"Ready?" he asked Jenny after they were gone.

"Almost," she said.

So he cast a mildly wicked look in her direction, just to let her know what he was thinking about. Talking to Sophie hadn't made him forget what he wanted to do with his wife when they got home. "Almost? 'Cause me, I'm ready to roll. I've got plans for you."

She bit her lip, offering up a slightly-innocent-yet-sexy expression that made him go hard. "You were sweet with Sophie. I saw you holding her hand."

He just shrugged. "Only being nice. She just looked a little lonely, that's all."

"Watching you with her gave me this feeling," she began, suddenly seeming more serious than sexy, "this feeling that . . . I've been having a lot the last week or so."

And something in Mick's chest tightened, but he wasn't sure why. "Um, what feeling?"

"The feeling of . . ." She stopped then, swallowing visibly, nervously.

Which made Mick a little nervous, too. Normally, he would urge her to go on, try to put her at ease. But right now, he didn't—because he wasn't exactly sure he wanted to hear what she was thinking. Only then he heard it anyway.

"The feeling that I want to have a baby, Mick," she said. "With you. I want us to have a baby, a family."

He just looked at her, instantly frozen, as all the blood drained from his face. Shit.

This was . . . this was completely out of the blue.

Because she knew, she understood, how he felt about that. And up to now, they'd had . . . well, a pretty damn perfect marriage in his opinion. And he hadn't expected that to change—he was wild about her, she was wild about him, and they wanted the same kind of life. But what she'd just said . . . it meant that suddenly she *didn't* want the same life he did. How had this happened?

"Did . . . you hear me?" she asked, her expression cautious now.

He wished he hadn't. Because he felt a little sick. "Jenny," he finally began, "you know—you've always known—how I feel about that. And you agreed that was okay with you."

"I know I did," she said, but her eyes . . . in them he saw a yearning he'd never seen before, something sweet and desperate that clawed at his heart.

"And . . . we don't even know if we can *have* a baby," he pointed out. Jenny had never gotten pregnant during her first marriage, and she'd not felt strongly enough—at least then—to look into the reasons why.

"But maybe I can," she said. "And maybe if we just tried to . . . well, if I didn't get pregnant, then we'd know it wasn't meant to be. But if I did, it would be like . . . fate. Destiny."

Mick just looked at his wife. He loved her with all his heart. She had . . . saved him, in so many ways. She had given him a life, and a love, he'd never even hoped to have. She was the best thing that had ever happened to him.

And yet . . . she'd assured him she understood how he felt about being a parent. His own parents had been walking nightmares. He didn't have the faintest idea of how to *be* a parent, a good parent, and he'd never experienced the desire to have kids.

Hell, hadn't he just been thinking about how uncomfortable he generally felt around children? A guy like him . . . no, it just didn't make sense. You couldn't force what you didn't feel. And he already knew it wasn't meant to be, *without* trying to get Jenny pregnant.

The beginning of their relationship had been rough—really rough. But after that, it had been smooth as silk. And now, for the first time since they'd worked through all those early problems, he felt a little bit like . . . like he didn't know her. And like, just as in the beginning, he was about to let her down. But he couldn't figure a way around it—he could only tell her the truth.

"Jenny," he said, the muscles in his chest stretched so tight now he feared they might snap, "I'm sorry. But I can't do that. I can't have a baby with you."

As Sue Ann drove home, Elvis sang "Blue Christmas" on the radio and she replayed in her head the conversation she'd just had with Jenny.

"It was agonizing," she'd told Jen, feeling an actual physical pull in her heart. She'd been talking about avoiding Adam's kiss. Even while he'd been wearing that silly Santa beard, it had been one of the hardest things she could ever remember doing, resisting. And she was still enduring that same gnawing want even now.

Jenny had shaken her head and said, "I just don't get it. I know you've only been divorced a little while, but I still think Adam is exactly what you need right now." She'd sounded downright exasperated. "Why won't you let yourself have fun with him?"

But the answer remained the same as before. It was simple. "Because I'm afraid to trust him."

"I still don't get it," Jenny had said. "Because if he's as crazy about you as it seems, he's not going to help Jeff in any way that would hurt you. I mean, he's Adam, for heaven's sake."

Yeah, good guy Adam. Mr. I-always-do-the-right-thing Adam. Jenny was thinking of the Adam they'd always known. But, again, she wasn't aware of Adam's dalliance at that wedding when he'd still been married to Sheila. And it wasn't that Sue Ann thought he'd cheat on *her*—it was simply that, right now, she just wasn't sure if *any* man could be counted on. She'd counted on Jeff and he'd let her down. And Adam had proven, at least once, that he wasn't infallible, either. And how could she possibly get involved with someone who might soon testify against her in a court of law?

She knew no one—well, Jenny and Adam—thought of it that way, as testifying against her. But if he testified for Jeff, it was *against* her. He'd be choosing sides. At the very least, he'd be helping Jeff increase her hardship. And at the worst, her daughter's custody could end up at risk. And yeah, that last part probably wouldn't happen, but what if it did?

"You don't really think Santa will bring me a reindeer, do you?" Sophie asked her then, her sweet but skeptical voice echoing from the backseat and shaking Sue Ann from her reverie.

Sue Ann just let out a sigh. She really did understand why Adam had told Sophie he'd try to get her a reindeer—she knew he'd been put on the spot—but the fact was, now, on top of everything else, her little girl was going to be severely disappointed come Christmas morning.

"Well," she finally said, "I just think that maybe . . . you shouldn't get your hopes up. Santa said he would try, right? That's different than a promise. So maybe you shouldn't count on it. And I'm sure if Santa can't come through on the reindeer that he'll bring you lots of other nice things." Like the stuffed reindeer she had picked up for Sophie today at the toy store in Crestview, somehow hoping that would be enough. After tonight, though, that stuffed deer had some big hooves to fill.

"I know all that," Sophie replied very stoically from the darkness behind Sue Ann, "but I'm not worried. He's going to bring me my reindeer. I just know it."

\* \* \*

Sue Ann had wanted that kiss as badly as he had—Adam knew it to the marrow of his bones. He still suffered the stirring desire to bring his body together with hers just thinking about it, remembering that moment when her soft lips had been so close to his . . . and yet so far away.

A few days had passed since then—it was Tuesday afternoon now and he worked in the tree lot outside the landscape supply. Christmas was only a week and a half away, so he'd watched the offerings in the lot grow thinner, yet they'd stayed busy, too, since some people waited until right about now to put up their live trees. And in one sense, he was glad he had plenty to occupy his mind—but in another, he felt weirdly as if he'd been moving through life in a fog.

His time these last couple of days had been spent in one of three ways: thinking about Sue Ann, remembering their hot nights together, and wishing—hoping—there could be more. Thinking about his boys and wishing they were here at home with him. Or snapping at people.

By now, Chuck Whaley seemed almost afraid to be in his presence—and Adam guessed he couldn't blame the guy. He'd yelled at Chuck more in the past two weeks than in the entire time they'd known each other. And Tyler Fleet no longer even made eye contact with him. He probably seemed like some kind of Dr. Jekyll and Mr. Hyde. He'd taken the time to explain that missing his boys had him in a crappy mood, but he guessed that after the third or fourth time, no one really cared, if they kept having to put up with it. And, of course, the situation with Sue Ann was adding to his rotten disposition, too—but that was no one's business.

Now, having decided maybe it was better to let Chuck and Tyler deal with the customers today, Adam had isolated himself in the lot, quieter this afternoon than normal, consolidating the remaining trees into one central area to free up more parking space. It felt good to start breaking down the now-empty stands of nailed-together two-by-fours where trees had leaned until they'd sold—the task required a little muscle, some physical labor, and as he worked he could even feel some tension beginning to leave his arms and shoulders.

A few minutes later, as he used a push broom to sweep up fallen needles and bark, it began to snow. Damn, what was it with all the snow this year already? The temperatures had stayed around freezing or below since Thanksgiving, so while the roads and most lots had been cleared, the ground remained blanketed with white. And now it looked like another fresh coating was on the way.

If it accumulated, it would mean a late night or possibly an early morning of plowing parking lots with one of the company trucks. And though he was thankful for work that helped fill the winter months, he didn't usually have to do so much of it until after Christmas.

Aw well—again, better to stay busy. The busier he was, the sooner this Christmas would be over and his kids would be home and he could put this cruddy mood behind him once and for all.

*But quit kidding yourself, Becker.* Yeah, having Jacob and Joey back would definitely improve that part of his life—yet he knew he'd still be wishing things were different with Sue Ann. When his Grinchiness had started, it had been all about the boys—and, as Sue

Ann had made him see—his regrets. But now he was forced to realize that even when the boys came home, he wasn't going to feel completely better. Nope, not by a long shot. He was still going to want her. And if her response to his near-kiss the other night was any indication, he wasn't going to have her.

And it wasn't just about sex. With Sue Ann, he wanted the whole package. From the pushy, know-it-all mom-about-town to the sweeter, more vulnerable woman he'd seen since Jeff's departure. From the girl next door to the lover who soaked up every pleasure she could.

Shit. This thing with her—it really wasn't going away. Yeah, he'd kind of known that by the time he'd delivered her tree, and he'd known it even more after what had happened between them in his truck—but damn. When had he gotten this caught up in her?

But then . . . the when didn't matter so much as the fact he couldn't run away from: The longer this wanting stretched out, the more powerful it became.

It had seemed so simple back in that cabin when she'd said they should forget about what had happened between them. Even if he hadn't necessarily liked it, it had sounded easy enough to accomplish. But now, as fluffy snow began to cover the very ground he swept, he experienced that familiar, pervasive, almost agonizing ache you got when you . . . fell for someone.

That was when he had to stop—stop sweeping, catch his breath, rest slightly against his broom. *I've completely fallen for Sue Ann. How the hell did I let this happen?*

*And how did it get so screwed up so fast?* After all, things were officially awkward between them right now. Plus she'd just gotten divorced from his best friend. And despite what they'd shared that night in the truck, it was pretty clear she wasn't interested in a relationship with him.

And he had to accept that, abide by her wishes. Didn't he? Because he understood how badly Jeff had wounded her, and in the big picture of their lives, it had only happened like . . . yesterday.

Adam sighed, then looked to the sky as if seeking an answer—but all he found there was the blank white slate of a snowy winter day, thick flakes now wetting his face.

Yet . . . could there be some way to win her over, to make her forget or look beyond her reasons for pushing him away?

And then something hit him, something new. The first time he'd kissed her, as a kid, he'd been dressed up as Joseph for the nativity play at school. The first time he'd flirted with her, just a couple of weeks ago, he'd been behind a big, stuffed reindeer head. And on Wednesday night when he'd tried to kiss her, he'd been in a Santa suit. So it seemed like he was always making moves on Sue Ann when he was . . . somebody else. Not on purpose—but it just worked out that way sometimes. Yet in the cabin, and in the truck—the times things had gotten really good with her—he'd been just . . . himself. For better or worse.

So maybe that was the key—just being real with her. Could be that those masks made it a little easier sometimes, easier to get flirty and make a play. But they'd known each other all their lives, and if there was anyone he should be able to be his real self with—whether that was his normal self or his Scroogy self or something in between—it should be Sue Ann. So if he did that from now on, maybe . . . something good would happen. Maybe.

Just then, Adam looked up to see an SUV rumbling into the parking lot, leaving wet tracks in the thin covering of new snow. *Jeff's* SUV. Damn. What timing.

Six or seven months ago, he'd have been happy to see Jeff—they'd been best friends since high school, the best man in each other's weddings. But since his breakup with Sue Ann, things just hadn't felt the same. And now the guy showed up right when Adam was plotting how to win his ex-wife's affections?

The SUV pulled up to where Adam stood working, and as Jeff came into sight through the windshield, he flashed a smile and lifted his hand in a wave. Adam tried to smile in return, but he suspected the effort didn't quite work.

Jeff didn't seem to notice, though—he hopped out, slammed the door, and merrily said, "What's up, bud?"

"Not much," Adam replied, fearing he sounded as sour as he felt. Things had been tense between them ever since he'd told Jeff, months ago, that he thought leaving Sue Ann was a mistake. But maybe for Jeff, the tension had passed. "What's up with you?"

"Haven't gotten around to putting up a tree yet at my new place with Ronni—so I took off work early to come get one. Christmas is right around the corner now, and it being our first one together as husband and wife, I want to make it special." Or maybe Jeff was still so smitten with the new woman in his life that he just didn't take in anyone else's reactions. He'd seemed to be in his own little world ever since parting with Sue Ann in June.

Despite Jeff's holly jolly attitude, Adam still couldn't manage a smile—so he just motioned at the remaining trees in the distance. "That's what I have left. Getting pretty picked over, though."

"Okey doke. And, uh, listen—have you decided if you can help me out at the hearing?"

Adam's chest tightened. "Um . . . afraid I'm still on the fence. Just feel sort of caught between you and Sue Ann, you know?" But he didn't go into further detail than that—he'd known Sue Ann their whole lives, too, so he hoped it made sense to Jeff that it counted for something, even without knowing that their relationship had become romantic—and sexual.

"I get that," Jeff said. "But I'm really hoping you can come through. My lawyer says it would help a lot. And like I told you on the phone—it's the only way Ronni and I can move forward with having a baby, and it's important to her. Her biological clock is ticking hard."

Damn, now Jeff was making him feel like he was preventing a woman from having a child? Sheesh. Despite himself, that tore at him a little. He'd only met Ronni a few times, but enough to know that he actually liked her. Still, he just nodded and said, "I'll let you know."

Jeff smiled in thanks, and that, too, dug at Adam's emotions a little. Maybe it reminded him of better times in their friendship—easier times. "You know it would mean a lot to me." After which he pointed toward the remaining evergreens. "Guess I'd better go find a tree. Then I gotta get home and get some lights up outside, too."

"I put up Sue Ann's lights," Adam heard himself say then, sounding more rigid than he'd meant to.

At which Jeff stopped, looked back. And maybe he sounded a little less merry and a bit more awkward when he replied, "Uh, yeah, Sophie told me. Been meaning to say thanks."

"It was no problem. And she needed the help," he added. Maybe he shouldn't have. And maybe he shouldn't risk making Sue Ann look . . . needy or something, since for the most part, Adam thought she was doing a great job of being on her own. But clearly Jeff had completely forgotten about the woman he'd once loved, about how hard his departure had made her life. He already had a full-time job, financial security. And he already lived with someone else who could help with the daily chores that came with being an adult.

Now Jeff obviously heard the stiffness in Adam's voice. Yet he only said, "Well, it was good of you to pitch in," and let it go.

And as his old friend walked away toward the trees, Adam was sorry he'd brought Sue Ann up at all. The fact was, people got divorced, and they learned to manage life by themselves—it happened all the time. And it wasn't his place to pick a fight with Jeff over this.

But he just thought, as he had from the start, that his old friend was inconsiderate. After all, during the first year after he'd split with Sheila, he'd still made sure she had what she needed. He'd delivered a free Christmas tree from his lot that year, he'd put up her lights as well, and more than once he'd repaired a broken toilet or dishwasher for her. It hadn't meant they forgave each other—it had just been the decent thing to do for a woman he'd once loved and the mother of his kids.

Now he watched as, across the way, Jeff was already

laughing with Johnny Fulks from the Destiny town council, who'd pulled into the lot behind him, also tree-shopping. Jeff shook Johnny's hand and then even slapped him on the back. Once more, Sue Ann and his old life had been forgotten, that quickly. Something about it made Adam's stomach sink like a lump of coal.

And suddenly he couldn't blame her for not wanting to jump into a relationship with him. Because how could he expect her to open her heart again so soon? How could he expect her to put that kind of trust in him? Especially after what he'd told her about Sheila. It was like he'd thought once before—she surely figured that birds of a feather flocked together. Even if he wasn't flocking much with Jeff anymore.

He spotted Lettie Gale then, trying to drag her own tree to her car—while Tyler Fleet, who'd just shown up for his after-school shift, stood flirting with his girlfriend, Cara, next to her mom's car. "Tyler!" he barked, then motioned toward Lettie—who'd also flinched at the sharp sound. "I'm paying you to work, not flirt! Help the lady with her tree."

And even though all three of them stood gaping at him like he was the Grinch himself, ready to descend on Whoville, he didn't bother apologizing this time. Despite himself, he was feeling Scroogier by the minute.

"Leave me! Take me back! Haunt me no longer!"

Charles Dickens, A *Christmas Carol*

# Twelve

*A*dam was in the room—and yet he wasn't. When he walked into the Dew Drop Inn, the bar on the edge of town, not one person inside looked up—and he knew instinctively that they didn't see him, didn't realize he was there.

A few of his friends sat around the bar, while others occupied nearby tables. Sue Ann sat prettily at one of them wearing a winter white skirt and a cozy-looking sweater the color of cranberries, a bottle of beer in her hand. The simple sight made him smile because no one would expect the well-put-together mom to be a beer drinker, but he'd knocked back more than a few with her over the years and had always liked that about her.

Jenny and her husband, Mick, shared the same table, while Chuck Whaley and Amy Bright occupied the next. His buddies, Mike and Logan, were at the bar *with another guy who worked with Mike on the Destiny police force, Raybourne Fleet. Red foil tinsel and tiny colored lights were strung above the bar, and a small artificial tree with too many ornaments weighing down its branches stood by the jukebox.*

*Despite himself, he suffered an instant surge of loneliness to be in their presence, yet to still be, effectively, alone. Instinctively, he lifted his hand in a wave and said, "Hey guys," but yep, just as he expected, no one heard him.*

*Except . . . to his surprise, Sue Ann glanced toward where he stood, then blinked uncertainly.*

*"What's wrong?" Jenny asked her over a glass of wine.*

*Sue Ann shook her head. "Nothing. Just . . . weird— I thought I heard Adam's voice." The two exchanged looks, and Adam could tell that Jenny knew they'd slept together.*

*Raybourne Fleet swung his head around. "Adam Becker? That's the last guy I want to run into tonight. He's been giving my kid a hard time at work." Besides being a by-the-book cop, just like Mike, Raybourne was also Tyler Fleet's father.*

*"Yeah, I don't know what's got into him," Chuck volunteered with a disgusted sigh, "but he yells at me every time I move lately. Keeps sayin' he's sorry, but he don't mean it. If he meant it, he'd knock it the hell off."*

*"It's because the boys are gone for the holidays," Sue Ann offered, "and he just misses them. I know he doesn't mean to be so harsh."*

*Adam's heart started to warm, pleased she'd taken up for him—when Mick Brody said, "Did he really tell Sophie that Santa would bring her a reindeer?"*

*Now Sue Ann let out a troubled sigh, but at least*

*she didn't sound as put out with him as everyone else.
"Well, he said Santa would try, and under the circumstances, I understand why."*

*"Still," Mick said, "that's gonna be tough come
Christmas morning, isn't it?" and Sue Ann replied
with a small, conciliatory nod that made Adam feel
like sludge anyway.*

*"You know, I don't like to talk bad about my friends,"
Logan piped up, "but he was pretty damn hard to work
with at the Christmas tree lighting, that's for sure."*

*"You can say that again," Chuck muttered.*

*"He keeps this up," Mike said from next to Logan at
the bar, "and he won't have any friends left."*

*Logan just drew back and gave Mike a look—which
Adam appreciated. Although he was a good guy at
heart, Mike was known far and wide for being brusque
and hard to get along with, even with his friends and
loved ones. Yet Mike simply replied to Logan's glance
by saying, "With me, people are used to it. But with
Becker—hell, on him it's just not right. Even I don't
like hanging with him lately."*

*"Yeah, if things don't get better," Chuck added, "I
might have to start looking for another job. I've always
liked working for Adam, but when your boss turns into
a jerk, going to work sucks."*

*And when even sweet Amy spoke out against him . . .
God, it felt like he was doomed. "I didn't want to say
anything because Adam is usually so nice, but . . . he
practically growled at me when he delivered my trees.
He was fine with the one for the bookstore, but he
seemed pretty snarly about carrying the other one up
to my apartment. Like, after all these years, he doesn't
know I live above the store?"*

*"Stop," Adam said then. "I'll try to be nicer." But of*

*course, no one heard him. In fact, they started going around the room, sharing more tales of how horrible he'd been the last few weeks. And even Sue Ann didn't hear him this time.*

*"I heard him get snippy with Mabel at the diner," someone said.*

*"And sure, he filled in as Santa, but Caroline Meeks said he was grumbly about it."*

*"Aw, come on, guys—give me a break," he said, trying again—but his words got no response, and damn, if he'd felt lonely when he walked in here, it was nothing compared to now.*

The shrill ringing of the phone seemed to slice into Adam's brain, jostling him roughly from sleep.

And—oh. Damn. It was a dream.

*Of course it was a dream, you numbskull—you were invisible.*

Okay, where was the phone? He thrust a hand out from under the covers toward the bedside table but didn't find it—and the sharp trill was about to shatter his eardrums. What time was it anyway? And who was calling him this early?

He reached farther and at last found the cordless receiver, but he knocked it off its stand. Eventually, it was in his grip and he finally pushed the answer button to snap, *"What?"*

"Dad?" Aw hell. It was Joey. And he clearly wondered why he was being yelled at for calling home.

"Hey Joe, I'm sorry," Adam said quickly, softening his voice. "Just couldn't find the phone. How ya doin'? What's up?"

"I got some sniffles, so I couldn't sleep. Grandma said it was probably late enough there that I could call."

"Of course it is. And hey, you can always call me—you know that. Any time, day or night." Adam glanced to the clock to see it was 8:00 A.M., which made it six in Colorado. And he should damn well be up by now anyway—what was it with him and all the oversleeping these days?

"Even if it's not important, though?" his son asked, still sounding doubtful.

"Absolutely. Even if it's not important. Just hearing your voice is important enough for me."

"You know what's cool?" Joey asked, punctuating the question with a big sniff.

"What's that?"

*All this snow. Skiing. The mountains.* Those were the things that had usually been cool lately, so Adam was waiting to hear more of the same when Joey said, "That even on the phone, you know me and Jacob apart without even trying."

Huh. He never knew the boys even noticed that. Because he was their dad, after all. Even if they were mostly identical, right down to their voices, and even if no one *else* could tell them apart—yeah, of course he knew without trying, without even thinking. "Well, you're my kid, buddy. Now tell me about these sniffles keeping you up."

As Joey filled him in, Adam listened intently and felt that parental *ping* of concern because he was so far away and couldn't take care of his boy while he was sick. And he kept remembering the hurt tone in Joey's voice when he'd barked into the phone instead of answering it like a normal person.

Shit, this had to stop. If that bizarre dream hadn't sent a strong enough message, yelling at his innocent kid over the phone sure as hell had. This Scroogy attitude was taking its toll, not only on the people in his life, but on him, too.

He didn't like himself this way. So how could he expect anyone *else* to like him?

The problem was, he just didn't know how to change it. After all, his bad attitude had started when the boys left, and since then, other parts of his life had only gotten more complicated, and more out of his control. The best friendship he'd ever known was fading, and though he didn't let himself think about it a lot, when he did, it stung. And he wanted a woman who wanted him back but wouldn't let herself have him. And then there was Jeff's request that he testify on his behalf, which mucked it all up even worse.

Just then, though, as Adam lay in bed staring out the window at a snow-covered hillside in the distance, it occurred to him that Jeff's request was the one and only thing in the mix here that he did actually have some control over. He'd been trying like hell to avoid thinking about that, too, but maybe making a decision, one way or the other, would help improve his whole general demeanor.

And the more time that passed, the more he knew in his heart what the right answer was.

Once he gave it . . . well, it would probably damage one of his relationships further. But at the same time, maybe it would help repair another.

On Friday, Sue Ann left Destiny Properties to walk around the corner and across the town square to Dolly's Main Street Café. She was having lunch with Tessa, who always cheered her up. Tessa herself had been through a lot in recent years, yet she went through life with a positive attitude Sue Ann admired.

And as they chatted over the next hour, Tessa's upbeat mood once again lifted Sue Ann's spirits. Mainly because Tessa had an answer for everything.

"What am I gonna do about money, and a job?" Sue Ann had complained over a plate of chicken and dumplings. She'd made no secret among her girlfriends that her need for a full-time income had become more immediate, and why.

"Okay, first," Tessa replied, "I think you should set a deadline. Like Christmas. If nothing comes through by then, I'll call my buddy, Greg, over in Crestview." Tessa had recently done some interior design work for Greg, who owned a steakhouse, and they'd already discussed that fact that Tessa felt sure he could use another waitress. "And I know that's not what you're really looking for, but you'd just have to think of it as temporary."

"But what if I get so bogged down that I never get my real estate license, I never take the those steps that will help me move ahead?"

Tessa just shook her head. "It'll be hard, but you'll just have to make the time. You'll have to see this as a period in your life where you just keep your head down and power through it—until it's better. What does Dory say, after all?"

Dory from *Finding Nemo*, she meant. All of Tessa's friends knew her favorite piece of advice came from an animated fish, yet no one could fault the suggestion. "Just keep swimming," Sue Ann answered dutifully.

"Right. Just keep afloat, keep pushing forward. That's really all you can ask of yourself right now."

Sue Ann tilted her head to one side, trying to see

it from that perspective, and something about the idea calmed her. "You're right," she finally said. And as usual, by the time she parted ways with Tessa, bundling up for the short walk back to the office, she truly felt better. *You're strong, you're capable, and everything will be okay.*

If she had to wait tables, she'd wait tables. If she had to lose some sleep to study, she'd lose sleep. It would all be about building a good life for her and Sophie. And though she'd never imagined she would become a single mom who had to worry about these things—well, this was where destiny had delivered her, and Tessa was correct: She had to power through it and know she'd come out better on the other side. Life was full of unexpected twists and turns, and all she could do was keep her eyes on the road and navigate it as well as possible.

Of course, she still didn't know what she was going to do when Sophie didn't get a reindeer on Christmas morning, but . . . one day at a time. One problem at a time.

She'd just hung up her coat, changed from her snow boots back into her pumps, and taken a seat at her desk—when the owner of Destiny Properties, Dan Lindley, peeked out from his office and said, "Sue Ann, can I see you for a minute?"

Hmm—Dan was calling her into his office? Sue Ann didn't hesitate to scoop up a notepad and pen to head that way, but she felt a little uneasy. She usually took direction from the office manager, Shirley Busby, and had little actual work contact with Dan—her conversations with Dan were usually small talk, and truthfully, the well-dressed, well-spoken middle-aged Destiny transplant intimidated her a little.

"Sit down," he said, motioning to the chair across

from his desk when she walked in. A handsome man in his forties, Dan's gray suit accentuated his salt-and-pepper hair. And as Sue Ann did as he instructed, she found herself taking a seat only on the edge, not leaning back—something about his clipped, all-business tone added to her growing sense of nervousness.

"Sue Ann," he said then, "it's come to my attention that you've been looking for another job."

And—oh no, oh God—why hadn't it occurred to her that the people she worked with might hear she'd been asking around town about full-time employment? *This is Destiny, dummy, where everyone knows everyone else's business.* She supposed she'd just neglected to think that far ahead amid her panic and worry.

"Aren't you happy here at Destiny Properties?" he asked. "Given that, last I heard, you were studying to get your real estate license, I was under the impression you planned to stay with us for a long while."

*Oh crap. He's going to fire me. He's going to fire me and then I won't have any income at all.* Her stomach churned and she could barely breathe—yet she had no choice but to spill the whole unpleasant truth to him now. "I'm sorry, Dan. The only reason I'm looking for other work is because my ex-husband is petitioning to stop his alimony payments and I can't make ends meet on a part-time salary. I'd hoped getting my license would solve that problem, but I no longer have time to wait for that. And while staying here would be my first choice, I know there are no full-time openings or any need to expand my current position. And whatever happens, well . . . I had hoped that when I get my license I would still be able to have a work home here. And the way things are going, I might just end up getting an additional part-time job waiting tables. Which I would in no way let interfere with my work here, I promise. And, okay, I guess I should have discussed my situation with Shirley, but I'm just so tired of people talking about me and my divorce that I was trying to deal with this quietly."

She'd rattled all this off without quite focusing on his face—instead she'd planted her gaze on the fancy silver reindeer on his tie. Ugh—again reindeers! Now, though, she looked him directly in the eye. "Please don't fire me, Dan. This job is the only bit of security I have left right now, the only thing in my life I wasn't worried about."

"Sue Ann," he said calmly, "don't worry—I'm not going to fire you."

"You're not?" Relief rushed through her like a brisk winter wind.

"No. I actually wanted to offer you a promotion."

She expelled the breath she hadn't quite realized she was holding. "A promotion?"

"This is very hush-hush in the office for now, but Shirley has just given me her notice. As you know, her daughter's pregnant, and she's decided to retire and babysit so her daughter can return to work. She's recommended you to replace her as office manager, but when we heard you were looking elsewhere, we were concerned you were unhappy."

Sue Ann felt as if all the blood had drained from her cheeks as she said, probably too softly, "I would love to be the office manager." Then she swallowed. "If you still want me for the position."

"I do. Especially now that I understand why you were making the rounds at other places. I need to know you're dedicated to staying with us."

"I am—oh, I am! And I still intend to get my license, too."

He nodded, smiled. "Good, that's great to hear. The office management job, as you know, is eight to five, Monday through Friday, and comes with a twenty percent raise over your current hourly wage. Will that work for you?"

Fighting off the urge to literally leap for joy, Sue Ann instead managed to stay in her chair, do the math in her head, and quickly reply, "Yes. Definitely."

"Shirley will be with us through mid-January, so you can start full-time at the beginning of the year and that will give her some time to train you."

Sue Ann was back to not being able to breathe again, but she tried desperately to hide it. "That's . . . amazing! Thank you!"

And it suddenly got a little easier to stay afloat.

On Saturday morning, Sue Ann and Sophie woke up to a few new inches of snow, but the roads were cleared early, so Sue Ann didn't let it change their plans for shopping. After all, she was in far too good a mood to let anything get in her way today. Her mouth hurt from smiling. And her throat was even a little sore from all the talking she'd done on the phone last night. Not only had she called her mother and Jenny, she'd then also called Tessa, Amy, and Rachel, too. Her friends had been so supportive throughout her divorce—how could she not share her great news with them?

And for some reason, a part of her also wanted to share it with Adam, but she'd resisted that urge. *It's only because you've shared some closeness with him lately.* And probably, too, because he was more connected to the situation than any other man in her life. But getting a job didn't mean her challenges were completely over—*and he still might testify on Jeff's behalf, and you still don't know where that could lead.*

Following a trip to Crestview, where the stores were filled with holiday crowds, she and Sophie then returned to Destiny, where things were a bit more pleasantly quiet. After parking on the town square, they needed only to stop by the Daisy Dress Shop—where Sophie picked out a scarf to give Jenny, especially from her—then headed on to Under the Covers. When she'd called Amy last night, Amy had mentioned that a gardening book Sue Ann had ordered for her mother had arrived.

When they stepped inside, it was a regular party—the whole gang was there. Amy stood behind the counter, ringing up a customer's order, while Jenny, Rachel, and Tessa all sat drinking eggnog in easy chairs. And Sue Ann was actually in the *mood* for a party for a change, happy to accept all the merry congratulations from her friends, and thankful for all the warmth and comfort that greeted her and Sophie when they walked through the door.

After Amy's customer left, she joined them and they all gabbed about shopping and holiday festivities and Sue Ann's new position, sometimes sharing one conversation, at other moments branching off into a couple—and Sue Ann appreciated how they all included Sophie, asking her about Christmas parties at school, and Rachel fawned over her new snow boots with the fur around the top. Although everyone, Sue Ann noticed, judiciously avoided asking what Sophie wanted for Christmas or even mentioning Santa, so she assumed word of Adam's reindeer promise had made it around.

"Dickens!" Sophie exclaimed when the gray kitten peeked out from a bookshelf at her exact eye level.

"I think he's missed playing with you," Amy said to Sophie—then cringed softly when she saw the look on Sue Ann's face, mouthing the words *Sorry, forgot* in her direction. Despite her good mood, and even despite what she'd told Adam about how maybe she should have taken the cat, Sue Ann still wasn't willing to make that leap. She hadn't given the cat a lot of thought with everything else vying for attention in her head, but now that she'd be working so much more and would be at home so much less, the idea sounded less prudent than ever.

"Where are his bells?" Sophie asked Amy, who then pointed behind the counter, and a moment later, with jingle bells in hand, Sophie went scampering off after the cat, who appeared to like being chased.

"You're lucky to be a mom," Jenny said on a sigh, watching as Sophie disappeared between the tall shelves.

Sue Ann supposed that meant Jenny's baby quest wasn't going well, but she didn't feel she could ask at the moment since their other friends might not know about that. *Oh, wow, look at* me—*not blurting something out before thinking.* She really was getting better at keeping secrets and not being a bigmouth all the time!

Maybe the flipside of the equation, though, would make Jenny feel better. "Yeah, but sometimes it's really tough. Like right now, for instance." She lowered her voice to make sure Sophie didn't hear. "I mean,

I'm still really anxious about keeping her happy this Christmas."

"She seems happy enough to me," Tessa said, glancing back through the bookshelves where Sophie's giggles could be heard.

But Sue Ann only sighed. "Well, she has a lot of ups and downs. And I'm concerned about how all this will affect her, you know, in the big picture of life." The fact was, having one big problem solved didn't mean the others just went away.

"It seems to me," Jenny said with a tilt of her head, "that you've always felt a lot of anxiety about Sophie's happiness. And don't take this the wrong way, but sometimes I'm afraid you overworry it."

Wow. Jenny had never said anything like that before, so the words left Sue Ann stunned. "But I'm her mom—of course I'm going to worry. I mean, you hear every day about people who are screwed up because of stuff in their childhood. And we know people who've . . . well, struggled due to things that happened when they were kids." She knew she didn't have to point out that she was talking about Mick, and also Rachel's and Tessa's fiancés, Mike and Lucky Romo. "I just consider my number one job in life keeping her safe. Emotionally."

"But . . . maybe you can't do that," Amy said. "I mean, that's how we grow, how we live—we have emotions. And sometimes they're hard, or rotten, but we learn from them and get through it."

Sue Ann just cast her friend a sideways glance. "Listen to Miss Psychologist over here."

"Yeah, Miss Matchmaker who never makes a match for herself," Tessa said.

And Amy's face went red. Because they never talked about that, about the fact that Amy hadn't dated anyone in a very, very long while. But apparently Tessa had decided it was time to confront that particular elephant in the bookstore.

"Well, who would I match myself up with around here?" Amy finally replied, clearly trying to downplay it with her light tone. "I mean, you girls have already taken most of the hot men off the market."

Rachel just rolled her eyes as the others flashed looks of disbelief. There were still more than one or two attractive single men running around Destiny. And Rachel finished her eye roll by pointing to Amy and saying, "Okay, I'm turning the tables on you, Miss Matchmaker. What about Adam Becker? He's the nicest guy in town, and you're the nicest girl, so that seems like a good match to me."

And in response, Sue Ann's stomach wrenched. *Because Adam is mine! Mine, mine, mine!* Not really, of course—but that was her gut reaction. Which threw her a little.

Thankfully, no one besides Jenny noticed the look on her face because they were all too caught up in what Rachel had just suggested. And Sue Ann's heart beat too hard as she sat waiting for Amy's response.

"Adam? And me? Gosh, I don't know," she finally said, sounding blessedly skeptical. But already Sue Ann's mind raced. Could Adam be attracted to Amy? Amy was much prettier than she realized, and such a nice person, too. *And what kind of creep am I to not want my dear friend to find love? Oh Lord, I don't want to be one of those I-don't-want-him-but-you-can't-have-him kind of women.*

"He's a great guy," Tessa chimed in.

"But he's been kind of testy lately," Amy pointed out.

"True, he has," Sue Ann heard herself agree. *Oh God, I* am *one of those women.*

"I'm sure it's just holiday stress," Rachel said, then shifted her attention to Sue Ann. "You know Adam really well. Don't you think he and Amy would make a nice couple?"

Everyone looked at her now, waiting for her answer—even Amy, darn it. So she glanced at Jenny, as if for rescue—rescue that didn't come—and then made herself say the right thing. "Sure. He's a great guy, like Tessa said." Even if the words didn't come out quite as strong and clear as she'd hoped. And her stomach churned, wondering if she'd just set something in motion that she would regret.

Yet then Amy replied, "Even so, I've just never felt that thing with Adam, you know? That spark. So I don't think it's in the cards." And Sue Ann was torn between wanting to jump for joy and giving Amy the real truth of the situation: *Just because you've never felt a spark with Adam before doesn't mean it won't suddenly happen—trust me, I know.* But she settled—wisely, she thought—for doing neither and just sitting quietly in her chair and taking a sip of eggnog.

After that, fortunately, the discussion moved on to other topics, and though Sue Ann tried to pay attention and occasionally add some pithy remark that would make her friends think she was acting normal, she felt far from normal on the inside. Her reaction to the idea of Adam being with someone else was . . . startling. And a little frightening.

She'd forgotten. How this felt. To have that powerful

pull toward a new man in your life. Lord, she hadn't gone through this since high school—half her life ago. It was at once exhilarating and agonizing.

But for her, right now, agonizing was winning, hands down. It seemed like no matter what she did regarding Adam, she was going to be miserable. To let herself start a relationship with him would be . . . to worry, to be wary. And was she even emotionally equipped to have a relationship right now? She didn't think so. And there was so much to do, so much to consider. There was Sophie. And Christmas. There was her new job and her real estate license. And whether or not to keep the house. She loved the house. She'd put a lot of blood, sweat, and tears into the house. But she and Jeff had refurbished it *together,* and now some of those tears were the really sad kind, and so wouldn't the place always be tainted with memories of a past she needed to put behind her?

"I'm going to sell the house," she said out of the blue. It suddenly seemed so clear, like something she shouldn't have been waffling on all this time.

"Huh?" Tessa asked, and Sue Ann realized she'd interrupted something Tessa had been saying about her Christmas present for Lucky.

"I'm sorry," Sue Ann said, "I didn't mean to be so rude. But it just hit me, hard—I should sell the house. For a while it seemed like something I needed to hang onto, but I think hanging onto it was like hanging onto Jeff, and the past, and even as much as I love that house, I need someplace new, a truly fresh start. You know?"

All her friends chimed in with their agreement and support, but soon enough the conversation drifted to yet another new subject, and that's when Jenny leaned over to put her hand on Sue Ann's knee. "This is big," she said quietly. "Especially since you just became more financially equipped to stay where you are."

"I know," Sue Ann agreed. "It just shot through me like a bolt of lightning. That I don't need the house anymore. I don't need that part of what used to be my marriage. In fact, maybe I don't need any of it anymore. Well, other than Sophie, of course. But the rest . . . I think I'm really, finally, beginning to let go."

Jenny's smile reached all the way to Sue Ann's core. What she was feeling right now was real, and solid. Jenny was right. It was big. She suddenly felt braver, and more ready to face life. Maybe it was the new job helping her see that she could make changes, be successfully independent, do things on her own. And she realized it was as if holding onto the house, even just in her own mind, had somehow been . . . weighing her down.

"Beginning to let go and starting to move on?" Jenny asked.

"Yes, and starting to move on," she said. "Definitely."

"With Adam?" Jenny whispered.

And Sue Ann's stomach began to churn again, pushing her to say, "Look, one big step at a time, okay? I have a new job, and I'm ready to sell the house—that's enough for today. And I think it's pretty good progress."

"Okay, okay—you're right, it is," Jenny agreed. "And I'm proud of you."

And Sue Ann felt pretty proud of herself, too. "New life, new beginnings," she said. "But one step at a time."

A few minutes later, she announced it was time to get her mom's book and depart. "I promised Sophie we'd make cookies this afternoon and that we'd try sledding on that hill at the end of our street—you know, the one that runs down to Sugar Creek." As she stepped up to the counter and opened her purse to pay Amy, she called back through the bookstore, "Soph—it's time to go!"

And by the time she'd picked up her bag and was buttoning her coat, Sophie appeared from between the shelves—of course carrying fluffy little Dickens in her arms. "I love him so much, Mommy," she said, peering up. "Can't we take him home? Pleeeease."

*Oh boy, here we go again.* It was starting to seem dangerous to bring Sophie to the bookstore. "Soph, honey, we've discussed this. Having a cat takes a lot of work—and money, that we just don't have right now."

"But . . . " Then Sophie flashed her best pouty face and sad eyes—almost enough to do Sue Ann in. Yet she refused to let it. Even if the kitty did start looking a little cuter to her every time she saw it. "You got a new job yesterday. That's more money, right?"

Sue Ann could only sigh. "More money that we need for other things. And between my schedule and yours, we'll barely be home. Come on, honey—say goodbye to Dickens for now and we'll go home and make cookies like we planned. Then we'll get out the sleds—remember?"

She saw Sophie struggling, trying to decide if she should keep arguing or just look forward to the fun afternoon ahead, and eventually her little girl gave a soft nod and said, "All right." Then she hugged the gray kitten to her chest and said, "I'll see you soon, Dickens. I'll miss you. Bye."

Okay, good—another bullet dodged. At least for today.

Next mission: Get Adam Becker out of her head.

Because, again, there was so much else occupying space there that needed her attention—and heck, now she had a house to put on the market, too. Which would take a hellacious amount of work in the new year. And then she'd need to find a new place, figure out what kind of home she and Sophie actually wanted—and all while settling into a new job and studying for her real estate exam, too. So yeah, this was no time to add a pet to the mix. And this was no time to keep letting herself pine over a man. *My God, I just stopped pining for one and now I'm already pining for another?* What kind of madness had her once simple, settled life become?

So even as she said her goodbyes and gathered up her bags and her child, she lectured herself. *No more Adam. No more thinking about his kisses. Or the hot, hot sex we shared. It was getting-back-on-the-horse sex, that was all—all it* can *be. No more feeling jealous at the mere mention of his name.* Oh Lord, she'd practically behaved like he'd told her Sheila once had. So it stopped. Now.

Pushing through the door and out onto the sidewalk, she glanced back as she held it open for Sophie behind her, then started forward—only to barrel straight into a solid, sturdy male body. They both let out little *oomph* noises at the impact, and then she looked up—into the warmest, sexiest blue eyes she'd ever seen.

. . . they were happy, grateful, pleased with one another, and contented with the time . . .

Charles Dickens, A *Christmas Carol*

## *Thirteen*

*U*h oh. So much for her "no more Adam" plan.

As his gloved hands rose to her shoulders to steady her, his gaze widened. "Sue Ann."

"Adam," she breathed. *Oh brother—don't breathe at him. You sound like a smitten schoolgirl.* "Sorry. I wasn't watching where I was going."

And when he smiled at her and said, "Not a problem, sugar plum," she felt it squarely between her thighs. Talk about madness.

*Oh Adam, why do you have to be here, now, for heaven's sake?* Because she might have dodged a bullet with the cat, but *this* bullet was hitting her, hard, embedding itself straight into her heart. He stood before her, his dark hair mussed, jaw stubbled, bundled in a winter jacket and blue jeans, a striped scarf of hunter green and burgundy circling his neck. His cheeks were slightly red from the cold, but . . . oh my—those eyes of his were like hot blue flames, making it so she didn't even feel the brisk December wind. And that fast, her heart beat too hard and she was wanting him again.

*But wait, stop. I can do this. I'm a big girl—I can push down my desires and stick to my plan.* And she was going to start by . . . acting more normal than smitten. Even if the last time she'd seen him she'd been dodging his kiss.

"So . . . what's up?" she asked.

"Not much," he told her.

"Christmas shopping?"

"Um . . . actually, to be honest," he said, taking on that slightly sheepish look she found so inexplicably endearing on him, "I'm heading to Dolly's for a piece of pumpkin pie. Because I'm done at work for the day and not in the mood to go home to a quiet house."

"Oh." Damn, that made her sad. "Still missing the boys?"

His simple shrug said it all—then he changed the subject by reaching down to ruffle Sophie's hair. "How's it goin', kiddo?"

Sophie tilted her little blond head and replied, "Okay, I guess. Mommy still won't let me have a cat, but we're gonna go home and make cookies, and then go sled riding, too!"

"Well, that sounds fun. Who needs a cat when you've got all that to keep you busy, right?"

Glancing down at Sophie, Sue Ann saw that she truly seemed to be considering his words. "Yeah, I guess Dickens wouldn't be very good at that stuff."

"Dickens is the cat in question?" Adam asked,

switching his look briefly from Sophie to Sue Ann. She nodded, and he looked back to Sophie to say, "Cat hair and cookies don't go too well together. And cats are terrible sled riders. Now—my dog, Pepper, though, is great on a sled."

Sophie let out a giggle, smiling up at Adam. "No he's not. You're teasing me."

"Would I do that?" he asked playfully.

And Sophie gave a big, emphatic nod that made them all laugh.

"Kid's got my number," Adam said, lifting his gaze back to Sue Ann.

She didn't answer, just smiling a bit more, busy commanding herself, *Don't want him, don't want him, don't want him,* until he said, "Well, guess I'll head on to Dolly's. You girls have a fun afternoon, okay?"

And—hell. She couldn't stop herself. "Are *you* any good at cookies? Or sledding?"

A sexy glint shone in his eye when he said, "It so happens I am a master sledder. Cookies—not so much, but I can promise not to get any hair in them."

Sophie giggled once more, and—holy crap—Sue Ann felt his response tingling through her like softly falling snowflakes. If snowflakes were tingly. And hot. Though maybe it wasn't his response so much as the flirtation in his gaze. "Well, if you can bear to pass up Dolly's pie, you're welcome to join us for cookies and sledding."

"Hmm," he said, eyes narrowing as he appeared to weigh it carefully. "It's pretty good pie. But . . . " He glanced back and forth between her and Sophie. "All right, you talked me into it."

They made plans for Adam to follow them home, and

on the short walk to the car, with Sophie's little mitten-covered hand in hers, Sue Ann girded herself. She'd only invited him over because she felt bad for him, that was all. And if Sophie were away for a whole month, this month in particular, she'd be moping around like crazy. And if she'd learned nothing else lately, it was that Adam was going to be in her life. He just was. So having him over seemed like a good chance to prove she could be with him without . . . *being with him.*

*It's not because I want him. It's not.*

Even if her thighs ached as she walked to the car.

Even if her heart beat harder with the mere knowledge that they'd soon be spending time together again.

Then—dear Lord—a little shiver actually shook her, and she felt it all the way through her body, and in some key places more than others. Yikes.

"Cold, Mommy?" Sophie asked, peering innocently up at her.

"Um . . . yeah, that's it—I'm cold." *Uh-huh, you just keep telling yourself that.*

Adam wasn't very good in the kitchen, but he tried. Mainly, he liked being close to Sue Ann, and without planning it, he kept finding reasons to touch her in small ways as the three of them maneuvered about the space. A touch on the shoulder as he stepped around her to grab more dough from the fridge, a hand on her waist to keep her from backing into him with a hot tray of cookies.

They found a rhythm—Sue Ann rolled out the dough, then let Sophie cut out the shapes of trees, snowmen, stars, and stockings with Adam's help. He removed the excess dough from around the shapes before Sue

Ann gently scooped them onto the baking sheet with a spatula and into the oven. He and Sophie were also in charge of decorating after the finished cookies cooled—and of eating any that ended up broken or burnt. Holiday music echoed from the living room the whole while, and beyond the kitchen window a light snow began to fall.

Of course, he knew Sue Ann had invited him over because she felt sorry for him. And that kinda would have sucked except . . . he sensed it was about more than just pity. He sensed that she might be starting to care for him, too, in just the way he wanted her to. But he didn't plan to push that with her today—nope, he just let himself enjoy the afternoon. And more than that, he made sure he was being real with her, being his real, everyday self, just as he'd realized he should. And as a result, he was pretty sure they were *all* enjoying the afternoon.

And just to reassure her, on one particular occasion when both his palms closed lightly over her hips to keep them from colliding, he leaned near and softly said, "I'm not trying to put the moves on you here, by the way."

"I know," she said pleasantly over her shoulder.

Then they went on about what they were doing, Sue Ann bending to put a tray of cookies in the oven while Adam grabbed milk from the fridge to mix up more icing. Of course, the fact that he wasn't putting the moves on her didn't stop him from enjoying the view of Sue Ann from behind.

Once all the cookies were baked and decorated, Adam asked, "So are we ready to break out those sleds?"

"Yeah!" Sophie yelled.

But Sue Ann, looking pretty damn adorable in a frilly red and white Mrs. Santa themed apron with flour smudged on one cheek, put her hands on her hips and said, "Well, not until we get this mess cleaned up."

Okay, so he hadn't noticed the mess until that moment. But now that he looked, the kitchen table was covered with racks of freshly decorated cookies—with drips of icing and colored sugars sprinkling the spaces in between. The counter was spattered with flour, as well as dirty cookie cutters and a rolling pin. And greasy cookie sheets set stacked atop the stove.

"Make ya a deal," he said.

She tilted her head and didn't quite smile, but a playful gleam entered her gaze. "Let's hear it."

"You forget about this and go sledding with us, and when we come back, I'll do clean-up duty."

In response, she tilted her head the other way, and just when he thought she was going to insist on not leaving the mess for later, she said, "Well, that's an offer too good to pass up, so you got it, mister." She whipped off the apron as Sophie cheered.

Adam headed to the storage shed in the backyard in search of sleds while Sue Ann and Sophie changed into snow clothes and got bundled up. He was pleased to find several old-fashioned, wooden Flexible Flyers, complete with their signature red runners, well-aged and probably passed down through Sue Ann's or Jeff's family—and one of them was even kid-sized. Steel runner sleds weren't great for fresh powder, but today's new snow was light, and a slower ride for Sophie wasn't a bad idea anyway.

Given that he worked outdoors most of the time,

often even in winter, he kept extra gear in his truck, so after dropping the sleds in the driveway, he found himself a hat and a thicker coat to put over the winter jacket he already wore. The snow was really coming down now—but he was actually starting to enjoy this snowy December. At first, it had come far too early for his liking, but he couldn't deny how pretty it looked draping the boughs of evergreens like white icing or lying like a thick blanket now across Sue Ann's rooftop with the Christmas lights he'd put up peeking out from the edge.

And when Sue Ann and Sophie exited the front door, he was reminded that this early snow was what had brought him and Sue Ann together in the first place. So . . . yeah, now that he thought about it, he was suddenly liking the snow a lot.

Within a few minutes, they'd dragged the old sleds up quiet Holly Lane, where the dead end met with an old fence and a thin line of trees that gave way to a vacant, rolling hillside. Sugar Creek, which wound past the Farris-Romo Family Apple Orchard before carving a path south of town, gurgled past somewhere at the foot of the incline.

Adam quickly figured out that Sophie hadn't done much sledding before, so he gave her some pointers and stuck close by her side, taking one of the bigger Flyers down the hill right behind her. Other than a couple of minor spills, she did great, and her laughter made it clear she was having a good time.

Sue Ann didn't seem particularly skilled with the sled herself, and after one or two slow, choppy trips down the hill, she mostly just watched from the top. Adam didn't say anything, keeping his focus on watching out for Sophie, but he couldn't help being amused—she'd acted like she was such a cookie *and* sledding expert earlier.

Once Sophie had really gotten the hang of things and the two of them had just reascended the hill together, wooden sleds pulled behind, he said to her, loud enough for Sue Ann to hear, "You keep going—I'm gonna go help your mom out, make sure to give her a good ride." And Sue Ann's face bloomed a bright pink color in response, from more than just the cold.

Adam couldn't hold in his laughter, which was probably a little lascivious, even as he added, "Down the hill." To let her know she was the only one who'd taken his words in a naughty way—and teasing her about it.

She bit her lip, looking appropriately embarrassed, even as she tried to squelch the grin sneaking out—and Adam wasted no time situating himself on the sled behind her. Which meant pressing his body up against hers, of course. Which was damn nice. "Hi," he whispered low in her ear, leaning close as he reached his arms around her for the Flyer's rope.

"Hi," she whispered back, her voice barely audible, and tinged with a timid ardor that made him just want to wrap around her even closer and pull her into a warm embrace. *But that's not what today is about. Today is about just being with her and Sophie, not pushing the sex, or even the romance.* Even if she felt perfect cuddled in front of him. And even if he feared he was starting to get a little hard against her ass.

"You're not much of a sledder," he said, pointing out the obvious.

"I guess I haven't really gone sledding much since I was a kid. I guess I remember it being easier."

"Well, no worries, sugar plum," he said deeply. "Just hold on and enjoy the ride."

"Hold on where?" she asked.

But Adam had already put the sled in motion and they were beginning to descend the hill, gaining speed, so he said, "Wherever you can." And Sue Ann gripped onto both his knees through the denim and he liked having her hands on him as he maneuvered the sled down the slope.

With so much weight on the Flyer, it picked up speed more rapidly than on other trips, and before he knew it, Sue Ann was letting out a high-pitched squeal, latching her arms around his legs as if for dear life, and expecting him to control the sled at the same time. Not that he minded—while she screeched, he chuckled, the wintry wind brisk on his face and snow flurries flying in his eyes; it was the best damn run down the hill he'd had.

Until—whoops!—the sled flew over a rise too fast, hit the curving slope of snow unevenly, and they both went tumbling off into a rolling heap of flailing arms and legs.

When they came to a stop, they were covered in snow, and Adam lay on top of Sue Ann. They were both laughing—until their eyes met, only a few inches apart. Damn, she felt good under him. "Hi," he said again, low and deep.

"Hi," she returned.

"I'm still not trying to put the moves on you."

"I know." She gave him a small, pretty smile. "But, um, maybe you should get up now."

"Uh—yeah," he said, pushing up off her warm body. He really *hadn't* been trying to put the moves on her—

but laying there in the snow with her had felt too nice, and it had stolen his senses there for a few seconds.

As he reached his gloved hand down to hers, pulling her to her feet, she said, "Thanks for the ride."

When the pale light of the snowy day turned to dusk, they gathered their sleds and headed back to Sue Ann's, where she invited Adam in for dinner. She did it without even weighing it, because it just made sense. "I've had beef stew cooking in the crock pot all day," she told him teasingly, as a lure. Really wanting him to stay. Just not quite ready to be away from him yet.

Because . . . maybe things were slowly changing. Was she crazy to let that happen, to let herself be tempted? Yet to her surprise, she found herself thinking that maybe, just maybe, she could begin to look past what stood between them, to trust in him not to hurt her in any way—by testifying for Jeff or otherwise. And maybe Jenny was right—maybe it wasn't too soon. Maybe she could handle this. Maybe.

Part of her couldn't believe she was starting to let down her guard on this, but a bigger part began to wonder how she'd kept it up for so long.

Still, she planned to move very slowly here—she wasn't sure of anything yet.

"I knew I smelled something good earlier before we started the cookies," Adam said, holding the front door open for her and Sophie.

He never actually said he was going to stay—he just followed them in like it was natural, normal. And though it felt good to step into the cozy warmth of her house, having him there warmed her heart in a whole different way.

As Adam built a fire, Sue Ann lay out wet gloves

and scarves on the big brick hearth, and they decided it was too cozy next to the blaze to leave—after baking up some refrigerated biscuits and dishing up plates of stew, they ate next to the fireplace.

"Who wants cookies?" Sue Ann asked after they were done.

"Me!" Sophie said.

"Me, too," Adam chimed in.

Although Sophie's eyes suddenly bolted open wider. "But be sure to save some for Santa!"

"No problem—I'll make sure we have some on hand for the big guy. If we run out, I'll just make more."

Sue Ann was taking up plates as Sophie turned to Adam to say, "Guess what? Santa's bringing me a reindeer!"

And just like every time Sophie brought up this subject, Sue Ann's heart froze a little, even despite the warmth of the now-blazing fire just a few feet away. She felt Adam's guilt, as well, as they exchanged looks. But she didn't say anything—she'd officially run out of ways to dissuade Sophie from counting on a reindeer on Christmas morning.

"Wow," Adam said, "a reindeer, huh? That . . . sounds like a pretty tall order for Santa."

"No it's not, silly," she said, all confidence as usual when this was discussed. "Santa has lots of reindeer."

"But . . . probably none to spare. It takes eight to pull his sleigh—nine if you count Rudolph," Adam reminded her. "And he probably needs to keep a whole second string on hand, too—in case of . . . injuries or illness. Or maybe they just get worn out from all that flying sometimes. So . . . you should try not to hold it against him if he doesn't bring one."

Sue Ann had headed toward the kitchen, dirty plates

in hand, but she paused at the doorway to listen to her daughter's response. "That's what everybody keeps saying," Sophie told him, "but I know he'll come through. He's Santa. He won't let me down."

That's when Adam promptly changed the subject back to cookies, and she guessed she couldn't blame him because what else could he do? What could *anyone* do? Sophie believed Santa Claus would bring her a reindeer, and nothing was going to change her mind until her heart broke on Christmas morning.

By the time they'd scarfed down a plateful of cookies between them, a glance at the mantel clock told Sue Ann it was later than she'd realized. "Miss Sophie," she announced, "it's just about your bedtime, so you'd best get ready for your bath, and I'll be right up to help." Then she looked to the handsome man sitting by the fire, now stripped down to his blue jeans and a thermal pullover of waffle weave, his dark hair mussed, having gotten wet and then drying that way. "And you, mister, have a date with my messy kitchen."

"Kitchen?" he said in playful denial. "What are you talking about? I, uh, gotta go. My dog is home alone and probably misses me."

"Adam," Sophie said, crossing her arms just like Sue Ann sometimes did before a scolding, "you promised Mommy you'd clean up the cookie mess."

He gave his head an innocent tilt. "I did?"

She nodded emphatically.

"Okay, okay—ya got me," he finally surrendered. Then he pushed to his feet. "Guess I'd better get busy."

And he'd just started to trudge toward the next room when Sophie grabbed onto the tail of his thermal shirt. "Wait."

He turned back, looking down at her.

"Thanks for making cookies and sled riding with us today. You make everything more fun." And then she hugged him.

Wow. Sue Ann hadn't seen that coming. Watching filled her with an overwhelming thankfulness for having him in their lives—and in that moment it had nothing to do with her, with the warmth she felt in his presence or the new ways she'd come to know him recently. Right now it was all about Sophie, and simply being glad he made her happy.

Adam stooped down and returned her daughter's hug, saying, "I had fun, too, kiddo. It was a nice afternoon."

*Indeed it was.* And sometimes that was all you needed in life. A nice afternoon. A good day. Good people in your world. And Sue Ann realized just then, with full clarity, that she was more fortunate than she'd stopped to realize for a while.

. . . the only time I know of, in the long calendar of the year, when men and women seem by one consent to open their shut-up hearts freely . . .

Charles Dickens, A *Christmas Carol*

# *Fourteen*

When Sue Ann walked back downstairs after tucking Sophie in, the sleeves of her turtleneck laden with pastel snowflakes pushed up from helping with the bath, she felt pleasantly tired, the kind of tired that comes from a day well spent. The fire still crackling in the hearth combined with the glow from the Christmas tree to cast warm light across the room, and holiday music played softly. She paused at the foot of the staircase to spend a moment taking it in.

Then she lifted her gaze to see Adam, sleeves also bunched on his forearms, wiping his hands on a dish towel as he entered the living room. "What's up?" he asked quietly.

Sue Ann looked again at the cozy space, then back to

Adam. "Guess I was just thinking that . . . maybe this Christmas isn't so horrible after all. It's still hard, sure, but . . . it's not turning out nearly as awful as I thought. And I couldn't have dreamed I'd say that a few weeks ago."

Coming to stand next to her, he gave a small nod. "For me, too. God knows I'm missing my kids, and I haven't exactly been merry, but . . . at times, the holidays have been . . . downright nice this year. Like tonight."

His gaze locked on hers in the firelight and she suffered a familiar stirring low in her belly—but she wasn't going to let it get the best of her. Even if a part of her wondered if she could let herself ease into a relationship with Adam, for now it was best to keep things simple. So she stepped around him toward an end table where a bowl of popcorn sat. "Want to help me string popcorn? Sophie's class is decorating a tree in the schoolyard with all edible items, for the birds. I'm on popcorn detail and I started last night but didn't get to finish."

"Sure," he said. "I haven't strung popcorn since I was a kid. My grandma used to put it on her tree. Cranberries, too."

"Yeah, it's actually really pretty on a tree. Very light and fluffy-looking. My mom and I used to always put a couple of strands on our tree, then drape it outside after Christmas for the birds to take—but I guess I stopped the tradition after I got married."

Taking a seat on the couch, Sue Ann passed Adam the partial strand she'd already started, then threaded another needle to begin a new string of her own. They worked in companionable silence for a minute before she finally announced, "Guess what? I got a job." She'd had plenty of opportunity to share the news with him through the day, but maybe she'd somehow wanted to save it for a time when it was just the two of them.

His eyes lit up when he looked at her. "Really?"

With her enthusiasm remaining in full swing, she proceeded to tell him all about the promotion to office manager, concluding with, "I still want to pursue selling, too, but I'm excited about this! Not only the increase in income, but also the new challenge—I feel really ready for that right now."

Even as he cast a grin her way, it surprised her when he raised his eyebrows. Until he pointed out, "You mean you haven't had enough challenges lately?"

But she just shrugged, smiling. "Different kind of challenge. *Better* kind of challenge."

"That's great, Sue Ann, really," he said. "I know how worried you were, so I can imagine what a weight that must lift off your shoulders."

She nodded again, still pleased with the change in circumstance—and then grew bold enough to ask about the other big topic they hadn't yet discussed. "So, um . . . what did you decide about testifying for Jeff? Or have you?"

And his grin faded to something more solemn before he replied, "The truth is, guess I've been avoiding giving him an answer—because the more time that goes by, the more I know I don't want to do it. Since you and I have gotten closer than we used to be, it just doesn't seem right."

That warmed her heart for lots of reasons, yet she still felt the need to confirm. "So you're going to tell him no?"

"That's the plan," he said. No hesitation.

And Sue Ann just nodded. Because she didn't want to make a huge deal of it. But wow, what a colossal relief! Between her new job and this . . . well, it was enough to make her think all of Tessa's positive thinking and Amy's book mantras were paying off. Slowly but surely, it seemed the things that had frightened her the most lately were beginning to work themselves out.

Still, she knew this was big for Adam, and she didn't want to downplay that part. "I'm sure it'll be hard to feel like you're letting him down."

He tilted his head to one side. "Yeah, it will. And we might not be friends anymore afterward—that'll be up to him to decide."

Sue Ann said nothing in reply, as no answer seemed needed; she simply resumed working on her popcorn, torn between her own relief and the difficulty the decision had caused Adam.

"So," he said a moment later, "Sophie's doing okay? With all the changes?"

The shift in subject threatened to dampen Sue Ann's mood, but as she pondered the question that still haunted her daily, she tried to view it more logically than emotionally. "She seems fine most of the time. But there are moments when she gets easily upset or seems more . . . needy than before. Like over the kitten at Amy's store. I so want to make this first Christmas without Jeff at home a nice one, to show her life is still good. But the fact that I can't give her what she wants is just going to be one more disappointment."

"And I made things worse with my reindeer promise," he said, sounding guilty.

Though that hadn't been her intent. "You didn't

promise, and I really do understand why you caved on that, so I don't blame you. I just think Christmas morning might be . . . a little rough around here."

"You could always let her have the kitten. That would probably make up for the reindeer."

Yet next to him, Sue Ann sighed. "Sometime I think I should. But . . . I just don't know if I can deal with a kitten right now. Because no matter how you slice it, most of the work would fall to me. And I'll be home a lot less soon. And . . . hell, Adam, some days I don't feel like I can handle even one more thing, you know?"

The look of bewilderment in his eyes, though, caught her off guard. "No, I *don't* know. Because you say stuff like that, but you seem like you're handling everything fine from where I stand. With grace and dignity. You can handle a lot more than you think, sugar plum."

Wow. She was handling her divorce with grace and dignity? Her?

But then, on second thought . . . maybe she was. Maybe in some moments she still saw herself as she'd been at her worst; maybe she couldn't quite stop remembering herself as that hysterical woman who'd shown up barefoot at Jenny's house in the middle of the night. Maybe she'd come a long way toward healing and was only just slowly beginning to realize it.

"Thank you," she finally said, her voice small in the quiet room, barely audible above the hiss and pop of the fire. "So how are the boys?" she asked then, louder, because she didn't want to start acting mushy or fragile.

"Still enjoying their time out West," he said, "but . . . I think they're also starting to miss home. Seven's pretty young to go away that long, which is something that concerned me in the beginning."

"It really is a long time at that age.. Heck, a month is a pretty long time at any age. But Christmas is right around the corner, so they'll be back soon."

"I won't lie—I still miss 'em like crazy," Adam told her. "But . . . days like this help."

"I'm glad," she said. "And they help me, too—because, well, you heard Sophie. Having you here made everything more fun for her."

"More fun for you, too?" he asked speculatively.

And Sue Ann felt a little put on the spot. She didn't like admitting her answer, or the reason for it. She wanted to pretend they were just friends, that this was all just strictly platonic. That was what she'd wanted this to be when she'd invited him over, after all. But as the day progressed . . . well, lying to herself about it seemed pretty fruitless at this point. And she couldn't quite bring herself to lie to him, either—finally saying, "Yes, more fun for me, too." But she kept her eyes on her popcorn and needle, even as her skin prickled at the small confession.

"You know, you were right about what you said that night in the cabin," he told her, the statement seeming to come out of the blue. "Trying to save my marriage would have been futile. There was too much wrong with it. And in fairness to Sheila . . . I know I blamed it all on her, but when things started to fizzle, maybe I became emotionally . . . distant or something. Maybe that's why she started getting jealous and paranoid."

"All this just suddenly hit you?" she couldn't help asking. Especially given that he'd originally been so close-mouthed about his divorce. But maybe this meant he felt he could confide in her now.

"Well, I've had a lot of time to think with the boys

gone—more time than usual in a quiet house, just me and the dog." He fished in the big bowl sitting between them on the couch for another piece of popcorn. "And figuring out that part of the fault lies with me, too, was kind of a revelation. Nobody's . . . completely blameless."

Sue Ann sucked in her breath as the idea permeated her—and stung a little. She paused, a fluffy kernel between her fingertips, and lifted her gaze cautiously to his. "Do you think part of the fault lies with me—when it comes to Jeff?"

"That's not what I meant—I was only talking about *my* marriage."

"But what you said . . . sort of makes sense. About no one being blameless. I just . . . haven't let myself think much about that up to now."

He shrugged and said, "I thought he was happy. He always seemed like it."

"I thought he was happy, too," she agreed. "Life was good. Sex was good. But . . . maybe there was something he needed that I wasn't giving."

The room felt unusually quiet then, even despite the music and the crackling of the fire. She'd spent all these months being angry at Jeff, feeling so beat up and abandoned—and she'd even wondered if those little things about her had somehow driven him away, things like her loud laughter and tendency to blab. But she'd never once allowed herself to truly ask what she was asking now: *Was it somehow my fault, too? Could I have been a better wife in some way?* It was a scary moment for her, especially when Adam gently asked, "Like what?"

Sue Ann swallowed past the small lump swelling in her throat, and let herself speculate out loud. "Maybe

I . . . got too wrapped up in my own life, or in being a mom. Or maybe I didn't appreciate him enough in some way."

"Or maybe," Adam began slowly, "it wasn't you at all. Maybe . . . he just got tired of being perfect."

She blinked. "Huh?"

"You guys were pretty perfect," he pointed out. "Perfect couple in high school. Perfect little family. But it gets hard being perfect. Always doing the right thing, making the right moves, the moves everybody expects. So maybe it wasn't even about you. Maybe it was about something bigger. Maybe he just didn't want to be perfect anymore."

Adam sounded clear-minded on this, but Sue Ann remained confused. "I'm not sure I get it."

That's when he abandoned his string of popcorn in his lap. "I'm just thinking . . . you always thought *I* was awful damn perfect, right? Until I started acting like an ass a few weeks ago. And until I told you what happened with Sheila."

"I guess," she said, his point still lost on her.

"The thing is, on the night of that wedding, that's part of what I was feeling. I was tired of always being the guy who did the right thing, who was always responsible, dependable, who never did anything wrong. It's a lot of pressure. I mean, sometimes I feel like people hold me to a higher standard than they hold themselves—just because they think I'm such a good guy. They expect me to always, always be that good guy, no matter what. And I was so fed up that I just . . . wanted to do what I felt like doing in that moment, for once in my life, without weighing all the right and wrong of it.

"And I regretted it—because I *am* a good guy. But

I'm just saying . . . maybe there were things in Jeff's life that he wished he'd done differently. And when he finally broke down and did something different, it happened to be something that affected you severely."

Sue Ann swallowed, a stab of guilt attacking her out of nowhere. "He wanted to go away to OSU with you after high school, remember? And I talked him out of it. I talked him into staying here with me and going to the community college in Crestview because I was afraid I'd lose him if he left."

Adam's jaw went slack. "Wow. I didn't know that."

She bit her lip, nodded. "I asked him not to tell anyone. Because I didn't want his parents or friends to think I was holding him back. And Prince Charming that he was—at the time—he took total responsibility for the decision. Even with me—he told me he'd decided he really didn't want to go. But deep down, I knew he had doubts. I was just too selfish and insecure to ever explore them—I was just happy he was staying here with me."

"Well, even so, the choice was his," Adam replied, clearly trying to make her feel better. "He must have wanted you more than he wanted OSU."

She let out a sigh, thought back through it all. "He never seemed unhappy with the choice," she agreed. "Still . . . if he'd gone to OSU, maybe it would have worked out that he'd have been more satisfied with his life *now*."

Yet Adam just shrugged. "Who knows? Maybe, maybe not. And . . . don't think I'm taking up for him, okay? I've told you before, I don't like the way he's handled anything about this situation."

But now Sue Ann had delved deeper into this idea

that Jeff wasn't the only one to blame, and it was making her ask herself still more questions, continue to examine it in this new way. "Maybe I quit working—at my marriage," she suggested. "Maybe I thought everything was so perfect that I didn't even have to try anymore."

After a moment, Adam blew out a long breath and said, "Yeah . . . like I said, I quit working at mine, too." He stopped then, staring into the fire—yet he appeared to see something more. "I think marriage is . . . a constant work in progress. Like it's always changing and evolving, and if you take your focus off of it for very long . . . "

"It collapses," Sue Ann said.

"Yeah," he replied quietly. But she didn't expect the sour expression that came over him. "Damn, I'm sorry I even brought up the subject of marriage now."

"Why?"

"When I started this, I wanted to tell you that what you said in the cabin helped me realize some stuff, like that my marriage wasn't really meant to be saved, and that I probably even knew that all along but just couldn't admit it to myself. But I didn't want to make you feel bad, like anything that happened with Jeff was your fault."

"I . . . don't feel bad, though," she said, tilting her head as she realized the whole truth. Lowering her string of popcorn back into the bowl, she turned sideways on the couch to face Adam, pulling her legs up under her. "In fact, maybe I'm finally starting to find a little clarity. I mean, for so long I just felt abandoned for no reason and couldn't stop wondering why. So . . . maybe this is weird, but just knowing that there might be an answer that makes sense, even if I don't know exactly what it is, actually helps."

"Well, I'm glad. Because I want you to be happy, Sue Ann." As his warm gaze met hers, he turned toward her on the couch, too—and she had a feeling it was a good thing the popcorn bowl sat between them or that he might be kissing her. And that she might be letting him.

"Thanks," she said, perhaps a bit too breathily. And it seemed like a damn good time to change the subject, and to quit all the meaningful mooning into each other's eyes that had just started. "So . . . I'm going to sell the house. In the spring."

"Wow," he said. "That's huge. Especially after all the work you guys put in on it."

She nodded, still totally at ease with the decision. "Yeah, but . . . I don't need it anymore. I don't need all this space. To heat or to clean. And I don't need to hang onto it—because it's part of a life that was in my past. I need a new place . . . and a fresh start."

He nodded in return, looking pleased. "That's great. And if there's anything I can do to help, just let me know."

"Be careful," she teased, smiling now, "or I might decide I need a fix-it man to whip things into shape around here and take you up on that."

"I'd be happy to be your fix-it man, Sue Ann," he told her smoothly, his voice going a bit deeper, his eyes once again making her feel as if he'd actually reached out to touch her—and she felt that invisible touch everywhere. *Whoa.*

"Well, it's getting late," she said—maybe too abruptly. Because yeah, it was a huge relief that he'd decided not to testify for Jeff, and even more enormous if he'd done that for *her*. And she definitely felt a real connection with him tonight. But none of that meant it would be wise to suddenly go rushing headlong into this.

And he clearly got the point and wasn't going to fight her on it. "You're right," he replied easily, slowly beginning to get to his feet. "It's been a long day, and I'm sure you're tired. I am, too."

"Yeah," she murmured behind him, standing up herself, moving the popcorn bowl to the coffee table, then following him toward the foyer, where his coat hung and his boots sat waiting from when he'd taken them off after sledding. But then she glanced over her shoulder to the fireplace, remembering. "Oh, your gloves and hat—I'll go get 'em."

When she returned, he'd put on his boots and jacket, and he clutched the collar of the bigger parka he'd worn for sledding in one fist. Sue Ann found herself reaching up with both hands to pull his knit hat onto his head, then playfully wrapping his scarf around his neck, twice, as he smiled down at her.

"Okay, I think I'm all bundled up, Mom," he said.

She laughed softly, then turned to open the door, now—suddenly—feeling oddly . . . hesitant. Since, inside, she didn't really want him to go. She just knew that he should, knew it was best.

*Best, best, best,* she told herself. Even when he stepped up into the open doorway, looking incredibly cuddly and warm. Even when the cold air rushed in around them and made her want to snuggle in his arms.

Just then, Shemekia Copeland's sexy "Stay a Little Longer, Santa" began to play, echoing into the foyer, reminding her of that moment in the church basement when she'd wanted to kiss Santa Adam so badly that her whole body had tingled with it. And oh Lord, it was tempting—everything *about* him was tempting. And maybe someday—maybe even sooner than she'd thought—she'd be able to open her heart to him more, to get past her fears.

But for now—best, best, best. *Just let him go. Just let the night end.*

Adam knew he should just walk away. They'd had a nice day together—more than a nice day—and it was time to leave. Hell, she'd even put his hat on for him, and as much as he liked having her that close—well, it was a pretty big hint. *She wants you to go. So don't be an idiot and blow this nice thing you've had with her today.*

And yet . . . damn. She looked so pretty standing there just a few inches away from him, all the snowflakes on her close-fitting turtleneck seeming to hug her body, transforming her into a living snow angel before his very eyes. And with everything in him, he burned to make her believe he was a good man who could be counted on, a man she should have in her life. And his body ached for her.

It wasn't a decision he made so much as a driving compulsion that led him to lift his hand to her cheek, chilled now from the cold night wind swirling around them. And he could see in those pretty brown eyes that he wasn't the only one wanting more. Even if she was sending him away. His heart beat faster with the knowledge, the knowledge that made him lean slowly down . . . until his mouth pressed against hers.

She sucked in her breath as he kissed her—but then she relaxed into it and began to kiss him back, like an invitation to stretch it out, deepen it. So Adam took his time, moving his mouth on hers, drinking in the taste and feel of her, wanting her in a more profound way than he ever had before.

When finally he ended the passionate kiss, it left him a little breathless—and he leaned his forehead over against hers, trying to get hold of himself. They stayed that way, silent, still, until he raised his head back up to peer down at her. And his next words came straight from the heart—he didn't weigh it, he just said it. "Sue Ann, I think we could really have something together if you'd give me a chance."

Again, the woman standing so close to him pulled in her breath, let it back out. Then she whispered up to him. "I want to, I really do. I'm just . . . not sure."

"I know," he told her. "I get it, I understand."

And then—God help him—he kissed her again. Once more, it wasn't planned, it wasn't a choice—it was just the chemistry between them, smoldering hotter and hotter. It was simply what his body told him to do, and he was beyond fighting it. He wanted to simply be close to her, listen to her breathe, touch her face, kiss the little shell-shaped ear she'd just shoved a lock of hair behind.

And so when the kiss was over, that's what he did—he found himself pressing his mouth to her cheek, then moving to kiss the rounded edge of her delicate little ear. He drank in the scent of her hair, let it swirl in his senses along with the aroma of the pine wreath on the open door and the much more vague smell of winter, and snow. She clutched at his jacket now, her fingers curling into fists at his chest as he stopped himself once again but didn't move, his mouth still touching the tender flesh

of her ear. "I'm sorry," he told her, sounding—feeling—
a little shaky now. "I don't mean to . . . "

"I know," she whispered below him—but like him,
she didn't move, didn't let go. They stood frozen that
way, like an ice sculpture in the doorway, for so long
that Adam finally began to feel the cold seeping into
his skin, and he figured Sue Ann must be freezing.

"Are you cold?" he asked.

"Yes." She nodded.

"I can keep you warm, Sue Ann."

She drew back slightly, looked up at him. "I know,
but . . . " She still grasped at the fabric across his chest
like she was gripping a lifeline. "I still don't know if
I'm ready to trust somebody again, Adam."

"Do you want me to go?"

"Yes," she murmured—and he was crushed. Until
she added, "No," and he understood. She was torn. And
it was his fault. And God, he was sorry about that, but
right now . . . damn, right now, if she wasn't going to
make him go, if she wasn't going to push him away or
tell him to stop . . . he couldn't. He just didn't possess
the will.

So he kissed her again—but not as slowly as before,
and not as soft. And as she returned the kiss, as her
arms looped sweetly around his neck, he found himself
shifting their bodies away from the door and using one
foot to kick it closed and finally shut out the cold.

He backed her out of the foyer—still kissing her the
whole time, needing her wildly—and toward the living
room. She stopped the kissing then, just long enough
to untwine the scarf from around his neck and begin
working at the zipper on his jacket. He'd dropped his
bigger winter coat somewhere along the way in order

to free up his hands, both of which he lifted to her face as he moved in for another hungry kiss—and then he found himself letting them glide downward, his touch skimming over her chest, her round breasts, finally stopping at her waist.

They both breathed heavily now, and Sue Ann pushed his jacket from his shoulders. He let go of her only long enough to free himself of it—and then he was closing his arms around her waist and shifting their position once more, until they fell back on the couch, her underneath him, right where he wanted her.

He resumed their kisses as he gently lowered his weight, nestling his hard cock at the perfect juncture of her thighs. She pulled in her breath, the sound at once lovely and urgent, as he kissed her yet again, hot and sweet, pressing his tongue between her lips as one palm molded gently to her outer thigh. God, it felt good to touch her, to get to explore her curves again. And as they made out, his hand slid smoothly up over her hip, into the feminine indention of her waist, and back onto her breast—where he let it stop. Her soft, heated gasp only fueled him and he began to massage the soft mound—slow, deep, thorough.

Oh yeah, this being-real-with-her thing—it was working. Big time.

When he spoke, his voice came out raspy near her ear. "I, uh, might be trying to put the moves on you now," he admitted, half teasing, half not. Yet then he immediately recanted, rethinking it. "But . . . not really *trying*. So they're not really moves. I don't plan it. It's just what keeps happening when I'm with you. I keep wanting you."

"I want you, too," she breathily confessed, the words

stiffening his erection even more. "But . . . Sophie's right upstairs."

"How about your bedroom?" he suggested. "We'll lock the door, but you'll be right there if she needs you for anything."

"Spoken like a true parent," she said, peering up at him, voice still weak with passion.

"No," he told her. "Just spoken like a guy who wants to make hot, sweet love to you."

"Pray come to me."

Charles Dickens, A *Christmas Carol*

# *Fifteen*

Adam trailed after her up the stairs, eager to get behind that bedroom door with her as fast as humanly possible, his every male sense in overdrive. *Thank God she didn't make me leave. Thank God the bedroom suggestion worked for her. Thank God we're almost there.*

Once at the top of the old wooden stairs, he followed her silently past the darkened doorway he knew to be Sophie's, then down the hall and into the bedroom he'd been in only once before, on the day he'd helped Jeff and Sue Ann move in almost ten years ago. This room, too, was bathed in darkness until Sue Ann flicked on a dim bedside lamp to reveal a room done in pale shades of pink and green, a log cabin quilt adorning the big four-poster Shaker-style bed.

When she turned to face him, he nearly gulped at the

sight of her. Yeah, he'd spent the whole afternoon and evening with her, but it was the look in her eyes right now: some combination of innocence and hunger, of caution overridden by want. And again, he hated that he'd made her feel she had to be cautious about him— but he was pretty damn excited by the want.

"Shut the door," she whispered, reminding him.

"Oh," he mumbled—that quickly, he'd forgotten, too caught up in his desire. So he turned to quietly close it, flipping the old lock, and it felt like isolating them in a private cocoon together.

He spent another hushed moment just looking at her then, aware that their previous encounters had been fraught with uncertainty or surprise, awkwardness or hesitation—and this wasn't like that. This time there was no reason to rush, or to feel uncomfortable. Now they could take their time.

"Take off your clothes for me," he requested with calm confidence. "I want to see you. The other times, I barely got to enjoy that part."

His admission brought a small, brief smile to her face—just before she crossed her arms toward her hips and removed the turtleneck over her head. Underneath, she wore a lacy ice-blue bra, the rounded curves of her breasts swelling provocatively from the cups, so pretty that it almost took his breath away. Or maybe it was still the expression on her face making him harder by the second—she bit her lower lip, the color of ripe berries, looking at once shy but ready, her eyes burning on him in invitation.

Tossing the turtleneck aside, she then reached for the button on her jeans and soon began to slither out of them, wiggling her hips until they dropped, then step-

ping free of the denim. When he saw her panties—
simple white cotton but sporting little pale blue
snowflakes—he couldn't resist a grin. "I like the way
your panties match your turtleneck."

She smiled timidly back. "Believe it or not, a complete coincidence."

But he didn't care. Coincidental or not, he still
thought of her as his own personal snow angel now.
And he knew exactly what he wanted to *do* to his snow
angel. "Lie down," he whispered, his voice coming out
deeper without planning it. He wanted to make her feel
good.

She sucked in her breath lightly at the command,
perhaps a little caught off guard—but then sat on the
edge of the bed, soon lying on her side, propped on one
elbow as she continued looking at him.

"Aren't you gonna get undressed, too?" she asked.

"Right now is all about you," he informed her.

"Then you should take off your clothes, because
that's what I want."

Okay, that he could get into. In fact, it sent a fresh
wave of heat all through him. For some reason, it reminded him of that first night they'd spent together,
of the moment she'd turned quietly more aggressive,
going down on her knees and taking him in her mouth.
He *liked* Sue Ann getting a little aggressive. So as he
moved toward the bed, he didn't hesitate to rip off his
thermal pullover and throw it aside, then undo the
button on his jeans.

Yet after that he forgot about getting his jeans off—
because that's when he reached her. And other urges
took over.

Placing one knee on the mattress next to her, he

climbed atop the quilt, near her feet. He hadn't noticed, but she still wore socks, fuzzy ones the same pale blue as her lingerie. Another grin snuck out as he lifted one ankle in his hand. "These are sexy," he told her.

She flashed a playful smirk. "Shut up and take them off me."

"That'll be my pleasure, sugar plum."

Yet he didn't just take them off—as he flung the first blue sock aside, he kept her ankle balanced in his hand, then bent down to kiss the top of her foot. She pulled in her breath in response and the look in her eyes was more than welcoming. Oh yeah, he liked Sue Ann this way. Finally.

Tossing the other sock away, he dipped down to rain gentle kisses across that foot as well, which made her bite her bottom lip as her gaze narrowed sexily on him. *And I'm just getting started, babe.*

From there Adam made slow, thorough work of kissing his way up Sue Ann's smooth calves and ascending the top of one silky thigh. Her sharp little intake of breath as he passed over her hip to reach her stomach stiffened the bulge in his jeans further, especially when she began to thread her fingers through his hair. Her skin tasted slightly salty and sweet.

Soon he kissed a path between her breasts, letting his hands play over their outer curves, brushing his thumbs across her nipples just one soft, teasing time. He loved her hot, gentle gasp, but he didn't let it stop him from easing more kisses upward, onto her slender neck, which she bent to one side to accommodate him.

When he reached the spot just below her ear, he whispered, "Feel good?"

"Mmm, feels good," she promised. Still all sexy and inviting. Still no doubt.

Of course, he couldn't be that near her face without kissing her pretty lips, so that's what he did next, just following the instincts of his mouth. As he pressed his tongue inward, her own joined the sensual fray, and they continued that way for a few long, languid moments while he used his hands to slowly, tenderly explore her—caressing her neck and shoulders, her stomach and waist, and the perfect breasts hidden under lace.

And yeah, he wanted to go slow right now, but he was getting harder by the second and he wasn't a saint, so it wasn't long before he found himself lowering one icy blue bra strap and kissing his way down onto the mound of flesh within the cup. And mmm—oh God, yeah. Her soft little moan told him she was as excited as him, especially when he closed his mouth over her beautifully taut nipple—a firm, tight bead on his tongue.

As he got lost in the pleasure of suckling her, Sue Ann lifted slightly, reaching behind her to undo her bra. When it loosened around her, it felt, again, as if she was . . . giving herself to him, freely, willingly, without apprehension, for the first real time. He eased back just enough to pull the bra away and peer down on her. "You're so beautiful," he said, and—damn—his voice actually trembled a little.

That's when their eyes met. She'd heard it, too, the quiver in his voice. He didn't know why he was embarrassed exactly—he'd already been honest with her, he'd told her that he wanted something with her, he'd made no secret of how hot she got him—but maybe a shaky voice showed just how much. Maybe a little *too* much.

That's how he felt—weirdly exposed, at risk, and like maybe he wanted her even more than he'd realized up until this very moment. Yet his vulnerability faded quickly when she dropped her eyes from his face to his bare chest, lifting one palm flat against it, then gliding her touch downward toward the waistband of his jeans to say, "You're pretty damn beautiful yourself, Mr. Becker. And I want you so, so much."

But it wasn't just sex. He could see in her eyes and hear in her tone, as well, that it was more. That even though she'd been trying like hell to fight this, it wasn't only the physical part she'd been fighting; she'd been battling the bigger part, too—the relationship part. And now he sensed that she was giving in, starting to believe in him, finally starting to believe it was safe to let this thing between them happen.

Adam sucked in his breath, then lowered his body over hers—and his mouth back over hers, too. He kissed her deep and thorough, first taking her face in his hands, but then letting his touch drift south to caress all those sensuous curves below. Sometimes it was still hard to believe this was Sue Ann, the Sue Ann he'd been around for years without ever a real sexual thought—you just didn't let yourself go there with your best friend's girl—but slowly, he was starting to get used to the idea. This was Sue Ann, and she'd been walking around this town his whole life with this beautiful, responsive body hidden beneath her clothes, and now, for tonight anyway, it was his.

The thought inspired him back to kissing her all over again—since he'd kind of stopped his own progress before with the whole trembling voice incident. But within seconds, her soft, round breasts were in his grasp and he was kissing and licking them with passionate abandon. He twirled his tongue around one turgid nipple, making her moan, and lifted his gaze to see her leaning her head back, eyes shut, body stretched out in pure oblivion. Oh yeah.

And as much as he hated to leave her perfect breasts behind, soon he found himself kissing his way farther down, back over her smooth stomach dotted with just a few freckles, and onto the little rise of flesh below her belly button that led to her panties.

This time, though, rather than bypass the delicate blue-flaked bikini undies, he curled his fingers into the elastic at her hips, urging her to lift her ass, then began to peel them down. His chest tightened and his heart beat too fast as he went about getting them completely off her and dropping them over the edge of the bed—and then he moved back in, using his hands to part her legs.

After allowing himself the indulgence of studying her there for a moment, his eyes met hers and he didn't try to hide his lust. "You just lay back and relax, sugar plum," he told her, "because I'm about to make you feel so damn good you won't be able to stand it."

A small, sexy smile formed on her face, and her voice came like a purr. "And you think I'll be able to relax through *that*?"

He grinned. "Good point. You won't. So just lay back and enjoy instead."

"All right," she whispered, soft and sweet, and Adam couldn't wait another second—he bent to begin kissing his way up her inner thigh.

She sucked in her breath in response, and when he saw how it affected her, he made himself slow the hell down, remember that he wanted to stretch this out, give her every conceivable pleasure. And when her hot sighs

turned to sexy little whimpers, he knew he was suc-
ceeding.

When finally he reached the juncture of her thighs, he
kissed her there, gently, eliciting a high-pitched moan.
Aw, damn—part of him, the hungry part, just wanted
to take her, hard, right here and now. But the part of
him who liked being a good lover, pleasing his partner,
continued to kiss her, lick her, pleasure her, sinking
into the task until he knew he was just as aroused from
it as she was.

Her breath came harder, heavier, as she let herself
move against him, lift herself toward his ministrations.
It made him relish tasting her that much more. He fo-
cused now, though, on the sensitive little nub that was
swollen with need, licking it, then closing his mouth
around it to suck.

Above him, her panting breath turned to moans and
her moans to hot little sobs that fueled him. He sensed
her moving closer to orgasm with each passing second.
At moments she held onto his head, threaded her fingers through his hair; at others she curled her hands
into fists in the quilted squares beneath her. Adam got
so deeply into laving and suckling her moist flesh that
at some point his eyes had fallen shut, but when she
began to cry out, he opened them, watching her come
even as he continued working his tongue on her.

Partway through the orgasm, she clamped her mouth
closed tight, clearly trying to be quiet, remembering
Sophie—but as far as he could tell, it didn't dampen
her pleasure, and in fact, the climax seemed to stretch
on and on, Sue Ann undulating against his ministrations the whole time.

When finally she went still, silent, she seemed breathless, completely spent, and he liked it.

"Wow," she breathed. "That was nice."

Crawling up alongside her on the bed, he slanted her a look, half grinning. "Again with the nice? Come on, woman—be serious."

She giggled prettily and pointed out, "I said 'wow' first."

But he just kept the same doubtful, prodding look on her, until she finally drew him into a warm, easy embrace and said, "Okay, that was the most incredible, mind-blowing, heartstopping orgasm I've ever had. I saw fireworks. The earth moved. And I heard angels sing. Happy now?"

He gave her a short—and maybe slightly arrogant—nod. "Damn straight."

And more of her soft, trilling laughter filled the space around him, making him just . . . happy. Happy to be in her arms.

But being happy shifted quickly back to being aroused when Sue Ann's expression went more sultry and she reached for his zipper. "Fireworks or not, though," she said, "I still want more."

"And you're about to get it," he promised her, pushing his jeans and underwear down with her help.

He loved the little gasp she emitted when she saw his erection—he was pretty sure it made his cock stand a little stiffer between his legs. And he loved it even more when she boldly took him into her hand, warm and firm and perfect as she squeezed and caressed.

"Oh God, honey, that feels nice," he rasped.

"Nice?" she teased—and a short laugh escaped him.

"Amazing," he corrected himself. "I meant hot and amazing. Seriously. Completely perfect."

"Well, if that's so great," she teased him, "I wonder what you'll think of *this*." And then she eased down in the bed and didn't hesitate to lower her beautiful, soft mouth over him. And—damn—he loved that the most so far. And he let himself lay back in bed and watch her, let himself drink in the hot, naughty pleasure as Sue Ann Kinman made love to him with her mouth.

But the truth was, the part he ended up loving best of all was when, a few minutes later, he rolled his body on top of hers and sank his erection into her wet warmth. "Aw, damn, sugar plum," he rasped, "now *this* is perfect." Because besides the deep pleasure it sent roaring through his body, it felt . . . well, like exactly where he was supposed to be, like where he belonged.

Sue Ann was almost overwhelmed by the fullness, the utter sense of completion she experienced with Adam inside her now. After the day they'd spent together, all the laughter and the talking, this was . . . mmm, the most fulfilling culmination of it all that she could imagine. Thank God she hadn't been able to resist. And now, somehow . . . something was changing inside her where he was concerned.

And it was about more than just Adam—it was about her, too. About her way of seeing the world, of looking at life. For months now, her viewpoint had been shadowed—downright sullied—by divorce, loss of trust, loss of faith that she'd ever really be happy again. But Adam was truly helping her look beyond that.

And then—wow—something hit her. Where they were. Should it matter, should it be a big deal to her that this was the bedroom, the very bed, she'd shared with Jeff all those years? Because . . . it didn't. In fact, it had taken this long for the thought to even surface. And now, well, the bed felt like it was hers, only hers, and like she was free to do whatever she wanted here. And right now she wanted to roll around with Adam Becker. She wanted to feel him moving in her, sliding, thrusting deep, making her moan.

Oh God, she was crazy about him. She'd known that all along, of course, ever since that night in the cabin, but she'd just been unable to let herself accept it, to let herself trust in him. And she wasn't sure how exactly this had happened, how she'd ended up in bed with him tonight finally feeling like . . . like it was okay to be here, okay to enjoy him, okay to soak up all that pleasure without also soaking up the fears. But as their bodies connected—again, again, his strokes deep and potent—she knew he was slowly wiping away her doubts.

And what was happening between them now was . . . more than it had been before. Before, they had shared good, hot sex—but this, now, had also become exactly what he'd called it earlier, downstairs: making love.

And yes, she'd let him seduce her again—but this time it was about more than lust and physical need. She was so tempted, so close, to putting her faith in him that she could taste it in the kisses she gave him as they moved together.

Sure, he was Jeff's best friend, and that could cause problems—but the fact that Adam had decided to refuse Jeff's request changed things. After all, the main issue she'd been worrying about the last couple of weeks seemed to have faded away with Adam's plan not to testify. And sure, the similarities in the ways their marriages had ended still bothered her a little, and it still seemed far too soon to dive into another relationship. But maybe the time had come to just push such logical thoughts aside. Maybe it was time to let her heart, and her desire, guide her.

When Adam pulled out of her, she gasped, stunned and disappointed by the sudden emptiness. But then he let his gaze sweep over her body as he gently rolled her onto her side, facing away from him, and when his erection nestled against her ass, a low moan erupted from her throat. "Just want to make you feel me deeper," he murmured in her ear. And then he was pushing tightly back into her warmth, and a satisfied sigh left her as the fullness returned.

"You feel so, so good, Sue Ann," he told her as he began to thrust again.

"You, too," she whispered, happy to be sharing this with him, and still amazed that her holiday season had taken such a shocking turn. Not only was she having sex with Adam—but she was having sex with Adam *freely, joyfully.* Joy to the world.

That's when Adam's drives into her most sensitive flesh grew harder, more intense, and Sue Ann had to fight to hold back her sobs of pleasure, biting her lip, absorbing each hot plunge all the way to her core.

Behind her, his heavy, panting breaths turned to low groans as he gripped her hips tight, *thrusting, thrusting, thrusting*, and Lord—she did almost see fireworks.

"Aw God," he rasped, "I'm gonna come, honey. I'm gonna come." And Sue Ann closed her eyes and loved having taken him there, loved having him adore her, loved the power she felt bursting from his body into hers.

When she rolled to her back a moment later, she sighed. "Mmm, that was—"

"Please don't say nice."

"That was magnificent," she promised with a smile.

He gave her a small, sexy grin as they lay facing each other on the same pillow. "It was pretty damn magnificent for me, too, honey."

Turning farther toward Adam, she cuddled against his broad chest as he curved one arm snugly around her. They hadn't gotten to do this part in his truck, so it took her thoughts back to the cabin. Except . . . at the same time it reminded her that everything was different now—in a good way. No more worry. No more big questions. Just the sweet afterglow of pleasure.

"I liked that you were . . . " he began, then paused, "I don't know, more about enjoying it this time than trying not to."

She bit her lip, a slight blush warming her cheeks. "I . . . I feel different now."

He shifted to look down at her, meet her gaze. "Yeah, I could tell that, but . . . what changed?"

"I guess I'm starting to get used to the idea. Of me and you. Together."

"I like hearing that," he said with a smile both sweet and sexy. But then the smile paled, leaving behind an earnest, almost vulnerable expression. "You can trust me, Sue Ann. You know that, don't you?"

She blinked, still a little overwhelmed by her own feelings—and even a bit surprised when she heard herself say, "I'm starting to. I'm really starting to."

On Monday, Adam took the day off. He was the boss— he could do that, and he trusted Chuck to handle the not-very-busy tree lot.

Feeling more energetic than he had for the past few weeks, he did some work around the house—some cleaning and overdue laundry—and actually found himself smiling through the tasks. He realized he didn't mind the quiet for a change. And he found himself playing with the dog more than he had lately, and scratching behind Pepper's ears every time the lovable collie's claws clicked across the hardwood floor in his direction.

Of course, he knew his mood was thanks to Sue Ann. And again, it wasn't just because they'd had fanfreaking-tastic sex Saturday night—it was because she was beginning to come around. Maybe she wasn't *all the way* around just yet, but she was getting damn close. And he wanted to keep showing her that she was making the right decision, that he wouldn't let her down. Hell, he just wanted to make the woman happy.

After a nice phone conversation with Joey and Jacob—a little later than usual, as they were taking a day off from the slopes for schoolwork—Adam headed into his home office and turned on the computer. He wasn't sure he should get Sue Ann a Christmas gift, but as he'd left her place the other night, quietly padding past Sophie's door, down the stairs, and out past the still-lit tree in the bay window, an idea had hit him, an idea of something he'd love to give her if he could. But it might not be easy to find.

*So if I don't find it, maybe it just isn't meant to be. And if I do, it is.* That seemed like a wise enough way to look at the situation.

Heading to the Google site, he typed in a few words to start his search. And though what he sought didn't appear on his screen immediately, within five minutes there it was. He thought it was the right one, anyway. And as he completed the transaction, he hoped it would make her Christmas a little brighter.

And then it struck him. Damn, Christmas. It was suddenly right around the corner. And though he hadn't succeeded in getting in the holiday spirit so far—well, now he found himself bundling up, heading out to his own tree lot even after taking the day off, and toting home a tree.

He'd be having a late celebration with the kids when they got back, after all, and it wouldn't be right if he didn't have a tree for them. And as he draped the garland and hung the ornaments, he realized maybe he wouldn't mind having it around, either. It would make the place more cheerful until the twins came home, that was for sure.

He finished the task an hour later, and when he glanced out the window to see it was snowing again, he got yet one more idea. And a damn good one, he thought. Of course, Grampy Hoskins, who was home from visiting his sister now, might not think so, because it would require the old man loaning him something pretty sizable. But then again, the way he saw it, Grampy owed him for that whole Santa gig, big-time.

So he didn't hesitate to pick up the phone and dial up the General Mercantile, the old-fashioned grocery store the friendly old guy owned not far from the town square.

"It's Adam Becker," he said when Grampy answered. "And I think you owe me a favor."

Sue Ann nearly floated through the day at Destiny Properties. She answered the phone merrily. She typed up memos and contracts with a smile on her face. And she felt lighter, happier, than she had in . . . well, in almost as long as she could remember. Suddenly that nagging, gnawing pull when you were nuts about a guy didn't seem quite so agonizing. *Because you're letting yourself go. With Adam. You're letting yourself feel it. All of it.* And she still wasn't a hundred percent sure that was wise, but after Saturday night . . . well, it was too late to turn back now.

Rather than grabbing a quick sandwich at Dolly's and bringing it back to the office as she did on many days when she worked, she whisked into Under the Covers and insisted Amy go to lunch with her instead.

"What has *you* so happy?" Amy asked, looking a little dumbfounded as they walked up the street bundled in their winter coats.

"Um . . . Christmas," she fudged.

But Amy very decisively said, "That's not it."

That Amy—sometimes she was too smart for her own good. But Sue Ann just smiled, insisting, "That's my story and I'm stickin' to it."

Over lunch, Amy brought up the topic of Sue Ann selling her house. "Any idea where you and Sophie will move?" she asked.

And even as Sue Ann gave her head a soft shake, she felt . . . a fresh sense of renewal inside her. A new sense of hope for the future. Part of that had been brewing in her ever since she'd learned about her upcoming promotion, but now she wondered if the inner joy she was experiencing today could possibly be attributed to Adam, as well. "I'm not sure," she replied merrily. "But someplace smaller. And probably a fixer-upper. I'd like to do more of that, you know? The way I refurbished the one I have now."

And yes, she and Jeff had fixed up the Victorian *together,* but the ideas had all been hers, and she'd just recently started recalling how much she'd enjoyed taking something old and giving it new life. And even as she returned to the real estate office a little while later, the idea kept her energized and continued spurring still more fresh, hopeful thoughts in her head.

It began to snow in mid-afternoon, heavily, and though everyone else at Destiny Properties moaned and groaned about the drive home, Sue Ann stayed quiet. Of course, the trip to Holly Lane was short—only a few blocks—but the snow suddenly seemed even prettier than she'd noticed recently, and it reminded her of that first encounter with Adam at Bear Lake.

Sophie would be with Jeff tonight, but even that didn't bring her down. She was capable of having a perfectly pleasant time on her own, and it looked like it would be a good evening to curl up next to the fire with a blanket and a book—maybe even her real estate manual. Time was about to become a commodity for her, so no time like the present to start using it wisely.

Most of the office's small staff all trickled out early due to the weather, but Sue Ann offered to stay behind, finishing up a few tasks before locking up. After which— wrapped in coat and hat—she stepped down from the small building's snow-covered front stoop, lifted her gaze, and . . . oh, she couldn't hold in her small gasp.

Adam stood leaning up against a streetlamp just a few yards away, hands in his pockets, clearly waiting on her. And even bundled in a thick winter jacket, scarf, and a hat, he still looked just as hot and hunky as usual.

Despite the cold and snow, a wave of heat traveled the length of her body. "Adam," she said, their eyes meeting. "What are you doing here?"

"Since it's snowing, thought I'd come by and take you home."

She gave her head a playful tilt. "That's sweet, but believe it or not, I really am capable of driving a few blocks in bad weather."

He only shrugged, grinned, and something about it warmed her even further.

"Where's your truck?" she asked then, not seeing it parked along the street or in the small adjacent lot where her car sat.

"I, uh, brought something else," he replied, sounding just a little mischievous. Then he took her hand and led her around the corner, where—oh my!—before her, right on the town square, set a red horse-drawn sleigh, looking like it had come straight from a Currier and Ives print.

"And we're taking the long way," he said.

. . . a ripe little mouth that seemed made to be kissed—
and no doubt it was . . .

Charles Dickens, A *Christmas Carol*

## Sixteen

"Is that . . . Grampy Hoskins' sled?" she asked, wide-
eyed at the sight.

"Yep," Adam said. She recognized it because the old
man pulled the antique sleigh into his front yard as a
decoration every December. "It's mine for the night,
though, complete with the horse."

Sue Ann couldn't hold back her smile, her pulse
kicking up a little. "You did this for *me*?"

He simply gave a short nod, like it was nothing. "I
just remembered you saying once or twice over the
years that you thought it sounded romantic to take a
sleigh ride. And . . . as far as I know, you never got to
take one, right?"

Her heart warmed all the more—what a sweet,
thoughtful gesture. "Right—never did."

"Well," he said, motioning to the big red sled, "your chariot awaits, milady." Then he took her hand and helped her climb up onto the black leather seat.

Once he was sitting beside her, he draped a fleece blanket over their legs, then scooped up the reins. And now Sue Ann felt a little like she'd stepped beyond the Currier and Ives print—right into a fairy tale fantasy. And sure, it was only little old Destiny, all the same buildings and streets she'd seen her whole life—but maybe it felt different from inside the sleigh, nestled up against a handsome man. The town square lay silent and still, today's snowfall heavy enough to send most people home already, and as the sled proceeded up the street past the fire and police stations, then town hall, the buildings and storefronts all adorned in a glistening mantle of white, Destiny felt . . . enchanting. And like it was theirs alone, their private little winter hamlet. Grampy's horse, a dark brown mare named Clara, even wore bells on her harness, which jingled with every trotting step she took through the fresh snow.

Soon the snowfall lightened until the fat, fluffy flakes only sprinkled down softly upon them, and Adam drove the sleigh out of town toward Blue Valley Road. "I've always thought this route was pretty in the snow," he told her, and he couldn't have been more accurate. Snow clung like lace to the boughs of tall pine trees along the roadside, and when they rounded a bend, bringing Blue Valley Lake into sight, the cottages along the shore looked like tiny gingerbread houses dripping with white, velvety frosting. Ice rimmed the lake's edges in curving scallops, and the water's surface shone a glassy midnight blue even in the flat light of a cold, snowy day.

Adam steered the big sleigh off the road at a quiet spot next to the lake, then pulled up on the reins with a deep "Whoa" that brought Clara to a halt.

And though it was a lovely view, Sue Ann asked, "Why are we stopping?"

"I brought a light dinner—thought we'd have a little in-sleigh picnic," he told her with his usual sexy grin.

She couldn't get over it—Adam had done all this just to give her a special afternoon. And it *was* special. And if any doubts about putting her faith in him still existed on the periphery of her mind . . . well, this all but swept them away. Yes, trust was hard for her right now. But as Adam hoisted a picnic basket from a small chest on the back of the sleigh, she could no longer find any good reasons *not* to trust him.

Of course, maybe doing something sweet didn't have much to do with being trustworthy—but how could a guy prove something like that? And in that moment, she realized that maybe it was about believing, the same way Sophie believed in Santa Claus to bring her a reindeer. Only, while she knew Sophie would be disappointed in the end, she trusted Adam not to let her down. Yes, all this was happening fast—but she was caught up in it now, and finally embracing it, giving herself over to it completely.

Spreading a red and white picnic cloth over the blanket on their laps, Adam served up turkey sandwiches on paper plates. "Like the ones you made us that night at the cabin," he reminded her. With them came pretzels and some potato salad, then slices of pumpkin pie and pumpkin bread, and as she began to eat, it really did remind her of the mishmash of a post-Thanksgiving meal they'd shared.

After doling out all the food, he poured hot chocolate from a thermos into two mugs—and then even produced a plastic container of marshmallows. "The tiny ones you like," he told her.

And that's when her jaw dropped. Because . . . "How do you know that?" She never served marshmallows with hot chocolate at her house—never had. Jeff and Sophie had both always preferred whipped cream, so she just didn't bother with the marshmallows.

"You told me once," Adam said. Grabbing a small handful of marshmallows, he plopped them gently in both cups, which she held. "When we went ice skating on New Year's Eve. Remember?"

Ice skating? Wow. That had been . . . years ago. Before either of them had had kids. The two couples had driven to Cincinnati and gone skating downtown on Fountain Square before ringing in the new year. She recalled now a moment when she and Adam had left the ice to get hot chocolate from a concession booth, and that she'd been so very pleased when it came with little marshmallows.

"You told me how the tiny ones were the best," he went on.

She smiled and sipped from her mug. "They are."

"And I remember how happy they made you."

She bit her lip, a smidge embarrassed, recalling it. "I think I'd had a couple of beers with dinner," she felt the need to say on a laugh. "Marshmallows don't always excite me that much."

"Well, if they excite you at all, that's good enough for me." He raised his eyebrows teasingly, then licked some hot chocolate off his upper lip in a way she felt between her thighs.

And as she took another drink, the little marsh-mallows melting to create a creamy foam on top, she peeked at him from beneath lowered eyelids. " 'Excite' might be a strong word. When it comes to marshmallows, I mean. It takes more to really, you know, *excite* me." Then she bit her lip, and her next words came out huskier, unplanned. "*You* excite me."

"Okay, you know I have to kiss you now, don't you?" he said before taking her cup and setting both of them on the floor of the sled.

And she didn't answer, but there was nothing in the world she wanted more in that moment than to be kissed by Adam Becker.

He gazed deeply into her eyes in the still gently falling snow, then took her face in both his hands, tilted it slightly upward, and lowered a slow, smooth kiss to her lips. Oh God, it was just like in the cabin, in the snowstorm—kisses so thoughtful and sure that nothing else mattered. It wasn't about rushing toward sex—the kisses were intoxicating enough on their own and something in them made her feel . . . treasured. Or maybe it was all of this making her feel that way.

When his tongue eased into her mouth, a small moan echoed from her throat up into the cold, early evening air. And when finally the kissing ended, he leaned over, pressing his forehead against hers, their chilled noses touching, and said, "That was better than hot chocolate."

"Even better than tiny marshmallows," she agreed.

"Thank you," he told her then.

"For?"

"Giving me a chance. We've come a long way in a short time, Little Miss Sugar Plum."

"Well, you're very . . . persuasive," she said breathily.

From there, they resumed their picnic, the hot chocolate warming them, and they talked. Adam told her about his phone call with the twins earlier in the day, and how it had inspired him to finally put up a Christmas tree.

"If you'd waited 'til tonight," she pointed out, "I could have helped you."

He gave his head a sexy—even if regretful—tilt in response. "Damn, that would have been nice." Though after that he narrowed his gaze on her, a slight grin sneaking out. "But then again, I might have better plans for you tonight."

A few minutes later, she found herself sharing with him some of the ideas that had hit her throughout the day. About wanting to get a new little house she could revitalize. "And then I was thinking—maybe I could eventually do that as a sideline to the whole real estate thing. Fix up and remodel old houses. And maybe, if I had enough money, I could flip them—you know, actually buy them, then refurbish and resell them. I think I'd find that really satisfying, you know? Besides liking the work, it would be nice knowing someone else would enjoy the homes for years to come."

"You'd be great at that," he told her without hesitation, and she could tell he meant it. "You did a damn good job on the house you live in now—and, well, I think it's important to do something you love if you can."

The thought made her smile. "You know, two weeks ago, my future didn't feel very . . . inspiring. But now it's hit me how much I really love dealing with homes and home-buying. And I suddenly have more ideas,

more opportunities, than I even have time to explore—
I have too many exciting things to do with my life!"

He raised his eyebrows. "Excited again, huh?" he
teased.

"Down, boy," she scolded, laughing. Then said, "Do
*you* love landscaping?"

He nodded. "Yep. Love working outdoors, love working with plants and trees and earth. I even still love the
smell of fresh mown grass, despite how much of it I've
mowed over the years," he added with a grin.

"You never talk about your work much," she observed.

But he only shrugged. "Guess it's always been such
a big part of me that I don't even think about it. I knew
I'd do something like that, here in Destiny, from the
time I was young."

As a few snowflakes continued gently wafting
around them, she gave him a long, hard look as something new struck her. "You and I . . . we're really a lot
alike in ways. I mean, we've both always valued simple
things, appreciated a simple life. I never wanted to
leave Destiny, and even when you went off to college,
you knew you'd come back. Whereas Sheila wanted
something different, and deep down, I'm pretty sure
Jeff did, too."

He gave his head a thoughtful tilt. "Guess I've always
known that, about us being alike. That's probably why
I've always been so comfortable with you."

When she gave a little shiver, he said, "Cold?"

And she nodded.

"Drink up," he said, motioning to the warm mug she
still held, "and I'll get us on the road home."

The shortest days of the year were upon them, so it

was dark by then, but a bright moon was beginning to shine down now that the snow was finally tapering off, and reflecting off the snow, it lit up Blue Valley Road for the romantic ride back to town. Sue Ann didn't hesitate to snuggle against Adam as he guided the horse, Clara's bells jingling the entire way.

And when finally the red sled came to a stop on Holly Lane, she looked into his eyes, close to hers now, and said, "You've got this thing for the rest of the evening, right?"

"Right."

"Then that means you don't have to leave right away. It means you can . . . come in and warm me up."

And warm her up he did. In more ways than one.

Once inside, Adam built a fire in the old brick hearth, and Sue Ann poured more of his hot chocolate into fresh mugs from her kitchen—adding the marshmallows, of course. They sat near the fire and talked more, about nothing in particular—the kids, Christmas, snow—being interrupted only briefly when Adam had to take a call on his cell phone and stepped away, into the kitchen.

While he was gone, Sue Ann hugged a throw pillow to her chest and felt more caught up in romantic passion than since she'd been a teenager. As she'd acknowledged before, romance could be agonizing when it held problems or didn't go the way you wanted—but she was now remembering how absolutely, soul-stirringly amazing it could be when it all fell into place. She bit her lip, her body aching for his return, and her heart was definitely getting into the act, too. She couldn't have dreamed six months ago—or heck, even six weeks ago—that she could be so happy by Christmas.

Though when Adam came back in the room, shoving his phone into his pocket, she thought he looked troubled. Rising to face him, hugging her mug in both hands, she said, "Problem?"

He tilted his head, squinting lightly, as if weighing it, and said, "Uh . . . nothing I want to let dampen the evening."

She didn't want anything to mess up the night, either, but felt compelled to ask, "Are you sure?"

"Yep, completely."

"Nothing's wrong with the boys?"

And his expression lightened as he rushed to say, "Oh no, nothing like that. Everything's fine." Then he even smiled. "Stop worrying so much, sugar plum."

"All right," she said, relieved and deciding it was probably some issue related to his business or something.

Then a look she liked even better entered his gaze— the sexy expression he wore when he was feeling seductive. "But I think we've had enough hot chocolate," he said deeply. "And I'm ready to move on to a new activity." Standing next to the fireplace with her, Adam confidently took the cup from her hand, set it on the mantel, and began to kiss her again.

But now, as smooth and perfect as his kisses were, kisses alone were no longer enough—for either of them. He wasted little time before sliding his hands beneath the hem of her sweater—at the precise moment she reached for the button on his blue jeans.

As they made love by the fire on another braided rug, for Sue Ann it was as if everything that had happened since Thanksgiving was coming together, melding into one hot, wonderful moment that left no questions, no worries—only happiness. The setting took her back to that snowbound cabin, but the most wonderful part was—now it wasn't just sex; it was so much more. And just like the other night in her bed, she didn't hold back, she let herself and her inhibitions go completely in his arms.

The pleasure was wild and intense, and as much as she adored her daughter, she was thankful they didn't have to worry about being quiet this time. Being alone with Adam, feeling utterly free with him, filled her almost to overflowing. When he kissed and licked between her thighs, she could moan and purr. And when he turned her onto her hands and knees on the rug, plunging into her, hot and hard, she could cry out at will—no holding back.

Before it was over, he'd given her another two ecstasy-filled orgasms, and when he came in her, knowing she'd taken him there left her feeling . . . whole. Complete. For maybe the first time in months.

He collapsed gently atop her naked body and they lay quietly for a few moments, until she smiled into his eyes and said, "You give an entirely new meaning to the idea of Christmas joy."

A rich, hearty laugh echoed from his throat, and they kissed and cuddled together for a minute before he rolled onto his side next to her, caressing her stomach with warm fingertips and saying, "I like this new you."

"New me?"

"This you who isn't pushing me away and telling me it can't happen and all that. This you is much more fun," he teased with a wink.

She bit her lip. This her was *having* much more fun, too. In fact, this her was just a plain happier person than she'd been a week or two ago. She was glad she'd stopped fighting her feelings for him. "I guess . . . you're pretty hard to resist, Becker."

He cast a sexy grin down into her eyes, then leaned in to lower a soft kiss on the ridge of her breast. "Damn straight," he rasped.

She leaned her head back then, just basking in the moment. "And I guess I've . . . quit dwelling on my trust issues so much. I'm starting to look at those in a new way, too."

"What new way?" he asked absently, studying her breast now as if he were examining some amazing work of art, then lowering another tiny kiss, this one to the very tip of her nipple. It made her shiver.

Still, even as good as that felt, she rolled onto her side to face him—she couldn't concentrate on what she was saying otherwise—and peered into those gorgeous blue eyes that had held her so captivated in recent weeks. "Well, with a more . . . positive attitude, I guess. Because it seems the more I relax and let things happen, the better my life goes. And yeah, I was surprised when you told me what happened at that wedding, because I'm very sensitive about any sort of cheating right now, and I always thought of you as so . . . flawless before that. But like we discussed the other night, none of us are perfect. And I was worried, too, about the idea of you testifying for Jeff in the alimony hearing—afraid of things that could come out, about me—but that's one more thing that turned out not to be a problem. I didn't tell you this the other night because . . . well, I didn't want to make a big deal of it at the time—but finding out you weren't doing it lifted such a burden, Adam. It just changed . . . everything. So all that makes it a lot easier to just be brave, not back away from this anymore, and put my trust in you."

When he said nothing in reply to this, though—in fact, exhibited no reaction whatsoever—she found herself looking more deeply into his eyes, trying to read them.

And she wasn't sure how, but that quickly—almost in the blink of an eye—it had turned into . . . a strange moment. A sudden uneasiness filled the air around them.

*Maybe you're only imagining that.* But why would she imagine something so unpleasant when everything else was so wonderful? And had his body just stiffened slightly next to hers? Whether she was imagining things or not, she just wanted him to confirm what she was saying, to assure her that she wasn't just being . . . naïve or something.

Now his gaze had narrowed on her as well, and—damn—she still couldn't quite interpret his expression. Though she began to fear that he appeared more . . . concerned than she liked. What was that about?

Propped on her elbow, she tilted her head, their eyes still connected—and she knew he saw the growing question, the uneasiness, on her face.

"What's wrong?" she finally asked. "Why are you being so quiet?"

His mouth flattened into a straight line—and her stomach churned lightly. "Thing is, honey . . ." He stopped, sighed. "That phone call I got before . . . "

"What?" she asked nervously. What was he holding back from her?

He looked away for a second then, not answering, and she saw him swallow—uncomfortably.

Her chest tightened and her throat went dry.

And then Adam blew out a long breath and shut his eyes, finally reopening them to say, "It was Jeff on the phone. He wanted to tell me that if I say no, his lawyer plans to subpoena me. So . . . looks like I'll be testifying after all."

She often cried out that it wasn't fair, and it really was not.

Charles Dickens, A *Christmas Carol*

# Seventeen

*S*ue Ann simply gaped at him. How was this possible? She felt as if someone had just lowered an anvil onto her chest. She barely managed to whisper, "You're testifying for Jeff? Against me?"

"It's not *against* you," he insisted, shaking his head. "And I have no choice now. But it has nothing to do with you, so don't worry."

She simply let out a heavy breath, stunned. "How can you possibly say it has nothing to do with me? It has everything to do with me. If they ask you questions about me, you'll have to answer. And God knows what could come up or how it could make me look."

He just tilted his head and narrowed his brow, as if she were being unreasonable. "I would never say anything to make you look bad, Sue Ann. How could you even think that?"

"Because it's not up to you what the lawyer asks! And though I think of Jeff as more selfish than vindictive, who can say anymore? For all I know, he could be angling to take Sophie from me!"

"That's crazy—that's not what he's after."

She sat up next to him, incensed now, and feeling the need to tower over him. "It's not crazy. If there's even a tiny fraction of a chance that my custody of Sophie could be at risk, it's not crazy. And you're just now telling me about this? Why on earth didn't you tell me before, when he called? You said everything was fine! How could you keep that to yourself?"

Another big sigh left him as told her, "I meant everything was fine with the boys—that's what you'd just asked me about then. And damn, Sue Ann—I just didn't want either one of us to have to think about this right now. I knew you'd make too much of it and I didn't want to upset you."

Sue Ann simply sat before him astonished, speechless. She'd felt so close to him just a minute ago—but suddenly that had changed into feeling . . . almost betrayed. She'd slowly worked up to being ready to proceed into a relationship with him—hell, to having already proceeded there. And she'd been so . . . open with him just now, during sex. She'd given him so much of herself. Because she'd begun to trust him so much. And yet he'd come back into the room without telling her about that phone call?

"More like you didn't tell me because you figured you wouldn't get laid," she murmured under her breath.

And now he looked angry, too. "Shit—that's how you think I see this? As getting laid?"

She knew it was harsh, knew it wasn't true, and

yet . . . "Why else hold back on news you knew would upset me?" She glanced away from Adam then, even shifting her body away, too, and hugging her knees to her chest—an urge to cover herself up a little. She was tired of feeling confused, and tired of analyzing all this—but she couldn't stop herself.

And when he answered, his voice sounded small coming from behind her, as if he were as drained and exasperated as she was. "Because we were having a nice night and I didn't want to ruin it. I didn't figure waiting an hour or two to tell you would change anything."

She sucked in her breath and felt herself almost begin to tremble with all the emotion running through her. "You should have told me before. Because now it feels . . . almost like you weren't honest with me by not sharing it the second you found out."

Now even his sigh was racked with weariness. "It was an hour, Sue Ann. One fucking hour. And a damn *good* hour, too, I might add."

Yes, it had been an absolutely amazing hour—but that didn't matter to Sue Ann at the moment. What mattered was how much she'd let herself go with him, because she'd begun to feel so sure they saw things the same way in life. What mattered was that he thought she was "making too much of it," and that he'd made the conscious decision to keep something important from her, even if only for a little while. What mattered were the things he could be forced into saying about her under oath. What mattered was her daughter. Her life. Her heart.

She shut her eyes, tight, willing back tears. She had no intention of letting Adam Becker see her cry. She'd opened herself up to him so much these last two nights, in so many ways—and now she'd become far too vulnerable, let him see far too much.

He sat up next to her, touched her arm. And she could smell the sexy, musky scent of him right beside her, but she kept her eyes closed. "Sue Ann, you gotta know I'm crazy about you. If that helps at all."

A lump had grown in her throat. And that stark vulnerability now hung around her like a blanket, heavy and stifling, made worse by the fact that she was naked. "It . . . actually makes it worse," she managed.

"That doesn't make any sense," he said softly.

*Yes, it does. It makes me care about you even more. It makes me envision this perfect thing we could have together.* But now that was soiled. And if he hadn't been completely honest about this, right up front, what else might he choose to hold back from her in the future? What else might he decide she was "making too much of"? It was hard to weigh—maybe at any other time of her life this one transgression wouldn't matter so much, but right now, it did. She'd put her trust in him and he'd promptly shown her that was a mistake.

"I think you should go," she finally said in a hushed tone. But at least her voice hadn't quivered. *Hold onto your dignity, above all else.* Despite Adam's previous observation about that, she still thought she'd lost enough of her dignity in the divorce—she couldn't bear to lose even an ounce more.

Next to her, he expelled a heavy breath. "Can't we talk about this? Can't we talk through it?"

She just shook her head briefly. "I don't think so. I just want to be alone."

"I told you before that I would never hurt you, and I meant it."

And at this, she lifted her eyes briefly to his to softly point out, "You just did."

"Sue Ann—" He touched her arm again, but this time she pulled it away—and he flinched, clearly surprised.

"Please, Adam," she snapped. "Please just go."

"Really?" he asked. "You won't even talk to me about this?"

She simply shook her head.

And he went still, silent, and a few seconds later said, "Fine."

As he got up and went about getting dressed, Sue Ann followed the instinct to climb up onto the sofa, pulling an afghan from the back and burrowing under it, curling her body to face away from him. She waited, biting her lip, still willing back tears, angry at herself, angry at him, angry at all her emotions—emotions she'd thought she was coming to grips with, but now, here they all were, suddenly flooding back through her like a brand new river of pain.

Only when the front door closed quietly behind him a minute later did she finally let herself begin to cry. She'd told him everything in her heart, honestly. And each time they'd been intimate, she'd given him a deeply private, personal piece of herself she could never get back.

And only now was she realizing how much trust that had taken, how much trust she'd already given him before even fully deciding to do so. She'd thought she was easing into something with him slowly, carefully, but now that it was suddenly over, she understood that she'd already let herself go way too far to come out of this unscathed.

*Oh God, why did I ever let this be any more than sex? Why did I have to start having such deep, wrenching feelings for him? How did I let myself get hurt again this soon?*

Adam tried to hold crookedly cut snowman-laden wrapping paper in place with one hand while he wrangled a piece of tape from the roll with the other. But by the time he managed to tear off the tape, the paper had slipped. He let out a small growl, sending Pepper trotting from the room. Damn it, he really was "all hooves" when it came to this.

"Pepper," he called, then whistled softly. "You can come back in the room, boy—I'm not mad at *you*." No, he wasn't mad at Pepper  he was mad at everything else. *But when my mood drives away even my dog, man's best friend . . .* Hell, it felt like a new low in Grinchiness.

Timidly, the collie re-entered the living room, where Adam sat on the floor attempting to wrap the boys' gifts. Exasperated, he abandoned the task, lifting both hands to scratch behind the dog's ears. "That's right, you're a good boy, aren't you?" he murmured. "Of course you are. Without you, I'd probably be stark raving mad by now."

Because one of the things that had him back in a bad mood was the utter emptiness of his own house. Yeah, that had started not to seem so bad the other day, but now it was back, again making him aware of how quiet the place was without the kids. Even now, the only sound was the crackling fire in the hearth across the room. Of course, he hadn't bothered to turn on lights in other rooms the last few days, or music, or even the TV. So maybe it was his own fault.

And so he was mad at himself, too. For the way he'd been acting since Jacob and Joey's departure, and for the Scroogy attitude that had taken hold of him yet again after what had happened with Sue Ann the other night.

God, why didn't he tell her about the call right when it had come in? Looking back, he supposed that hadn't exactly reeked of him being an honest, up-front guy. He just hadn't thought that far ahead at the time.

It had actually been a split-second decision—he'd walked in the room, seen her pretty face, and had simply chosen to think about better things. After all, it wasn't exactly fun for him to find out he was getting subpoenaed. But apparently Jeff's lawyer was bent on Jeff's lifelong best friend, Adam Becker, taking the stand—because Adam was so respected in the community. *Lucky me for being so damn well-liked.*

On one hand, he couldn't help feeling Sue Ann was blowing this out of proportion. She'd practically acted mad at him for having to testify, even though it wasn't his fault. But . . . hell, maybe he wouldn't be in this fix right now if he'd just refused Jeff's request from the beginning and not hemmed and hawed so long. And he knew Sue Ann was fragile right now when it came to trust—how many times had she told him that in the past month? So, on the other hand, when he looked at it from her point of view . . . well, maybe the answers suddenly didn't seem as clear.

"All right, boy, all right," he said when he'd had enough making up with Pepper. "Go lie down for a few minutes and let me finish this, then I'll give you a treat."

The word "treat" worked its usual magic, and the

dog retreated to the rug in front of the fireplace. "Good boy," Adam praised him. Then he looked back to the wrinkled paper around the new gaming system he was trying to wrap. "Learn to wrap presents," he said absently to the dog, "and you'd *really* be man's best friend."

Finally, Adam succeeded in doing his usual sloppy job on the gaming system, then reached for the two large boxes containing new winter play coats, one in red, the other blue. *Oh boy,* these *should be fun to wrap.* Letting out a sigh, he grabbed a roll of paper featuring snow-skiing Santas. He'd picked it up at the drugstore knowing the boys would like it since they were such expert skiers now.

God, making love to Sue Ann, in her bed and then again in front of the fire, had been so good, so freaking perfect—and it killed him to know he'd blown it all to hell in the blink of an eye. One mistake had cost him a woman he really thought he could have a future with. And shit—having to drive that damn sleigh away from her house and all the way back to Grampy's place had made him feel pretty fucking ridiculous given the way the evening had turned out.

Though as he used the first big coat box to measure the amount of paper he'd need, he realized there was someone else he was mad at, too—he was mad at Sue Ann. For not listening when he'd wanted to talk through it. For not realizing that he *was* a damn good guy. For not even trying to look past his mistake. After all, hadn't they just agreed that neither of them were any more perfect than anyone else?

But at the same time, he knew that for her to be with him, the way he wanted her with him—for something real—she needed to believe in him wholeheartedly. And he'd made that impossible for her.

After using scissors to cut a big swath of Santa paper—more jaggedly than he'd meant to, of course— he wrapped it around the box . . . only to find it wasn't quite big enough, after all.

*Great—that's just fucking great.*

He let out another growl, sending Pepper running from the room once more.


Jenny let go of Mick's hand to peer down into the heavy-duty stroller Betty Fisher pushed up the sidewalk near Under the Covers. "My, who's this?" she asked.

Betty was a longtime family friend who, along with her husband, Ed, hosted an annual Fourth of July picnic at their farm every year. And Jenny occasionally took her telescope to their large, wide-open yard for stargazing. Now Betty flashed a big smile in response to Jenny's question. "My grandbaby, of course. My daughter and her husband just came into town yesterday and now Grandma has until the day after Christmas to spoil this perfect little one."

Jenny bent down, pulling back a snow white blanket to reveal a tiny infant girl, fast asleep. A small red bow was clipped into a tuft of dark hair, and she wore a sweater proclaiming, I LOVE SANTA! Something in Jenny's heart curled inward at the sight as she breathed in that soft, warm baby scent. And then her stomach pinched. Because of the ongoing strain between her and Mick lately. Because she wanted a baby now and he didn't.

"She's beautiful, Betty," Jenny told her, aware that Mick stood somewhere behind her, probably with his hands in his pockets, not even stepping up to look. And normally she wouldn't have a problem with that—Mick had just never been a baby person. But now, suddenly, it seemed rude and disinterested, and it even embarrassed her a little.

Yet Betty didn't seem to notice, or at least she didn't seem to mind. "Thanks, Jenny," she said as Jenny gently covered the baby girl back up. "You two have a nice evening."

So maybe the problem was hers—not Mick's or anyone else's. And she couldn't deny that she was the one who'd changed here—not him. But somehow that just broke her heart all the more as she and Mick continued up the street toward Dolly's, where they were meeting Tessa and Lucky for a casual dinner.

When Mick took her hand again, she stiffened—then realized what she'd done. It made her draw in her breath. They never got mad at each other, never fought. And she wasn't sure she'd ever reacted that way to his touch before.

So she relaxed her hand into his—but it was too late; he'd noticed, and he pulled back to look at her. His dark eyes blazed with hurt, and maybe a hint of irritation.

She considered saying something, but couldn't conjure any words. Nothing felt right at the moment. So finally, she just let out a sigh, then looked back ahead of them, starting to drag him forward in the cold. "Come on, we're late." Yet she feared the tension suddenly stretching through her body could still be felt in her grip.

And she found out she was right when Mick pulled up short, stopping them again.

She looked back at him. "What?"

"Jenny," he began slowly, "I'm sorry I don't feel the way you want me to about this."

For some reason, she played dumb. "About what?" Maybe she just didn't want to talk about it right now. They were only steps away from the café, after all.

"You *know* what."

Okay, this meant she couldn't get out of having the discussion—and as another large sigh left her, her chest began to ache. Biting her lip, searching for words, searching her heart, she gazed up into the eyes of the man she loved more than anything in the world. "But couldn't you just try?" she asked him. It probably wasn't the right thing to say—yet it was what had come out.

"Why isn't this enough, just you and me?" he asked. "You and me and Trouble? It was enough up to now. And I thought we'd agreed it would be enough forever. It's still enough for *me*. I like our life the way it is."

Oh Lord—how could she explain this? Because it was true—up to now they'd been like-minded enough on the subject. Mick hadn't wanted children, and she hadn't felt strongly about it either way, trusting the outcome to fate. And fate had definitely been doing things right not to create a baby during her first marriage because she'd been with the wrong man then. But now that she was with the right one . . .

"I'm just . . . having maternal urges." *Strong ones.* "I never really had them much before, but now . . . here they are, and they won't leave me alone. And the thing is, Mick," she went on, now reaching out to take both his hands in her gloved ones, warmly this time, "part of why I want a baby is because . . . I want one with *you*. I want a baby that you and I made, together, that's part of us both. Can you understand that?"

Mick squeezed her hands in his, but at the same time, he looked down, let out a breath. And Jenny's hopes crumbled. She already knew she hadn't gotten through to him—that his feelings on this outweighed his usual desire to make her happy. "Jenny, honey, I just . . . don't want kids. And I'm sorry, but I can't pretend to want something I don't."

"I know, but . . . " *I'm suddenly not sure if I'll ever be complete now without a child. Everything inside me is changing. Why can't you feel the same way? Why don't you want to share that with me?*

"But?" he asked pointedly, urging her on.

"Why can't you just think about it? Consider it? Maybe if you really thought about it, you'd realize you feel differently now, too." She sounded desperate, she realized, stopping. And he was looking at her like she wasn't quite making sense, like she was almost scaring him.

She saw her husband swallow visibly, then he slowly took her hands again in his. When he spoke this time, his voice came low and deep. "Jenny, I love you, you know that. But . . . no. I can't. That's just all there is to it—just . . . no."

Jenny stood before him saying nothing, biting her lower lip so she wouldn't start to cry.

It was his right to feel this way. And yet—somehow she just couldn't quite accept it. Suddenly, she couldn't quite figure out how she was ever going to be truly, deeply happy again if she knew with certainty that she'd *never* be someone's mother, and that Mick didn't even want to try. And what if she grew to resent him for it? And what if he resented her, too? How on earth had her once-perfect marriage suddenly gone so wrong?

"Come on," he said then, his voice low and a bit wooden, "Tessa and Lucky are waiting."

Sophie sat on the floor watching the brand new Lionel train circling the Christmas tree—Sue Ann's mother had insisted on giving it to Sophie as an early gift just a few days ago. "Otherwise," she'd told Sue Ann, "she won't get to put it around the tree this year. So why not let her have it now?" Sue Ann knew, though, the gift was really her mother's way of helping keep Sophie's mind off the fact that everything was different this Christmas.

As dusk turned to dark outside, Sophie loaded the tiny people from her favorite dollhouse into an empty train car—Sue Ann had passed her love of dollhouses, and a few of the houses themselves, on to her daughter. Then Sophie switched the train on again as Sue Ann leaned back, trying to get comfy on the sofa, her real estate study book open in her lap.

Between getting ready for Christmas, going to holiday events, and . . . well, Adam, she'd devoted very little attention to studying the last few weeks. And she was still trying to start using all her time wisely. Now that Christmas was almost here and all the work surrounding it was done, it was a good time to refocus. And Adam was out of her life—romantically and sexually anyway—so she was doing her damnedest not to waste any more time or emotion on him.

"Can Adam come over and see the train?" Sophie asked then.

*Oh boy, think of the devil.* Not that Adam was actually the devil, but . . . "Oh, I don't think so, honey—I'm sure he's busy. It's only a few days 'til Christmas, after all."

"It's only a few days 'til Christmas for us, too, but *we're* not busy."

Well, crap. True. And maybe Sue Ann wished she were *more* busy—just as she had in the cabin after Thanksgiving. But again, everything was done. Gifts were bought and wrapped. Cards and packages sent. Now, other than studying, there was nothing to do but sit around and wait . . . for Santa not to bring Sophie a reindeer. She let out a sigh. "Well, I need to study, and you, young lady, have homework of your own." Christmas break hadn't started just yet. "And we'll need to bake some more cookies for your class party, too—maybe tomorrow after school. How's that sound?"

Sophie smiled. "Fun."

"Good. Now go grab your books. You have math problems to do and a spelling test to get ready for."

But even as she and Sophie both buckled down and got to work, Adam stayed on Sue Ann's mind. And she couldn't even blame it on Sophie having mentioned him—the truth was that he stayed firmly in her thoughts most of the time now anyway, despite her best efforts to banish him from her brain.

She'd let herself slowly begin to trust in him, just for a short while, and even just that—God—had left her much more vulnerable than she'd been before. Their conversation after sex the other night had simply felt like having the rug pulled out from under her all over again. And it hurt worse than she thought it should have.

Maybe that was how she knew she'd been right from the start. Putting trust in someone too soon was dangerous, and she was too emotionally fragile to venture into a relationship right now. So it was settled. Once and for all. Finally.

But if everything was so settled . . . why was she still so freaking miserable about the whole thing?

Sue Ann stood in yet another few inches of fresh fallen snow helping Sophie and the other second graders decorate the small evergreen outside their classroom window. After draping garlands of popcorn and cranberries, the group began hanging the edible ornaments: thinly sliced fruit that had been cut into the shapes of small stars, bread cut into snowman shapes, strawberries sprinkled with sugar to make them glisten, and chunks of pound cake coated in a mixture of birdseed and cornmeal.

It required a ladder to reach the top, as well as a few parents who didn't mind climbing in slippery conditions, but when the task was done, adults and children alike marveled at how lovely such a simple, natural Christmas tree could be. And like a reward for all their hard work, barely a moment had passed before they were treated to a visit by a male cardinal who looked breathtaking against the snowy backdrop of the schoolyard.

It was the end of the day, the final activity of the class party, and Sue Ann had enjoyed the whole afternoon—full of cookies and gifts and games—more than she'd anticipated, making her extra glad she'd rearranged her work schedule to be here. And not one other parent in attendance mentioned anything about her divorce.

Still, when Jeff pulled up at three on the dot to get Sophie, Sue Ann felt the glaring reminder. And she was glad she had plans this evening to keep her from feeling lonely or whiny. Tonight was her annual Christmas dinner with her girlfriends.

A couple of hours later, Jenny picked Sue Ann up from

home—they were headed to the Farris/Romo Family Apple Orchard, where Rachel's grandma, Edna, was hosting their event, cooking a big, old-fashioned meal for them all. They'd drawn names for a gift exchange, so as she left the house, Sue Ann clutched a wedding planning book for Rachel, wrapped in bright red paper, as well as a small gift bag containing a gingerbread-scented candle as a hostess gift for Edna.

*Hmm, gingerbread. Like my gingerbread man panties.* Which made her think of Adam, of course, every time she wore them. And hell—apparently now it only took gingerbread in general to remind her of Adam. Come to think of it, what *didn't* remind her of Adam?

Even a glimpse back at her own house as she reached the car did it. Since, of course, he'd put up the lights glowing around the eaves and windows right now. And the remains of the snow cat he'd built with Sophie still stood in a vague, lumpy cat shape only yards away. She couldn't help recalling with a wistful sigh what a nice evening that had turned out to be.

*God, stop thinking about him already!*

"Hey," she said, trying to sound cheerful as she got in and pulled the door shut.

"Hi." Jenny glanced over, but her eyes were uncharacteristically downcast, and she sounded downright morose.

"Um, why do you look so grim?" Sue Ann asked. "I'm supposed to be the grim one here, remember?"

Putting the car in reverse, Jenny turned to peer over her shoulder to back from the driveway. "Well, you've been less grim lately. Kind of. So I guess I'm taking over on grim duty."

Then Sue Ann remembered. "Is it Mick? He still doesn't want to have a baby?"

"Yep," Jenny answered, shifting the car into drive. "And I know it's not his fault, and I know it's not fair for me to go back on my word—but I'm still mad at him. I can't help it."

Sue Ann pondered the situation a moment, then simply said, "I'm so sorry you're going through this, Jen."

Until Jenny said, "You think he's right, don't you? You think it's okay for him to refuse me this."

Sue Ann pursed her lips—and then prepared to spit out her thoughts. She might have to hold back with Jenny on a few things about Adam, but when it came to anything else, she could lay it on the line. "Look, it sucks to want a child and not be able to have one. But it's early days here yet. You just decided you wanted this, like a week or two ago. He could change his mind at some point in time. Or you could change yours back. And Mick's a good guy. I mean, there's a lot to be said for a guy who is completely and utterly devoted to you, a guy who's as true to you as the day is long."

Sue Ann had never seen Mick so much as even glance at another woman—for him, Jenny was clearly everything. Then it struck her that Jenny must think she was comparing Mick to Jeff, but in fact she was thinking about Adam. Who had let her down at the very moment she'd felt closest to him.

Jenny navigated the small grid of residential streets that led from Holly Lane to the heart of town, where the only lights at that hour were the ones aglow on the large tree in the square. Then she finally said, "I hate to admit it, but . . . you make some good points there."

"I know I do. And you should be *glad* to admit it. So you can calm down and act normal now."

"You're right," Jen said. "I'm going to do that. Calm down and act normal."

"Good."

But then she cast a disparaging glance in Sue Ann's direction. "But inside, I still don't *feel* normal. I still have that horrible ache inside me that I can't seem to run away from." And she was back to sounding just as emotional as she had a minute ago.

Sue Ann could only sigh. "Listen, Jen—take it from me. No matter how you feel on the inside, act normal anyway. It really does help. And if nothing else, it saves your dignity."

Jenny nodded, then acknowledged, "You *have* stayed pretty dignified through all this—publicly, I mean."

"Thanks," Sue Ann said, and honestly meant it. If Jenny and Adam both thought that, maybe it was true. And dignity hadn't been easy at times—but it had slowly started getting better, in most ways, especially since she'd forced herself to start getting out and about again.

"So how are things with Adam?" Jenny asked then.

Ugh—her least favorite subject right now. Even if he was always on her mind. "Um, over. Definitely over for sure," she said with a raw conviction that made her proud.

As Destiny gave way to the more open road that led to the orchard, Jenny peered across the dark car at her. "Something else happened, didn't it? Something I don't know about."

Okay, maybe she'd gone a little overboard on the conviction. But she'd have told Jenny the whole thing anyway, any moment now, whether she'd asked or not. "Well, we had sex again. A couple of times. Really great sex," she confessed, feeling a little bittersweet about it.

"And somewhere along the way I guess I started having . . . stronger feelings for him than I realized."

"Really?" Jenny asked, clearly pleased. But she didn't know the rest yet.

"Yeah, and he even decided to tell Jeff he wouldn't testify as his character witness," Sue Ann said, remembering how happy that had made her. "But then he found out he was being subpoenaed. Only he didn't tell me that right away—he waited until after we had sex. And he thinks I'm too worried about the whole thing anyway."

"Oh Lord, you're kidding," Jenny said, and Sue Ann appreciated the sneer her best friend cast in her direction.

"Wish I was, but no, it's true." And while, at the time, every worry she could imagine had gone tumbling through her brain—like Adam's testimony somehow causing her to lose Sophie—she knew that was highly unlikely now. She had a better job on the horizon, after all, and if anyone brought morals into question, Jeff's own behavior would be put on trial, too. So, for her, this was simply about Adam betraying her trust a little. And right now, even a little was too much. Plus he'd made her feel like an overreactive nut at the same time.

"Did he have any explanation for that?" Jenny asked.

"None that mattered to me," Sue Ann replied, in no mood to go into detail about it. "And the upshot is that I instantly realized I was right all along and it was far too soon for me to start trusting in another man. But somehow I still managed to get hurt by him." She scrunched her brow, feeling the sting inside that, so far, hadn't even begun to weaken. "I don't know how the situation got away from me so quickly."

And Jenny said simply, "I think it's like that with love. It can sneak up on you fast."

But . . . love? Jenny thought she already loved Adam? Surely not. Surely it took longer to fall in love with someone. Yet she was also in no mood to hash through such a complicated subject right now, so she chose to say nothing in reply.

And as they exited the car and tramped through the snow to Edna's little white farmhouse with the lacy cookie-cutter trim, she pasted on a smile even though she hurt inside. Because what she'd told Jenny was true—acting normal was the next best thing to *feeling* normal sometimes. And she sensed Jenny doing the same thing.

A minute later, the two were walking in through Edna's back door—it was the kind of house where anyone who knew Edna just naturally came in the back way—and the place felt busy and alive as soon as they stepped in. Rachel, Tessa, and Amy were already there, and Edna was cooking up a storm, filling the air with rich, heavenly aromas. A tall tree sparkled with old-fashioned ornaments in one corner of the front parlor, and Bing Crosby's "White Christmas"—scratchy because it came from a piece of vinyl spinning on an old record player—echoed through every room.

"I hope you girls brought your appetites," Edna was saying. "We've got us a big ham with homemade gravy, mashed potatoes, green beans, corn, cinnamon apples, cranberry relish, and three different kinds of pie for dessert. And I don't intend to be loadin' up my fridge with a bunch of leftovers, neither."

Meanwhile, their girlfriends were smiling and hugging them hello, setting the gifts they'd brought beneath the tree. Sue Ann was saying how lovely everything looked, and Jenny said how good it was to see everyone, even though they all saw each other fairly often.

But Sue Ann couldn't have agreed with Jenny's sentiment more. It truly *was* good to see them. It was good to be swept into this lively, cheerful party and let it make her feel better. Acting normal usually *became* feeling normal when she was with the girls like this. *Thank God for my friends*. Without them, she wasn't sure what would have held her together lately.

Sadly, though, she also wasn't quite sure what was going to *keep* holding her together when all the Christmas festivities were over and she ran out of distractions once and for all. She'd been getting herself together after the divorce, finally. But now, that gnawing ache she suffered in her heart for Adam made her fear that, if she wasn't careful, she could end up on an emotional downward spiral all over again.

It didn't make sense.

*But love doesn't always make sense.*

And then, standing by herself for a moment, peering into the glow of the Christmas tree lights until they almost began blending together, she realized what she'd just said in her head. Love. *Was* she in love with Adam? Already? That fast?

She swallowed around the lump that had just grown in her throat. Oh God. Yes. She was. In love. With Adam. That fast.

*Okay. Regroup. Think through this.*

*I'm in love with a man I don't feel I can trust at a time when I'm more fragile and vulnerable than I've ever been in my life.*

*And in a few days my daughter is going to wake up*

*on Christmas morning brokenhearted—in more ways
than I can possibly begin to mend.*

*And I have no idea how to fix any of this.*

"All right, dinner's served," Edna called from the
dining room.

And Sue Ann knew her only choice was to simply
keep on distracting herself—at the moment, with food
and friends—and to keep on acting normal. It was her
only answer to anything right now.

" . . . hear me! I am not the man I was."

Charles Dickens, A *Christmas Carol*

# *Eighteen*

*Adam* sat in a rocking chair in his living room, but everything around him was dusty, and the room smelled . . . stale. It was cold in here, cold and dank—he should make a fire. But as he started to get up, his joints ached and he felt deeply fatigued, all the way to his bones. So maybe a fire could wait. Maybe he'd just sit here a little while longer.

It was a gray winter's day outside—no sunlight came in through the windows, and no lamps lit the room, either. But even in the dim, somber lighting, his eyes caught on some pictures atop the mantel.

His boys—with their families. They were grown up now, men. How the hell had that happened? But he knew it was them, knew it to his very core, just at a glance. And that's when Adam realized—he was old. He was old and alone.

*A stark sense of pride in both his sons ran through him as he studied the framed eight-by-tens—each appeared to have a wife, kids. In one of the photos, the whole family wore white and stood outside on a bright summer's day. In the other, everyone dressed in sweaters or long sleeves and gathered around a brick hearth. They all looked happy.*

*But Adam suffered the faint sense that he hadn't seen his sons in a while, and that maybe he barely knew their children. Maybe he hadn't been the kind of grandpa their kids had wanted to know. Inside now, he felt vaguely snarly, mean—and perhaps that's how they saw him, too.*

*When he heard a noise from the kitchen, he barked, "Who's in there?"*

*"It's just me, Uncle Adam. Sophie," a female voice said. "I'm just getting your meals for the week put in containers and labeled. And you'd best quit yelling or I'll stop doing even that for you."*

*Sophie. Dear little Sophie. But she was grown up now, too. And labeling meals for him? How old was he, for God's sake? Or was he just too ornery and broken down to take care of himself and his own food? "I . . . didn't mean to yell," he called to her softly.*

*"Really? Well, that's a switch. You usually don't mind yelling at all."*

*He didn't? That was who he'd become? An old man who yelled at everyone?*

*No wonder he hadn't seen his boys in a while. No wonder he was sitting in a dusty, closed-up house, cold and alone. Well, alone except for Sophie.*

*A moment later, she came into the room, drying her hands on a dish towel and looking . . . oh so pretty.*

*Like her mother had when they were young. His heart fluttered a bit at the thought—but then it clenched tight. He couldn't remember how things had turned out with Sue Ann, yet he instinctively knew it was bad. "Sophie, why are you here? Why are you helping me?" he asked.*

*She looked at him like he was becoming addle-brained. And he probably was, or he wouldn't have to ask, and he wouldn't find his own life so much of a surprise. "Well," she said matter-of-factly, "somebody has to. And nobody really wants to. But . . . you were good to me when I was a little girl, and despite how mean you are, I guess I've kept a soft spot for you all this time."*

*"That's good of you," he said, only now becoming aware that his voice had turned gravelly over the forgotten years.*

*The lovely young woman before him appeared stunned at his words. "You're right—it is good of me. You've never even acknowledged that before. Thank you."*

*He felt embarrassed—by this bitter person he'd apparently become, so bitter that no one wanted to be with him, so bitter that he'd somehow blocked it all out. So he only nodded in reply.*

*"Well, you're set for the week, and I have to go."*

*"Where's the phone?" he heard himself asking. "Maybe I'll call Mike. Or Logan. Or maybe even your dad. Maybe we could all get together, play some cards, drink a beer."*

*Again, Sophie just tilted her head, her expression one of confusion. "Uncle Adam, you haven't talked to Mike, Logan, or my dad for years."*

*He blinked, dumbfounded. "I haven't?"*

*She shook her head, still looking worried that he was losing it. And he felt like he was, more with each passing minute. "You had a big falling out with them when I was a kid—don't you remember? They got tired of your attitude."*

*Adam sighed, feeling all the more weary. Yet he didn't want to just keep sitting here—he had the impression he'd been doing that for far too long. "Well then . . . maybe I'll go into work for a while. I could use some fresh air."*

*But Sophie only appeared all the more concerned. "You haven't worked at the landscape supply in a long time, Uncle Adam."*

*"No?"*

*"Jacob and Joey took over the business years ago. And you're darn lucky they're good enough to keep a roof over your head and food in your mouth." Then she stopped, looking sad, and she almost seemed to be talking to herself when she said, " I might need to let them know, though . . . "*

*"Know what?" he asked when she trailed off.*

*She gave her head a short, troubled shake. "Well, you don't seem quite yourself today. They've talked about it for the last few years, but now it might really be time for them to consider moving you to . . . "*

*Again, she didn't finish. But he heard her unspoken words clearly enough. He was old. He was useless. He was bitter. And now he wasn't even in his right mind. His boys wanted to put him in a home.*

*And he suffered the urge to argue—but the more he talked with Sophie, the more he began to understand the pain he must have heaped upon all the people in*

*his life. It was all murky, distant-feeling, and yet . . .
he instinctively knew that the angry fist squeezing his
heart had been there for so long that he couldn't even
remember why, only that it wouldn't let go and was
something he'd lost control of decades ago. He wasn't
sure he deserved any mercy.*

*"I'll see you next week," she finally said, turning
to go.*

*"Sophie, wait," he rushed, stopping her.*

*She paused at the doorway, looking back.*

*"Your mother. How's your mother? What's she doing
now? Did she ever remarry? Is she happy?"*

*Grown-up Sophie looked more stunned by this than
by anything else he'd asked. "You don't remember?"*

*Even the effort required to shake his head left him
tired.*

*"Mom's doing well enough," she said, but her
pursed lips and shaded eyes told him there was more.
"She's still running Destiny Properties and making a
killing. And she's bought and refurbished another Victorian in town—that's the seventh one now. But no, she
never remarried. No matter how many men pursued
her over the years. And deep inside, she's never really
been happy since she divorced my father. But the funny
thing is . . . growing up, I always got the idea that her
unhappiness had more to do with you than with him."*

*Adam's heart broke. He'd so wanted to find out that
Sue Ann had ended up happy, leading a full life brim-
ming with passion and love. "Tell her I said hello?"
he asked.*

*But Sophie's eyes darkened further at the request. "I
don't think so, Uncle Adam. The very mention of your
name always makes her sad."*

Adam flinched awake on his sofa. Then he looked around the room. Low flames burned in the fireplace across the way. Nothing smelled musty or looked uncared for. And the scent of pine from the tree he'd put up—for the sole purpose of having a late Christmas with the twins when they came home, he recalled—filled his senses.

Whoa. It had all been a dream. He wasn't old. It wasn't too late.

It wasn't too late to stop himself from becoming a crusty old geezer no one wanted to be around.

Like other dreams he'd had lately, this one had felt startlingly real—*frighteningly* real. He even raised his head to take a good, thorough look around the room to ensure once again that the place was fairly tidy, not dust-covered, and that everything was as it should be. On the mantel he spotted both his sons' second-grade pictures. Okay, good. And out the window in the driveway he caught sight of the truck that said BECKER LAND-SCAPING on the door. He'd driven it home from work today because his parents had borrowed his pickup to bring home a new mattress. Okay, also good. He was still only thirty-three. He had plenty of life left ahead of him. And plenty of time to treat the people around him right.

Which meant, plain and simple, that he had to snap out of this Scrooge thing once and for all. Maybe his holiday season hadn't been everything he'd hoped, but that didn't mean he had to take it out on everybody else. And it hit him then that facing his troubles with anger was like . . . well, not really facing them, period.

Sitting up, he gave his head a brisk shake and tried to wake up completely. Only problem was, he still felt pretty Scroogy. Happier than he had a minute ago, of course, when he'd thought he was a crotchety, lonely old man. But sometimes you couldn't just shake a mood simply because you wanted to.

*Okay, how do I shake it? Really shake it? For good this time?*

His first move, he decided, would be getting out of the house. At the moment, Adam felt like being around people. Whose heads he would try not to bite off. Because being around people was a lot better than sitting in a dusty rocking chair watching the paint peel off the walls.

Grabbing his keys and a coat, he walked out the door not really knowing where he was headed. Sue Ann's? Nope, bad idea. He was still crazy about the woman, but he hadn't seen her since she'd thrown him out of her house, and he was pretty sure he wasn't even welcome on her doorstep right now. The landscape supply? Nah—there was work he could do in the office, but it was getting dark out and it would be as quiet there as it was here.

Finally, as he backed out of his driveway, he decided he'd go where all Destinyites headed when they needed to socialize a little after dark: the Dew Drop Inn.

Ten minutes later, he pulled into the gravel parking lot, much of it covered with a thin layer of packed snow. The simple one-story building sat outside town and looked surprisingly inviting with Christmas lights in the window and a blanket of snow dripping from the roof to form a few icicles on one side.

The parking lot was moderately full and when Adam stepped inside, he found several tables taken and a few people at the bar. Springsteen's "Santa Claus Is Comin' to Town" played on the jukebox near the door. And unfortunately, though he spotted plenty of people he knew in passing, he saw no one at the Dew Drop tonight who he'd generally sit and drink a beer with or shoot the bull.

Okay, so much for socializing. Still, lifting a hand to return a couple of waves from guys he knew as customers of Becker Landscaping, he eased onto a bar stool—then found himself taking in the shiny red garland lining the mirror behind the bar. It seemed familiar for some reason.

And then he realized why. It was the same as in his dream, the dream he'd had of his friends talking him down here at the Dew Drop. The same, even though he hadn't been in the place since before Thanksgiving. Okay, that was officially weird. But he quickly decided not to ponder that too hard or he might start feeling like he had in that *last* dream a little while ago, like he was losing it. When, in fact, his goal was to finally start getting it back.

"What'll ya have, darlin'?" Anita Garey asked him. As usual, the lady bar owner sported a tight top that showed off her shape, this one green and sparkly—for the holidays, he guessed. She was a flashy sort of woman, not the norm for Destiny, but folks here had taken a liking to her since her arrival a couple of years ago—and especially since she'd started dating Police Chief Tolliver—and Adam was among them.

"Bud Light," he told her.

Reaching under the bar, Anita grabbed a bottle, smoothly removed the top, and placed it before him. "Cheer up," she said. "It's almost Christmas."

Damn, that was how ingrained his mood had apparently become—he was clearly wearing it on his face without even knowing it. "I'm trying," he told her honestly. "That's why I'm here. Thought it would do me some good to get out, be around people." Then he met her gaze. "I haven't had the best December."

"I've heard," she said.

He sat up a little straighter. "You have?"

The lady barkeep just shrugged. "Well, I've heard you, uh, haven't been yourself lately. Something about your little boys being away for the holiday?"

And then—damn. He remembered. He remembered the hush-hush secret he'd heard: that Anita Garey had once had a little boy herself, and that he'd been abducted by her ex-husband over twenty years ago.

And he thought about the years of pain she'd endured if it were true.

And the words Sue Ann had once imparted about his boys, that night at the cabin—*At least you know they're coming back*—echoed through him in a whole new way, like the resonating clang of a bell.

God, he'd been selfish. And small. And sure, his Grinchiness had extended beyond just missing the twins—it was about divorce and the state of his life in general, and then it had become about Sue Ann, too—but still . . . Sue Ann was so right. His boys would be home soon. His life would be back to normal. And yeah, not having *her* in his life was kind of killing him now that he realized how badly he wanted her there—but when he thought of what the woman standing behind the bar had suffered, was still suffering, it just put everything in a new perspective.

"Um, yeah," he finally said, but felt almost ashamed to have griped about that when Anita's little boy hadn't *ever* come home. "And . . . some other stuff, too. But

I'm realizing that I need to count my blessings and snap out of it, you know?"

Anita nodded knowingly. "Me, I find that life is about ninety percent attitude. You just gotta keep your head held high and focus on the positive."

"You're right," Adam said, admiring her more than he could fathom. "You're absolutely right." If he ever lost his boys . . . God, he couldn't even imagine it. But something that felt a little miraculous to him had just happened. In that moment when he'd remembered Anita's son, he'd really snapped out of his mood. That last dream had started it, for sure. But this . . . this went beyond that. His kids would be home soon. And until then, they were both healthy, and safe, and happy, and with people he trusted. Not everybody had that. Anita didn't have that. The realization of just how fortunate he was, in so many ways . . . well, it suddenly felt like a heavy weight had been lifted off his shoulders, once and for all.

Anita crossed her arms over her ample chest. *"That* was easy. Usually takes me a little longer to talk somebody out of their troubles."

"Well," Adam told her, suddenly feeling a lot more like himself—like he'd been with Sue Ann at times recently, like the guy people knew and liked—"I guess I was on the verge. And I just needed to take that last step."

When the bar's front door opened again, Adam looked up to see Mike and Logan walk in. As they shook off the cold and Mike unzipped his jacket, they both caught sight of him—and merely lifted their hands in casual waves, then took a couple of stools at the end of the bar, nowhere near him.

He started to feel pissed—but then he remembered.

"I still have one problem, though," he said, switching his focus back to Anita. "I've been treating people like crap. I mean, look—my friends walk in here and don't even want to talk to me."

Again, Anita just shrugged. "So make it up to them."

"How?"

She just gave her head a saucy tilt and told him, "Guys are easy, darlin'—send 'em a couple of beers. It's how men kiss and make up."

"Huh," he said. Then, "All right. Two Bud Lights for my buddies."

A few minutes later, Anita delivered the beers, and Mike and Logan lifted them in his direction. In response, he picked up his half-empty bottle and joined them at the end of the bar.

"Thanks for the beer, dude," Logan said.

"Consider it a peace offering," he replied.

Mike angled a glance his way. "This mean you're back to normal?"

He could only shrug. "Trying to be."

Mike narrowed his gaze on Adam then, to ask, "So what's been your problem lately anyway?"

He could have dished up a few different answers. But for some reason he decided to go with the most recent. "Woman troubles."

Both guys balked, clearly surprised since they didn't know he was seeing anyone, and Logan said, "What woman?"

"You wouldn't believe me if I told you."

"Try us," Mike said, and Adam instantly decided he'd picked the wrong problem to share. Because, yeah, there wouldn't be any crime in telling them about his involvement with Sue Ann, but she'd probably feel funny about it—even if he knew he could trust these guys not to say anything. And he'd always been the type to keep romantic difficulties to himself anyway—it just seemed private.

So he finally said, "Nah—let's talk about something else. You guys ready for Christmas?"

The next day was the last day the landscape supply was open before the holiday, and since the following day was Christmas Eve, Adam planned on closing early. Besides the fact that customers were few—only the occasional person who needed a last minute wreath or greenery for a mantelpiece—he figured Chuck wouldn't mind having an extra half day to himself. Unlike Adam, Chuck had a big family to spend time with over the holidays—and in fact, his older brother was on leave from the Marines and had gotten in to town just a couple of days ago. But Adam was truly no longer bitter about his own holidays—he was glad Chuck would enjoy his Christmas; he deserved it.

So when Chuck came into the office around noon after sweeping the parking lot, and asked, "Mind if I take my lunch now?" Adam said, "Sure, and in fact, take the rest of the day off."

In response, Chuck's eyebrows shot up. "Really?"

"Really. Go spend the afternoon with your brother."

"Um, okay—and thanks," he said, face red from the cold.

Adam then reached into a drawer at the desk he sat behind and pulled out an envelope, which he held out to Chuck.

"What's this?" Chuck said cautiously as he drew it, almost hesitantly, from Adam's hand.

Adam gave his head a slight shake. "Nothing big. Just a little . . . Christmas bonus, guess you might call it." The truth was, he had never given a Christmas bonus in the past because business was lean through the winter months and it hadn't seemed prudent. This year would be just as lean, but he needed to show his employees that he appreciated them, especially after this past month.

Adam hadn't necessarily intended for him to open the envelope right now, but Chuck tore into it anyway, then pulled out a hundred-dollar gift card for the large grocery store in Crestview. His jaw dropped. "Wow, Adam. That's . . . generous."

Maybe. Kind of. But he knew Chuck still lived at home and that his family had suffered from the hard economic times of the past few years. And he wanted to ensure that Chuck's mom could make a nice Christmas dinner for them all. So he just said, "You're a hard worker. You always show up on time. You never complain. So just want to show my appreciation."

Chuck's mouth remained open in surprise, but now it was probably because Adam hadn't been this nice to him in a while. "Well, um, thanks."

Just then, Tyler Fleet walked into the office. He was off today, but Adam had called him that morning and asked him to stop by. "Hey," Tyler said, lifting his hand in a wave.

"Hey—thanks for coming on short notice," Adam told him, then dipped into the same desk drawer to extract another envelope. "Christmas bonus," he said, passing it to him.

"Really? Wow, cool," Tyler said, also ripping right into his. Inside were two tickets to an upcoming Xavier University basketball game. The school was a couple hours' drive away, but Adam happened to know Tyler was a fan of the team that consistently made it into the NCAA tournament. He also knew Tyler had never been to one of their games. "Holy crap," he said when he saw them. "This is freaking awesome."

Adam just shrugged. It had been easy enough to get his hands on the tickets, and . . . "Well, I know I haven't been the easiest guy to have as a boss lately. Truth is, I've been taking my personal problems out on you guys—and lots of other people, too—and that sucks. So I hope maybe this'll do something to make up for it and show you both that I'm glad to have such good workers."

"Um . . . hell yeah," Tyler said, still clearly excited over the basketball tickets.

And Chuck said, "Could happen to anybody, man," then held up the gift card. "This'll make my mom real happy. In fact, maybe my brother and me'll go get a big turkey to surprise her with."

After Chuck and Tyler left his office a few minutes later, Adam got up and turned the lock on the building's front door, as well as flipping the OPEN sign in the window to CLOSED. And it was quiet again. And he was alone again. And the overcast day outside—damn, looked like it might snow some more—left the office dimly lit.

But to his surprise, Adam didn't feel that same sense of loneliness he'd suffered so much lately. Funny— seemed like doing something for somebody else, and mending some fences, had truly kept his mood changed for the better. Apparently, focusing on others instead of only on himself was good for him. And he was pretty sure he used to know that, but he guessed he'd needed a reminder.

When his cell phone buzzed in the pocket of his Levi's, he reached to pull it out. A quick glance revealed it was the number of the condo where the boys and their grandparents were staying in Colorado—and when he answered, he heard Sheila's father on the other end.

"Wanted to let you know we've had a change of plans," his ex-father-in-law said.

"Oh? What's that?"

"Looks like we're coming home a little early. As in tomorrow."

Tomorrow? Tomorrow was Christmas Eve. "Really?" Adam said, trying not to sound too excited—at least not just yet.

"Yep. Turns out the boys are missing you and their mom awful bad. I think they really want to have Christmas at home. We probably should have thought of that when we planned all this, but it's easy to forget how it feels to be seven."

"Well, I'll be damned," Adam said, his heart pinching up to hear that his kids missed him, too, even enough to end their trip early. "I'm sorry it's probably causing you a headache or two, but I can't lie—I'll be real glad to have 'em home for Christmas myself."

"Can't blame ya for that," the older man said.

And as Adam pushed the disconnect button a minute later, he leaned back in his desk chair and let a big smile spread across his face. His boys were coming home for Christmas. It felt sort of like God giving him a reward for making things right with the people in his life. But maybe it was just . . . things falling into place, things beginning to straighten themselves out here and going the way they should.

Of course, there was still one part of his life that hadn't straightened itself out. And maybe he should just keep right on leaving Sue Ann well enough alone since he'd let her down. But on the other hand . . . well, he definitely had some amends to make with her, too.

Adam sat relaxing on the couch, Jacob curled under one arm, Joey under the other. The boys wore the brand new Bengals' football-themed pajamas Adam's mom and dad had gotten them—among many other things— for Christmas. Just like every year, they were spending Christmas Eve with him, and then Christmas day with Sheila. The three of them had gone to his parents' for a big holiday dinner and presents, along with his older sister's small family—then they'd come back home and sat around the tree opening gifts Adam claimed Santa must have delivered early. It was technically his year to have the boys stay over 'til Christmas morning, but since they'd been gone so long and he knew Sheila was missing them, too, he'd offered to bring them to her place later tonight—and they'd already be wearing PJs when they got there.

After presents, they'd roasted marshmallows in the fireplace and made s'mores—Adam's way of giving them all a little bit of that trip to Snow Valley the boys had missed out on. And now all eyes were glued to "Rudolph the Red-Nosed Reindeer" playing on the DVD player, which had become a tradition the last few years. Reindeer games were taking place at the moment—and of course, even as cozy and content as Adam felt right now, it made him think of the very different sort of reindeer games he'd played with Sue Ann.

*You should quit thinking about her.* So he hugged his

kids both a little tighter and tried to banish her from his mind.

But soon Rudolph was meeting Clarice, and Adam's stomach was curling up in a funny way—and then it hit him. *Oh God. She's my Clarice. Sue Ann is my Clarice.*

But she *couldn't* be his Clarice. Because Clarice trusted Rudolph, never doubted Rudolph. And he didn't have that same thing going for him with Sue Ann.

*Good God, dude, take a deep breath. Quit getting so invested in your kids' animated show. And speaking of your kids, focus on* them *now. Yeah—the two little boys finally nestled in your arms.*

And so he did.

Except for when Clarice was on the screen—sadly, then, all bets were off.

When he thought through the events of the past month, all of the good ones had included Sue Ann. Being with her had been the only thing to melt away his Grinchiness—until he'd finally come to his senses a couple of days ago—and despite the problems between them, he still couldn't help crediting her for keeping him sane these past weeks. And as he'd realized yesterday, he needed to figure out a way to make up for his mistakes with her now, too—but he hadn't found one yet. For Sue Ann, it would take more than a beer or a gift card, after all.

At one point, Rudolph had to be put on hold so Jacob could go to the bathroom, after which Adam chatted with the boys about their gifts from Santa and what else they hoped they might find at their mom's from the big guy tomorrow morning.

And hell, before the conversation was done, he remembered that Sophie wouldn't be getting what she wanted from Santa, and that while he was having a great homecoming with his kids, Sue Ann's Christmas Eve was probably filled with a lot less joy when she anticipated the morning to come. His stomach sank as he watched the rest of Rudolph. And not because he felt responsible so much as . . . he just didn't like to think of Sophie suffering through yet one more disappointment this year.

"Dad, what do you think Santa's reindeers do on Christmas morning?" Joey asked as they watched the team led by Rudolph come in for a smooth landing on the Island of Misfit Toys.

"Sleep in," he said, and they all laughed.

But as he watched the final minutes of the DVD, he got to thinking about that question a little harder, about other possible answers he could have concocted.

And an idea began to form in his head.

Maybe it wouldn't work. Maybe it was as impossible as Sophie's wish for a reindeer of her very own. But then . . . maybe not.

Could be that if he put his mind to it and pulled a few strings . . . well, perhaps he'd just figured out a way to give Sue Ann and Sophie a Christmas morning they'd never forget.

" . . . for it is good to be children sometimes, and never better than at Christmas."

Charles Dickens, A *Christmas Carol*

# *Nineteen*

It seemed to be a week for calling in favors.

After getting the boys safe and sound into Sheila's house in Crestview an hour later, where it was just starting to snow, Adam climbed back in his truck, turned up the heat, pulled out his cell phone, and looked up a number. He knew it was awfully late to call, and on a holiday, too, but fortunately Charlie Hopper was an easygoing guy who would hopefully understand when Adam explained why he was bothering him.

"Hello?"

"Charlie, it's Adam Becker." Charlie owned the Christmas tree farm about an hour west of Destiny that supplied him with the trees for his lot each year. And trees weren't the only things he raised on his farm, either.

"What can I do for ya on this fine Christmas Eve, Adam?" Charlie asked. He didn't even sound perturbed, for which Adam was grateful. Because if anyone deserved to act Scroogy right now, it was probably Charlie.

Then Adam took a deep breath. Here went nothin'. "Thing is, Charlie, I need a huge favor. And I'm hoping you can help me out."

In the early dawn of Christmas morning, Sue Ann sat in her living room in pajamas, a soft pink terry robe, and thick, fuzzy socks, staring at the Christmas tree. After a big family dinner at her mother's, she and Sophie had set out cookies and milk for Santa. Then she'd tucked Sophie in, read "The Night Before Christmas," and stayed up past 2:00 A.M. putting out Sophie's gifts, including the stuffed reindeer she'd bought—the best she could do to give her daughter what she'd asked for.

*Damn, I should have broken down and gotten that kitten from Amy.* It would have made a wonderful gift and, as Adam had suggested, it would probably have been enough to make Sophie forget there wasn't a live reindeer in the room. But it was too late for that. All she could do now was deal with the fallout.

God, this was wrong, all wrong. Christmas was supposed to be a magical time for a child—it always had been for her as a little girl. It was supposed to be the time of the year when families were together, when wishes came true, and when miracles happened. *Well, Soph, it's gonna take one hell of a miracle to give you a merry Christmas, and I'm fresh out of them right now.*

Some years on Christmas morning, she and Jeff had gone into Sophie's room, actually waking her up because they couldn't wait to see the joy and excitement on her face as she rushed down to find what Santa had brought. This year, though, Sue Ann almost dreaded seeing Sophie come down those stairs. She had no idea what she could possibly do to explain why Santa had let her down, other than spout more of the same stuff about him needing all his reindeer and reminding her that he'd only said he'd try.

*Adam* had said he'd try. The thought of him made her heart contract as a fresh sense of loneliness wafted over her. She missed him. She missed what they'd started to have together. But what she knew now, without a doubt, was that if she took one step closer to him she'd be even deeper in love than she already was—and if she risked letting herself be hurt further, she wasn't sure how she'd recover. One world-shattering heartbreak was enough for a lifetime.

And she had more important things to do than risk her emotional well-being in exchange for a man's company.

And, well, for great sex, too.

Both of those were important, but it was far more vital to focus on Sophie's happiness, and her new job, and to get herself to a place where she felt truly strong and independent.

She reached down to the cookie plate where one remained, not eaten by her last night, and nibbled at a yellow-frosted star, crumbs dropping down onto her robe. Brushing them away, she realized she had on the same snowflake-covered flannel pants and cami she'd worn that night in the cabin. And she remembered how Adam had called her his snow angel when she'd stripped off her snowflake turtleneck the night they'd made love in her bedroom.

Wow, made love. That was what he'd called it. That was what it had been. It wasn't getting laid, like she'd so meanly said that night by the fire—she'd just been angry and hurt. Now she shut her eyes, trying to blot out the memories, attempting to crush the nagging flare of arousal between her thighs. *Don't cry. Don't cry about Adam. Don't cry about the-reindeer-that-wasn't.*

When she opened her eyes a few minutes later, the glow of dawn beyond the bay window had brightened into full early morning. More snow had fallen overnight and now blanketed the yard, fresh and untouched. That's when she heard the first stirrings of life up above her in the big, old house and knew the moment of truth was at hand. Sophie was up.

Up and running, in fact—Sue Ann could hear the *thump, thump, thump* of her little feet as she barreled toward the stairs and down. She looked up to see her daughter bright-eyed and beaming from ear to ear in fleece pajamas covered with pink candy canes. "Did he come? Did he come?" she squealed.

Sue Ann's heart nearly rose to her throat as she forced a smile and said, "Of course he did—just like always."

Sophie came trundling into the room, taking in the scene—checking out the gifts around the tree. She didn't appear upset yet—instead, when she didn't see what she wanted there, she just shifted her attention out the wide window into the yard. Where, of course, there was still no reindeer. Stark silence punctuated the moment as the expression on her daughter's face pierced Sue Ann's heart. She should have turned some Christmas music on to create a distraction.

But then she realized she'd been trying to create distractions for herself and Sophie all holiday season long. And sometimes it even worked. It got them through tricky moments, helped them keep moving. But something as simple as music wouldn't have fixed this, not even close. Sophie just had to go through this, that was all. She had to feel the pain—she had to suffer the disappointment. Just like Sue Ann had to feel the pain of Adam's brief betrayal, and then of letting Adam go.

When Sophie spoke, her voice came as a mere whisper. "I thought he'd do it. I thought he'd bring me a reindeer."

Sue Ann tried to catch her breath, stay strong, be the sensible mom. "He said he'd try, honey, and I'm sure he did. That's all any of us can do. Something must have kept him from being able to part with one of his herd or I'm sure he would have."

Sophie just sighed, and again, Sue Ann tried for a smile as she motioned toward the gifts. "But look at all the other presents Santa left for you. I'm sure there's some good stuff! Why don't we see?" Then she moved down onto the floor, next to the merrily lit tree, reaching for Sophie's hand so she would join her.

Sue Ann quickly pointed out a new dollhouse she'd spent quite a bit of time assembling last night. Though she'd passed some of her old dollhouses on to Sophie already, this would be her daughter's first brand new one. "Oh, look—Santa must know you like dollhouses. Wow, look how pretty this one is!"

Sophie shifted her gaze to the small Victorian house filled with miniature furniture, her eyes brightening some. "Yeah," she said. "Look at the girl's room." She leaned to peer inside, clearly enamored of the pink décor in what was designed to be a teenager's bedroom.

"Maybe one day we'll do *your* room like that," Sue Ann offered, and Sophie smiled.

"That'd be cool," she said.

After examining the dollhouse a bit more, leaving Sue Ann pleased that it was a hit, Sophie began to open wrapped gifts one by one as Sue Ann raved over how pretty the packages were. Maybe distractions *could* work here.

Though when they reached the stuffed reindeer in one corner, Sophie's gaze saddened all over again and Sue Ann realized her error. She shouldn't have brought reindeers into the mix at all.

"Isn't he cute?" Sue Ann asked. "You should give him a hug."

"He's a stuffed animal," Sophie said, sounding far too world-weary for a seven-year-old. And despite knowing it had been a lame attempt to fill the void, it wounded Sue Ann a little to hear that this particular gift was such a flop.

"I'm sure Santa thought you'd like it, even if it's not the real thing. It shows he remembered what you wanted, right? And look at him," Sue Ann said, motioning to the deer. "I think he's adorable. So if you don't want him, I'll just let him come live in my room with me."

She said the last part in a teasing voice that brought Sophie around—she appeared troubled for a quick second, then laughed and said, "No, he's mine."

Sue Ann lowered her chin and gave her daughter a look. "I thought you didn't like him."

"No, I like him a lot," Sophie insisted, finally reaching out to pull the stuffed deer toward her for a hug.

"I think he has a real reindeer's spirit inside him," Sue Ann offered up, the idea just hitting her.

But at this, her daughter only looked at the deer and said, "Maybe." And her expression again turned glum. "I like him—I just wish he was real. Really real. Like the ones we saw at the zoo last year."

Tired, Sue Ann was at a loss. But maybe another distraction would work. "Why don't we see what Santa left in your stocking."

Of course, as they got to their feet and headed toward the mantel, Sue Ann was reminded how much lonelier two stockings looked compared to the three that had hung there on previous Christmases. Still, Sophie's bulged with candy and a few other small gifts Sue Ann had stuffed inside, so hopefully something within it would capture her attention.

Though just as Sophie reached it, Sue Ann realized that it looked a little different than when she'd gone to bed last night. She'd left a small teddy bear in a Santa hat poking its head out, but the bear was nowhere in sight. What the hell? Instead, a small plastic bag with something grainlike inside stuck out the top of the red velvet stocking, bearing a big green tag.

"Hmm," Sue Ann said, her curiosity sincere. "What's that?"

Then, as Sophie extracted the bag, Sue Ann saw the handwritten label on the outside: *Reindeer Food*.

She swallowed nervously, not sure what to make of this. Where had it come from? And why?

That's when Sophie opened the big, folded green tag attached to the bag and gasped. "Mommy, look! Help me read this!"

Taking the bag from Sophie's hand, Sue Ann recited what was written inside the tag out loud, more stunned with each word that passed through her lips. "To Sophie, from . . . Dancer. I'm waiting for you in the backyard. I can only visit for a little while, but I wanted to wish you a merry Christmas."

Sue Ann and Sophie just looked at each other, both equally taken aback. Sue Ann tried to reason it through. *Okay, I know there's not really a Santa Claus, and I know a reindeer can't really write notes. So surely there can't really be a reindeer in my backyard. Can there?*

But Sophie had already snatched the bag of reindeer food and raced toward the back door, so what else could Sue Ann do but follow? Heading into the kitchen, she watched her little girl nearly skid out the door in her socks, so she rushed after her, catching the door before it fell shut, then stepping out onto the back porch into the fresh snow, also in socks. And she was just about to tell Sophie they needed to get their snow boots on—when what she saw silenced her.

A reindeer.

A real, live, honest-to-goodness reindeer stood in her backyard.

How could this be? They both just gaped, ignoring their wet, freezing feet.

Apparently, miracles really did happen at Christmas—Sophie's impossible Christmas wish had somehow come true! And at this point, Sue Ann wouldn't have been surprised if the reindeer stepped up and said hello.

The animal standing near the storage shed appeared docile, unmoving—and that's when Sue Ann realized it was firmly tethered on a short rope, which stretched into the bushes next to the shed. Okay, good. The reindeer hadn't just come here of its own volition, and Santa hadn't left it behind. She wasn't losing her mind.

"Mommy! Santa did it! Santa brought me a reindeer!"

"Looks like he did," Sue Ann murmured, still in awe.

Then she spotted Adam crouched down in those very same bushes. And—oh God—he was the one making this happen; he was the one saving Sophie's Christmas and making miracles to boot!

As their eyes met through the winter-thin branches, a lump rose to her throat—she wasn't sure anyone had ever done anything so special for her or Sophie, ever.

And as the seconds stretched out into a long, wondrously golden moment, tears welled behind her eyes. Because this wasn't a small thing. It was closer to huge. And she didn't know how he'd done this, but what she did know was that he didn't have to. She knew he'd done it because he was a good guy; he was that good man everyone knew him to be. Their gazes stayed connected and she could feel her heart stretching, bending, yearning, wanting.

Sophie, however, hadn't spotted Adam—she had eyes only for the big shaggy caribou twenty feet away out in the snowy yard. When she finally got over her shock enough to start toward the edge of the porch, Sue Ann had the wherewithal to grab onto her little shoulder, pulling her back to say, "Wait." Then she reached inside for the kid-size snow boots that had last been left on a small rug by the back door. And as Sophie struggled to step hurriedly into them in already soaking wet socks, Sue Ann grabbed her daughter's old play jacket from a hook inside, along with an old pair of gym shoes for herself.

When Sophie began to approach the reindeer, Adam looked to Sue Ann again, giving her a slight nod, silently indicating that it was safe, and indeed, even as she stepped right up to it, the reindeer stayed still, and Sue Ann could have sworn the animal's gentle eyes locked with her daughter's awestruck ones.

"Careful," Sue Ann called anyway as Sophie reached up to softly pet the deer's neck. But—oh God—it was quite a sight, and in reality, Sue Ann experienced no fear at all; the moment was that perfect.

"Untie the ribbon on the bag," Sue Ann said when she sensed the reindeer eyeing the grain Sophie still held. "Then hold some in your hand, flat. Like when we fed them at the zoo, remember?"

Sophie looked back, nodding, and Sue Ann allowed herself to dash back into the house, quickly, just long enough to get her camera.

It was clear to see how Sophie delighted in feeding and petting "Dancer" for a few long and wonderful minutes, occasionally whispering something to the deer that Sue Ann couldn't hear but found heartrending anyway. And when the reindeer food was all gone, Sophie looked up at Sue Ann on the porch, wearing a great big smile, and exclaimed, "This is the best Christmas ever!"

Sue Ann swallowed the lump in her throat, still trying not to cry. Oh Lord. Adam had done the impossible—he'd taken what could have been Sophie's worst Christmas and turned it into her best. Talk about

Christmas miracles. The reindeer visit—appearing to come straight from Santa—had seemingly wiped away the sadness of not having a normal Christmas with her father there.

So Sue Ann watched for another few minutes, continuing to take pictures, as Sophie spent time with her new friend—and then finally, when she was chilled to the bone and felt certain both Sophie and Adam were, too—she called, "You should say goodbye and come back inside, honey. Remember, the note said he could only stay a few minutes, so I'm sure it's time for him to go."

At this reminder, Sophie looked sad and Sue Ann realized her daughter hadn't even noticed the cold—but still Sophie said, "Okay," and turned back to "Dancer," this time actually giving him a hug. Sue Ann bit her lip at the utter poignancy of it, then flicked her gaze back to Adam, still crouched in the shrubbery. And what she saw in his eyes as they met hers . . . oh God, that nearly made her weep, too.

He still wanted her. And he cared about her. And his heart was breaking, too. She knew all that, knew it to the marrow of her bones, just from the expression on his handsome, unshaven face right now—it was all there, nothing held back. Funny, she hadn't really thought much about that part of it before—his part. She'd thought of her own fears, her own anger, her own emotions—yet she hadn't much considered his.

*But that doesn't change anything. It doesn't make you any safer, any more secure. You have to protect yourself.*

"Bye, Dancer," she heard Sophie saying, and shifted her focus back to her daughter and the reindeer standing in her backyard, looking like some figment of her imagination. "Thank you for coming to see me. It's the coolest thing that's ever happened to me and I'll love you forever!"

The reindeer let out a slight snuffle then, as if in reply, and Sophie reached up to give him one last gentle pet, just above his nose. "Bye," she whispered again, then began walking slowly back toward the porch, even as she looked over her shoulder at the deer, their eyes still seeming to connect.

When she climbed the steps, Sue Ann stooped down to give her a big hug, and after a moment whispered in her ear, "See, Santa came through. He didn't let you down."

And Sophie pulled back to smile and nod, though there were tears in her eyes now, as well.

Sue Ann gave her daughter another squeeze, then said, "Go back inside and get warmed up. I'll be right behind you in a minute."

Once Sophie was safely back in the house, Sue Ann ventured carefully down the snowy steps and through the yard to meet Adam, where he emerged from the bushes. His cheeks were red with cold and he looked so warm and cuddleworthy bundled in his winter coat and hat that it was hard not to give him a hug, too—but she resisted, and instead said, "Thank you. So, so much. You have no idea what this means to her."

He gave his head a slight tilt and replied, "Actually, I think I do. That's why I did it. I couldn't bear the idea of you guys having a bad Christmas."

Sue Ann just bit her lip, more touched than she could say. Then she asked the obvious. "But . . . how did you do this? How the hell did you come up with a reindeer?" She glanced over at the animal a few yards away, still a little amazed.

Adam simply slanted her a playful look and said, "Come on now—you know I have reindeer connections."

Then he explained that he'd enlisted Sue Ann's mom to sneak the reindeer food into Sophie's stocking late, after they'd gone to bed, and that the man who provided the trees for his lot also raised a few reindeer on his farm. "I totally forgot about that, though, until just last night." Then, looking over at the deer himself, he said to it, "You and me, we've gotten pretty close now, haven't we?" And when Sue Ann gave him a questioning look, he said, "Truth is, I've spent all night with this guy."

"Huh?" She cocked her head to one side, perplexed.

But he just shrugged. "Takes a while to get a reindeer loaded in a truck. Takes a longer while to get a reindeer *un*loaded from a truck, by myself, quietly. Thank God this guy's gentle. And we've been out here a few hours now."

She flinched, her eyes bolting open wider. "A few hours?"

"Wasn't sure how early Sophie would get up. I mean, it's Christmas morning. For my boys, sometimes it's so early that it's really the middle of the night. And I couldn't risk not being ready."

Sue Ann stood before him, dumbfounded, as she took in everything that meant. "You must be exhausted. And freezing."

He offered up only another easy shrug. "I can sleep all day."

Oh God. How sad. "On Christmas?"

He must have read her thoughts, though. "Hey, don't worry. Turns out I've already had my Christmas. The boys came home early—yesterday. Got to take 'em to dinner at my parents' place and then spent the whole evening with 'em."

Sue Ann let out a happy gasp, truly as thrilled for him as she was for Sophie right now. "Really?"

"Yep." A large smile spread across his handsome face. "And damn, was it ever good to see those two little rug rats."

"I can only imagine," she said with a smile of her own. "I'm so glad for you, so glad they were here for Christmas."

"So—yeah, as far as Christmas is concerned, things turned out good. And I'm putting my Scroogy ways behind me once and for all."

And then she realized he was looking at her—in a different way than he had a moment ago. Before, it had been a pleasant exchange between two parents, but suddenly, now, his expression had transformed into the one she'd seen when their eyes had met a few minutes earlier—an expression that said he still yearned for her the same way she yearned for him.

And it sort of took her breath away. Enough that she didn't bother trying to eke out very many words—only said, perhaps too softly, "Well, good."

As that wanting gaze of his continued to pour over her, she thought for a second he might kiss her, standing right there in her snowy backyard as she hugged her big pink robe around her. And she wondered if she'd be able to resist right now. After all, the man had made her daughter's Christmas wish come true. And he looked good enough to eat.

But then he suddenly went a bit stiffer, standing up a little straighter, and said, "I better get this guy back in the truck."

"Yeah, right, of course," she murmured.

"Think you can keep Sophie from looking out the windows for a little while?"

"No problem. We're going to make Christmas pancakes before Jeff comes to pick her up, so I'll keep her in the kitchen until I'm sure you two are gone."

"Sounds good," he said, then lifted his hand toward the reindeer's lead line, which she could now see hooked to a strong branch in the shrubbery.

"And Adam," she said then, fending off the urge to reach out and touch his arm through his winter coat, "thank you again. This was . . . "

He grinned. "Don't say it was just nice."

And a small giggle escaped her as his words drew her back to their post-sex conversations. "It was spectacular," she said, teasing him. "Amazing. Phenomenal."

"The earth moved," he supplied for her.

"And I saw fireworks," she added with a smile.

But then the humor faded and they were edging back into that nagging, gnawing desire again—only this time *she* was the one to make them move past it, returning to what he'd done for Sophie. "It really was . . . the most special thing that could have happened for her. She'll never forget this. And neither will I."

And still, she nearly melted in the heat from his warm brown eyes as he said, "I was glad to do it, Sue Ann. And glad . . . it made you happy."

They stood together for another slightly-too-long moment before Adam said, "Well, I'd better get this reindeer back home. And you'd better get inside before your feet freeze off." He motioned down toward the canvas tennis shoes she'd put on.

"Yeah," she said. "They're pretty cold. And I'm sure you are, too. Thanks again."

He just nodded. And she turned to go, her heart beating far too fast, as usual lately when she was with Adam.

She only allowed herself to look back when she'd reached the porch—and when she discovered him still watching her, she raised her hand in a short wave just before rushing inside, shutting the door, and then leaning back against it. *Oh God, he's sweet. And hot. And still sexy as hell, damn it.*

*But it's Christmas. Get back to Christmas. Sophie. Presents. Pancakes.*

She found her daughter in the living room, now hugging her stuffed reindeer tight under one arm as she sat on the floor playing with her new dollhouse. She looked more content than Sue Ann had seen her in months.

"Ready for pancakes, my girl?"

Sophie hopped to her feet with a smile, still clutching the stuffed animal. "Yeah."

But as they headed back toward the kitchen, Sophie said, "Hey Mommy, look—I think Santa must have left something in your stocking, too."

And, glancing over, Sue Ann realized that, indeed, her red velvet stocking bulged just a little, hanging differently than when it was empty. "Hmm," she said, figuring perhaps her suddenly sneaky mother had decided it was a good opportunity to leave her some additional small gift while skulking around her house in the middle of the night.

"Let's see what's there," she said, padding over to the

fireplace. Then she reached down inside and pulled out
. . . an old-fashioned glass Santa ornament, identical
to the one that had been broken. As her heart swelled,
she saw it had a tag attached, too, just like Sophie's
reindeer food:

*Merry Christmas, Sugar Plum.*
                    *Love, Adam*

"He was very much attached to me."

Charles Dickens, A *Christmas Carol*

# *Twenty*

---

*J*enny, Rachel, and Tessa were all busy with family gatherings that day, of course. But Amy, knowing Sue Ann would be at loose ends, had invited her over to her apartment above the bookstore to watch Christmas movies and nibble on holiday leftovers from a family dinner the night before.

It felt strange to be parking on the now quiet town square, preparing to climb the steps to Amy's place on Christmas Day. Normally it was her family on Christmas Eve and Jeff's on Christmas, where Sophie was now. And she couldn't shake the sense that life felt a little emptier when you had nowhere you particularly needed to be on Christmas Day. Thinking of Adam at home now, sleeping through it, she almost wondered if she should call him up and invite him over, too.

*But it's just another day. You'll get used to it. Maybe you'll even like how low key it is.*

*And Adam clearly needs some sleep, so let him. You don't need to be spending time with him anyway. Even if what he did this morning was amazingly sweet and special, you can't let yourself be drawn in like that.* Because even if he'd turned down Jeff's request, the fact that he hadn't told her about that subpoena the moment he found out, when she'd felt the very closest to him no less . . . well, her trust issues with Adam were alive and well.

And it wasn't that she thought Adam was *trying* to draw her in, only that it could happen if she didn't keep her guard up. And somewhere along the way, self-protection had become the all-important thing here, the thing she couldn't afford to lose sight of.

As for that antique ornament, she'd been stunned and pleased to have an exact replacement for her grandmother's, and despite herself, was touched that he'd gone to so much trouble. She couldn't deny that Adam seemed more than willing to go to extra effort just to make her—and her daughter—happy. But she'd tried to banish those thoughts as she'd hung the ornament on the tree—after removing the tag, of course. *Love, Adam* it had said. *Love.*

But lots of people wrote *Love* on their cards and it just meant "with strong affection." Although . . . did *guys* write it that casually?

Well, it didn't matter—she'd made herself throw the tag in the trash with the wrapping paper Sophie had ripped off her gifts from Santa.

Of course, this meant her mother knew. Well, at least it meant she knew Adam was calling her Sugar Plum, which had probably tipped her mom off that *something* was going on. And that felt a little weird. After all, what had Adam told her? And what did her mom think about it all? Well, whatever the case, she hoped Adam had also filled her in on the fact that anything that had taken place between them was already over.

Tonight was the big annual Destiny Christmas party at town hall—a tradition Chief Tolliver had started many years ago after his wife had died when Jenny was just thirteen. The idea behind it had been to make sure everyone in town had something to do on Christmas—but now no one ever missed it. So if she didn't talk to her mom before that, she would see her there. And she figured Adam would be there, too. But him she would just make a point of avoiding. For the sake of her heart. She'd come far too close to kissing him this morning—and God knew she'd wanted to.

A minute later, Amy was greeting her with a hug, pulling her into the apartment, and showing her the treasure trove of classic Christmas movies she possessed. And soon they were stretched out on the couch watching *It's a Wonderful Life,* a spread of food on the coffee table before them: pumpkin pie, fudge, Amy's buckeyes, Sue Ann's Christmas cookies, and half a cheeseball with crackers.

It was about the time George Bailey rescued his brother Harry from the hole in the ice that the kitten, Dickens, decided Sue Ann's shoelace would make a good toy. Amy's beloved pet, Mr. Knightley, was already curled up with her at the other end of the sofa, but Sue Ann was surprised to see Dickens. "What's *he* doing up here?" she asked.

And Amy just looked at her like she'd lost her mind. "Well, I couldn't very well leave him down in the store by himself on Christmas." As if the gray kitten could read a calendar and knew it was a holiday.

Sue Ann pulled her foot away from the silly cat. "Well, he's annoying."

Amy just rolled her eyes. "He's playful and a little mischievous. But that's his charm."

"You call this charm?" Sue Ann asked dryly, still trying to regain control of her shoe.

Finally, she just kicked her shoes off and pulled her feet up onto the couch with her. "Ha, guess I showed *you*," she whispered triumphantly down to the kitten. Which was when he rose up and took a swipe at her fingertips where they hung over the edge of the sofa cushion. She gave him a look of warning, then pointed one narrowly missed finger at him. "You're a trouble-maker, pal."

Dickens let out a small meow, as if defending himself—then noticed the strap of Sue Ann's purse hanging over the arm of the sofa. Within seconds it became his newest toy, so she gathered up the strap and shoved it under the purse with a sigh. "Take that," she whispered smartly.

And Amy said, "Shush—I'm trying to watch a movie."

Sue Ann slanted a glance in her direction. "Yes, it's important to hear every line of a movie you've seen thirty times."

"Shhhh," Amy said anyway.

It was when George and Mary were doing the Charleston on the edge of the pool that Dickens leapt silently up onto the couch and started walking around on Sue Ann like she was part of the furniture. She said, "Sheesh," and set him beside her on the middle cushion.

But by the time George and Mary were singing

"Buffalo Gals" on the front walk, the gray kitten found a spot to settle—right in Sue Ann's lap—and she decided to let him stay. And that maybe, just maybe, he wasn't so bad. Maybe the little guy was actually pretty cute, even if she didn't like to admit it.

And it was exactly when Mary said, "Welcome home, Mr. Bailey," that Sue Ann realized she'd absently begun to pet him a little. "Hmm," she said, glancing down.

"Hmm what?" Amy asked her, eyes still glued to the TV.

"Hmm, I guess maybe I'm starting to get what Sophie sees in this cat. A little anyway." Then she thought out loud. "I wonder if maybe . . . I should think about taking a leap of faith."

"What leap of faith?"

"That maybe Sophie can take care of a cat. That maybe he wouldn't be just an expensive headache. Maybe I should reconsider."

When Amy finally drew her attention from the screen to flash a big smile across the space between them, Sue Ann thrust a pointed finger in her direction. "But don't get your hopes up. I still need to think about it."

"No problem—my hopes are in check." She still smiled, though. Then asked, "How was Sophie's Christmas morning?" Everyone knew how concerned Sue Ann had been about that.

And while the easy answer was that it had turned out great, that reply would require a lot of explanation, which she knew Amy would dig for if she didn't supply it, so instead Sue Ann said, "I thought you were watching a movie."

"I am," Amy said, reaching for the remote, "but we can pause it. I need a bathroom break anyway." And the picture on the screen stilled, leaving the room quiet. "So, about Sophie's Christmas. How did she take it when there wasn't a reindeer under the tree?"

"Not very well," Sue Ann said, realizing she'd have to tell the story whether she liked it or not. "But things got a lot better when she discovered that there *was* a reindeer in the *backyard*."

Amy blinked. "There was a reindeer in the backyard?"

"Yep," Sue Ann said, still a little awed by the memory. Or maybe it was the sweetness involved on Adam's part that left her feeling overwhelmed. "Incredible but true."

Amy just gaped at her. "Well, are you going to give me any details? I mean, I'm pretty sure a reindeer didn't just come conveniently wandering up Holly Lane to your house on Christmas morning."

Okay, this part would be a little tricky, but she could handle it. "Adam brought it," she said.

"Adam brought it?" Amy asked.

"Because of how he semi-promised it to her when he was playing Santa. And of course, he *is* Sophie's godfather." Then she explained about him knowing a man with some reindeer. "And naturally, Sophie thought it was the best thing ever, and it really *was* pretty amazing, so . . . Adam definitely saved the day."

"What else?" Amy asked.

"What do you mean, 'What else?' "

Amy tilted her head and cast a speculative look Sue Ann recognized. "There's more. More you're not telling me."

Oh, for heaven's sake. Usually it was her and Jenny who knew when the other was holding something back. But with Amy . . . well, her sixth sense generally pertained to romance. Which meant that Amy some-how sensed what Sue Ann's mom already knew—that something was up between her and Adam. Still, she fibbed, on the off chance Amy would believe her and let it go. "No there's not."

But letting it go was not to be. "You like Adam," Amy concluded after a pause. "*Like* like him. Not just as a friend anymore."

Sue Ann simply sighed, blinked. "You got that from the fact that he brought a reindeer to my yard?"

"I got that from the look in your eyes when you said it."

Damn it. "I was trying to be nonchalant yet apprecia-tive of his effort."

"You failed on the first part. I mean, the delivery was okay—if we'd been on the phone, I'd have never known—but it's your expression. And you blushed a little when you said he saved the day."

Now Sue Ann let out a much larger sigh and said, "Don't tell anybody, okay? Only Jenny knows. And I feel very weird about it."

"No problem—I can keep a secret. But this has been going on awhile, hasn't it? Because I even thought you were acting a little odd that day Rachel suggested *I* hook up with Adam."

Sue Ann let her mouth drop open in disbelief. "God, you have an uncanny ability to recognize crap like this."

"It's a gift," Amy said with a shrug. Then she leaned in closer, eyes widened and hopeful. "So does he like you back? And is it serious?"

Oh hell. Why lie at this point? Amy would eventually weasel it all out of her anyway. "Yes, he likes me back.

And yes, it feels . . . horribly serious to me. And to him, too, I think. Only . . . " She shook her head, still sad about the whole situation. "We can't be together."

Amy looked stunned. "Why not?"

"Because . . . it's just so soon after my divorce. And there are trust issues. And besides, there's so much going on for me right now—big, life-altering things."

"Which would probably be easier to handle with the love of a good man in your life, don't you think?"

Lord, she and Jenny both made this sound so simple. But it wasn't. "Amy, I've thought long and hard about this, believe me, and I just can't deal with it right now. I mean, I'm barely over the last man in my life, you know?"

"You're afraid," Amy said softly.

Hmm, funny. Sue Ann could spend all day postulating all the reasons she couldn't be with Adam, but yeah, when she got right down to it, it was indeed as simple as that one little word. "Yes, I'm afraid," she admitted.

Amy stayed quiet for a minute, clearly thinking this through, and reaching for a buckeye to help her. After she'd eaten it, she said, "I don't want to discount your fears, Sue Ann. I mean, I get it, and I know you have a lot on your plate right now. But . . . "

Sue Ann bit her lip. "But what?"

Amy met her gaze and looked suddenly, profoundly serious. "I've only been in love once in my life. It was a long time ago, and it didn't last long enough." Sue Ann remembered—Amy had had a boyfriend from another town for a couple of years after high school, and everyone had assumed they'd get married—only they didn't. They'd broken up, and as far as Sue Ann knew,

Amy hadn't dated anyone since. It always made her sad to think about.

"You've been with the same guy since we were young," Amy went on, "so maybe you don't know this, but . . . love, real passion, doesn't come along just every day. You went from loving Jeff right to having these feelings for Adam, yet it just as easily could have been years—or never—before you found someone you felt this way about. To pass it up because you're afraid is . . . almost criminal. It's a terrible waste. For both of you."

Whoa. Sue Ann just sat there, trying to absorb everything her friend had just said. Amy was usually so upbeat, happy, fun—but right now she looked more somber than Sue Ann could remember seeing her in a very long time.

And she knew what neither of them were saying—that Amy would probably give anything to have a good man like Adam fall for her. And she wouldn't take it for granted. She was reminding Sue Ann that she was actually pretty damn lucky to already have a great guy like Adam wanting a relationship with her.

"I . . . I know that. But the timing . . . "

"Sucks a little, yeah. Or maybe it's actually perfect. Whatever—doesn't matter. I just think it's too precious and valuable a thing to pass up over something like fear. And besides, if you love him—" She stopped then. "Do you? Love him?"

Sue Ann's chest tightened with her gasp. What a question. "I—I don't know."

"Well, the thing is, even I, with my limited experience, know that if you do love him, you can't stop just because you want to. Love doesn't work that way. It's not that easy."

*   *   *

Other than a few years between high school and adult-
hood when he'd thought he was too cool, Adam had
attended the annual Destiny Christmas party at town
hall without fail. Besides being a nice way to catch up
with everyone in the community after the busy holiday
season, it was usually just a damn good time.

Of course, it was snowing for this year's party. Again.
"For God's sake," he muttered, looking skyward as
he stepped out of the house heading for his truck. A
few new inches had fallen throughout the day and the
weatherman had reported that it would keep right on
coming until daybreak. He'd never seen so much snow
in December in his entire life.

But he tried to remember that people loved a white
Christmas and that some considered Christmas snow
more of a magical thing than a nuisance. His boys, to
name two. He'd talked to Jacob and Joey earlier and
they'd convinced their mom to let them go sledding
in lieu of sitting around with her extended family all
afternoon. And a part of him was definitely wishing
he could be there with them, playing in the snow—but
lately he'd come to accept that this was just a condition
of his life now. He wouldn't always have every moment
with his sons that he wanted. Which simply meant he
had to make the time he did have count. And overall,
he was just glad they were home. They wouldn't be at
the party tonight, but he'd pick them up tomorrow for
a couple of days, and he'd have them again over New
Year's.

As for now, dealing with the snow in practical ways
meant a lot of people were having a hard time getting to
the party tonight, but everyone with four-wheel-drive

vehicles was pitching in to help out—including him. Currently he was on his way to pick up not only Edna Farris, but also "a slew of apple pies," she'd told him on the phone an hour ago. "Get me there in one piece and there's a whole pie with your name on it."

Given how good Edna's apple pies were, he'd said, "Now that's an offer I can't refuse."

After that, he'd make another trip out to transport Willie Hargis, Grampy Hoskins, and anybody else who called needing a ride by then.

And as he turned on his windshield wipers to battle the snow, falling in thick, heavy flakes, he realized that a week or two ago, calls asking him for help would have had him growling and snarling his way into Grinchville—which must mean he'd truly, finally, shaken that off now, thank God. Because he was happy to help, happy he *could* help.

Part of that, of course, was because his kids were home and Christmas had turned out pretty damn nice after all. And part of it, too, had to do with this morning, with delivering that reindeer to Sophie. The truth was, it had been a hellacious amount of work and he'd been just as exhausted and cold as Sue Ann had suspected. But he hadn't minded a bit, especially when he'd seen the look on Sophie's face. And also the look on Sue Ann's.

It had been truly gratifying to make Sophie's Christmas special.

And . . . illuminating to realize how much Sue Ann still wanted him.

She hadn't said that, but she hadn't needed to. Somehow, even despite the facts that she'd been in a bathrobe with her hair pointing all over the place and that he'd been unable to feel his fingers by then . . . the expression on her face had warmed him inside and made him realize he wasn't alone in his feelings here, he wasn't the only one suffering. And yeah, he'd understood that before, but given that the last time he'd seen her she'd been throwing him out of her house, maybe he'd forgotten. Maybe he'd forgotten just how sexy and sweet she could look when she felt that invisible pull between them. Maybe he'd forgotten the caring went both ways.

Yet now he remembered. And he still hadn't had any strange dreams today as he'd slept off his reindeer-related exhaustion, instead waking up feeling . . . happy.

He wasn't sure why. He still didn't have the girl he was pining for, after all. But maybe . . . well, maybe something had happened inside him that he hadn't expected.

Over the last few days, people had forgiven him for being a first-class jerk this month. And without quite realizing it until today, somehow, at the same time, he thought *he'd* finally forgiven himself, too. But not for his Scroogy attitude. For what he'd done at that wedding.

God knew he'd been carrying the weight of it for a while now—three long years. And through everything that had happened over the last few weeks, he realized he was at last ready to stop mentally beating himself up for it. And that—along with all the other good tidings of the last few days, including a call to Jeff's lawyer today that he thought might allay some of Sue Ann's fears about his testimony—was indeed enough to make him a happy guy on this snowy Christmas night.

All of which made him cautiously begin to wonder

if maybe, just maybe, it was possible for Sue Ann to forgive him, too.

Could be that he was a glutton for punishment, but he'd realized he still wasn't quite ready to take no for an answer from her. The emotion in her eyes this morning had reminded him how much there was between them, and that it was just too damn precious to let go.

She didn't think she was ready to trust him? Understandable.

But he'd just have to change her mind.

Tonight.

As to her, she was worthy to be his partner in every sense of the term.

Charles Dickens, A Christmas Carol

## Twenty-one

When Adam hung up his coat and stepped into the party, Bryan Adams' version of "Run, Run Rudolph" rocked through the large town hall meeting room. The place was aglow with white mini-lights and filled with Destiny residents celebrating the holiday. Long tables overflowed with both new dishes and leftovers from celebrations at home: cookies and candies and fudge, stuffing and cranberries and mashed potatoes. Chief Tolliver stood carving a turkey Jenny had baked for the occasion, and Adam even spotted a couple of fruit-cakes people had undoubtedly received as gifts and were hoping to rid themselves of here.

Little kids danced around a twinkling Christmas tree near the wide front windows, where snow could be seen falling outside. Ladies mingled and admired each other's holiday fashions while men stood around drinking beer and slapping each other on the back, many of them clearly uncomfortable in new sweaters they'd gotten just today. He spotted Tyler Fleet kissing Cara Collins under a sprig of mistletoe that hung from a light fixture.

Everything was as it should be on this snowy Destiny night, and taking it all in gave him a warm feeling.

Except . . . well, okay, not *everything* was as it should be. The night wasn't perfect. Yet. But he'd be working on changing that, with Sue Ann, very soon.

As he grabbed a festive paper plate and began to load it with food, Mike and Rachel meandered up. "Thanks for bringing my grandma, Adam," Rachel said. "We'd have done it ourselves, of course, but we had to pick up half the Romo population in the county."

After plopping a helping of potatoes onto his plate and returning the spoon to the bowl, he smiled and told her, "Happy to help, and Edna's even sending a pie home with me for my trouble."

Mike joined the conversation by giving his head a small shake and saying, "Damn, I'm glad you're back to normal, dude. I couldn't handle you walking around—"

"Acting like you?" Rachel cut him off.

"Something like that," Mike said on a sigh. "One of me's enough."

Adam only laughed, adding, "I couldn't agree more."

As the two went on their way, looking for Edna, Adam continued filling his plate, hungry since he'd slept through lunch, but at the same time he kept an eye out for Sue Ann and Sophie. Not just because he wanted to take another shot at romance with Sue Ann—and

also tell her his new news about the alimony hearing—
but because he was planning one more special thing for
Sophie, too, one more Christmas surprise. He'd hoped
to pick them up for the party as well, but he'd found out
from Mike on the phone earlier that Jenny and Mick
were already giving them a ride. And they still hadn't
arrived when he took a seat with Mike, Rachel, and
Logan to eat his dinner.

Before long, the CD player was turned off and people
gathered around the piano in the corner of the room
to sing carols while Caroline Meeks played. "Hark the
Herald Angels Sing" rang out through the air when
Adam looked up to see Sue Ann and Sophie step in
from the cold, Jenny and Mick on their heels. His eyes
met Sue Ann's across the room even as she began to
untwine the scarf around her neck, and he experienced
that all too familiar tugging sensation inside him that
stretched all the way from his heart to his groin. Damn,
she made him feel everything. Everything tender and
sweet. Everything hot and sexy, too.

He had to battle the urge to go bolting from his seat
to go see her. *Be cool, dude.* Not only because he didn't
want to overwhelm her the second she walked in the
door, but also because—just like when he and Sheila
had broken up—he wasn't particularly open about
spreading personal news, and he still figured Sue Ann
didn't want the whole town tuned in to their romance,
either. He understood now that Sue Ann's divorce had
taught her the value of keeping private things private.

So he calmly finished his meal, even though he
stayed completely aware of where she was in the room
at every second, in a way that made him feel all of sixteen. But that part he didn't fight. There was something

surprisingly exhilarating about experiencing that sensation again for the first time in a long while.

A few minutes later, he stood up and headed to the kitchen to discard his plate, and when he turned around, Sue Ann stood before him in a sparkly white sweater along with dark jeans and boots. She looked warm and wintry, and he suffered the sudden urge to curl up next to her under an afghan, in front of a fireplace.

"Hey," he said, offering up a small grin, and not trying to hide anything that might be showing in his eyes, like that he was still completely into her.

"Hey," she said. Her blond hair was drawn back from her face, giving him a clear view of her pretty brown eyes and berry-colored lips, her cheeks still a bit pink from the cold.

They both started talking at once then, after which they both stopped, and Adam said, "You first."

"Well, I just wanted to thank you again. For making Sophie's Christmas so perfect. She got home from Jeff's a little while ago and she still can't stop talking about the reindeer. You took what could have been a heartbreaking Christmas for her and made it the most special ever." And then she leaned in and hugged him. Not a long hug, not a passionate hug, yet enough of a hug that the warmth of it moved all through him and he wanted more when it ended.

Huh. Maybe winning her over wasn't going to be as hard as he thought. Maybe he'd won her over with the reindeer. That hadn't been his goal, but if it was enough to make her decide to give him another chance, he'd take it.

"I'm just glad I could do it," he told her. "And I'm glad it took Sophie's mind off her troubles."

"And . . . the ornament. In my stocking. Where on earth did you find it?"

He shrugged, offered a small grin. "EBay. Is it the right one? I thought it looked right, but . . . "

She nodded. "Identical. Pretty amazing. And it's nice to have it back on the tree again."

"Um, listen, I wanted to tell you about something I did this afternoon, a phone call I made—"

And just then, Edna stepped up to say, "Sue Ann, your little girl claims you had a reindeer at your house this mornin' and that you got the pictures to prove it. Now, a regular deer, yep, that I can buy, but I'm gonna have to see it to believe Santa Claus dropped off a reindeer in your yard."

Clearly distracted by Edna, Sue Ann smiled at the old woman and said, "It's true. It was a real reindeer. And it just so happens my digital camera is in my purse, so I can show you right now."

And then Edna had Sue Ann by the arm, whisking her away, and Sue Ann waved to him as she was dragged off.

*Damn it, Edna—what timing.* Yet he held back the small growl of frustration he wanted to let out, because it would take more than this to kill his renewed Christmas spirit—or his plan. And as the carolers burst into "Up on the Housetop," Adam decided it was time to give Sophie her next surprise—and hope like hell Sue Ann would be okay with it. It was probably a little presumptuous of him, but when he'd called Amy to ask her opinion while on his way to pick up passengers for the party, she'd claimed she had insider information that made her think it was a great idea.

Spotting her now, talking with Tessa Sheridan and

Lucky Romo near the Christmas tree, he motioned her over and she broke away to head in his direction. "What's up?" she asked with her usual friendly smile.

"I'm ready to put Operation Dickens into action," he said.

"Heard about Sophie's special Christmas present."

Sue Ann turned away from her current conversation with Lettie Gale and LeeAnn Turner to find her beloved mother standing before her grinning like a Cheshire cat. "And I heard *you* were sneaking around my house in the middle of the night," Sue Ann said pointedly. "That's not like you." Her mom didn't have a sneaky bone in her body. Or at least Sue Ann hadn't thought so.

"Well, I didn't want to spoil Adam's surprise."

"It was for Sophie, not me. The both of you could have filled me in."

"Part of it was for you, too," her mother said knowingly, and of course Sue Ann was well aware of that, but she'd been trying to be practical and not think about that aspect of things.

Now, she couldn't even summon a reply for her mother.

But apparently she didn't have to, since her mom kept going. "Adam's a good man," she said.

*Oh boy, here we go.* "I know he is," she replied dryly.

"And though he never exactly said so, I think it's very clear that he's quite taken with you."

Why did that make Sue Ann's breath catch? Perhaps because it hadn't been said out loud too many times? Maybe that made it feel more real. "Mom," she finally said, "it's just . . . awfully soon, you know?"

And to her surprise, her usually conservative, cautious mother just shrugged. "We can't always pick when things happen, dear. Sometimes we just have to go with the flow."

It sounded to her like an abbreviated version of the lecture Amy had given her today. And maybe this was the universe's way of trying to tell her something.

But she just wasn't sure she was ready to hear it.

In fact, she was starting to get tired of everyone pushing her toward Adam. First Jenny, then Amy, now even her own mom? She was tired of feeling so torn, so pulled apart over it. She'd made the decision to part ways with him that night in front of the fireplace. And reindeer or not, ornament or not . . . none of it was enough to make her believe she should give her heart to someone again this soon. Even Adam. Maybe especially Adam.

Because it had turned out he was pretty damn wonderful. Except for the fact that he'd already managed to hurt her. And she'd already had enough of wonderful men who ended up hurting her. Maybe she should just be thankful Adam had done it so quickly.

Ten minutes after sneaking away from the party, Adam and Amy left Under the Covers, Amy turning out the lights and locking up behind her. Adam carried Dickens in his coat pocket to keep him warm, and despite Amy's warnings that he was full of mischief, the kitten seemed fairly content there, at least so far. Together, they made the return trip across the Destiny town square in the falling snow and back into the bustling party.

All he'd told Amy was that he wanted to make Sophie's Christmas complete by giving her the kitten and that he hoped he could win Sue Ann over to the idea. Seeing how happy the visit from "Dancer" had made Sophie had reminded him how attached his boys had gotten to Pepper, and that having a pet to love and focus on during the divorce had been a source of comfort to them. And he thought maybe after this morning, Sue Ann would see the logic in that, too.

Of course, that wasn't his *whole* plan. First, he would fill her in on his talk with Jeff's attorney today, who'd fortunately agreed to take his call on a holiday. And then . . . he was going to tell Sue Ann he was in love with her, and that he was sorry, and then just hope like hell she'd be willing to look past his mistake. He was just gonna go for it. Because he had to. Because his soul was telling him to. And the thing was—his soul hadn't told him to do too many things in life; he wasn't a guy who often sat around thinking about his soul, let alone feeling it. But it was driving him to do *this,* and surely that meant something.

As he and Amy were about to part ways, she whispered, "Good luck," and he scanned the room.

He found Sophie playing with some other kids near the Christmas tree, and Sue Ann stood chatting with Jenny and Tessa—but as luck would have it, she started walking away from her friends then, toward the bathroom.

Reaching down to pull his pocket open and glance inside, he said to the gray kitten hiding there, "Get ready, we're on. We play this right and you get a new home and I get a new girl."

"Meow," the cat said in return, and Adam let go of his pocket and strode ahead, boldly meeting up with Sue Ann—even blocking her path.

"Hey," he said, "do you have a minute?"

She looked slightly taken aback, but stopped. "Um, sure. What's up?"

Okay, this was it. Even in the busy room, they stood relatively alone. And it suddenly hit him that maybe he should have figured out what he was going to say, since he didn't have a clue—but a lot of good things had happened naturally with Sue Ann, without a plan, so maybe this part should, too. No masks, no disguises, just being real.

"Okay, first things first. Today I called Jeff's lawyer. And I explained to him that Jeff and I aren't all that close anymore and that I wasn't particularly in favor of his petition and that my testimony might ultimately do more to hurt his case than help it. And magically enough, he thanked me for filling him in and decided not to subpoena me after all."

He watched as her jaw dropped, her eyes growing large and round. "Seriously?"

"Seriously."

"Oh Adam, that's great. Thank you! Wow—I can't believe it was that simple."

"Me neither. But I got to thinking about it, and since all that's true, I figured filling the guy in might change his tune, and it did. I'm just sorry I didn't think of it before now. But I think I felt extra motivated after seeing you this morning."

Still smiling at him, she just blinked and said, "What do you mean?"

*Okay, here we go—the moment of truth.*

"Sue Ann, when we first got together, it was as big a surprise to me as it was to you. But now it seems like it was . . . destiny. Like fate slapping us in the face, telling us to open our eyes and pay attention to what's right in front of us. Because I couldn't have dreamed then how much I would care about you now, and yet at the same time, I've *always* cared about you, you know? You've always been a part of my life, and I guess that's what's made this change in our relationship come so fast, so naturally. And I know you're angry with me, and I understand why. And I didn't quite get why it was such a big deal at the time, but now I do, and—"

"Stop," she said.

It caught him off guard, made him go silent. He just looked at her. "Huh?"

Her chest rose and fell as she expelled a heavy breath, and when she met his gaze, he could see—oh God—the pain filling her eyes. And even as she kept her tone low, her words came out with a sad, futile certainty. "Adam, what you did for Sophie this morning was wonderful. And the Santa ornament was very thoughtful. And you getting out of the subpoena helps put my mind at ease. But none of that changes how I feel."

Adam took a deep breath and looked her in the eye. "How do you feel? Exactly?" he asked. "Because you can say what you want, but I know you care about me, too. I saw it in your eyes this morning."

She stood before him, mouth half open, blinking, and now looking . . . well, as desperate as she did sorrowful. "You want to know how I feel?" she finally said. "I feel . . . like I'm drowning."

"Huh?" he asked, dumbfounded.

"Okay—I've demanded honesty from you about various things, so it's only fair I'm completely honest, too, right? So here it is. Every time you and I are . . .

intimate, I open myself up to you a little more. And . . . that scares me to death. And that's probably why I almost always pull back afterward."

He just peered into her eyes and wished he could make her see things the way he did. "But there's nothing to be afraid of with me. I promise."

"Yes, there is. So much is changing so fast in my life—it's too much, and sometimes I feel like I can't even catch my breath. And then you come along, and you make me feel so close to you and then you . . . " She shook her head. "I'm just not ready for this. I've tried, and I can't do it. I'm sorry."

"But—"

"No buts," she said, sounding firmer now, a little more in control. "In fact, we shouldn't see each other anymore. At least as much as we can help it, living in the same town and having the same friends. And now that the holidays are almost over, it'll be a lot easier."

Damn, he hadn't seen this coming. He knew he'd let her down. But maybe he hadn't quite understood how deeply that one moment in time had affected her until this minute, and it was punctuated with the silent tear trailing down her cheek that she'd just reached up to wipe away. Hell.

It wasn't easy to bare your heart to somebody, but he'd been doing it. He'd done it with her a *few* times now. Yet this time, unlike any before, she'd convinced him that it didn't matter, that there was nothing he could do to change her mind. He'd done everything he could think of—from the heart—and it clearly wasn't enough.

"Okay," he finally said, a small lump rising in his throat. "I get it. I'm sorry, too, Sue Ann." Then he turned around and walked away.

God, that stung. More than stung. It was like taking an ice pick in the heart.

His chest ached and his eyes burned, so bad that he shut them for a few seconds, opening them again only because he was heading for the door and needed to see the way—he needed to get outside, be alone for a minute before anyone noticed something was up and asked him what was wrong.

A moment later, standing out in the falling snow, he peered up into it, as if asking God for some sort of answer, some sort of reason this made sense. Maybe it was karma. But in his heart he really felt that he'd paid for his past mistakes and had grown beyond them. And now that Sue Ann had come along . . . hell, he'd been foolish enough to start believing he could truly have something special with her, something solid, something that would bring back what was missing in his life.

Only when he felt a gentle movement at his hip did he remember that he had a kitten in his pocket. Crap, he'd never even gotten to that part. *Guess, for Sophie's sake, I should have done the kitten part first.*

Reaching down into his coat, he extracted the miniature cat and held him in both hands. "Let me give you some advice, dude. Don't fall in love. All it does is screw with your head, screw with your life."

"Meow," the gray kitten said.

"Now I almost wish that night in the cabin had never even happened, ya know?" he said to Dickens. "I wish I'd never ended up in bed with her, never started realizing I could care for her this way, never found out I could love her this way." He'd been a happier person not knowing that than he was now, knowing and not being able to have her.

"And as for you, buddy," he told the kitten on a sigh,

"guess you're going back to the bookstore. Sorry I got your hopes up."

Just then, he glimpsed a couple in the distance, rounding the corner of the building hand in hand. He remained in the shadows, keeping a low profile, still not in the mood to talk to anyone. This wasn't like before, though—he wasn't back to being Grinchy; he just felt depleted and . . . hell, sad.

When the couple passed under the lights above the town hall's front door—he realized it was Jeff and Veronica. Shit.

Jeff shouldn't have brought her here. It was Christmas, after all. And he knew Sue Ann and Sophie would both be inside, trying to have a nice time—and not wanting the recent changes in their family life shoved down everyone's throats.

And Jeff probably hadn't even thought about that, how coming here tonight would affect anyone else—he was probably just trying to enjoy his holiday like the rest of the people here—but Adam still thought it was in damn poor taste. Seemed the divorce truly had turned his one-time best friend into a selfish jerk. Why again had he almost felt obligated to Jeff regarding the hearing?

His first urge was to step forward, block their way, question Jeff's judgment, and perhaps suggest he and Ronni find something else to do tonight. But then— look what he'd gotten for stepping into Sue Ann's path a few minutes ago. He'd thought he had a handle on the situation, thought he understood it and had some idea what to expect. But he'd obviously been overconfident; he'd clearly misread that hug she'd given him earlier.

And what it came right down to was: Jeff showing up here wasn't any of his business. He and Jeff weren't really friends anymore if they were both honest about it. And even he and Sue Ann weren't really *anything* anymore. So maybe the best move he could make was to just stay out of it.

"Do you believe in me or not?"

Charles Dickens, A *Christmas Carol*

# *Twenty-two*

"Are you having a nice evening, Miss Ellie?" Sue Ann shouted toward the old woman who had been Jenny's neighbor on Blue Valley Lake for their whole lives. In her eighties, Miss Ellie was hard of hearing and sat in a chair in one corner of the room where everyone could come up and say hello.

She put a hand to her ear. "What's that you say?"

"I said—are you having a good night?" Sue Ann yelled louder.

In response, Miss Ellie shook her head. "Oh, it's awfully early to say goodnight, but if you're leaving already, be careful out in the snow."

Sue Ann just sighed—conversations with Miss Ellie usually went this way and you just had to roll with it. "Okey doke, I'll be careful," she said, more to herself than the old woman.

Then she felt a tug on her sweater and turned to find Sophie at her side, her face scrunched up. "What's wrong, honey?" Sue Ann asked, almost recognizing the look even before Sophie replied.

"Daddy and Ronni are here."

*Damn it.* Jeff had told them both, just hours ago, that they would be celebrating with Veronica's family tonight in Crestview, and Sue Ann knew that even though Sophie had begun to accept the situation, she'd also seen this as a safe zone, a place where she wouldn't be confronted with the fact they were no longer a family and that her father had a new wife.

And she'd put up with this for the last six months, with Jeff bringing Ronni wherever he damn well felt like it. Because it was a free country, and because she didn't feel she had much choice but to suffer through it. And personally, she no longer even cared. Maybe she remained a little embarrassed, because their presence reminded people he'd dumped her for another woman—but otherwise, she'd finally gotten past the hurt.

To Sophie, however, it still mattered. It was one thing for her to go stay at Ronni's house with them—she'd gotten used to that. But seeing them out, together, in the same place as Sue Ann, still upset her.

And something in Sue Ann just broke. She'd already been struggling to stuff down her feelings after her confrontation with Adam—especially since she'd been working just as hard to convince *herself* they shouldn't be together as she'd been working to convince him. But this was it—the thing that ripped off the cork that had been holding her emotions inside.

Looking around, she quickly spotted Jeff and Ronni not far from the front door. Narrowing her gaze on their oblivious, smiling faces, she said to Sophie, "You go play with the other kids, honey," then she made a beeline for her ex-husband.

She didn't hesitate to march right up to him, fists clenched, until they were eye-to-eye, practically nose-to-nose. He appeared a bit startled, even before she spoke.

"What the hell do you think you're doing showing up here?" she bit off sharply. "On Christmas, Jeff? Really?"

Jeff's eyes widened on her in bewilderment. And she sensed Ronni shrinking next to him in humiliation, but she couldn't have cared less, keeping her gaze narrowed vehemently on her ex.

"Our plans changed. What's the hell's wrong with you?" he asked as if *she* were the rude one here.

"What's wrong with me is that it's one thing to divorce me, but it's another to constantly parade your new girlfriend—wife, whatever—all over town, and now, even on Christmas, here, with everyone we know."

Jeff simply looked disgusted, clearly not getting it. Then the usually quiet Ronni spoke up, saying—quite rationally, Sue Ann thought, "I knew this was a bad idea, Jeff. Let's just go."

But Jeff ignored her, still focusing on Sue Ann. "Look, I grew up here, too," he argued. "Destiny is as much my home as it is yours."

"I don't think you know what the word 'home' means anymore. But that aside, the important part you're missing—that you always miss—is that it bothers Sophie."

Jeff then drew his gaze from hers to peer down next to her, and Sue Ann realized Sophie had followed her across the room, darn it. "Is that true, Sophie?" he asked brusquely. "Does it bother you for me and Ronni to be here?"

He sounded angry, and even if that anger was directed at Sue Ann, Sophie had no way of knowing that. She looked frightened, instantly sending Sue Ann that much more deeply into mama bear mode. "You can't just put her on the spot like that! How can she possibly feel comfortable being honest?"

And that's when Sophie turned and ran away.

Jenny had heard the raised voices and recognized one of them as Sue Ann's, but she didn't quite put two and two together until Sophie came dashing across the room, eyes welling with tears. She froze in place, not sure what to do—then watched as Mick, standing next to her, immediately bent down and scooped Sophie up into his arms, briskly carrying her as far away from the yelling as possible. Jenny followed behind, anxious to help calm Sue Ann's little girl.

Whisking Sophie into a small office off the main room, Mick lowered her to the floor but kept his hands at her little waist as he sat down in a chair facing her. "Hey there, honey," he said soothingly, "whatcha cryin' about?"

Sophie sniffed and struggled to say through tears, "Daddy and Ronni are here. And now Mommy and Daddy are fighting. And Daddy's mad at me."

Jenny was about to swoop in and take a stab at some comforting words—but Mick beat her to the punch. "Aw now, I'm sure nobody's mad at you. Nobody could be mad at anybody as cute as you." He concluded by giving her a little poke in the tummy, à la the Pillsbury dough boy, and it made her smile a little through her tears.

"Grown-ups are silly sometimes," he went on. "We can always find stuff to yell about. But you can't let it bring you down on a day like today."

"Why not?" she asked, sniffing again, and reaching up to wipe away a tear.

Mick leaned closer and said, "Because you got the best Christmas present ever, remember?" Sophie had told them about Santa's surprise for her on the short ride from Holly Lane, Sue Ann whispering who was responsible for it, and it still blew Jenny away that Adam had come through with a real live reindeer. "So how can you be sad on the day when Santa brought you a reindeer? I mean, Santa never brought *me* a reindeer. What was it like?"

This, of course, brightened Sophie's eyes considerably, and she launched into telling Mick even more about the reindeer visit, how she'd talked to him and petted him and how her mother had taken lots of pictures.

Jenny watched the whole conversation in awe. Turned out that Mick hadn't needed her help at all. God, why didn't he know, why couldn't he see . . . he'd make such a good dad. It was bubbling up from somewhere inside him right now, at the moment when Sophie needed it, and Jenny knew he didn't even realize it.

But she simply drew in a deep breath, then let it back out. Like it or not, she had to accept that it just wasn't what he wanted, that it wasn't meant to be.

"He couldn't stay, though," Sophie went on about the reindeer. "He had to go back to the North Pole. But that's all right, because at least he came to see me, and it was the coolest thing that ever happened to me. Ever!"

"I can't wait to see those pictures," Mick told her with a grin that, even under these circumstances, Jenny found sexy as sin.

Sophie smiled and said, "They're on Mommy's camera. We'll show you later."

Just then, Sue Ann's mother poked her head into the room. "There you are," she said to Sophie. Bickering could still be heard beyond the door, and Jenny knew Sophie's grandma had probably been worried about her when she'd run off.

"I was just telling Mick about Dancer," she said.

"Pretty exciting stuff," Mick added, and Mrs. Kinman smiled.

"Exciting indeed." Then she refocused on Sophie and said, "Will you go for a walk with me. To my car? I forgot a container of cookies there."

Jenny knew Mrs. Kinman just thought it was best to get Sophie outside for a few minutes until things blew over in here, so she rushed to the big rack near the front door to find Sophie's coat.

A moment later, she looked for Mick behind her—yet she discovered him still sitting in the office, just staring straight ahead. She couldn't make out his expression but said, "You were great with her, Mick."

He just shrugged, sighed. "Guess I've sorta gotten attached to the little munchkin or something."

Jenny had been trying her damnedest to work through her recent problem the last week or so, trying to make peace with it. She'd refused to let it ruin their Christmas, and it hadn't—but she knew the unresolved topic still hung over them. So maybe right now was the time to say what needed to be said, even if saying it was going to break her heart.

"Even so," she began, "I know how you still feel about the idea of having kids, and so I wanted to tell you—I understand and I'll make the best of it. Because you're right—you said up front how you felt and I thought that was fine with me, and now . . . I just have to deal with it. So I won't bother you about it anymore—the subject is closed." And she tried to ignore the lump that had risen in her throat by the time she finished.

Mick didn't answer for a minute—he didn't respond at all, just kept staring off into space—and Jenny was starting to wonder what on earth was going on in his head when finally he glanced up and said, "What if I'm wrong?"

She blinked, confused. "Wrong about what?"

She watched him let out a sigh, looking wholly uncertain. "Maybe I . . . I don't know—maybe I'm starting to . . . have a change of heart or something."

Jenny's jaw dropped and her face went numb. What was he saying? "About?"

"About this—kids, having a baby," he said, suddenly sounding a little exasperated.

After which she simply stood before him speechless. What had just happened here?

Fortunately, he went on, since she couldn't muster the will to ask him. He gave his head a short shake and said, "I don't know—what happened with Sophie just now . . . I can't explain it, but . . . hell, Jenny, maybe I want more of it, more of how that felt. I just kinda . . . wanted to take care of her, keep her safe or something. And at the same time, I felt . . . close to her, like there for a second, I wanted her to be *our* little girl." Now he shook his head more vigorously. "God, I can't believe I just said that. But . . . damn, maybe it's been, I don't know, bubbling up a little here and there lately and I've just refused to see it."

Jenny bit her lip to hold back the smile that threatened to sneak out, then told him quietly, "Sometimes things change." It seemed impossible—so, so impossible—but Mick was beginning to want what *she* wanted. He'd been so adamant that she truly hadn't believed it could happen, even when Sue Ann had pointed out that it could. But now—oh Lord—he was making *her* Christmas wish come true just like Adam had made Sophie's wish come true.

"Well, I don't want to rush into anything here, but . . . maybe *this* is changing," he said softly, still sounding uncertain as he got to his feet. Yet for Jenny, his words confirmed it, as sure as snow fell from the sky tonight.

Circling her arms around his neck, she said, "Mick, you have no idea how happy that makes me. Even if you're not sure, it means the world to me that you're just willing to consider it." And then she gave him a kiss, small at first, but it quickly deepened into something passionate.

He kissed her back, his hands curving warmly over her hips as he leaned in closer, pressing his body to hers. "I think I do know," he insisted against her lips.

And she guessed that was probably true. Not just because of how emotional she'd been lately, but because it suddenly felt as if a heavy weight had been lifted off of them, as if all the tension of the past few weeks had just been stripped away like so much holiday wrapping paper.

"You know," she said, "I love the Destiny Christmas party, but . . . what do you say we ditch it and head home?"

Even with his eyes half shut in passion, Mick let out a knowing chuckle. "You just want to get started on this before I have a chance to change my mind."

She laughed softly in reply, still in his intoxicating embrace, and said, "Maybe I just want to go to bed with my hot, hunky husband because I'm completely in love with him and want to give him one last Christmas gift—ever think of that?"

He gave a playful shrug and said, "Either way, doesn't matter—I can't resist you when you want to have your way with me. Let's get outta here, Mrs. Brody."

Finally, Adam dropped the kitten—who seemed far more agreeable than the rumors about him—back in his pocket and stepped inside from the cold. The first thing he heard? Sue Ann and Jeff arguing. Damn.

No one stood anywhere near them—apparently trying to give them some privacy, or maybe just not wanting to let their squabble put a damper on the party. The singing around the piano continued, although it struck him as ironic to hear the makeshift choir harmonizing on "Silent Night" at this particular moment—since he thought they were singing louder than before in an attempt to drown out the spat.

Then Sophie and Mrs. Kinman came back in—he'd seen them depart a few minutes ago, and now he realized why. Mrs. Kinman probably thought she'd kept Sophie away long enough for the argument to end, but Sophie's sweet little face instantly puckered in distress.

*Damn it, Jeff, why'd you have to come here tonight?* He couldn't help feeling it was almost as if Jeff was trying to rub his happiness in Sue Ann's face. And yeah, Adam was still hurt by her rejection earlier—but mostly, he just wanted her to be happy. He thought she could be happy with *him*, but if she didn't see it that way, he still wished her every joy—and she sure wasn't getting that right now.

He couldn't make out most of their words—the carolers continued working pretty hard to overpower the bickering—but then Jeff raised his voice above the music to say, "You're really being a bitch, Sue Ann!"

And that was it.

Adam's blood began to boil.

Especially when he took a few steps closer and saw that Sue Ann looked ready to cry.

He'd tried to stand back, tried to mind his own business here—but he couldn't take it anymore. His jaw clenched and his muscles tensed, his hands curling into fists.

He never considered his actions; he simply followed his instincts. He strode right up in between the two of them, his tone low and menacing as he faced Jeff to say, *"Listen, you need to back off and quit talking to Sue Ann like that."* He knew he was pretty much ending what little remained of his longstanding friendship with Jeff, but that didn't matter.

In response, his old friend drew back, clearly stunned. "What business is it of yours?"

And Adam didn't fight the urge to raise his voice. "For one thing, you're clearly upsetting your daughter! And for another, I love this woman!"

As a collective gasp blanketed the room, Adam realized what he'd just done, said.

Whoa. Okay, so it was out. There was no taking it back now. So, not having much choice, he went on, speaking loud enough for the whole room to hear since they'd already tuned in anyway. Even the singing had gone silent. "That's right," he said, "I'm in love with Sue Ann! She's sweet and funny and gorgeous, she's a great mom, and she deserves better than to be treated like this!"

Then he turned to her, lowering his voice as much as possible now that he'd drawn so much attention back to them. "I didn't meant to say it, to just blurt it out like that—I'm sorry. And I'll leave you alone now—I just couldn't stand by and let him talk to you like that."

"Adam," she breathed. She'd lowered her gaze at some point, obviously embarrassed, but now she peered up at him from beneath long, pretty lashes, looking bashfully beautiful. "I . . . I'm just . . ." She stopped, shook her head, then continued in that same hushed tone. "I'm just terrified. Terrified that one day you and I will be standing here behaving like . . . like this." She motioned back and forth between her and Jeff.

"That'll never happen. Ever," he promised her. He had no idea what Jeff was doing now, how he was reacting to this, and he didn't care. He only cared about the woman whose hands he now took in his. "I can't make you many guarantees, Sue Ann—life is too uncertain for that—but that's one thing I can promise you without a doubt." Because no matter what, he'd never treat a woman he'd *ever* cared about that way.

Standing before him, Sue Ann said nothing—but she bit her lower lip, looking to him as if maybe, somehow, he might be starting to sway her, to make her see the light. So he went on. "I want to make you happy, Sue Ann, you and Sophie both. And I promise I'll do my best to never let you down again, to never hurt you again, no matter what. All I need, sugar plum, is for you to trust me, to believe in me. That's the only part missing." He stopped, let out a breath, and realized exactly how true his words were, how close he and Sue Ann were to having what he knew they both wanted. "Just give me a chance to love you, honey, the way you deserve to be loved."

Sue Ann peered into Adam's eyes, trying to weigh it all—everything that had happened to her in the past six months. It was funny how life changed sometimes without your permission; you thought you had it all figured out and then—kapow!—everything disintegrated around you. It was funny how one unexpected event led to another, how one *person* led to another.

How had she ended up falling for this man? And so very soon, too. Was it all chance, or—as she'd always believed—did things happen for a reason? She wasn't sure about any of that anymore—it was easier to believe in things like fate when everything in your life was good, and solid, when you had control over it all.

But control, she'd learned, was mostly just an illusion. And now . . . now she was realizing that the only thing she could truly control was her happiness in this very moment. She could go on denying her desire, telling herself she needed to focus on Sophie, or on her career, or on a million other things. She could go on being miserable, wasting more days that way. Or . . . she could choose to be happy.

She could choose to have faith. In Adam. To take a *leap* of faith, just as she'd been contemplating with Sophie and that kitten.

She could choose to take a risk and believe in him.

Really believe in him. From this moment forward. The way she'd started to on that sleigh ride.

She didn't want to be naïve; she didn't want to be vulnerable. For so long now, protecting her heart had felt like the only sane move she could make, the driving force in her life. But this sudden moment of clarity was forcing her to realize that the brave thing to do was to *take* that leap, give him her faith, stop hiding behind her fears. And she wanted to be brave, wanted to be a brave, in-control woman.

And—Lord, maybe it was just hitting her, really, truly hitting her—the man had brought a reindeer to her house! To make her daughter happy! Sophie's happiness had been Sue Ann's number-one priority since the divorce, and Adam had seen that and made it happen! And for her: a special ornament, a sleigh ride, tiny marshmallows. None of them huge things, and yet, in her mind . . . they were. Huge. Enormous. Maybe she'd been trying not to see that up to now, trying not to feel it.

Sometimes being in control meant . . . following your heart, allowing yourself to do something courageous, and . . . giving someone your trust. *You're strong, you're capable, and everything's going to be fine.*

"I believe in you, Adam," she whispered. "I believe in . . . us."

He blinked, looking utterly stunned. "Really?"

She just nodded, smiled. And felt incredibly free inside as she watched the joy rushing through him.

Only then he was suddenly pulling her by the hand, dragging her across the floor, right out the door and into the still gently falling snow.

"What are you doing?" she asked, laughing.

"Avoiding a public display of affection. They've seen enough in there," he told her—right before he kissed her.

Oh God, she hadn't realized how much she'd missed this—kissing him, feeling the warmth of his body next to hers. She kissed him back for all she was worth and knew to the marrow of her bones that she wouldn't regret this. He'd made a few mistakes, but in every other way, he was the most amazing man she could ever hope to know. His hands threaded through her hair as his tongue pressed into her mouth and Sue Ann let herself become completely engulfed in him in every way.

That's when Adam's body went suddenly rigid—and they both looked up to see that, despite trying to find a little privacy, they actually stood in front of the town hall's large plate-glass window and that the entire population of Destiny was watching anyway.

But the fact that Adam had at least *tried* to be discreet—when Jeff, conversely, had shouted their troubles all over town—was one more thing that told her, in her heart, he would treat her and Sophie right. Overcome by it all, she simply laughed at realizing the whole party was gaping at them—until Adam pulled her away from the window to kiss her some more, snow gathering in their hair and on their shoulders.

She'd just sunk into those heavenly kisses of his once again when she—dear Lord—felt something moving in his coat and pulled back to say, "What the hell is this?"

"There's a cat in my pocket," he murmured, still trying to kiss her.

"A cat in your pocket?" she asked. "Is that some weird euphemism for . . . ?"

"No," he said, laughing, "there's really a cat in my pocket. I just sort of forgot about him in all the excitement." He finally stopped kissing her then to reach in and draw out—oh my—it was Dickens!

"I wanted to give him to Sophie," he said. "And that might have been a bad call, but I just thought, after seeing how much she loved the reindeer this morning, that having a pet might really help her right now. If you still don't want a cat, I'll give him back to Amy. Or I'll take him myself or something."

Sue Ann peered down at the gray kitty in Adam's hand, who meowed sweetly up at her now, and—oh hell, how could she say no? "Yes, I want the cat," she told him, reaching to pet Dickens while Adam held him, her hands finally closing over his around the kitten.

Then she smiled up into his gorgeous eyes, incredibly blue even in the dim light of streetlamps struggling to shine through the snow, and said, "It looks like I'm getting *lots* of things this Christmas I didn't know I wanted."

"God bless us everyone."

Charles Dickens, A *Christmas Carol*

# Epilogue

Sue Ann and Adam relaxed on the couch at her place on a quiet Saturday afternoon, watching Sophie and the boys. The kids sat on the floor near the fireplace playing with Dickens, who was growing rapidly. Sophie had done an admirable job of taking care of her new kitten, and it turned out Adam had been right—having a pet gave her something she really cared about to focus on. And yes, the little kitty was a troublemaker for sure—even if Adam was always defending him—but the truth was, Sue Ann enjoyed having him around even when Sophie was with Jeff and the caretaking duties fell solely on her.

And as Sophie began to seem happier and more acceptant of the changes in her life, Sue Ann was making every effort to be a little less overprotective of her daughter. Of course, it helped that Jeff had begun making more effort to respect Sue Ann and Sophie's space since the blow-up at Christmas, and also that Sophie enjoyed having Adam and the twins around so much.

"I'm thinking we need to tackle the kitchen tomorrow," Adam told Sue Ann, drawing her attention from the children and the cat.

In addition to getting adjusted to her new job, Sue Ann had also succeeded in getting her real estate license, just last week, and now Adam was helping her fix up the house so she could put it on the market and act as her own first client. They'd been putting off painting the kitchen because it was a big room with lots of nooks and crannies, so her first response was to sneer, before she said, "You're right."

"All the kids'll be gone—it'll be a good time for it."

And the truth was, she knew she'd enjoy the project once they got started. In fact, as soon as she and Sophie were moved and settled, she planned to embark on her plans for a little home remodeling side business—so long as she could find the time.

It had continued to be an unusually snowy winter, in which Adam and Sophie, often with the help of Jacob and Joey, had built many snow cats in the front yard. Sue Ann's gaze drifted to the mantel, to a framed photo of Sophie and that first snow cat, accompanied by a larger one of Sophie and Dancer, as well as a picture of Adam and Sue Ann holding hands in the snow—it had been taken outside at the Destiny Christmas party after all the excitement died down.

"And speaking of the kids being gone," she said, "isn't it about time we start delivering them?" The boys were due at Sheila's, and Sophie at Jeff's.

"Yep," Adam replied. "I hate to tear all that attention away from Dickens, but it's getting late."

"Well, I can think of one good thing about it," Sue Ann said softly, running her fingertip gently across the palm of his hand.

When he met her gaze with those sexy blue eyes, it made her bite her lower lip as she began to tingle below. "Are you getting fresh with me, sugar plum?"

"Indeed I am," she whispered.

At which point he turned to the children. "All right, kids, time to go." He clapped his hands together to hurry them along. "Chop, chop. Get movin'."

Sue Ann only laughed, watching as Adam herded the children into coats—and then she glanced out the big bay window at the last mounds of snow, now melting in her yard to reveal the ground underneath for the first time in months. The calendar page had turned to March and the weatherman was predicting sun and spring temperatures over the coming days, so she suspected the snow might finally be finished for the year.

And even though most folks in Destiny had seen enough snow this winter to last them a lifetime, Sue Ann thought she might actually miss it. Snow had first pushed her and Adam together, after all, and it had reunited them on more than one occasion. But on the other hand, she was looking forward to spending time with him in all the coming seasons, too—and she knew they'd be together long after the spring thaw.

"What are you guys gonna do without all us kids tonight?" Joey asked as they began filing out the door. Indeed, with three between them, there were usually at least one or two of them around. "Won't you be bored?"

Adam met Sue Ann's eyes over the children's heads, his gaze sparkling seductively on her, then said, "Oh, don't worry about us. I'm sure we'll find *some* way to spend our time." Then he mouthed the words: *Me and you. Later. Reindeer games.*

One more thing, Sue Ann decided with a private smile at her man, that she planned to enjoy all year round.

And though she truly was ready to leave her home for a new one, to go along with her fresh start in life and in love, she knew she'd always cherish certain memories she'd made at the house on Holly Lane, including the ones that had helped bring her and Adam together.

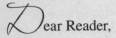Dear Reader,

While writing the Destiny series, I often find myself pulling small bits of inspiration from memories of my own life growing up in a rural small town area. Some of these things make their way into the story, while others just stay in the back of my mind. And when I was writing *Holly Lane*, I knew without even thinking about it that Sue Ann's Christmas cookies were *my* family's traditional Christmas cookies, made from a recipe passed down through my Appalachian grandmother's family.

Some of my earliest memories include standing on a step stool in my grandma's kitchen helping her roll out the dough for these cookies, which we called Grandpa Cookies because my grandfather liked them so much. Later, I helped my mother make them, as well, rolling out the dough and cutting out the shapes of trees, stars, bells, stockings, snowmen, and reindeer every Christmas. (Although be warned: The reindeer shapes were often difficult to maneuver onto the cookie sheet.) Throughout my school years and then into my work years, everyone I knew looked forward to my mom's cookies—she's gifted at rolling out the dough very thin, making them light and airy but still very tasty. Now I sometimes make Grandpa Cookies myself, but so far I haven't achieved quite the perfection with them that my mother has.

These cookies have been a memorable part of my

life and are definitely a long family tradition—and I'm happy to pass the recipe on to you with hopes that your family will enjoy them as much as mine does.

Wishing you and yours every joy this holiday season!

*Toni*

P.S. And for more recipes from Destiny, visit *www.ToniBlake.com*.

# Grandpa Cookies

### (also called Butter Cookies)

2 sticks butter or margarine
1½ cups confectioners sugar
1 egg
1 tsp cream of tartar
1½ tsp vanilla
2½ cups flour
1 tsp baking soda
¼ tsp salt

Cream together first five ingredients. Combine salt, soda, and flour in separate bowl, then mix gradually into creamed mixture. When well-blended, cover and chill for eight hours or overnight.

Preheat oven to 375 degrees. Roll dough to approximately ¼ inch or less, if possible. Cut into desired shapes and place on a nonstick cookie sheet. (Or the dough can also be shaped into a log for chilling, then sliced for simple round cookies.)

Bake on lower oven shelf until cookies are slightly puffed, then move onto upper shelf and bake until edges begin to turn lightly golden. Entire baking time is approximately four to six minutes, depending upon cookie thickness. Do not overbake. Cool on rack.

Eat cookies plain or cover with glaze:

2 cups confectioner's sugar
dash of salt
1 tsp vanilla
add milk to desired consistency (but be careful not to
   add too much)

Stir ingredients together, then add food color if desired. Apply to cooled cookies with pastry brush.

*Next month, don't miss these exciting new love stories only from Avon Books*

**A Scottish Love**  by Karen Ranney
Shona Imrie should have agreed to Gordon MacDermond's proposal seven years ago—before he went to war and returned a hero—but though she loved him, she would accept no man's charity. MacDermond has everything he could ever want—except for the stubborn beauty he let slip through his fingers.

**Within the Flames**  by Marjorie M. Liu
When pyrokinetic Dirk & Steele agent Eddie goes to Manhattan to investigate a string of murders, he comes upon a shapeshifter, Lyssa, with powers over fire similar to his own. Hiding from brutal memories, Lyssa is reluctant to trust Eddie. But with flames at their fingertips and evil forces at their heels, will the fire between them conquer all?

**Beyond the Darkness**  by Jaime Rush
Shapeshifter Cheveyo walked out of Petra's life when his mission to hunt evil jeopardized her safety. But when he discovers that Petra is the target of a deadly enemy, he struggles to keep his emotions in check as he draws near to protect her. The closer the danger, the deeper the devotion . . . and the deadlier the consequence.

**Brazen**  by Margo Maguire
When Captain Gavin Briggs informs Lady Christina that she's the long-lost granddaughter of a duke, she refuses to meet with the old man who abandoned her as a child. But she knows Briggs needs the reward money and she agrees to go only if he helps her rescue her endangered brother. Peril and treachery await them . . . as well as sizzling attraction, lustful temptation and unanticipated passion.

**Visit www.AuthorTracker.com for exclusive information on your favorite HarperCollins authors.**

REL 1111

Available wherever books are sold or please call 1-800-331-3761 to order.

The gold standard for women's fiction—
*New York Times* bestselling author

# SUSAN ELIZABETH PHILLIPS

## Glitter Baby

978-0-06-143856-1

Fleur Savagar is an ugly duckling who can't believe
she's turned into a swan. Jake Koranda is a tough-guy
movie star with a haunted past. In a land of broken
dreams, can two unlikely lovers trust their hearts?

## Ain't She Sweet?

978-0-06-103208-0

Sugar Beth Carey's come back to Parrish, Mississippi,
and she's brought her reputation for wreaking havoc
with her. She's broke, desperate, and too proud to
show it, even with her old enemies lining up for a
chance to get even.

## Breathing Room

978-0-06-103209-7

Dr. Isabel Favor, America's Diva of self help, meets up
with Hollywood's favorite villain on a magical night in
Tuscany. A good guy wouldn't think of seducing such
a tidy-looking woman . . . but Ren Gage never saw
the fun in playing the hero.

Visit www.AuthorTracker.com for exclusive
information on your favorite HarperCollins authors.

Available wherever books are sold or please call 1-800-331-3761 to order.

SEP2 1009

*Give in to Impulse . . .*
*and satisfy your every whim for romance!*

### Avon Impulse is

- Fresh, Fun, and Fabulous eBook Exclusives
- New Digital Titles Every Week

The best in romance fiction,
delivered digitally to today's savvy readers!

*www.AvonImpulse.com*

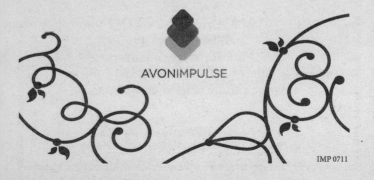

AVONIMPULSE

IMP 0711

*New York Times* bestselling author

# RACHEL GIBSON

## NOTHING BUT TROUBLE
978-0-06-157909-7
Chelsea Ross's acting career has been a total bust.
But leaving Hollywood to become the personal
assistant to a famous hockey player could be her
stupidest career move ever.

## TRUE LOVE AND OTHER DISASTERS
978-0-06-157906-6
Faith loathes Ty on sight, but she can't stop thinking
about him all day . . . and night. Soon she sees there's
more to him than sex appeal.

## NOT ANOTHER BAD DATE
978-0-06-117804-7
Adele Harris has had so many lousy dates, she's sure
she's cursed. She goes back to her hometown, only to
run smack into Zach Zemaitis . . . the one who got away.

## TANGLED UP IN YOU
978-0-06-117803-0
When Mick Hennessy discovers why
Maddie Dupree is back in Truly, Idaho, he can't
resist getting tangled up with her.

Visit www.AuthorTracker.com for exclusive
information on your favorite HarperCollins authors.

Available wherever books are sold or please call 1-800-331-3761 to order.

RG1 0211

**#1 *NEW YORK TIMES* BESTSELLING AUTHOR**

# DEBBIE MACOMBER

## One Night
978-0-06-108185-9

*Morning deejay Carrie Jamison is skyrocketing in the ratings, and her quick wit has won her the admiration of everyone at KUTE radio—except Kyle Harris, a serious, no-frills newscaster.*

## Someday Soon
978-0-06-108309-9

*Cain McClellan knew that just seeing Linette Collins from afar could never be enough.*

## Sooner or Later
978-0-06-108345-7

*When Letty Madden asks Shaun Murphy to help find her missing brother, he makes her a very indecent proposal.*

## A Season of Angels
978-0-06-108184-2

*Three women, each with a special wish . . .*
*Three angels make their dreams come true.*

## Touched by Angels
978-0-06-108344-0

*When the need is greatest, three divine angels will be the answers to your prayers.*

Visit www.AuthorTracker.com for exclusive information on your favorite HarperCollins authors.

Available wherever books are sold or please call 1-800-331-3761 to order.

DM 0711

*At Avon Books, we know your passion for romance—once you finish one of our novels, you find yourself wanting more.*

May we tempt you with . . .

- **Excerpts** from our upcoming releases.

- Entertaining **extras**, including authors' personal photo albums and book lists.

- Behind-the-scenes **scoop** on your favorite characters and series.

- **Sweepstakes** for the chance to win free books, romantic getaways, and other fun prizes.

- Writing **tips** from our authors and editors.

- **Blog** with our authors and find out why they love to write romance.

- **Exclusive content** that's not contained within the pages of our novels.

Join us at
**www.avonbooks.com**

**AVON**

*An Imprint of HarperCollinsPublishers*
www.avonromance.com

**Available wherever books are sold or please call 1-800-331-3761 to order.**

FTH 0708